Praise for *My Perfect*

'A slow-burn thriller with a great sens
characterisation where almost no one is ~~quite who they~~
Tense and shocking.' Catherine Cooper, author of *The Chalet*

'An intensely gripping thriller, with astute characterisation,
a cleverly woven plot that keeps you guessing all the way,
and a story that is both suspenseful and moving. A hugely
satisfying read.' Philippa East, author of *Little White Lies*

'Sarah delivers such a smart and beautifully taut novel in *My
Perfect Friend*. Full of intrigue and delicious betrayal. Just
how I like my thrillers.' L.V. Matthews, author of *The Twins*

'A gripping read, exposing the dark lies at the heart of a
supposedly perfect life. Pacy, with well-drawn characters you
care about. The perfect thriller!'
Louise Mumford, author of *Sleepless*

'An incredibly tense psychological thriller that grips you from
the very first page. The suspense is utterly breathtaking.'
Victoria Dowd, author of *The Smart Woman's Guide to Murder*

'A carefully crafted, clever novel with plenty of twists, suspense
and red herrings. A sparkling and satisfying read.'
Diane Jeffrey, author of *The Silent Friend*

'A dark and clever thriller that kept me turning the pages
late into the night.' Sophie Flynn, author of *All My Lies*

'A really tense and atmospheric read with distinctive voices
and a satisfyingly twisty ending.' Mira V Shah, author of *She*

SARAH CLARKE is a writer living in South West London with her husband, children and stubbornly cheerful cockapoo. Over fifteen years, Sarah has built a successful career as a marketing copywriter, but her dream has always been to become a published author. When her youngest child started secondary school, she joined the Faber Academy Writing A Novel course to learn the craft of writing psychological thrillers. Sarah graduated in 2019 and joined HQ Digital two years later. *My Perfect Friend* is her third novel.

Also by Sarah Clarke

A Mother Never Lies
Every Little Secret

My Perfect Friend

SARAH CLARKE

ONE PLACE. MANY STORIES

HQ
An imprint of HarperCollins*Publishers* Ltd
1 London Bridge Street
London SE1 9GF

www.harpercollins.co.uk

HarperCollins*Publishers*
Macken House,
39/40 Mayor Street Upper,
Dublin 1
D01 C9W8
Ireland

This paperback edition 2023

1
First published in Great Britain by
HQ, an imprint of HarperCollins*Publishers* Ltd 2022

Copyright © Sarah Clarke 2022

Sarah Clarke asserts the moral right to be
identified as the author of this work.
A catalogue record for this book is
available from the British Library.

ISBN: 9780008494940

For my family
Chris, Scarlett, Finn
& Mika

Prologue

January 2022

Simon sits up tall. The soft cushion of his chair feels wrong in this setting, his expectation formed by childhood memories of hard wooden church pews. He plants both feet, rests his clammy palms on his thighs and tries to focus on the discomfort caused by his shirt collar cutting into his neck.

He wonders if he can keep up the façade throughout the whole service. Or whether he will slip to the floor at some point, bang his fists against the carpeted floor of the crematorium and scream for his life back, beg some higher power to tell him it's all a big joke – a dark prank performed for one of those toxic TV shows perhaps – and that Beth is going to waltz back into his life at any moment with a wink and a 'gotcha' smile.

There are many other people here, every chair occupied, the room thick with mourners. But it doesn't stop the intense ache of loneliness seeping through him. Or the desperate knowledge that things won't get better. That his future is now grey and empty.

He wishes Beth was here.

Of course she is here, he thinks as he stares at the coffin lying on the plinth just ahead of him. But not in any reachable way. She can't allay his loneliness, squeeze warmth into his fingers, lean against him and whisper something inappropriate for a funeral that makes them both look down at their feet to hide their smiles. She can't be his wife anymore.

Looking back, he can see the stepping stones of mistakes he made, and how they helped build the path that led to this day. If only he'd recognised the danger earlier, veered away from his middle-class beliefs that things like this don't happen to people like them. If only he hadn't believed Beth when she said she'd be fine on her own.

An older woman stands up and walks to the lectern, a piece of paper trembling in her grasp. It's so brave of Beth's mother to speak today. He sees the familiar features on her face, but she still looks like a stranger, lost in her own grief. He listens to her words of love, a fitting eulogy for a beautiful person, and finally gives in to his emotions. He cries for the wife he's lost, the life that was once so privileged and now lies in tatters.

And he cries for his daughters.

December 2021

Chapter 1

Beth

If she'd walked home via Thurleigh Road she wouldn't be here now, Beth thinks, staring at the three emergency vehicles lined up on the pavement, their flashing lights giving the normally quiet road an early Christmas glow. She would be in bed, Simon gently snoring next to her, wondering whether the magnesium that her nutritionist recommended will do its job, or if she'll need something stronger to help her drift off.

But no. Tonight, she chose the slightly longer route from Wandsworth Common train station via the main road because it felt safer. And here she is. Surrounded by police and paramedics.

A small gust of wind appears from somewhere and Beth shivers as it coils around her. It's always a dilemma, going to an upmarket restaurant in the wintertime, and she'd erred on the side of style over practicality this evening. Her floaty dress, leather bomber jacket and Veja trainers had looked good when she left home, and equally so when she arrived at Barrafina in Soho. But now she wishes she'd chosen something more in keeping with the early December temperatures, or even sneaked a pair of tights underneath her dress. Not that she could have expected her evening to turn out like this of course. Standing outside a vacant shop unit within a few feet of a corpse.

The relief when the paramedics finally arrived – about ten minutes after she made the 999 call – had washed over her so potently that it felt like a jet of warm water, albeit a temporary one. She was no longer responsible for the inert figure collapsed on the ground, the poor homeless man with a needle sticking out of his arm, whose smell she'd been trying desperately to ignore. She'd stepped back with an almost giddy sigh when they took over, and watched the performance like it was an episode of *Casualty*. The stocky older woman with short grey hair had flung her green rucksack onto the concrete paving slabs and pulled out various bits of equipment, while the younger one stretched on some latex gloves and crouched over the man slumped motionless in the doorway.

'Airway clear but not breathing; no pulse; pupils fixed and dilated,' she'd called out in a serious voice, carefully releasing the belt strapped around the man's bicep and picking up the needle by his side. 'Looks like a heroin overdose.'

It was at that point Beth started shivering again. When she'd first seen the man lying there, she'd acted without thinking, adrenalin overpowering rational thought. But once she learned that he wasn't breathing, and realised that her calling the ambulance hadn't saved his life, the chemicals quickly faded. It took a few more minutes for the grey-haired paramedic to officially pronounce the man dead, and by then Beth was struggling to not just feel grateful that it was all over.

Except it wasn't all over. The confirmation of death into the paramedic's radio had started a new flurry of activity. Another ambulance pulled up with two more paramedics, and two police officers arrived in a flood of blue light. They ignored Beth at first, heading straight for their colleagues and the man on the ground, but now one of them is walking towards her.

'I hear you're the person who called the emergency services,' he says, stopping a little too close for Beth's liking. 'I'm PC Curtis.'

'Beth Packard,' she whispers, taking a step backwards. 'Nice to meet you.' She must sound odd, exchanging pleasantries in these circumstances, but it's how she's programmed to behave.

'It must have been a shock,' he continues. 'Finding him like that. How are you doing?' He pauses a moment, taking in her summery outfit. 'I can ask one of the paramedics to get you a blanket from the wagon if you're cold?'

Beth smiles warmly at the pale-faced police officer. Not because she wants a hospital blanket – she wouldn't trust that it had been properly laundered after its last recipient – but because smiling warmly is her default. She probably did it on purpose once upon a time, when she first discovered the advantages it could bring. But now it's just a habit, a defence mechanism in uncomfortable situations.

And she's certainly feeling uncomfortable right now.

'I'm fine – thank you though,' she says, hoping that she sounds genuine. He seems nice enough, not one of those misogynist policemen that you read about in the press.

'My super just called. CID will be here in a sec. We need to check the property over, then they'll take your statement. Are you okay to wait?'

Beth smiles. It's the very last thing she wants to do, but of course she wouldn't admit that. Instead, she asks, 'CID? Is it normal for them to be involved in something like this?'

PC Curtis shrugs. 'Normal enough, I suppose, if they're quiet. We need some help to check the shop out.'

Beth starts to smile again, to regain lost ground, but they're both distracted by another car joining the line of vehicles on the pavement. It's a nondescript colour and model, made worse by the thin glaze of Wandsworth pollution covering its panels, and Beth isn't surprised when two almost identical men in jeans, hoodies and stab vests climb out.

'Excuse me,' PC Curtis says, dipping his head slightly and turning towards the detectives. Beth watches them talk on the pavement for a few moments, then move as a threesome towards the shopfront where the four paramedics and a second uniformed police officer are still loitering. The newly arrived ambulance will transport the body to the mortuary at St George's Hospital, Beth hears the older paramedic explain. She wishes they'd hurry up; surely the dead man deserves better than a grubby concrete floor and an audience of strangers for his final resting place. At last, the group fragments and Beth watches the uniformed officers, and one of the detectives, head inside the shop. The other detective, the slightly broader of the two, strides over in her direction. She smiles at him, warmly.

'Thank you for waiting. I'm DC Stone, Wandsworth CID. Mrs Packard, isn't it?'

'Yes, that's right. And no problem at all. It was the least I could do.'

'I don't agree,' the detective observes. 'A lot of people would have chosen to do considerably less than you've done.' There's an admiration in his tone that Beth wasn't expecting, and it makes the space between her shoulder blades widen a fraction. But now she feels like crying, so she blinks and draws them back together.

'I was just on my way home from a night out with my girl-friends,' she explains. 'A Christmas get-together before Christmas actually kicks in and we're all too busy to celebrate.'

He smiles, but it's a polite one. He doesn't understand her world.

'I live on this road, but further up towards Clapham Common,' she continues, wafting her hand eastwards and up the hill oppo-site. She can't help a note of pride slipping into her voice. When she and Simon first moved to London, they bought a flat in Fulham with a little help from Simon's parents. It was small and the mortgage used up most of their salaries (not that hers contributed much) but its location was what the estate agent called aspirational, and selling it smoothed the way for future house moves. Beth dreamed of having a family home between Wandsworth and Clapham Commons, so when they returned from a few years in Singapore with a baby in tow, it was the first place they looked. 'I was on my way home from the station when I saw him,' she explains. 'He was slumped in the doorway; I knew straight away that he was seriously ill.'

'And that's when you called the emergency services?'

Beth nods. 'A man walked past when I was calling them; I thought he was going to stop and help, but when I looked around, he'd gone.'

'And they say chivalry's dead,' DC Stone murmurs.

'The woman I spoke to asked me all these questions, whether he was breathing, if he was in the recovery position; I did what I could, but I was shaking all over.' She shudders and isn't sure whether it's the cold air or the memory of kneeling down next to the man that's causing it. The image is still so clear in her mind. His wiry beard, red-raw cheeks and rotten teeth. How badly he smelt. And she had to touch his skin, check his pulse, bend close enough to listen for breath. A wave of nausea rises with the image and Beth tries to ride it by imagining stepping into a scalding-hot shower. She scratches her left palm.

'That must have been very difficult for you,' the detective surmises in a low voice.

The tears are threatening again and she's so tired that she's not sure she can stop them escaping this time. She hears her tone harden a notch. 'DC Stone, I want to help, but I really don't know anything else. I'm tired, and I'd love to go home.'

'Of course, I understand,' he says, but his body doesn't move, and Beth knows she's not free yet. 'Just a couple more questions, then I'll get one of the uniforms to run you back.'

Beth thinks about turning down the offer of a lift, her house is only ten minutes away on foot, and a neighbour might notice her getting out of a police car. Like Saskia with her nocturnal habits and eagle eyes. But she's frozen solid and the thought of a warm vehicle is enticing. 'Thank you,' she says, surrendering. 'But I'm really not sure what I can add.'

'You mentioned that you live on this road. And it looks like the deceased might have been squatting in this property. I wondered whether you'd seen him before tonight? Or anyone else coming or going?'

Beth face stretches into another smile and freezes. She's been half expecting this question, but now it's arrived she's not quite sure how to answer it. Because she has seen him before tonight, sitting against the shop's front window, or just wandering around, clearly high, scaring the children. And she may have uttered the odd word under her breath. There have been conversations with neighbours too, the collective tutting and sighing about the presence of squatters on their affluent street. She even emailed the residents' association a couple of weeks ago to see if they could track down the owners of the shop (Delphine's used to sell French haute couture until everyone transitioned to joggers). But she feels bad about that now, after what's just happened. And it's not like it's relevant to the man's death.

'Not that I can think of,' she says, hoping that the white lie doesn't show on her face.

'Okay, well—' A noise bursts out of the shop, followed by a muffled shout. 'Excuse me,' DC Stone says, twisting his body. Beth watches him run inside; his shoulders hunched, ready for action. The paramedics have left now, the body too, so Beth's alone in the darkness. She eyes the hill opposite; her house is up there. She's told the detective everything she knows, and the police have clearly got their hands full inside the shop. She should just go home. She wonders if her legs will defrost if she moves them.

The noise gets louder, the shouting clearer, and Beth can't help turning to look. Four people went into the shop but five are coming out, and one of them is in handcuffs. He's more boy than man.

10

'Fucking pigs! I was fucking sleeping!' he screams, his voice slurring from drowsiness or alcohol. He's tall and skinny, with a mess of curls leaking out from a black beanie. 'You can't fucking arrest me!' he continues shouting. 'This place is commercial property! Don't you know the fucking law, Plod? And where's Jon? Have you nicked him too?' He dances clumsily towards the street as DC Stone holds his wrists behind his back with one hand and his shoulder with the other, trying to move him forward in as straight a line as possible.

'We found three wraps of heroin, mate. I know *that's* against the law,' the other detective says, walking next to him, his bored tone showing this kind of chat isn't new to him.

'That's not mine! I don't do smack. Do I look like a junkie?'

'Were you living in that shop?'

'I was having a kip inside an empty building because it's fucking arctic out here!' He pauses for a moment, then tilts his head and glares in Beth's direction. 'What are you staring at, lady?'

A second of silence passes, then Beth gasps when she realises that he's talking to her. She should look away, but her head appears frozen too now.

'Stop scaring the locals, Mark,' DC Stone says, giving him another shove towards the police car. But the boy resists, pushing back against his captor, and maintaining eye contact with Beth.

'Hey, I recognise you,' he says, his voice slowing. 'Jon always reckoned you'd be the one to get us kicked out. Looks like he was right.'

Beth makes the effort to drag her eyes away and tries to smile warmly at DC Stone, but his attention is elsewhere.

'I bet you did this, didn't you?' Mark goes on. 'Got the police to chuck us out onto the street? In the middle of the night too. Heartless bitch.'

'Look, you are talking out of your arse, mate,' DC Stone growls. 'This woman tried to save your friend's life, and that's how you thank her?'

'What? What are you talking about?' The boy sounds both angry and scared now, like a wild animal in limbo between fight and flight.

Everyone stops walking and DC Stone sighs. 'Look, sorry to tell you this, but a man was pronounced dead here a short while ago. Suspected overdose. Could that have been this Jon you mentioned?'

'Jon's dead?' His voice cracks. He shakes his head furiously, then lifts it skywards. 'I thought you said she saved him?'

'I said she tried to save him, but it was too late. He died before the paramedics arrived.'

Beth watches the boy's face crease, his eyes jam shut and his mouth stretch into a grimace. He breathes hard and his chest heaves, but no tears appear on his face. 'I bet she didn't try,' he snarls suddenly, tipping his head forward and staring at Beth again. 'She couldn't give a shit about us. She's probably glad he's dead,' he spits out.

Beth flinches and draws her hands up to her face, as though she needs to protect herself from his vitriol. Or his saliva.

'Don't be stupid, Mark,' the detective says, resuming his shuffle forwards.

'And then she gets me arrested, dragged off her precious street. One dead, the other in a cell. Problem sorted.' He laughs with such bitterness that it makes Beth shudder again.

DC Stone opens the back door of the police car.

'Well, think again, missus, because you don't get rid of me that easily,' Mark shouts. 'I'll be back, you stuck-up bitch!' His voice trails off as the detective shoves him into the car and slams the door shut.

12

Chapter 2

Beth

'Come on, girls, time to go, or we'll be late for school,' Beth says, not daring to look at the state of the room she's leaving behind. She likes the house to be spotless by this stage of the morning, but everything is out of kilter today. While she tried to hide it, she was shaken up by that second squatter and the anger he directed at her last night. Her attempt to cover up her distress clearly didn't wash either, because DC Stone insisted on driving her home himself, and then waking Simon to warn him to look out for signs of shock. That led to Simon making Beth a chamomile tea to relax her, while asking a multitude of questions that wound her up.

After a long, hot shower and half a sleeping pill (she knew magnesium wouldn't cut it) Beth had finally drifted off at about four in the morning, so when her phone started blaring Nina Simone's 'Feeling Good' (still her favourite song) three hours later, it had been almost impossible to get up.

Her hands are shaking as she pushes open the front door, and ten steps later, their ornate iron gate. She reaches down to squeeze

Martha's and Ava's hands in an effort to instil some resilience into her own, but they both seem to sense her ulterior motive and wriggle free. Her jitters could be down to lack of sleep, or the traumatic way her evening ended. But they could also be the result of catching eyes with Saskia when she climbed out of the detective's car last night. And knowing it's only a matter of time before her neighbour – and closest friend, she supposes – grills her about it. She would much prefer to put the whole experience behind her, but sadly Saskia isn't the type to let a drama go unscrutinised.

'Beth darling!'

She sighs. Saskia lives directly opposite and they usually walk to school together. Of course she wouldn't be able to avoid this. 'Hey, Sas, how are you?' she asks in what she hopes sounds like a casual, indifferent tone. Saskia in an ex-journalist and has an uncanny way of wheedling out any story that piques her interest; in the past Beth has appreciated this skill, but that's before the story centred around her.

Saskia's two children, Olivia and Angus, are stood either side of her, dressed with military precision in their uniforms. Normally, Martha and Ava would look equally well presented, but Ava's plait is looking a bit haphazard today and Martha's slightly grimy collar suggests she could be wearing yesterday's blouse. All four children go to Nightingales, a local primary school that's only a five-minute walk away. Martha and Olivia are in the same class in year two, and usually best friends (except when they're arch enemies). Ava is in year one – just 18 months younger than her sister – and Angus is the baby in reception.

'Never mind me,' Saskia says, too loudly for Beth. 'What's with the clandestine ride in a police car in the middle of the night? And don't deny it. They could tattoo the word POLICE onto that man's forehead and it wouldn't be any more obvious.'

'It was nothing—'

'Wrong answer!' Saskia cuts her off. 'Come on, Beth, I want all

14

the juicy details.' She giggles and her eyes dance with curiosity. But not concern, Beth notices.

'Okay, but keep your voice down,' Beth says quietly. She hasn't mentioned what happened last night to Martha and Ava; she doesn't need them asking what squatting or overdosing means. 'The girls don't know.'

A look of concern wafts over Saskia's face, as though she's belatedly realised that Beth could have been involved in something genuinely traumatic. 'Of course,' she says, dropping her voice an octave. This new deference gives Beth a moment to collect her thoughts.

'I was coming back from Soho,' she finally says. 'You know I was out with some of the mums from Ava's class?'

Saskia nods. Micromanaging their families' lives doesn't mean they don't have time to keep track of what the other is doing too.

'I tend to walk home from the station via Bolingbroke Grove when it's dark, which means passing the shops at the top of our road. And last night, outside the empty one …'

'The old Delphine's? With the squatters?'

'There was this man, unconscious, just outside the front door. Like he'd walked out of the shop and collapsed.'

'Shit,' Saskia exhales. 'So you phoned the police?'

'No,' Beth says, furrowing her brow. 'I phoned for an ambulance, and followed all their instructions. The police came after.'

'And was he okay, the man?'

Beth shakes her head. Her earlier frustration with controlling her bodily functions has returned because her eyes are getting hot. She blinks them a few times and pushes her lips together.

'He died? Wow, Beth, poor you. Talk about wrong time, wrong place. But you did what you could, and phoning for an ambulance is hero-level stuff. How are you feeling now?'

Beth hesitates; she doesn't know how to answer her friend's question. She knows that she should feel proud of herself for stopping for that man. And that it's not her fault he died. He was a heroin addict, homeless and must have been in his fifties at least, so the odds were already stacked against him. But she actually feels immensely sad, guilty even. Perhaps it's the other squatter's comments, and her previous less-than-charitable behaviour, preying on her mind. 'I suppose I just wish I'd taken a different route home,' she says eventually.

'You did something amazing last night, Beth. You should feel very good about yourself. I bet loads of people would have just walked straight past, assumed he was drunk, or that he was someone else's problem.'

'I just want to put it all behind me now,' Beth says. She can't help suspecting that Saskia is sweetening her up to extract more details.

They reach the school gates, and as they submerge into the crowd, Beth prepares for the inevitable onslaught of wide smiles and enthusiastic greetings. She knows this is entirely her own fault, a side effect of her being an enthusiastic member of the PTFA and running the face-painting stall at every summer fair, but it still makes her nervous. The sense of scrutiny it creates. But doing the right thing has been a feature of her life since she was forced to move schools for her A levels. She was given a chance to be someone new, someone better, and her gratitude for the opportunity has shaped every decision she's made since.

But after what happened last night, she can't cope with being that quasi-celebrity today, so she nods at the other mums, returns their smiles, but looks away before they have chance to strike up a conversation. It works until one of them – Nicole, mother of Rosie in Ava's class – goes one step further, and curls her fingers around Beth's arm. Her skin feels hot beneath the woman's grip.

'Beth, hi,' she enthuses. 'How was last night? Can't believe I couldn't make it; bloody Charlie late home from work again.'

Beth applies a warm smile to her face and swallows down bile. She pulls her arm away from Nicole's fingers and scratches her palms. 'Fun, yes,' she mumbles, nodding, wishing her heart rate wouldn't rise without warning. She wants to take a step backwards, but there are bodies there too; she can sense their heat. 'Got to rush, you know?' she manages. She turns towards Martha and Ava, but they've already slipped away, carried along by the tide of children tumbling into school. At least with the girls inside, Beth's job is done. She turns, drops her head and weaves her way through the crowd. But she hasn't fully escaped; Saskia is still at her shoulder.

'And can you put it behind you?' she asks, returning to the subject of last night as though there hadn't been an interruption. 'You won't need to go to the inquest?'

'I don't know,' Beth admits. DC Stone didn't mention anything about an inquest, but he did say he'd pop round again when the file was ready to be handed over to the coroner. He also gave her a card with his contact details on. He said it was just in case she had any questions, but Beth isn't sure he would have felt the need if that boy they arrested hadn't spoken to her so fiercely. Beth hopes it was just talk, empty threats made in the heat of the moment. She was scared last night, and grateful for the detective's card, but the reassurance of daylight is helping. Even if the police let him go, the squatter won't be able to go back to the shop unit now that the police have cordoned it off. He'll probably move on to another neighbourhood, become someone else's problem, and forget all about Beth. She'll throw the detective's card away when she gets home, she decides.

'Well, it will be months away even if you do,' Saskia says, shaking her head in mild exasperation. 'The wait times are a disgrace these days.' Of course Saskia would be familiar with the process, Beth thinks to herself. Without journalism to feed her hunger for a story, Saskia now spends hours backing various campaigns on social media – from allergy awareness to narcotics anonymous to supporting victims of domestic abuse. Beth is horrified by some of the comments Saskia gets on her Twitter feed, but her friend seems to love a spat, the feistier the better.

Luckily Beth didn't have a career to be wrenched away from when she had children. Nothing to miss when she's doing an Ocado order or tidying the girls' toys away for the millionth time. She met Simon at university and knew almost instantly that she wanted to spend the rest of her life with him. They moved to London from Bristol, and she worked in marketing for a few years. But then Simon's bank sent them to Singapore and the expat lifestyle kept her occupied until Martha came along.

They reach Saskia's house and pause on the pavement. 'Coffee?' Saskia says it more as an observation than a question because coffee together is a Friday morning tradition, but Beth can't face any more of Saskia's probing questions today.

'Sorry, can't today,' she apologises. Then before Saskia tries to convince her otherwise, she gives her friend a quick wave and retreats into her house.

Beth leans against the front door and breathes. She's so tired, she thinks she could stay like that forever, but there's too much to do. At least Simon took Luna for a walk before he left for work this morning, and it must have been quite a hike. While her eyes are staring adoringly at Beth through the sliding glass door that separates the entrance hall from the open-plan kitchen, her body is hardly moving, just her tail going up and down like a serpent dancing to a Nick Cave track. Beth pushes off, lines her trainers up in the shoe cupboard and goes to stroke the newest member of their family.

Beth was against the idea of getting a dog, but was outvoted, and they picked up their 8-week-old cockapoo from a breeder in Herefordshire in the summer. Beth has warmed up a bit since then; she likes the unconditional love and constant tail wagging that Luna provides, and the morning walk or run helps keep her in shape. But she still struggles with the muddy pawprints, the dog hair (whoever said poodle breeds don't moult is misinformed) and the dog smell that seems to emanate from all four corners of the house.

As Beth crouches down to stroke Luna, she takes in the view of her kitchen. A lidless carton of butter littered with dark crumbs, a mug smeared with a coffee rim and Ava's cloth tiger hanging over one of the two discarded cereal bowls. Twelve hours ago, her life was designer gin and tonics and Soho-style tapas. Now she's exhausted and her house is a disaster zone. There's a policeman's business card on the island unit, and her body hasn't quite stopped trembling. A surge of rage sweeps through her, anger with herself for letting things slide so badly.

She stacks the dishwasher, wipes the surfaces, polishes the appliances, runs bleach down the sink, and sweeps and mops the floor. She sprays and resprays the glass doors until every last smear is gone. By mid-morning, the kitchen looks perfect, but it's not enough. So she starts on the cupboards, emptying them out, spraying and wiping, returning the contents according to shape and size, until the inside looks as immaculate as the outside.

But it's still not enough.

With a sense of surrender, she walks up two flights of stairs and into her bedroom like a zombie. She tries not to look at the bed, but of course she can't help it. With a surge of annoyance, she removes the throw, four pillows and six scatter cushions. She straightens up the duvet and methodically replaces the accessories one at a time. When it looks perfect, she allows herself to turn away and walk the few steps into her dressing room. She opens the wardrobe door, and finally a veil of relief floats over her.

She keeps the pills inside the toe of a winter boot, an old pair that she never wears anymore. She was first prescribed diazepam before she met Simon, and it's always been her little secret. She weaned herself off it completely in Singapore, but there have been a few relapses since then – motherhood can be challenging – and over the years, she's managed to squirrel away a collection of foil strips in her boot. Just one, to get her through today; that's all she needs. She places a pill onto her tongue and walks into the en-suite bathroom, dipping down under the tap. The water is icy cold, and she enjoys the feel of it running into her stomach, carrying the much-needed crutch.

With her brain finally calming, she straightens up and stares into the mirror. People have been telling her that she's beautiful for half her life, and that should be enough time for the message to sink in. Her hair is just brown, but people say it reminds them of dark chocolate. Her eyes get lots of compliments too, for their size and the length of her lashes. And her skin tone is coveted by paler English roses; the smooth warm tan that she sports all year round.

She never gets complimented on her hands though. She lifts them up to her eyeline and turns them at the wrists. The jitters have gone, but her skin feels rough and raw from too much scratching and cleaning. She washes them one more time, then reaches for her Jo Malone moisturiser. As she rubs it over her fingers and across her palms, she thinks about the detective's business card now in her jeans pocket. And wonders why she didn't throw it away after all.

Chapter 3

Mark

Did he really admit to possession of a class-A drug this morning, just so that he could get released with a caution? Mark leans forward on the wooden bench, drops his elbows onto his knees and digs the heels of his hands into his eye sockets. He can't believe he was arrested in the first place, just because Jon checked out before he got to inject all of his gear. It was like that detective – DC Stone – was punishing Mark for his only mate in London dying.

Not mate in any accepted sense of the word, of course. He only met Jon a few months ago, and they weren't exactly alike. Mark is just between homes, not homeless, and has got big plans. Jon was the real-deal rough sleeper, on the streets for nearly twenty years, except for a few stints at Her Majesty's pleasure. Jon had done everything, slept everywhere and had stories that ranged from hilarious to completely disgusting. The bloke's cold on a slab and Mark still hasn't got over his graphic description of the foot infection he picked up last winter. It's why Mark washes his feet every day religiously, even if it's in some stinking public toilet block. His own stories are pathetic in comparison with Jon's. A few drinks and a bit of a temper were all it took for him to end up sleeping on Clapham Common.

But despite all that, they got on like mates. When they first met, Mark was still part of the rat race with a job and a roof over his head. It was a shit job, media sales for magazines nobody reads, and a tiny bedroom rented off the aunt of a mate from back home. But he was on the right path, at least that's what people said. Jon's only job was selling wraps of smack for some big-shot dealer from Battersea in exchange for free drugs, and his home was a fluid range of spots on Clapham Common (or Holy Trinity Church floor when it got really cold).

Mark started hanging out by the skate park on the common during the summer – with his salary, it was the only way he could escape the suffocating box of his bedroom after another shit day of working from home – and it turned out to be one of Jon's regular spots. Neither of them could skate – Jon struggled to walk half the time – but they'd watch the kids doing their tricks, and laugh when they fucked up. After a while, Mark started picking up a four-pack from Tesco's. Jon would make one can of lager last the same time as Mark's three, and Mark wouldn't comment if Jon disappeared to jack up.

When Mark turned up at the common a couple of months ago with a rucksack and the thin sleeping bag he'd only bought for a trip to V Festival a few years back, Jon didn't say anything much. He just found him a place to sleep and lent him a blanket.

So maybe they were mates after all.

Now Mark lifts his eyeline and slides his hands under his chin. His head feels heavy, and he wonders if it's grief, or just the after-effects of a night in a police cell. Although at least it was warm in there. That metal excuse for a bed was far from comfortable, but the radiator pumped out a heat that he hasn't felt since the day he found Jon on Clapham Common and slept under his blanket, the same day that Stew chucked him out. That was the final injustice after a shitshow of disasters, and the one that dealt a killer blow to his dream.

With a sigh, Mark leans back against the wooden slats of the bench and extends his legs over his rucksack. After he accepted the caution, Mark was free to leave Wandsworth police station, but it was made clear to him that the squat is permanently off limits. Which is pretty irritating because, after four weeks bedding down there, it was starting to feel like home. Jon had pleaded for the front room with the big window as soon as they arrived, and Mark had been happy to oblige because he wanted the storeroom out back, somewhere private to work out how the hell he was going to get his life back on track.

The electricity supply had been turned off, but there was running water and various extras like an old sofa (Jon won that in an arm wrestle but expected Mark to lug it to the front room for him) and a cardboard box full of biscuits and long-life milk. They'd been given an old camping stove by a day centre in Clapham, and Mark had been able to have a cup of tea first thing in the morning again.

It's gutting to think all that effort has gone to waste.

In a fit of frustration, Mark kicks at the hard concrete with his heels. Some part of his brain is telling him not to blame that woman, that she did a good thing, phoning the ambulance and trying to save Jon's life. But then her image takes over, her look-at-me dress and those big doe eyes, thinking she's better than him and Jon. Too blinded by her own arrogance to realise the only thing that separates them is luck. She's been trying to get them off her street ever since they moved into that shop, threatening them with some residents' association legal action, pulling her kids close every time she walks past. She's never once asked how she could help.

Even that night, earlier in the evening, she'd been at it. Mark had gone on a vodka hunt, and Jon was fuming about her when he got back. Then a few hours later, not only does she rid the street of them both, she has a ringside seat. The fucking irony of it.

But he knows he must stop dwelling on her, because he's got more immediate problems to solve, like where the hell he's going to sleep tonight.

Theoretically, Cambridge is an option – he's sure his parents would take him back if he asked – but he can't face his dad's mocking expression, or his mum's sympathetic one. There are his mates to consider too, how much they'd take the piss out of him. Big gaming genius back with his mama. Mark's still got a few quid in his account, the remnants of his last pay packet, so he could try Mrs Mason again, promise that he'll get a new job and be more respectful of her home this time. But she's probably got another lodger by now, and anyway, there's not much chance of her forgiving him after he kicked a hole in her wall.

So that leaves Stew. Would he have Mark back in his little flat in Tooting? Just for a few nights until he gets himself sorted? Yeah, things got a little out of control last time he stayed, and Stew's face did look pretty battered in the morning. But he must see it from Mark's point of view; Stew wasn't exactly the innocent party. Mark eyes the bus grunting down Garratt Lane. The 270 will take him all the way to Tooting, practically to Stew's flat. He knows it's a gamble, but it's not like he's flush with options. He picks up his bag, swings it over his shoulder, and uses the rear exit to climb on board.

'You've got a fucking cheek coming here.' Stew glowers at Mark from the doorstep, his arms crossed, and feet planted so wide that they're almost touching the walls of his hallway, as though he's transformed himself into a child safety gate.

'Look, I'm sorry for losing my shit that night,' Mark says, trying to sound conciliatory, which is hard because he's tired, hungover and still pissed off with the arrogant prick stood in front of him. 'But I was hammered, and it was ages ago now.' Mark smiles and hopes that the cold wind is carrying the stench of his unwashed body in the opposite direction.

'You kicked the crap out of me in my own home, even after I offered you a place to stay when that old lady threw you out.'

'I know, and I was grateful, but when you smashed my Mac, I just saw red. My whole future was on that computer.'

'It fell,' Stew snaps. 'It was an accident.'

'It cost me over a grand,' Mark explains. 'My game design portfolio was sat on its desktop.'

'That doesn't excuse what you did – I thought you were going to kill me.'

'Don't be stupid,' Mark scoffs, but Stew's claim ruffles him. Because he can't really remember hitting his old work colleague. He remembers Stew stumbling after too many beers, then falling heavily on Mark's Apple Mac computer, plus the sound of it crashing to the floor. And he remembers a tidal wave of fury raging through him. But the rest is a blur, until the next morning when he woke up on the floor. Surrounded by bloodstains, spilt booze and glass from his smashed screen. 'My mate died last night,' he tries. 'I was arrested and spent the night in a cell. I've got nowhere else to go.' He tries to keep his voice steady, not show how badly Jon's death has knocked him, but it's hard.

'I think you're confusing me for someone who cares. Listen, we hardly know each other. We worked together for, what, four months? We got pissed together a couple of times on those wanky company bonding nights; I thought you were all right and took pity on you when you had nowhere to stay. But that's it, and then you fucked it up. Goodbye, Mark.' Stew unfolds his arms and pushes the front door closed.

Mark stares at the wooden panels. He can't believe the guy isn't showing any remorse for smashing up his computer, or taking an ounce of responsibility for his role in their skirmish. It's like that woman last night. She didn't give a shit about Jon dying, even though she treated him like vermin when he was alive. Maybe that's why. Mark wonders how long it took for her to call the ambulance. Whether she hesitated. *The man's a junkie – no wonder he's out of it. Is he really worth helping?*

The anger is still racing through him, but he can't stare at a grimy front door all day. He eyes the VW Golf parked outside the flat. Dark grey and recently washed. Stew's car, but easy to imagine her face in its gleaming panels. Mark kicks out with his right foot, connecting with the driver's door. An alarm bursts into life and he laughs. The wailing suits his mood.

'Oi!' Stew's voice flies out of the front door. 'Get off my fucking car!'

'Don't worry, I'm going,' Mark says, grinning. It's the best he's felt all day.

'You're a fucking lunatic.'

Mark ignores the insult and turns right out of Stew's road. But the satisfaction he got from vexing his ex-housemate quickly evaporates as he realises that he's still got nowhere to sleep tonight. Stew was his only chance for finding a safe place to bed down, and it took him about three minutes to completely screw that up. What the hell is wrong with him? Why does his stupid temper always get in the way of him making a good decision?

Of course he knows Clapham Common is an option. He spent three weeks there before he found the squat, and it wasn't as bad as people with four walls and a roof might think. But while he hates to admit it, he's scared of sleeping there without Jon. The bloke was hardly bodyguard material, but he knew the streets. And he had a certain way about him; Mark felt safer when he was close by. But what other choice does he have? He feels the sting of tears burn his eyes again and he lifts them skywards to benefit from the breeze.

Chapter 4

Saskia

Unbelievable, Saskia thinks as she drops her phone and keys on the (much smaller than Beth's) island unit. It would have to be Beth, wouldn't it, who finds herself in a situation that requires a hero. As if effortless beauty and infinite wealth aren't enough for her. All she did was phone for an ambulance, for Christ's sake. Three demure taps on her iPhone 12. And that didn't even achieve anything – the guy died anyway. But she'll still have all the mums fawning over her at school when they find out, even more than they do already (if that's possible). Saskia volunteers for three charities, manages their websites and spends hours researching and writing blog posts, but however many times she drops her voluntary work into conversation, its value never seems to register with the other mums. Beth's Florence Nightingale routine will be a different story; she'd lay money on it.

Saskia sighs as she rifles through her coffee basket and picks up a Kazaar pod. A blend of Sicilian, African and Arabian beans, it says on the packet, which sounds like the sort of thing she needs after the extra bottle of Chianti she decided they all deserved last night – and then proceeded to drink almost single-handedly. Not that her night rivalled Beth's of course. Olivia's class night out was at a local pizza place, not Barrafina in Soho. Beth could have chosen to go to either – Martha is in Olivia's class – but she went for glamour over convenience, and Saskia supposes she can't blame her for that.

She drops the pod into the machine and slips a small cup into position. Saskia prefers the smell of coffee to the taste, and she breathes it in as a pencil line of brown liquid hits off-white china. She drinks her coffee black – quicker (she's impatient), easier (she hates mundane chores) and more efficient (she requires caffeine to function) – and as soon as the cup is full, she takes as big a mouthful as the burning temperature allows. Then she sinks down onto one of the two stools and stares out of the window.

She wonders how to fill her day. She's got an endless list of things to do, but absolutely no motivation to do any of them; constructing two perfect children before 8.15 a.m. has exhausted her goodwill in the domesticity department. She can usually postpone the dreary reality of life on a Friday because she and Beth always have a coffee together after drop-off. But of course, Princess Beth is too tired to socialise after her late-night misadventure. She'll probably be lying in bed, feeding herself age-defying goji berries as she reflects on what a saint she is.

'Saskia, you're such a bitch,' she murmurs to herself, although with a smile because it's not a label she's ever had a problem with. Beth is her best friend and of course she loves her; they have fun together, especially if there's a bottle of bubbly involved to loosen Beth up. She'll invite her over for kids' tea, Saskia resolves, with a glass of wine of course. It's the least she can do after Beth's stressful evening.

Taking another sip of coffee, she slides her phone open and wonders which social media account to get lost in for the next half an hour or so. She clicks into Instagram first, but closes it a second later; she's already had enough of beautiful mums with perfect homes and seemingly no financial constraints for one morning. She hovers her thumb over the Twitter icon next, but she'll need another coffee before venturing into that arena. So eventually she chooses MyNeighbour. There are the usual uncontroversial posts with legions of incensed comments underneath, and the worn-out cyclist vs motorist vs pedestrian debate. Saskia skirts over the dog poo posts – not relevant, she's way too selfish to fulfil her children's dreams – and the posts that pit her socialist values against her maternal instincts (kids mugging kids is both a social injustice and a terrible crime). But the post about a man chasing away an opportune Amazon package thief gives her an idea.

Saskia giggles as she hits 'new post' and decides how to start her story. Beth is going to get the adulation anyway, so it may as well be on Saskia's terms. And this way, she might get a slice of the glory too, as the pen behind the most exciting news to reach their area since Rosie Huntington-Whiteley moved in. Beth didn't give much detail this morning, but once Saskia starts typing, she finds it doesn't matter too much. As a journalist, she was a meticulous fact checker, so it's a joy to be able to stretch the truth a little in the barely regulated world of social media.

She finishes her post by adding a photo of Beth. She would never choose an unflattering one – that would overstep the mark of decency – but in Beth's case those don't exist anyway, so she picks the first one she can find and clicks upload.

Chapter 5

Kat

Kat scrapes the soggy cornflakes into the bin and looks at the clock on the wall. She's on late shift today, eleven 'til seven, which means she's got fifteen minutes before she needs to leave for work. She holds the empty bowl under the tap and waits for the water to run hot. It takes ages as usual, and she shifts from foot to foot, trying not to think about how much perfectly good water she's wasting in the process, all those different stages of purification, all that potential discarded. Finally the water runs warm enough to detach the last of the stubborn flakes, and she flips the bowl onto the drainer.

Her flat isn't big, and the rooms all merge into one. The kitchen is too small for cupboards, so Kat keeps her crockery in the living room. But that means there's no wall space for a TV in there, so she spends most of her time in the bedroom. Except her bedroom shares a wall – a couple of bits of plasterboard attached to a thin wooden frame – with the man who lives next door. She *thinks* it's gaming that he's doing, not *actually* shooting motherfuckers in the head, but either way, his shouting keeps her awake at night. So she falls asleep on the couch in the living room most evenings. It's a fluid space, her flat.

Kat sighs as she drags her duvet off the blue velour sofa – a second-hand purchase from Gumtree when she could finally afford to move from her bedsit in Streatham – and walks the few steps to her bedroom, rolling her shoulders in an attempt to dislodge the crick in her neck. She launches the duvet into the air, and it lands in a heap on her bed. Then she walks three steps to her left and slips into the bathroom, pulling the door closed behind her and twisting the lock. It's an unnecessary level of security for someone who lives alone, but her morning routine has always carried a sting of shame and it's a hard habit to break.

Her skin requires the most work – cleanse, tone, moisturise, treat, cover. As a teenager, she didn't see why her face should demand hours of attention while everyone else got by with a splash of water, but there have been plenty of lessons learned since then, and now she just gets on with it. Next, she pulls a new packet of contact lenses out of the vanity unit. She hasn't worn Seabreeze Blue before. She dabs one, then another, with her index finger, and places them over her corneas. She stares at her reflection in the bathroom mirror and allows herself a smile.

The colour reminds her of the Indian Ocean, somewhere her dad would take her every now and again when the farm work quietened down. But she hasn't got time to let those memories solidify, so she blinks them away and moves her focus to her hair. Deep ruby red, shorn at the back and spiky on top; she might be a lonely spinster, but at least she's got a badass hairstyle.

Work is less than two miles away, and on a sunny day she might walk it. But the weather is bitter today, bulbous clouds holding in last night's freezing temperatures, so Kat heads in the opposite direction towards Clapham North tube station. It's two stops on the Northern Line to Clapham South, then a fifteen-minute walk through an expanse of million-pound houses to her job at Groom & Bloom.

Amazingly, training as a dog groomer had been her mum's idea, when Kat was back from Australia and struggling to work out what to do next. Kat had spent fifteen years on her dad's farm in the outback, a place called Wandering two hours south-east of Perth. There were no professional groomers out there, so she became responsible for looking after the many dogs on the farm.

Life back in the UK had been so different that she couldn't imagine merging the two worlds, but as soon as her mum suggested getting a grooming qualification, she'd realised it was a way out of Newbury, and the suffocating side of her family. Her stepfather had paid for an intensive course – Javier is always happy to throw money at a problem – and a month later she was qualified. Her first job was as assistant to a mobile dog groomer, but without a driving licence, her career progression stalled as soon as she started, so when a role came up at Groom & Bloom, she applied.

Kat walks up the stairs of Clapham South tube station and onto the busy Nightingale Lane, where the green expanse of Clapham Common stretches out on her right. Before the road peels off towards its smaller neighbour, Wandsworth Common, Kat drops down into a gridwork of residential streets. She could walk down any of them to get to the salon at the end of Brookhill Road, but she always chooses the first one, Wroughton Road. Kat prefers the safety of well-trodden paths nowadays.

But her familiar route is different today. Because the empty unit at the near end of their short parade of shops looks like a crime scene. Kat doesn't slow down as she walks past the flimsy blue-and-white-striped tape encircling the building. She doesn't try to catch the eyes of the two women dressed in white overalls either, or even allow herself more than a cursory glance in their direction. But her heart still thuds with apprehension, the irrational fear that rises up whenever she gets close to a police officer.

The feeling started when she was 16 – when the fear wasn't so irrational – but eighteen years on, she still can't shake it.

She finally reaches Groom & Bloom and pushes on the Victorian-style front door. A bell chimes as she mumbles, 'Morning,' and Sally's head appears from behind the counter.

'Hey, Kat, you look blue; is it still freezing out there?'

Kat shrugs. Her parka might be a decade old, but it still works fine. 'New contact lenses,' she offers as an alternative. 'Maybe that's it?'

Sally squints and stares into Kat's eyes. It makes her feel uncomfortable, but it's over in a second and then Sally is pulling back and snapping her fingers with a smile. 'Yes! Oh my God, you look so different. I loved the green, but you know, I think I might like the blue even more. One day you might show me your real eye colour; I bet that's beautiful too.'

Kat feels embarrassed now. She's not good with compliments either. 'What's with the police outside Delphine's?' she asks, changing the subject.

'Ah yeah, that's sad,' Sally says, her voice dropping an octave.

'Oh?'

'You know there've been those squatters there?'

'Yeah, what about them?' she asks.

'Well, one of them died last night. He was found outside the front with a needle in his arm.'

'That's terrible.'

'Loads of drugs inside the shop too, apparently. You don't expect that sort of stuff to go on around here.'

Kat thinks about her own block of flats, so close geographically, but a world away in terms of expectation. There could be a whole gang of drug dealers inside one flat and no one would raise an eyebrow. 'How do you know? Did you speak to the police?' While Kat's voice would malfunction if she got anywhere near a police officer, she bets Sally has no such qualms. Her boss loves working front-of-house, swooning over puppies and giving

33

advice to owners as she hands dog treats out to their pets. It's what makes them the perfect working partnership, because Kat much prefers hanging out with the dogs in the grooming room.

'No, I read it on MyNeighbour. Put up this morning by that Saskia Tomes who's always posting stuff. She told a right old story, all about the woman who found the guy, how she tried to save him. There's even a picture of her, with a really cute dog. Hang on, take a look …' The work keyboard rattles as Sally's fingers fly over it. Then she swivels the computer screen around until Kat can see the familiar lilac logo on the web page. The top post shows a close-up of a beautiful woman in her mid-thirties with her arm around an apricot cockapoo. Kat's eyes widen and she leans closer.

'How did she try and save him?' she asks, staring at the photo, ignoring the body of writing underneath. The woman's eyes are striking. She reminds her so much of … Kat feels hot suddenly and has an urge to scratch her face.

'Phoned the ambulance, did chest compressions and all that. No first-aid training whatsoever, just her instincts kicking in apparently.' Sally screws her eyes in thought. 'Not sure I would have been brave enough.'

'She was all alone?' Kat asks, still staring. The similarity is mind-blowing. Could it be her? Nearly two decades on? She peers a bit closer. She looks more polished, and the name is different, but that doesn't mean anything; she could easily have changed that. And perhaps it's not surprising that she'd want to start over after everything that happened. But living in London? Near Kat's work?

'Yes, on her way home from a night out apparently. God, can you imagine? Having to get up close and personal, all on your own, not knowing if the man's going to die, vomit or mug you?'

Kat drags her eyes away from the screen. As she reaches for the long apron that she always wears at work, exposing the limbs of the cactus tattoo that sprouts from her left wrist along her forearm, she wonders how she would react if she found a rough sleeper

34

unconscious in the street. She would probably walk away. Not because she's heartless or thinks homeless people don't deserve her help. But because she's scarred, unwilling to be linked to what might end up as a crime scene again. Then she thinks about the picture of the woman in the MyNeighbour post, and how it's just the sort of thing her doppelgänger from two decades ago would do.

Is it her?

'She's stunning too, isn't she?' Sally says wistfully, interrupting her thoughts. 'Those eyes. She lives on this road apparently, in one of these double-fronted villas near the top, I think.'

'Really?' Kat blinks. She can't imagine the resolute teenager that she remembers living in such luxury now, but she's not sure why. Even back then, she never really knew her, however much she thought she did.

Sally looks at her quizzically, misreading her disbelief. 'She looks the type, don't you think?'

'Sorry, yes,' Kat mutters quickly, and luckily their conversation is interrupted by the bell chiming. Kat looks up to see a fluffy poodle dragging a woman inside, her high ponytail bobbing in time with his tail. As Sally beams her welcome, Kat uses the opportunity to slip through the orange-and-charcoal-striped canvas curtain and into the back room. Her heart is beating too fast, different memories rearing up, and she needs to calm down before she can start work. She uses her usual preparation routine to regain control – checking the water temperature, opening a fresh packet of treats to coax her four-legged clients through their grooming session – and it works to a degree.

Her heart rate settles, but her mind remains absent, remembering a teenage girl who changed the path of Kat's life forever, and wondering if the woman who stopped for a man lying in the street is the same person.

January 2003

Chapter 6

Katherine

Katherine feels hot suddenly, and claustrophobic, standing in the assembly hall surrounded by her year group, the breath of the boy next to her stinking of day-old garlic. It's freezing outside, but the radiators are on full pelt and the body heat from two hundred students is mushrooming. Her face starts to itch. She flares her nostrils and looks at the stage.

Her head of upper school, Mr Thomas, is leaning over the lectern, trying to look casual. There's a girl sitting behind him, a sixth former, with her ankles crossed. Her long hair is the colour of dark chocolate, and it falls in waves over her shoulders. Her eyes are a shade lighter, more like milk chocolate. And her skin is smooth and tanned. Katherine assumes she's one of those girls. Beautiful and bitchy.

'Quiet please!' Mr Thomas calls out. Then he turns his shoulder and flings one arm towards the girl, like a talentless ballerina. 'Some of you may already know Becca Fischer in year twelve,' he says. 'Becca only joined us for sixth form, but she's already making quite an impact.' He smiles at her, then returns his attention to his audience. 'Becca's come along today to talk to you all, so if everyone

can give her a warm welcome …' A smattering of claps reverberates around the room as the girl, Becca – and no, Katherine doesn't know her; they don't breathe the same air – uncrosses her ankles and pushes out of the chair.

'Thank you for having me, year elevens,' Becca calls out once she's arrived at the lectern. She's holding one wrist with her opposite hand, Katherine notices, tightly too, because her knuckles are turning white from the effort. 'I am the school's anti-bullying ambassador, and bullying is a subject I feel very passionate about.' This wasn't the speech Katherine was expecting; she tilts her head and stares more intently at the stage.

'Victims of bullying are often picked for no other reason than being a bit different from their peers,' Becca continues. A bit different like having a face half covered in eczema, Katherine thinks. She gives in to the urge, scratches her chin, then contorts her face and shoves her hands into her coat pocket when the itch grows exponentially. Becca is still talking, but it reduces to white noise as Katherine becomes transfixed by her hands. She watches Becca unfurl her fingers from her wrist and, with an almost imperceptible movement, scratch melodically at her palms.

Gradually the sound of scuffing feet and noses trying to breathe through winter colds breaks the spell. 'So it's easy to brush negative comments off as harmless banter,' Becca says. 'But they can really affect people's mental health.' She walks in front of the lectern and Katherine can see the whole of her now. Sixth formers don't have to wear uniforms and Becca is dressed in sage green cargo pants and a black top. She's slim, maybe a size eight, so one year older and three dress sizes smaller than Katherine. The top is sleeveless and reveals her tanned arms, which seem too exotic for a rainy day in January. She's not wearing make-up, but her eyes still seem to have a smoky frame.

'And, with immigrant parents, I have first-hand knowledge of that.'

Katherine wonders where her parents are from, what their story

40

is. She imagines them breaking free of a tyrannical regime, risking their lives, fighting for their freedom. Turning up in Britain with no clothes or money, just beautiful faces and a strong sense of justice.

'Anyway, next time you feel like laughing at someone who's different to you' – Becca's voice is speeding up, pulling Katherine back down to earth – 'please take a moment to think how you'd feel in their shoes. It really is that simple.'

'A powerful speech with a simple message.' She's sitting down, and Mr Thomas is back, Katherine realises with a heavy sigh of disappointment. 'Now, Jake is going to update us all on school sports news.'

Katherine switches on her internal mute button and lets her eyes track Becca to the chair at the back of the stage. She watches her recross her ankles and hold her hands tight until assembly is over and Katherine is filing out with the rest of her class.

December 2021

December 2021

Chapter 7

Beth

Beth pulls her full-length quilted coat tighter around her shivering body. She's not sure she's fully thawed out from Thursday night yet, and standing on the sidelines of a football game, icy rain pattering against the not-quite-waterproof material, certainly isn't helping. Plus it's not really a game either. Martha's under 7s team have finally worked out what direction to kick the ball in, but Simon is her responsible adult. Beth gets to watch Ava play with the under 6s, and half of them are still at the tripping-over-the-ball stage.

'Well, good morning, hero of the hour.' Beth's deep hood has robbed her of all peripheral vision, but she recognises the silky voice without visual input. Lara is one of the friends she was out with on Thursday night, and the mother of Ava's best friend Chloe, who's currently doing cartwheels down the pitch.

'Hi, darling,' she says automatically, then pauses as Lara's words sink in. 'Wait, what do you mean by hero?'

'You, roaming the streets, caring for the vulnerable like some modern-day answer to *Call the Midwife*. Hey, Chloe! Gymnastics

45

is this afternoon; try to keep your eyes on the ball, or at least stay the right way up,' she calls out towards the pitch.

'He was a homeless drug addict, not an East End mum-to-be about to go through life-threatening labour,' Beth murmurs in response. 'Anyway, how do you know about that?'

'Brilliant kick, Chloe!' Lara claps her hands then lifts her thumbs as her daughter scuffs the ball with the sole of her foot. 'I read it on MyNeighbour last night – it was trending as their top post. Your friend Saskia put it on there, I think, so it was full of her usual drama.'

'Saskia wrote about me on MyNeighbour?' Beth can feel her heart kick up a gear at the thought of strangers reading about her actions on Thursday night. 'What did she say?'

'That you came across a man lying unconscious in the dead of night. That his heart had stopped and you had to do chest compressions.'

'That's bullshit,' Beth whispers under her breath. 'I hardly touched him.'

'Saskia used to be a journalist, didn't she?' Lara asks, while simultaneously answering the question of why Saskia would embellish Beth's story. 'Look, I get that you're not one to boast, but you shouldn't feel embarrassed about people knowing how you helped that man.'

'I didn't help him in the end though,' Beth whispers, not daring to look at Lara in case she sees sympathy on her friend's face.

'Darling, even if only half of what Saskia wrote is true, you were an absolute legend that night. It's not your fault he died.'

'I know, but …' The image of that other squatter pops into her mind, his angry face bubbling with accusation. And of course there were the weeks leading up to that night, how she showed her disapproval of their being there. She just wants the whole thing over with. She walked past the empty shop unit this morning – it's on the way to Ava's football club on Wandsworth Common – and the police tape had already gone. Other than a new padlock on the door, there's no evidence that anything untoward had happened there less than forty-eight hours earlier.

Except for Saskia now spreading the details on MyNeighbour.

Beth scratches her palm. How dare Saskia write about her experience without even asking. Isn't she supposed to be a friend? Saskia is clearly feeding her desperate need to be in the thick of the drama without giving any thought to how Beth might feel about it. 'I'm going to tell her to take it down,' she says.

Lara lets out a resigned sigh, as though she was expecting Beth to say that. 'I think you deserve all the hero worship you can get, but I understand why you're upset. Saskia shouldn't have posted anything without your permission, especially the photo.'

Beth's heart freezes. 'What photo?' she asks, her earlier anger turning to dread. Did Saskia snap a picture of her when she was getting out of DC Stone's police car?

'I don't know,' Lara says with a shrug. 'You look gorgeous in it though, no surprise there, snuggling next to Luna. Chloe, that's the wrong goal for goodness' sakes!'

Beth's chest relaxes just enough for her heart to start beating again. But she still doesn't like the idea of her image plastered all over social media. She opens her WhatsApp and clicks on Saskia's face, half hidden behind a big glass of Aperol Spritz. *TAKE THE POST DOWN*, she types, hoping the capital letters will show Saskia how unhappy she is, and waits for the two ticks to turn blue.

'And has she?' Simon asks as he pops open a bottle of Cremant, their staple diet on a Saturday night when they don't have plans. Beth isn't in the mood really, but it's always easier to pretend. 'Taken it down?' he continues.

Beth sighs and takes a glass from Simon's outstretched hand. 'Not yet. She responded to my message saying that she'd delete the post as soon as she got chance. But that was ten hours and about eight hundred views ago, and the woman whose phone

47

is superglued to her hand doesn't seem to have found an opportunity.'

'Maybe it's not such a bad thing,' Simon offers cautiously. 'Getting some public recognition.' He shakes his head. 'I mean, it was such a brave thing to do, in the dark like that; I can hardly get my head around it.'

'Why not? Do you not think I'm the caring type?' Beth pushes, exasperated, but she shouldn't take her frustrations out on Simon. He's the perfect husband; she needs to remind herself of that.

'What? No! Of course you are. I just mean …' Simon's voice trails away. He picks up his phone and looks at the screen. In other marriages, this would be cause for an argument: important conversation interrupted by a damn device. But Beth knows it's different for Simon. His phone checking is a tick that he's developed over years of being at the beck and call of even richer, and considerably more arrogant, men than him. And now he uses the habit when he needs a moment to think. He places it back down. 'I suppose I see you putting the girls first, me a close second, all the time. Creating this perfect life for us. To step away from that, put yourself in potential danger, I guess it's an extra quality I didn't know you had.'

Beth takes another sip of the sparkling wine. It's true that she behaved differently on Thursday night, more impulsively. She didn't spend time weighing up the pros and cons of action or considering how it would look to her peers. But how can she explain that to Simon? How can she tell him that, in the moment when she saw the man lying there, she became someone else? Not a stranger, but the person she used to be before she met him and built a different kind of life. 'He just caught my eye, I suppose. His face was this deathly blue colour, so I knew he was in trouble. I couldn't leave him once I'd seen that, otherwise I'd have that image of him in my head forever.'

Simon reaches across the island unit and takes Beth's hand. 'I didn't think I could love you more,' he says, stroking her fingers and circling the large solitaire diamond of her engagement ring. 'But you've proved me wrong.'

His eyes look suggestive, Beth realises with a start. *The girls are fast asleep now,* they say, *we could take the rest of the bottle upstairs.* To buy time, Beth opens her hand and allows his fingers to slip between hers. Then she looks up at his face and tries a platonic smile. They have a good marriage. They've been together for sixteen years, married for ten, and she still loves him very deeply. She loves his loyalty, his strength of character. His ability to provide so handsomely for his family.

But she doesn't always love him touching her. She knows that's her problem, not his. And sometimes, like when he's fresh from the shower, damp hair glistening and white towel wrapped around his waist, his arms are welcome. But not tonight. She can't be that person tonight when there are so many thoughts swirling around her head. Did she really do enough on Thursday night? Will the other squatter follow through with his threat?

And why the hell hasn't Saskia taken down that post yet?

Her phone buzzes on the hard stone and they both jump. It's on silent, but the grind of the vibration is louder than any sound in her options menu. Beth expects it to stop after two buzzes, signifying a text or hopefully a WhatsApp message from Saskia confirming she's deleted the post. But it keeps buzzing and Beth belatedly realises it's actually a phone call. She stares at it another moment, wondering who it could be. No one phones her anymore.

No one except …

Beth lunges for the phone before Simon can see the name flashing up on her screen. It's an alias of course, but she still doesn't want him to ask who Eddie is. She's a good liar normally, but she's too frazzled to put on a competent performance this evening. Her fingers are shaking again, but she manages to press the red button on her iPhone to cancel the call and slide it away from Simon's eyeline.

'Who was that?' he asks, without a hint of suspicion; their

marriage is too solid for that. The interruption seems to have dampened his lustful intentions too, and Beth feels relief and disappointment battle inside her. Relief that she doesn't have to touch his skin in her current mood, but disappointment that he's not pushing harder for it. She knows every good marriage needs a healthy sex life, and it's not like this is the only sacrifice she makes.

'One of those 0800 numbers,' she answers. 'Probably someone trying to sell me life insurance.'

'Maybe they've heard about your new celebrity status,' Simon says with a chuckle. 'And think your life is more valuable now.'

'Or perhaps they think I'm more in need of insurance,' Beth whispers, more to herself than to her husband, thinking about the angry young man outside the shop.

'Sorry, what was that?'

She looks up and smiles. Takes a deep breath. She can do this, she thinks; perhaps it will even distract her. 'Nothing.' Then she lowers her voice to a purr and nods at the half-drunk bottle of Cremant in the ice bucket. 'Shall we finish that upstairs?'

Simon's face spreads into a beam, his desire back in an instant, and he takes Beth's hand again. He leans over and kisses her gently on the lips. He tastes of toothpaste and ethanol, a reassuring combination, and Beth finds herself searching for more. Perhaps this will be fine after all, she thinks, as he gently guides her out of the spotless kitchen, up the stairs, and onto the perfectly made bed.

Chapter 8

Kat

Kat reluctantly peels off her fleece. She knows she'll be hot soon, that her face will go bright red and sweat will drip from every pore. But right now, the garage is so cold that she can see the eerie glow of her breath in the gloom. With her arms exposed, hundreds of almost-invisible hairs lift up, pulling Kat's skin into miniature peaks. She swears, crosses her arms around her body and tries to rub some warmth into them.

As she does so, Kat allows herself to enjoy the deep curve of her arm muscles, and the feel of their hard strength underneath her palms. There was a time when she could sink her fingers into her flesh, and it would yield with pathetic acquiescence. But her dad had a punchbag on the farm, hanging in the centre of a dilapidated barn, and one night he invited her to train with him. Kat hated sport at school: the pressure of trying not to screw up in team sports, or the loneliness of losing individual ones alone. But Kat found that she loved boxing, as long as her only opponent was a heavy leather sack. She'd done enough damage to other people by then.

Her father had never married, preferring the simplicity of mates down the pub and dogs back home. But even though Kat was just the product of her mum's backpacking trip after finishing college, and lived half a world away from him, he'd always acknowledged his responsibility to her. There were cards at Christmas and birthdays, and even the odd phone call. And when Dr Sharp said she could leave the unit, he'd invited her to stay.

As a 16-year-old town dweller just released from a mental health clinic, Kat had wondered whether she could survive on a remote farm in the Australian outback. But in the end, she thrived. Her father, who'd only been a pen pal before then, turned out to be her kindred spirit, and the physical farm work helped toughen her body. The guilt didn't go, but it kept its distance. Even enough for her to meet someone special a few years in. Vic. Their relationship fizzled out in the end, but it was real while it lasted. Solid. Something she'd considered impossible before she fled the UK.

Kat might have stayed on the farm forever if her dad had noticed the cancer growing on his skin, or bothered to tell a doctor about it when he finally did. They buried him on the farm – that was never up for debate – and as Kat helped cover his coffin in red soil, she'd felt her connection with Australia snap like a dry rubber band. Three days after the funeral, she'd signed ownership of the farm over to her father's right-hand man and best friend – Shane had kept the farm going throughout her dad's illness and deserved that and more. Then she'd flown back to England to make a fresh start for a second time. She'd thought that her years in Australia would have made her strong enough to cope with the other side of her family, to not care about being the runt of an alien litter. But it didn't work out that way, so as soon as she could, she escaped again – to London this time.

She slides her boxing wraps over her knuckles now, then straps on her gloves. There's a row of garages at the side of her block of flats, rented out to any resident who has three hundred quid going spare each month. Kat doesn't fall into that category, but the two guys who live underneath her do, and they've chosen to use their garage as a makeshift boxing gym. It took Kat a couple of months to build up the courage to ask if she could borrow the space, but once she did, the rest was easy. Will and Jayden both work nights, so they gave her a key to the padlock, and said she could have free run of the place from 6 p.m. onwards. In return she grooms their dog every six weeks or so – a jack tzu called Jack, which Jayden assures her is an ironic name, not an unimaginative one.

The bag is attached to the roof by a thick metal chain. She jabs it once, rolls her shoulders as it swings away, then jabs again as the pendulum shift brings it closer. As she increases the speed of her punches, she stays light on her feet, gloves up at her face, protecting her features as the bag takes a beating. It twists and flies, but she's ready for it, spinning on her toes, varying her swing, hooking with her right, then delivering an uppercut with her left. She loves the feeling of power that it gives her, as well as the energy that it strips away. And she loves the total concentration that it demands, no room for any other thoughts to infiltrate.

Like why her mum had to marry a prick like Javier when Kat was 6, then bring Sofia and Gabriela into the world with their pretty names and glowing half-Spanish skin, so cruelly perfect compared to hers. And why her dad had to die when she'd finally found a place where she thought she belonged.

And of course why she's alone on a Saturday night, fighting a punchbag.

She keeps going until every muscle is screaming to stop and she's confident that her body is exhausted enough for sleep to come quickly tonight. Then she packs her gear into her sports bag, pulls her fleece over her damp Lycra and feels her body temperature start to drop again. She finished work at six and it's now eight o'clock, so she's killed two hours.

Only two hours.

53

How is she supposed to distract herself for the rest of the evening?

On Friday night she'd made the decision to forget about the MyNeighbour post. Even if she's right about who the woman is, revisiting those memories is too risky, the chance of redemption too slim. She'd cemented her choice by cooking some complicated recipe for supper and watching all three episodes of *Tyson Fury: The Gypsy King* on her laptop.

But she hadn't thought about the next day. Or how the urge to read the post might strengthen overnight rather than fade.

She pushes open the front door of her flat and heads straight to the bathroom. Once the shower is running hot, she climbs into the bathtub and lets the water rain down over her body. She closes her eyes and lifts her head into the path of its flow. She doesn't really believe in God, or karma or destiny. But there is something fateful about Beth living on the street where she works. As though it's a sign, a kick up the arse to be braver. She is 34 now, Kat reminds herself, not the naive 16-year-old unable to read signals anymore.

And anyway, all she wants to do is read an article about Beth on a social media website. Hundreds of other people will have already done that, so why not her?

It sounds so simple when she thinks of it like that.

Kat doesn't bother with her usual skincare regime, just roughly dries herself, then finds a pair of joggers and a hoodie screwed up at the bottom of her bed. Her dad wasn't one for house rules, so Kat's style of tidying hasn't matured much since she was a teenager. She pulls her laptop off the floor and places it carefully in the middle of her bed.

But suddenly she's not sure. Is she fooling herself? Is this the first step down a dangerous path, like an ex-smoker convincing himself one cigarette can't hurt?

She retreats to the kitchen and pulls a bottle of pale ale out of the fridge, her favourite craft beer that's brewed locally in Brixton. She grabs a fish slice from the drawer, lines its sharp end up against the bottle and flicks the cap off. She smiles as the shiny yellow disc sails up, then falls onto the laminate work surface with a clink. It's a trick her dad taught her on her eighteenth birthday, and it became part of the routine every time they had a drink together. Tonight, it's enough to give her the confidence to return to her bedroom, and the glowing laptop.

She takes a long gulp and opens the website. She clicks the 'Between the Commons' section and it's still the first post that comes up. Before she can stop herself, Kat runs her fingers over the woman's image on the screen. The sky behind is indigo blue and her chocolate brown hair is glistening under an out-of-shot sun. It's definitely her. Everything about her is familiar: the high cheekbones, huge brown eyes and tanned skin. Eighteen years have left their mark of course, but in some ways, Beth looks younger than her teenage self. Her hair is bobbed now, and her skin seems even smoother, if that's possible. Kat runs her hand over her own cheeks and feels the lumps and bumps of eczema scars. Her skin problems were so intertwined with her plummeting mental health back then that she's come to think of them as war wounds. Is she really contemplating opening them back up?

But she's a different person now. Physically, the wobbly flesh has gone, along with the eczema, watery grey eyes and lank, dark blonde hair. And she's stronger on the inside too, more stable. She can do this.

With a sigh, Kat forces herself to look away from the photo and focus on the post underneath it. It's long, five paragraphs, and reads more like a short story than an overview of the event. The author, Saskia Tomes, describes herself as Beth's closest friend. Kat wonders exactly how close they are. There's a tiny picture of Saskia next to her name, but she's mostly hidden behind a big glass of some orange cocktail and Kat can't see her features. She clicks on her name and scrolls through her activity, then onto her other social media accounts. Saskia Tomes is clearly a keyboard warrior, fighting for the vulnerable from the safety of her million-pound home.

Kat gets distracted for a while, clicking from one link to another until she has twenty-odd tabs open on her laptop. When she's satisfied that she knows enough about the woman who claims to be Beth's closest friend, she returns to the original post.

Sally had gone into lots of detail when she relayed the incident at work yesterday, so Kat doesn't learn anything new, but reading the words takes her to the scene, and she shudders as she wonders how Beth must have felt in the moment. Kat reads all the comments underneath the post too. The admirers and the critics, the fanatics, and the downright arseholes.

The forty-seventh comment is a video with just the words #localhero. It plays automatically as Kat hovers over it, and she realises that it's mobile phone footage of Beth. It's dark, and she's crouching down in front of Delphine's with her back to the camera. The deceased man is in shot too, but Kat can see only his legs, splayed out in front of him, as Beth's frame is obscuring his upper body. Even the grainy footage projects something warm about the scene, a well-heeled lady bending down for the lowest in society. Kat wonders if Beth was scared at all.

The post calls her a local mum, so there must be at least one child, maybe more, and she's bound to be married. Did she consider them before approaching the man? Kat feels sure that the teenager she remembers would have stopped, but she knows motherhood can change people. Not Beth though, it seems, and that makes Kat even more desperate to rekindle their friendship. Of course it's important that Beth doesn't find out who she is straight away, not after the way things ended, but there isn't any chance of that. Everything is different about her; even her Berkshire accent diluted to nothing in Australia.

No, the danger is not in Beth recognising her; it's whether Kat can keep her emotions in check this time.

February 2003

Chapter 9

Katherine

'Happy birthday, dear Katherine. Happy birthday to you!'

Katherine wishes she were dead. A faulty plane plummeting to earth maybe, or a flying tree root from a freak storm. Even a crazed gunman barging in through the front door, taking them all out in a blaze of glory. Anything to end the misery of celebrating her sixteenth birthday like this.

'Time to make a wish, love,' her mum says, holding out a plate weighed down by birthday cake, the glimmer from sixteen candles casting creepy shadows over her face.

'Kill me now,' Katherine wishes silently, before taking a couple of steps forward. She wants to be excited about the three tiers of chocolate sponge oozing with buttercream and her taste glands are playing ball. But she knows her mum will ruin the moment. Her eyes will shine with hope that her daughter demurely refuses a slice. And when she doesn't, they'll turn more desperate, silently plead for Katherine to slide the plate away after a couple of mouthfuls. For the sake of her skin. Or figure. Or long-term health. Or some other fun-stifling bullshit.

Katherine blows hard, determined to at least snuff all the candles out in one breath. But of course she can't even do that. Two stubborn bastards continue to taunt her. She flicks her two middle fingers at them and they drop, smoking with defeat.

'Katherine, why did you do that?' her mum complains, creasing her forehead as she plucks each candle out. Katherine considers saying sorry, but decides against it. The only time she's smiled today was when she opened the card from her dad. There was one hundred Australian dollars inside (for when you come visit me) and two photos. The first is of him hugging his dog, a short-haired Australian Kelpie called Hooper. In the other, he's with a massive tan-coloured cow, name unknown. But then the realisation hit – she's 16 and has never met her own father – and the gloom descended again.

'Me and Gabby made you a present,' Sofia pipes up, her little hand wound around her sister's. 'Would you like it?'

'You made it?' she asks. God, why do they have to be so nice?

'Well, sort of.' Sofia looks up at Javier, who nods his encouragement, his features slack with adoration. 'Daddy helped us a bit. It was his idea, but me and Gabby drew the cover all by ourselves.'

'Sofia, why don't you let Katherine open her present before you tell her all the details?' Javier suggests gently, an affectionate tease in his voice.

'Oops!' Sofia giggles, and Katherine tries not to notice how sweet the sound is. She watches Sofia pick the present out of the small pile on their dining room table and proffer it towards her.

She peels off the wrapping paper and pulls out a hard-backed book with blank pages inside. The cover is a blast of colour. Katherine's Journal *is written in large bubble writing, and there are drawings of flowers, trees and most of the cast of* Toy Story *spread across the front and back. She runs her thumbs gently over the designs. 'I love it,' she says, half meaning it.*

'They spent hours on it. Huddled over their little table in the playroom, heads together,' Javier says.

Katherine scratches her cheek.

'I hope you like the idea of a journal too,' he continues. 'I thought it would be good for you to have an outlet, somewhere to exorcise all that teenage angst.'

Rage shoots up Katherine's spine and splutters out of her mouth, disguised as a cough. What the fuck does Javier know? Any angst that she's feeling isn't to do with her age. It's caused by him, stealing her mum, looking down his judgemental nose at her. Making it obvious where she sits in their family hierarchy. Hot tears burn the backs of her eyeballs. She blinks and turns to face her mum. 'I'm going out.'

'But what about your presents from Javier and me?'

Katherine looks at her mum's face. Even tinged with disappointment, her porcelain skin and pale blue eyes look pretty. Why don't those features have the same effect on her? Why does her mum look like an English rose while she's a pallid lump, the only colour coming from her red-raw eczema? 'It's my birthday, my presents; I'll open them when want.' She knows that she sounds like a spoilt brat, but the words tumble out anyway.

'First entry for the journal,' Javier murmurs, the tease in his voice having morphed from affectionate to mocking.

'FUCK OFF! YOU FUCKING DICK!' she screams, panting with the effort.

'Katherine!' her mum cries out, her eyes wide with shock. 'What on earth …' But Katherine doesn't wait to hear the rest of her mum's sentence. She twists on her heels and stomps out of the living room, then out of the front door. She tumbles onto the driveway, then the street. Once she's far enough away, she slows her pace, because of course she doesn't actually have anywhere to go. And now she's stuck without a coat on a February afternoon.

Eventually she makes it out of her endless red-brick estate. She crosses the main road and climbs over a fence directly opposite. There's nothing but low-lying fields on this side, muddy and neglected, and that suits her mood.

'Hey.'

Katherine swivels round.

'Sorry, I didn't mean to startle you. I just thought I recognised you. You go to Newbury Academy, right?'

Becca Fischer. In black leggings and spotless army green wellies. What is she doing here? And how could she possibly recognise Katherine? No one ever notices her. She manages a weak smile and something close to a nod.

'I'm living over there.' Becca gestures towards a short row of narrow rendered houses on the perimeter of the field. Neat and tidy, but small. 'Needed a bit of fresh air,' Becca continues. 'What about you?'

Katherine blinks. She never confides in anyone; she made that mistake once in year seven, and the name of her first crush spread faster than an airborne virus. But for some reason her instincts tell her that she can trust Becca.

'It's my birthday today,' she starts cautiously.

'Happy birthday.'

'My mum did this big family tea. Cake, presents, my half-sisters ...'

'And you needed some time out?'

Katherine looks up, into Becca's eyes. 'Yeah,' she whispers, and feels the warmth of Becca's smile.

'I'm dealing with some stuff,' the older girl says. 'Needed a bit of a time-out too. I tried cleaning the oven, but it's a relentless task, you know? Never quite gets clean?'

Katherine doesn't know – she's never attempted it – but she nods anyway.

'I thought if I could master the oven, then maybe I'd feel better about the other stuff. Stupid, hey?'

Becca Fischer is saying everything like a question, Katherine realises, looking for validation from an ugly kid. 'Not stupid,' she whispers.

Becca smiles again, a smile that makes Katherine want to melt into the ground and fly into the sky at the same time. 'Fancy walking round the field with me?' she asks.

A walk with Becca Fischer. Her suggestion. Maybe this is going to be a special birthday after all.

December 2021

December 2012

Chapter 10

Beth

Even though it's only a five-minute walk from school, Beth breathes a sigh of relief when she crosses over the south circular and reaches the green expanse of Clapham Common. Luna has been straining on her leash since they left Nightingales, desperate for her morning run, and Beth's arm feels like it could be ripped from its socket at any moment. She leans down, unclips the lead from Luna's harness and watches her energetic fluffball zoom after two squirrels. The pair of them dart up a tree, leaving Luna staring forlornly, her front paws resting against the rugged tree trunk in hope.

Beth takes another breath, then picks her feet up into a run, immediately falling into her usual rhythm. It's been a long weekend, a busy Monday, and she needs this today. Saskia finally took the MyNeighbour post down on Sunday afternoon, but not before it had attracted over a hundred comments. A few were kind – other women commending her bravery – but most were derogatory. Plenty of the vitriol was aimed at the victim, taunts about a drug addict leech like him being better off dead, that he was doing society a favour et cetera. *I don't know why you bothered, love.* But there were at least a dozen that targeted her. Some of them mirrored her own discomfort. *A man's dead and you want praise? Disgusting.* But it was a different kind of message that got under her skin. *Hey, sweetheart, where do you live?*

The video was the worst though. Watching herself lean over the man from her crouched position, touch his filthy exposed arm as she tried to find a pulse. Without the benefit of adrenalin, or purpose, it had made her feel sick, and even more furious with Saskia. She was also horrified that someone had been watching her – the man she saw probably – but prioritised catching the saga on their smartphone rather than coming over to help.

At least there didn't seem to be any comments from that other squatter; no accusations or threats. She's spent the whole weekend trying to convince herself that his silence is proof that he was just reacting in the heat of the moment, shouting before thinking because he was half asleep, half drunk, and had just found out his mate was dead. That it's all over now.

Beth arrives at Clapham bandstand and pauses. The circular platform with its upside-down teacup roof is a central marker on the common, and six paths branch out from it like a pedestri-anised roundabout. She chooses the first path on her left, which takes her along the edge of woodland and towards the football pitches. She's careful to keep Luna in her eyeline – there have been too many stories about dog thefts for Beth to ever let her guard down – but otherwise she lets her roam free; that dog needs to be worn out.

The pitches are empty, no matches played on a Tuesday morning, and it's a lot quieter away from the playground and smattering of cafés. Dark clouds have formed in the sky, and the threat of rain seems to be keeping people away. Beth usually loves the solitude of running alone, but today she finds herself searching for the reassurance of others, of strangers doing familiar things. She shakes her head in annoyance. Is this how life is going to be now? Scared of her own shadow? That squatter kid will have forgotten all about his threat, so why can't she?

Especially with her background.

Beth started running when she was 14. It was an excuse to get away from the chaos of her home and forget about the gypsy taunts she suffered at school. Those streets were far more dangerous than where she is now, and as she'd pounded the pavements, she'd imagined running somewhere with views and fresh air and no one lurking in the shadows. Somewhere like Clapham Common.

And yet here she is, feeling like that scared teenager all over again.

The woods on Beth's left provide a thick barrier to soak up the pollution from the road, but in her current mood the towering oaks and horse chestnut trees look ominous in the low light. She sees two thick-chested men walking through them, heads together, deep in conversation. They're not interested in her, of course they're not. But what if they were? What if they tried to drag her into the woods? She looks at Luna, splashing through puddles, chasing birds. She'd be no help. Beth's skin is fizzing now, tiny needles of adrenalin pricking the back of her neck.

Damn it, and damn the kid who threatened her. She wants to run the fear off, but her heart is racing too fast, and shadows seem to be jumping out from every angle. She swivels on her toes and starts heading back towards the bandstand and the busier section of the common. A little faster, just in case. She's sprinting now, running away. Even though there's nothing there. She can sense Luna at her heels, thinking this is a game. Tears start to sprout, but they've become ones of frustration.

And of regret for choosing the wrong route home on Thursday night.

Beth sinks her key into the lock. She'd felt better as soon as her feet found concrete and Luna was reattached via her lead. But as she looks at Luna now, her grey belly and the clumps of mud hanging from her too-long curls, her mood dips again. 'Shit,' she murmurs under her breath. 'We really need an outdoor tap.' She pushes the door open, then reaches down to pick Luna up. But the dog is too fast; she pelts inside and runs across the entrance hall towards the kitchen, leaving smears of muddy footprints along Beth's light oak parquet floor. 'Luna, no!' Beth cries in exasperation, as she watches her once-cute pet spray tiny mud pellets out of the secret pockets of her fluffy coat.

'Is this a bad time?'

Beth gasps, spins around, her heart lurching towards her mouth.

'Sorry, I didn't mean to startle you.' DC Stone puts his hands up in apology and takes a step backwards. 'I thought I'd stop by, to give you an update,' he adds.

Beth looks at him. He's wearing jeans and trainers with a logo she doesn't recognise. He doesn't have a coat on, just a navy sweatshirt, and she wonders why that is. A way of guaranteeing an invite on this cold and drizzly day? Or did he just leave his coat in the car by mistake?

'Mind if I come in? It's freezing out here.'

'Of course,' she answers, smiling warmly, belatedly remembering who she is. 'Give me a second to banish Luna to the garden. As you can see,' Beth adds, gesturing to the floor as she walks down the hall, 'she's in my bad books.'

With Luna locked outside, Beth has no choice but to sit down next to DC Stone and look at him expectantly. She wants to banish him too really, to explain that she's not part of his world, not anymore, but of course she can't do that. 'How's the case going?' she asks instead. 'Have you found a next of kin?'

'Yeah, the deceased was on the system, been inside a few times over the years. His name's Jon Smith so it's lucky he was, to be honest. We checked the prison logbook and there's a sister; she came up from Plymouth to identify the body on Saturday.'

Beth can suddenly see the dead man's face, his blotchy red skin and rough beard. She wonders if his sister still loved him, despite what he'd become. She wants to take a sip of water, to hide behind her bottle for a moment, but she's worried DC Stone will notice her shaking hands. 'That's good,' she mumbles. 'That he has someone to take care of things.'

'The file will be passed to the coroner today,' DC Stone continues, nodding. 'Uniforms spoke to the neighbours; there's no sign the shop unit was being used as anything more dodgy than a squat, which means it's a civil matter. And the post-mortem didn't show anything suspicious, so there's nothing else for us to do our end.'

'That's good,' Beth says again. She wonders if the repetition makes her sound false. 'Poor man,' she adds. But she realises that she means it too. She's never personally been tempted by drugs, but they were always around when she was growing up, and she knew plenty of people who were. Some of them seemed able to control it, but it had devastating consequences for others. Not that she'd reveal any of that to DC Stone of course.

The detective shuffles on the stool he's perched on. 'I also wanted to let you know that we released the other squatter.'

Beth's stomach lurches so she crosses her arms to force it down. 'Oh?'

'To be honest, I think he was telling the truth about the heroin not being his; no sign of anything worse than a hangover when he woke up in the nick on Friday morning. He was clearly aware of his mate's gear being in the squat though – it appears they were quite close despite the thirty-five-year age gap – so we let him go with a caution for possession. He's only 18 and has no previous, so hopefully he'll use this as a warning to turn his life around.'

'And the shop?' Beth whispers. She sees the teenager's face again, how it seethed with anger that night. And also during those few weeks before, the times she's walked past their makeshift

71

home, catching eyes with him. 'He won't be allowed to go back there?'

'SOCO's finished their work, but we've left a message for the owners and the property's been made secure. And my colleague made it very clear to Mark, that's the other squatter, that he's not welcome there. Listen, I know he was an idiot on Thursday night, but I don't think you have anything to worry about. He won't be back.'

Beth lets out a long sigh of relief and it feels like she's been holding her breath since Thursday night. DC Stone sounds so confident, and she lets his words settle on her like a comfort blanket.

But now she wants him gone.

The detective has delivered good news and drawn a line under the incident, so he has no reason to be here anymore. 'Thank you for coming to see me,' she says. 'And for the update.'

Luckily, he reads her signal well and pushes himself to standing. 'No problem. The inquest will be formally opened this morning, but the main hearing won't be for months. And I doubt you'll be called anyway. There's a backlog so they're trying to keep them as short as possible. I imagine it'll just be us lot and the ambulance service asked to attend.'

The news keeps getting better; it really is all over. Beth feels an urge to punch the air, but she smiles warmly instead. 'Of course if I can help in any way, I'm happy to.'

DC Stone nods and mumbles his thanks. As he turns towards the hallway, he notices Luna, still half covered in mud, staring at him through the glass doors. 'I'll leave you to the dirty hound then.' He chuckles, then saunters towards the front door without waiting for an answer. But instead of reaching for the latch, he laughs again and bends down towards the doormat.

Beth frowns. His actions feel overfamiliar somehow. 'Is everything okay?'

'I think your prayers have been answered,' he says, handing her a leaflet. 'Either that or Big Brother really is watching.' Then he reaches for the latch, pulls open the door and disappears down the steps. As soon as she's sure he's out of view and she can peel the smile off her face, Beth looks down at the shiny piece of paper in her hand. *Groom & Bloom: pet boutique and grooming salon* is printed at the top. And there's a handwritten note underneath the title: *20% discount with this leaflet.* She looks at the pitter-patter of mud prints on the floor, the tangle of cockapoo staring at her through the glass, and smiles. She's not a fan of surveillance, but serendipity is a different matter.

Chapter 11

Mark

Mark stares at the imposing Georgian townhouse and hesitates. It seemed like such a good idea on Saturday night, a few cans in, and egged on by the others on the common. But now he's sober, he's not so sure. What even happens at an inquest? Ted is another regular rough sleeper, and he acted the know-all, shouting that it's a public building, and that Mark can just stroll inside. But the blood-red, two-metre-high, wrought-iron railings surrounding the building are giving him different vibes.

But it does look warm in there, which is enticing after three nights sleeping on Clapham Common, freezing cold and petrified. Mark knows there are hostels for rough sleepers, churches that open their doors in winter, but he doesn't want to go down that road. If he surrounds himself with hopelessness, chances are he'll get swallowed up by it too. What he really wants is the squat back, somewhere safe to sleep, and private enough to figure out his next move. The maggots with their evidence bags were gone by Saturday, but there's a new chain and padlock on the front door, and a replica on the back, so access is a problem. He's working on it, but for now, he's on the common, under a nest of old clothes and donated blankets.

With a mix of nervousness and forced swagger, Mark pushes on the gate and walks up the short path to the front door, a heavy slab of dark oak that would fit better in Hogwarts Castle than central London.

'Can I help you?' a muffled voice calls out as he steps inside. A woman is sat behind an antique desk. There's one of those plug-in heaters by her feet and it's glowing red, but she's still wearing a thick black jacket and a grey scarf that's wrapped so many times around her neck that half of her face is missing.

'I'm here for my mate's inquest,' Mark explains, trying to sound like he has every right to be there. Which he does. Ted said so.

'Name of deceased?'

'Uh, Jon Smith.' Mark isn't sure he'd have remembered Jon's surname if it wasn't the dullest name on earth.

'Sorry, no Jon Smith on my list.'

Mark hardens his expression. 'It's Tuesday today, yeah?' Sleeping rough can mess with your diary if your phone runs out of juice, but he's been charging his at the day centre every day on purpose, and it's definitely Tuesday, the date of Jon's inquest. No one told him formally when it would take place, but he overheard the plods mention it when he was waiting to be released on Friday. 'I was told Jon's inquest is today.'

The woman draws her perfectly shaped eyebrows together and pulls her scarf down under her chin. She's wearing dark red lipstick, and suddenly she looks like the mum in the Munster family. 'Who told you?' she asks. 'Did you get a letter from the coroner?'

Mark isn't keen on explaining that he overheard the news in the police station, but if he says it was a letter, she'll probably ask to see it and then he's screwed. 'I was there the other night, when my mate died,' he says, choosing to start with the truth. 'The police said I might be called to give evidence.'

'Did you say the other night?' Her tone has changed, softened a bit. 'Your friend died recently?'

'Last Thursday.'

'Ah, I think I know what's happened. And my condolences.' She dips her head and slides another sheet of paper across the desk towards her. 'Yes, Jon Smith is scheduled for an inquest *opening* later this morning. His full inquest won't be for a few months yet, I'm afraid. The police should have explained that.'

'So can I go in?' Mark doesn't care what type of inquest it is; he just wants to do right by Jon. And enjoy the central heating that he hopes is being pumped around the room.

'It's not usual for witnesses to attend, it's all over in five minutes.' The woman frowns for a moment, but then shrugs her shoulders and smiles a fraction. 'But seeing as you're here, you may as well stay. All inquest openings are taking place in Court 4 this morning, up one set of stairs and on your right.' She points at the set of polished wooden stairs just beyond her desk. 'The officer outside the court will let you in.'

'Thanks,' Mark mumbles, then grabs hold of the banister and hoists himself up one stair at a time.

By the time Jon's name is read out, Mark's bum is so numb that he's been contemplating leaving the courtroom for the last half an hour. He's already sat through six inquest openings – four blokes, a woman and a baby – and could do without another sad story. But this is what he came for, so he sits up straighter and looks at the coroner. Except she's not interested in him. She's flanked on both sides by two suits, one male and one female, and they're all shuffling paper between each other.

'I have his full name as Jonathan Augustine Smith,' the coroner says. Mark smirks at Jon's flamboyant middle name, but then, to his horror, feels a lump form in his throat. He'll never be able to take the piss out of the old guy for it, he real-ises, and the sense of loss feels brutal. 'And next of kin as Jane

Eliana Williams née Smith; his sister. I assume we'll be releasing the body to her?'

'That's correct,' the man in the grey suit and greyer tie says, his bald patch bobbing up and down like a skinned tomato on the boil.

'So he was found by a member of the public,' the coroner continues, running a pen tip down a piece of paper. Mark can just make out the Metropolitan police logo at the top of the page. 'Pronounced dead by the paramedics on arrival. Habitual drug user. Evidence of drug use at the scene,' she reads on. 'It all points to the cause of drug-related death, but of course that's not for today. Let's set a date of twenty-sixth May for the full inquest. Is that okay, Claire?' The coroner turns to the blonde woman on her left, who's staring at a laptop screen. She mumbles something Mark can't make it out, then starts clitter-clattering on her keyboard.

Mark feels a stab of disappointment when the coroner picks up her collection of papers, rustles them into an order, and places them to one side. He's not sure what he was expecting from today, but he knows it wasn't this. The police cared more about the drugs in the squat than the fact Jon had died, and now the coroner doesn't seem bothered at all. He can tell they're moving on to the next dead guy, so it's now or never. ''Scuse me,' he says, coughing to warm his voice up.

'Yes?' If the coroner isn't used to heckling from the public gallery, she doesn't show it.

'Is that it?' He doesn't wait for an answer before continuing. 'It's just that Jon was my mate,' he explains, trying not to let his voice wobble. 'And I was sort of with him when he died, except I was sparko and didn't have a clue what was going on.'

'I'm sorry for your loss,' she responds, her voice holding more respect than Mark has experienced since Jon died, and a while before that, to be honest. 'That must have been very shocking for you.'

Mark blinks, swallows, takes a breath. 'I thought I might get a few answers today, you know, if I came to the inquest. That's what Ted told me anyhow.' His voice drains away. He's not sure why he trusted a useless drunk like Ted.

'Can you come back on the twenty-sixth May?' she asks, but there's no expectation in her voice. Mark knows what she sees, his dirty clothes and unwashed face. If he doesn't have anywhere to sleep tonight, how can he know where he'll be in six months? He wants to clear his throat and explain. To tell her that he's got proper plans for his life, and that his not attending in May will be because he'll have a job by then, for some big-shot gaming designer, too busy to come to some old guy's inquest. But at best she wouldn't care, and at worst she wouldn't believe him, so he just shrugs instead.

'Dunno,' he mumbles.

She pauses for a moment, and the only sound is the rustle of her suited minions shuffling papers. 'What would you like to know?' she asks eventually.

What does he want to know? How Jon managed to give himself an overdose when he'd been shooting up for over twenty years without any trouble? Or is he looking for evidence that it wasn't the drugs that killed him at all, that it was somehow the fault of that witch with the pretty face. Death by contempt. 'How he died, I suppose,' he mutters into the cuffs of his coat.

'Of course you do. The cause of death is very important; that's why I make sure that I consider all the evidence before drawing my conclusions.'

'So it's not definitely the drugs then?' he asks, hope escaping through his tone.

The coroner is quiet for a moment, assessing his words. 'Do you have any reason to think there might be a different cause?'

How does he answer that? Suggest that bitch tutted Jon to death? 'He was a pro with the smack,' he chooses. 'And always used the same dealer. I can't see him getting the amount wrong, or the gear being dodgy enough to kill him.' As he says the words, he realises he means them too. Jon dying like that doesn't make sense.

The coroner's eyes dart towards the pile of papers, then back again. 'Drug-related deaths aren't always overdoses,' she says. 'Or the result of impurities, either.'

Mark screws up his face. 'What?'

'An error in the way the drug is injected can also cause death.'

Mark's eyes widen. 'Is that how Jon died?'

'If users are under the influence of drugs, or if it's been a while since their last injection and they're suffering from withdrawal, shaking hands and so on.'

'He fucked up the draw?' Mark blinks.

'Please don't …'

Mark shakes his head, an apology of sorts. Then a sense of realisation creeps in. 'What if he was drunk?' he asks, standing up and rubbing his clammy hands down his jeans. 'Could that have caused him to do it wrong?' He wants to throw the chair across the room, but it's attached to the floor.

'Sir, I want to help you make sense of your friend's death, but I'm afraid I can't talk about the specifics. If you can make it to the full hearing, I promise you'll get a much more detailed explanation.'

The room spins. Mark's suddenly roasting hot. He can't stop his mind slipping back to that night, the beers and vodka he and Jon shared before Mark hit the deck and Jon moved on to other things. Jon hardly ever drank more than a can of lager, but that night was different. When Mark was out getting booze, that woman had walked past, all dressed up, and told Jon that he scared her children, and that he should find somewhere else – somewhere more appropriate – to squat. Jon didn't usually care what people thought of him, but he liked kids and her words upset him that night. And now he's dead.

Because of her?

Jon wasn't going through withdrawal when he jacked up for

the last time, he was drunk, proper hammered, on Mark's stash of booze. Mark would laugh at the irony if he could stop the anguish contorting his face, the police arresting him for possessing a drug that wasn't his, while completely ignoring the empty bottles of alcohol that caused Jon's death. Does that mean this is his fault? Did he kill his only mate in London?

No.

It was her fault. Jon got drunk because of what she said, what she called him. And now she's acting like the local hero because she was there to watch him die. Mark looks up at the coroner, her concerned face, then he gives her a small nod of thanks and backs out of the courtroom.

Chapter 12

Kat

Kat rubs hard at her midriff, but it's pointless. She can't quell the sick feeling bubbling inside her belly. It's been building all morning, ever since she saw Beth Packard's name on the schedule when she first arrived, and now it's threatening to spill out. Fear and excitement mixing like oil and water.

It was Sunday morning when Kat decided she was going to try to orchestrate a meeting with Beth. But she didn't have chance to put her plan into action until her day off on Tuesday. She'd left the flat early, when the sky was still black, and walked over to Clapham Common. The darkness had eventually lifted as dawn broke, and Kat had tried not to see the splash of red across the horizon as a warning sign. She'd dropped onto Brookhill Road, and then wandered up and down the hill, watching people come and go from the big houses. Office workers looking smart and vaguely put out that they couldn't work in their pyjamas that day, teenagers with untucked shirts and heavy backpacks, grunting goodbyes and slamming doors, and younger children swinging book bags and skipping or scooting down the hill.

81

The door to one of the double-fronted houses had opened at exactly ten past eight and two little girls had walked out. They could have been twins except that one carried an air of leadership. With their matching dark hair neatly braided, they reminded Kat of her own half-sisters and she'd had to clench her teeth to stop any of the old emotions spilling out. A moment later, Beth had appeared with an apricot cockapoo by her side. The photo on MyNeighbour implied that the dog belonged to Beth, but Kat couldn't be sure, so she'd felt a jolt of relief at the sight; her plan was still on track. As Beth had paused by a black Mercedes to wipe a smudge from the back door handle, Kat had even managed to snap a few photos using her phone, something to fill the absence after the MyNeighbour post was taken down, and provide reassurance that Kat isn't going mad; it really is her.

The rest had been easy. She always has Groom & Bloom leaflets knocking around at home, and she'd dropped one in her bag before she left that morning. Scribbling down a discount offer wasn't a problem either because they do it regularly enough for local residents when bookings are slow. December doesn't fit that description – everyone wants their pooch to look their best in Christmas photos – but Sally almost always forgets to include a cut-off date, so the discount leaflets drift in at any time of year. Kat waited until Beth and her two daughters were out of sight on their way to school, and then slipped the leaflet through the letterbox.

And then she waited, part of her praying that Beth didn't take up her offer, and a much bigger part desperately hoping that she would. She checked the schedule when she arrived at the salon each day, and this morning, finally, she'd seen the booking. Mrs Packard was bringing in a 10-month-old cockapoo called Luna. She'd stared at the computer screen for a moment, then added Beth's phone number to her own contacts when Sally wasn't looking.

The bell of the front door jingles and Kat's stomach completes a full somersault. She takes a deep breath in, listens to it shudder out of her then walks into the reception area. Beth Packard is stood there, just a few metres away, her dog held close to her on a navy lead. She's facing Sally, who's sitting behind the desk, so Kat can see her only in profile. Her dark hair settles below her jawline; her lips, nose and eyelashes are all perfect. She's wearing one of those full-length puffer coats, like you see on professional rugby players or North London celebrities, with sparkly white trainers poking out at the bottom.

'Hi, I'm Beth Packard,' she says. 'I have an appointment for a dog groom.' Her voice is smooth and confident, posher than Kat remembers, and Sally is lulled by it for a moment before narrowing her eyes slightly. She's recognised Beth, Kat realises, but can't place her yet. Kat waits for the right memory to click into place. As it does, Sally's eyes widen again.

'You're the lady who found that poor man, aren't you?' she says, awestruck. 'The homeless man who was squatting in the old Delphine's? I read about it on MyNeighbour. It was truly amazing, what you did.'

'Oh, thank you so much,' Beth says with a warm smile. 'My friend posted it on there. Do I just leave Luna with you? It's her first groom, I'm embarrassed to say.'

It's the exact response Kat would have expected from her – deflecting the compliment – and the years seem to tumble away. She hasn't forgotten the trauma that ended their friendship, of course she hasn't, but she does think, after all this time, that maybe she deserves a second chance.

'No need to be embarrassed,' Sally assures Beth, slipping out from behind the desk. 'Luna's gorgeous, and she'll look even better after a bath and a trim.' She leans down, a treat in each hand, and deftly ingratiates herself into Luna's life.

Kat feels rejected when Beth closes the door behind her, which is ridiculous. Sally is handing her the lead to Beth's dog, which is the best way into Beth's life. Everything is working perfectly, and she should be euphoric. She does Luna's groom on autopilot, coaxing her into the bath with a couple of treats (washing always comes before trimming to avoid grit damaging the clippers) and letting her inspect the hairdryer before turning it on. Being quick with her nail trim and firm with her ear clean and teeth brushing. She wants to be more loving, to create a special bond with Beth's dog, but she's too distracted. Her hands are doing an adequate job, acting on the muscle memory that she's developed from the hundreds of grooms she's performed over the years, but her mind is elsewhere.

When she gets to the trim, she tries to be more focused. She wants Beth to be pleased with the finished result, grateful, and Kat imagines that she's got high standards. Cockapoos can have a wide range of coat types, from the tight curls of a poodle to the silky straight fur of a cocker spaniel. With her loose waves, Luna sits in the centre of that spectrum – a perfect specimen – and Kat needs her coat to be short enough to avoid matting, but long enough to preserve her cuteness. She chooses a grade 12 on her clippers, straps Luna comfortably on the grooming bed and sets to work.

By the time she's finished, Kat knows she's done a good job. Sally told Beth that Luna would be ready for collection at 2 p.m., which means she'll be here any moment. Kat leads Luna into the reception area and perches on the stool behind the desk. Sally is on her lunch break so it's just the two of them, and she nervously strokes Luna's soft ears. Waiting for Beth reminds Kat of before, all those times when she'd hang around, hoping for a sliver of Beth's attention. The elation when it worked, and the deep sadness when it didn't. She runs her fingers over her chin and tries not to scratch.

Through the window, Kat sees Beth walking towards the shop, tendrils of her hair spraying out in the wind. She clenches Luna's lead a bit tighter and starts a countdown in her head.

'Wow, Luna, you look so smart!' Beth takes the lead from

Kat's outstretched hand and gives her a warm smile. 'Thank you so much. I don't know how you managed to keep her still all this time; she goes crazy every time I go near her with a brush.'

Shit. Kat can't speak. There's a lump in her throat. What if Beth somehow realises who she is? Recognises her voice perhaps? How will she handle that?

'She's so clean and tidy,' Beth continues wistfully. 'I wish I didn't have to take her to the common ever again. Or at least until the spring.'

Kat manages a chuckle, then swallows hard. She looks completely different now, she reminds herself. There's no way anyone would recognise her from back then. And her voice is different too. 'It's a tough time of year if you're a dog owner,' she manages to say. 'But Luna was the perfect client. And she's beautiful too.'

'Gosh, thank you,' Beth says. 'We think Luna's special, but we're biased of course. It's lovely to hear someone new say such nice things.'

Kat's chest swells. Her plan is working. 'Oh yes, we really hit it off. She was a pleasure to groom.' She enjoys the look of maternal pride on Beth's face. 'And I think you have a discount for today, don't you?'

Beth doesn't say anything for a moment, but her eyebrows draw together and she looks confused. Kat's heart beats faster. What did she say wrong? Eventually Beth responds. 'Now you mention it, there was an offer written on the leaflet I found on my doormat. But I'd forgotten all about it, and I'm almost positive I didn't mention it when I booked. How did you know?'

The lump is back, but it's more like a boulder rammed up against Kat's throat.

'I must have mentioned it, I suppose,' Beth continues, looking away as though she's suddenly embarrassed. 'I'd had quite an eventful morning when I phoned.'

Kat leaps on her doubt. 'The discount was listed on the

schedule,' she says, silently thanking some higher power for Sally being on her lunch break. 'So I imagine you must have told my colleague at the time of booking.'

'Yes, silly me,' Beth mumbles quickly. 'And who would ever question a discount anyway?' She's flustered now, and Kat can't help enjoying seeing Beth's more vulnerable side. She pushes a little harder.

'You know, I do a bit of dog walking when I'm not working here,' she says while ringing up the discounted cost and proffering the card machine towards Beth. 'Do you ever use a dog walker for Luna?'

'I haven't done,' Beth says, dipping her card over the machine. But Kat can tell she's not against the idea, so she keeps going.

'Well, I'd love to walk her if it would help you out at all. And if it's after hours, I could even pop in here and wash her down before I drop her back at yours. Save you having to deal with muddy paws.'

Kat watches Beth's face light up with a mix of relief and something akin to joy, and realises with another jolt of adrenalin that the next stage of her plan may well be working too.

March 2003

Chapter 13

Katherine

Katherine wiggles her nose, then contorts her whole face. But it doesn't help. So she pushes both hands hard into the mattress and starts counting inside her head. She just needs to get to one hundred and twenty – two minutes – without scratching it. The dermatologist warned her about this, but he also promised that the new cream he had prescribed was revolutionary, that it would peel away the damaged skin and reveal something smooth and baby-soft underneath. It just needed time to perform its magic, and not be rubbed off prematurely.

Twenty-three, twenty-four, twenty-five …

BUT GOD, IT'S SO ITCHY.

Katherine shuffles down the bed until her body is horizontal, the back of her head sunk low into her pillow. It doesn't help that the cream is a toxic green colour. She stares at the white ceiling and wonders what her face looks like. The Italian flag maybe.

Forty-six, forty-seven, forty-eight …

No, it's too much.

Her hands fly up, but she forces them to stop mid-air; she needs her eczema gone. How can she stop herself surrendering? Read your journal! *her internal voice screams at her. That must be at least seventy seconds of distraction.*

She lurches over to her desk, and yanks open the drawer. She reaches underneath a pile of GCSE textbooks (all in suspiciously good condition) and pulls out her journal, the present from her sisters that caused her to erupt on her birthday. Since she's managed to erase Javier's involvement, she's started writing in it, and is secretly enjoying having somewhere to offload her thoughts, a place that doesn't have an opinion of its own, or a voice to remind her that eczema breeds in refined sugar, you know.

With a contorted face but deepening resolve, Katherine drops back onto her bed, but pushes against the wall and draws her legs up towards her. She picks up her pillow and shoves it between her stomach and knees to create a wobbly table for her journal. She doesn't want to write in it now – what would she say? I smeared toxic waste on my face today – *but she flicks through the pages to her favourite entry, almost two weeks old now.*

Thurs 2nd March
When Becca saved Katherine …
LUNCHTIME
Mum had made me this salad thing. It actually tasted okay, but I knew people would've taken the piss out of me if I tried to eat it in the dining hall, or say something like: 'yeah well, it's about time you went on a diet,' so I ate it at one of the picnic tables outside. But then Jade Carrington and her mates turned up. They were laughing at my Rugrats *lunchbox (FFS* Rugrats??*) then Jade got a pen out of her bag and said she wanted to play dot-to-dot on my face. She's such a bitch. An ugly, stupid, nasty bitch.*

Obviously I didn't tell her that. Too much of a wimp. I just kept pushing her hand away and trying not to cry. But the more I resisted, the more she forced the pen on me, and the more they all laughed. But THEN Becca showed up! She was with two of her friends and she still stopped, told Jade to quit being such a bitch, and said that she was embarrassing herself the most. Jade's face was hysterical. And her shoulders hunched over as she walked away. Hahaha.

And then Becca told her friends to go on without her, and she sat with me for the REST OF LUNCH. Turns out we like the same music (Radiohead and Björk) and the same TV shows (Dawson's Creek and Buffy the Vampire Slayer). She was so easy to talk to. She smelled amazing too. Apparently it was Impulse Free Spirit. I'm going to get some on Saturday.

And even better, I now know which house is hers. Maybe I should be a detective when I leave school because it was so easy to work it out. I waited until it was almost dark, then went out dressed in black, like in the films. Her street is only short, and I spotted her through her front window inside five minutes. It's one of those houses where the main room runs front to back, super tiny, so then I went into the field and spotted her again. There was even a hedge to hide behind there, so I could take my time. She lives with an older woman, maybe her grandma, and they don't seem to have any curtains on the back, which is good for me.

Anyway, that's me signing off. Hopefully next time I go to Becca's house, it will be through the front door.

Katherine closes the journal and straightens out her legs. That's at least two minutes, she realises with a rare swell of pride. Which means she can wash the shit off her face without feeling like a failure. She opens her bedroom door and scurries into the bathroom on the opposite side of the landing, like a soldier running for cover. But luckily there's no ambush. Javier is still at work and everyone else is downstairs; she can hear them murmuring to each other amidst the thrum of the washing machine and tinny sounds of Radio Two. She rinses her face in the sink with her eyes closed and pats it dry with a towel. Her skin will look terrible now, red and inflamed, but it will be better in an hour; that's what the dermatologist said. And if she keeps going with this new wonder cream, it should be better permanently soon. So if she could just work out a way of shedding her fat thighs she might even start to look somewhere close to half decent. Becca would probably like her more if she did.

Katherine retreats to her bedroom and listens to the satisfying click of her door closing. Shit, the journal is still on her bed, exposed. She grabs it by the spine. But with the pages loose, shiny paper slips out and drops to the floor. She swears again, then leans down and collects the dozen or so photos. But before she guides them back into her journal, she can't help flicking through them. Because Becca looks as beautiful on film as she does in real life.

December 2021

Chapter 14

Beth

As Beth leads Luna away from the dog groomer's, she realises that her neck isn't tight with tension anymore, and she's not jumping at every noise. It's been a difficult week, but little by little, she's starting to feel better. The squatter Mark hasn't returned, so he must have found somewhere else to stay. And he can't still be angry with her, not now he's had time to realise how crazy his accusation was.

And now seeing Luna so smart too. When they first brought Luna home, Beth was nervous that she'd never warm to her, that she would be too distracted by the horrors of what new germs Luna might be bringing into the family home. But her floppy ears and adoring eyes seemed to cast a spell, and after setting some strict hygiene parameters, Beth found she enjoyed having a puppy around, and even appreciated the excuse to wash the floor multiple times a day. But as Luna's grown older, and the seasons have changed, the balance has shifted. So it's a relief to see her looking cute again, and with the elegant edge of adolescence this time. Beth crouches down to give her a stroke, and breathes in her new scent. She smells delicious too. Whatever shampoo they use at the salon, she must remember to buy a bottle on her next visit.

As she resumes her walk home, Beth thinks about the groomer. Perhaps it's not surprising that she was so taken with Luna; she was the absolute stereotype of an animal lover. In fact, when she said her name was Kat, Beth had struggled not to laugh. She was very muscular, but in an outdoorsy way, like she dragged trucks up hills rather than lifted weights at the gym. Her hair was blood-red and spiky, and there was a striking cactus tattoo on her forearm. Her eyes were strange though, a bright tropical blue that didn't seem in keeping with the rest of her.

As Beth starts up the hill, she considers Kat's offer. Luna is used to having two walks a day, but ever since Tuesday morning, Beth has been finding excuses not to take her out in the evening. If she can feel scared in winter's excuse for daylight, how would she feel after dark? Her fears about the squatter attacking her might be receding, but not enough to convince her that night-time walks are safe. Simon takes Luna out when he's home, but he's got a work trip to Dublin next week. She wouldn't normally trust an offer made by a random stranger – she'd do research and choose a professional company with references and insurance – but Kat clearly loves dogs and knows how to handle them. And of course, there's the added bonus that she'd bring Luna back clean.

As she arrives home, Beth's phone buzzes in her pocket, and her mood instantly plummets. It might be Simon, she hopes, but she knows that's just wishful thinking. Because her phone has done this every day since Saturday; the one problem that is refusing to go away this week. She burrows her trembling fingers into her coat and pulls it out. The name lit up on her screen isn't a surprise, but a feeling of dread still grabs at her insides. Eddie. She concentrates on breathing as she pushes open the door, craving the privacy of an empty house. She's alone, so she could answer the call without any risk. But she doesn't want to. She knows that's selfish, but she hates being reminded of the invisible leash that tethers her to a life she walked away from.

Beth stares at the screen until it eventually clicks into voicemail. There won't be a message – Beth made that a condition early on – but they'll call again, and again, until Beth picks up. If only it was coming from a mobile number rather than a landline, Beth would have plenty of options then – text, audio, even video messaging – but sadly it's not to be.

Thankfully Luna is exhausted after her groom and flops into her daybed like a Renaissance muse. Beth wishes she could switch off like that. Even when she's doing something relaxing, a spa day with her girlfriends or a cosy night in with Simon, she's tense with the effort of performing relaxation to a high standard. The only time she feels close to calm is when she's either scrubbing her house to oblivion, or succumbing to one of her pills. It's a sad existence, she supposes, but she refuses to regret the choices she's made. She only has to look around her large, spotless kitchen to see what she's achieved.

Her phone buzzes again and she stares at it. She's only putting off the inevitable, and for what? To see if her heart might actually explode this time? She needs to be stronger, face up to her past. With one hand holding the work surface for support, Beth accepts the call and raises the phone to her ear. 'Hello, Mum.' She says it with as much lightness as she can manage, but the response is a short gasp followed by the sound of someone softly crying. Tears form in Beth's eyes too and she fights an animal urge to fling her phone across the kitchen. 'Don't cry, Mum,' she pleads. 'Sorry it's taken me a while to pick up. I've been busy.'

'I know, I'm sorry,' her mum whispers, her voice staccato between the sobs. 'I don't want to disturb you at work. Or wake you up. What time is it there?'

Beth closes her eyes and transports herself to her pretend job in her imaginary office in Singapore. Their roots may be international, but her parents haven't left England in decades, which luckily means they have no knowledge of different dialling tones or country codes for mobile phones. 'It's night-time,' she whispers. 'But I'm still at work. We had a board meeting this morning, so I'm catching up.'

'I wish you didn't work so hard,' her mum says, both fear and reproach in her voice. Beth's mum moved to England from West Germany when she was 18, nearly fifty years ago, and from Romania to West Germany four years before that, when the now infamous floods destroyed her home. But Beth can still hear the hard h's and rolling r's of her Eastern European accent. 'It is not good for you,' her mum continues. On one hand it's a hypocritical comment, the woman who worked at least two jobs throughout Beth's childhood admonishing her for having one. But Beth knows what her mum's referring to, the problem that sparked their separation and how it will never truly disappear. That Beth's job doesn't even exist makes her mum's fears even more heart-breaking.

'You mustn't worry,' she says on autopilot, her voice flat. 'I love my job, and it's not tiring like the physical jobs that you had to do.' She hopes that she doesn't sound patronising. Except what does it matter if she does? After all the terrible things she's done to her mum, what difference does a silent dig about her job choices make?

'I just miss you,' her mum continues. 'I wish you could come home, just once. Not for long,' she adds quickly. 'I know you don't like it here. But you've been away for so many years.'

Her mum's voice drifts away and with Beth's eyes closed, the silence feels like a black hole. She imagines herself spinning away from earth, from the phone call, from the hundreds of lies she's told her parents over the years. The big ones: the high-flying jobs and penthouse apartments in international cities. And the small ones: the anecdotes about made-up boyfriends, her friends' annoying children, the hobbies she's tried and rejected. 'It's hard, coming home,' she whispers.

'We're old now. We want to see you. We're scared that—'

'I know,' Beth spurts out, cutting the oxygen supply to her mum's warning. 'I will come, soon. I'm due a trip to the London office.' She's speaking without thinking now; she needs to stop but she can't. Perhaps it's seeing that man lying in the street, his dying on her. The way he died has brought back so many memories. Ugly ones, all the reasons she left. But also some happier ones from when she was younger, before everything went wrong. 'I'll come and visit you.'

'Don't leave it too long, *dragă mea fiica*. It's important.'

My darling daughter. How can her mum describe her that way after she abandoned her parents so brutally? She knows why of course, what makes it impossible for them to give up on her. 'I won't,' she hears herself whisper. 'I promise.' She clicks off the call, drops her phone and grabs the work surface to steady herself. The room is still spinning but she knows it will pass. That the anxiety will finally roll away, and she'll just be left with the messy residue, like the disrupted sand after the storm has gone.

Messy questions like can she visit her parents without Simon or the girls getting suspicious? Can she sit in her parents' sad front room – in the house she lived in for most of her childhood – and put on a good enough performance as a singleton in an Asian metropolis for them not to be suspicious? She and Simon lived in Singapore for nearly four years, so it's easy to describe the shops and restaurants, the clubs that expat life centres around. And pretending to be a senior banker isn't as hard as it should be – her parents have no context beyond the narrative she spins.

But how can she possibly hide that she's a mother from the woman who gave birth to her?

She didn't plan to tell so many lies. When Simon first asked about her parents, she didn't have time to think things through, to assess the potential damage of their polarised backgrounds, so she told him they were dead. Before starting at Bristol University, she'd been living with her elderly aunt, her dad's oldest sister, so it was easy to pretend she moved in with her after her parents suffered a tragic car accident. And lying to Simon about her parents meant lying to them about him. It was kinder than refusing to introduce him. She hadn't considered what might come next. Living together, marriage, becoming a family. But the further she climbed into Simon's life, the higher the stakes got. And the bigger the lies.

Beth scratches her palms and realises how sticky they are. She thinks about stroking Luna. Perhaps the shampoo the groomer used isn't so lovely after all. Or maybe Luna's fur has been cross-contaminated, carrying the germs of other, dirtier dogs. In fact, she can feel them burrowing through her skin now. She quicksteps over to the sink, flicks the tap round to the hottest setting and thrusts her hands underneath. The scalding water soothes her, the antibacterial soap even more. But now she can see smears on the glass surface of the induction hob. And two crumbs where it meets the white quartz worktop.

She feels sick, suffocated by the dirt floating around her. She holds her breath – she mustn't let the germs in – then she runs into the utility room, pulls out a freshly laundered towel and buries her face in it. It smells good, like the forest near St-Tropez that they visited last summer, and it allows her to breathe, momentarily shutting out the other terrors swirling around her kitchen.

But the reprieve is over in seconds. She needs more than a memory of fresh air.

She grabs her house keys and whips the sliding door closed. It's an involuntary action – they always shut Luna inside the kitchen when they go out – but today it also helps to create some distance between Beth and the dirt-infested space. She needs to make it clean, but she also can't bear to be in there. She takes a deep breath, and another, conscious that Saskia might be watching, then pulls the front door open and starts walking down the street. The girls have musical theatre club after school, so they won't finish for over an hour. But she could go to Northcote Road, get a takeout chamomile tea. Calm herself down.

Her skin feels like it's burning, but the cold air is a tonic, cooling her temperature, eventually allowing her to slow her pace. The sun is low in the sky ahead of her and even its weak winter glare is too much. She looks away, momentarily blinded, then back again.

And then he's there, in front of her, stopping her path.

'It's you,' he shouts, spit flying into the air. Did it land on her? Did it touch her skin? 'My mate's dead because of you.'

She stumbles backwards a few steps.

'You won't get away with this,' he warns. 'I won't let you.'

Beth pushes down on her trainers, darts across the road. She doesn't check for cars, but it still feels safer, more visible, than trying to outrun him on the pavement. Three women pushing buggies on the opposite side are like magnets, emitting an aura of safety, and Beth slips in behind them.

She doesn't want to look at him, but she needs to know where he is. She lifts her eyeline. He hasn't followed her across the road, thank God. But he's still staring. And then he shouts, *'I told you I'd be back, didn't I?'*

Chapter 15

Mark

It felt good, watching her run away, petrified.

After all, it's not right that she can just strut down the street without a care in the world, while Jon is in some funeral home stinking of embalming fluid, and he's freezing his nuts off under a bush on Clapham Common.

He wants to do more, go further, but it's hard to think straight when he's hungry and cold most of the time, and constantly knackered. When Mark first started sleeping on the common, he had Jon to look out for him. Veteran rough sleeper with a lion-shaped heart. Without Jon's protection, it's not the cold that wakes him up every five minutes, it's his imagination running riot. Expecting a gang of kids to turn up and give him a kicking, or some psychopath setting him on fire.

At least he's off the common as of last night, thank God, and back to having four walls to protect him. He'd worried that the chunky new padlocks at the back and front entrances of the squat might prove to be a permanent problem, but then he got lucky. He'd been at the day centre on Thursday and got talking

102

to a guy who turned out to own a set of bolt cutters. In exchange for a quart of vodka and the address of Jon's dealer (Jon wrote it down for him once, a kind of insurance policy) the guy had offered to lend them to Mark. Mark had waited on the common until two this morning, then walked to the squat and slipped down the adjacent alleyway. He snapped the back door chain on his first attempt. Bingo.

Mark moves a bit further up the hill. Brookhill Road is long and straight, so it's easy to keep her in his sights. After their exchange, the woman ran off and hid behind some mums pushing buggies. But they soon veered off down one of the side roads so she's on her own again now, scurrying back in the direction she came. He wonders if his presence means she's feeling the same insipid dread that has crept over him every night since Jon died; he hopes so.

And she can't stay out forever either. If he stays patient, keeps following until she pulls out a key and slips it into one of these fancy front doors, he'll soon know exactly which house is hers. She's slowing down now, but it's not a house that she pauses outside. As Mark looks at the building behind her, a kind of Victorian-era castle with red-brick turrets and ornate sash windows, he realises it's a school; it must be where her kids go, and that feels like currency somehow.

Other parents are also stood outside the gates, and Mark uses their cover to get a bit closer. The sky is murkier now; the sun has sunk behind the buildings, and heavy clouds hang low. But it's not dark yet. A mysterious white light is sneaking between the clouds, and Mark feels that's a sign, that someone up there agrees with him. Just because the woman didn't inject the gear into Jon's arm, doesn't mean she's not accountable for his death. If she'd been a bit kinder, shown some level of empathy rather than treating him worse than an animal, Jon wouldn't have got hammered, and he'd still be alive today.

Each led by a different teacher, groups of children start appearing at the gate, and one by one, they get distributed out amongst the adults. But the woman he's watching remains child-less. She just leans against the railings with a fake smile on her face, greeting other mums as they come and go, like the queen holding court. He wants to know her name – anything that might prove useful – but the mums who stop call her darling, or honey, or love.

Eventually a tall woman with a mane of blonde hair and crows' feet by her eyes stays for longer than the others. She doesn't stop jabbering – even spills that the woman's name is Beth – but there's a tension between them. After a while, the blonde gives up and disappears into the crowd of lookalikes, leaving the woman – Beth – staring after her, a blank expression on her perfectly designed face.

About half an hour later, a dark mass of overexcited kids appears in the playground. As it disintegrates into individual shadows, two of them are sent in Beth's direction. The sky is pitch-black now, so Mark can follow more closely. He watches the three of them cross the road and walk back down the hill. They stop outside a double-fronted house with three steps up to the front door, one of the biggest on the road. He listens to the click-clack of the girls' school shoes skipping up the steps, followed by a muted bark when their hallway is exposed for a moment, low lighting glowing on a patchwork wooden floor. He watches them all disappear inside, and the door slam shut behind them. So that's where she lives, he thinks, and takes note of the house number.

He'll be back tomorrow, he promises. And the next day. In fact, he'll be her shadow, a reminder of what she's done, until he decides how to properly avenge Jon's death.

Mark pushes on the back door of the empty shop unit and it swings open. The chain and padlock are still hanging there, but only for decorative purposes now. It feels so good to be back here, safe, surrounded by memories of Jon. The old man believed in him – knew that he had prospects and wouldn't be homeless for long – but he also had the patience not to push Mark too hard. He was worth a hundred of her, and he deserves his retribution.

He turns on the small battery-powered light – another gift from the day centre – and looks at the collection of Pret sandwiches he was given earlier. What he really wants is a hot meal, his mum's roast chicken or a lamb curry, but a ham and cheese on white will have to do. Then he walks into the main front room and sinks down onto the sofa. As an ex-dress shop, there are various mirrors on the walls, including a huge ornate one leaning on the mantelpiece of the Victorian-style fireplace opposite the sofa. Mark looks at himself with a growing sense of disgust. His stubble is getting unruly, and his hair must stink beneath his beanie. He used to spend hours in front of the mirror when he lived at home, trying on new clothes, and daydreaming about his future in the big city. He didn't think for a moment that it would look like this.

There's movement beyond the window and he turns to look. Two blokes are walking past, dressed in shorts and those poncy compression socks that sad fucks around here wear to exercise. One of them catches his eye, then looks away, not even prepared to admit Mark's existence. With a jolt of anger, Mark propels off the sofa and slams the flats of his palms against the glass. '*Look at me!*' he screams. '*See me!*' But the blokes just up their pace, and then they're gone.

He kicks the wall in frustration, and watches it crack. But as he keeps on kicking, the wall changes shape in his mind. It's no longer the straight surface of dusty plaster, but the softer ridges of a woman's face.

Chapter 16

Saskia

'Mummy, are Martha and Ava coming for tea today like you promised?'

Saskia swears inwardly, remembering the conversation she's just had with Beth outside the school gates. The invite extended and knocked back. 'No, darling, not today,' she says, in her best honey-coated voice. 'Beth thinks they'll be too tired after musical theatre club.' She counts silently, wondering if she'll get to five. Two, three, four …

'But that doesn't make any sense! They *always* come for tea on Friday. *After* musical theatre club.'

'I know, sweetie.'

'And they didn't come *last* week because they were too tired!'

'I understand why you're disappointed.' She tips her head to one side and tries to look sympathetic. But the watery film that's now spreading across Olivia's eyes isn't helping. Not because she's unmoved by her children missing out on their routine Friday playdate, the highlight of their week, but because there's a more dominant emotion wanting to express itself.

Because why the actual fuck should Beth always get her own

way? Why is it always Saskia, or Saskia's children, who have to make sacrifices, pander to the Packards' fragile dispositions? If Beth is in the mood for socialising, then Saskia is expected to be there, along with every other handpicked friend in the area. The three-line whip of high-end nappy valley. But the same rules don't apply when Saskia is sad, or lonely, or bored half to death by her inconsequential existence.

And now Beth is expecting an apology for the MyNeighbour post too. There was nothing but compliments in that piece, but still, Saskia's the bad guy, trampling on Beth's right to privacy or some such bollocks. And Beth was so overdramatic about the comments that the post attracted too. Of course there's going to be some nasty ones – that's why MyNeighbour thrives for Christ's sake – but there were loads of positive ones too. Someone even posted a video of Beth looking like Florence Nightingale in that floaty Whistles dress. And yet she's still pissed off.

'Mummy?'

Saskia snaps back to the moment and looks at her daughter. Olivia is worth ten of her. The girl has somehow managed to inherit all of Saskia's good qualities – strong principles, dogged perseverance, work ethic – and none of her bad. Not yet anyway. There's still time for the FOMO and penchant for cocktails to kick in, she supposes. 'Yes, honey?'

'Do you think it's because Martha doesn't like me anymore?'

Rage rises and circles inside Saskia's chest, like a lone shark. 'Olivia, darling,' she says, crouching down and taking her daughter's hands in hers. 'It is absolutely not because Martha doesn't like you, okay? In fact, it has nothing to do with Martha, or Ava,' she adds.

'Well, what is it then? They can't *still* be tired.'

Saskia sighs and straightens up. She opens the fridge and picks a half-full bottle of Sauvignon Blanc out of the door. 'Beth is upset with me,' she finally says, pulling a glass out of the cupboard (*God, that needs a wipe-over*) and pouring a generous measure. 'I think this is her way of punishing me.'

'That's mean of her.'

'Adults can be mean.'

Olivia screws up her face like a cartoon character, or more accurately, how everyone is born to express themselves before they realise life is a continuous game of poker and showing your hand must be avoided at all costs. 'But I thought Beth was your best friend?'

Saskia smiles and nods, then takes a large sip. Poker face. 'She is my best friend. We've had a little falling-out, just like you do sometimes with your friends. It's not a big deal; I only told you so that you don't worry about Martha. I bet we'll have made up by next week.'

'Do you promise?'

'That we'll be friends again?' Saskia takes another gulp. As the initial hit of alcohol spreads through her limbs, the idea becomes more palatable. Maybe she should just apologise, curtsey even. Then Princess Beth will forgive her, and they can both move on. Life's too short to hold a grudge, especially when the friend in question lives directly opposite, and their children are best friends.

'And that Martha and Ava will be allowed to come for tea next Friday,' Olivia goes on. 'I really want to show them my elf on the shelf, and it's the last day of term, so we might not get another chance,' she pleads.

Saskia draws her daughter into her midriff and strokes her hair. It's long and blonde, like her own but without the chemicals. Saskia's not the maternal type – when she first announced her pregnancy, the general reaction was more akin to shock than delight – but as it turned out, she's fairly passionate about it. Not the chores element – homework, washing, signing school trip waivers – but the fundamentals of motherhood. Loving, championing, protecting her children. She does that part like the stereotypical lioness. 'Of course I promise,' she whispers, and silently challenges Beth to dare turn her invite down again.

Chapter 17

Kat

'You're different now, Kat. Body shape, eyes, hair, even your name; everything about you. So this time, it's going to be different with Beth too, okay?' The words ring out in the small bathroom as Kat stares into the mirror. She thinks about the old saying, that talking to yourself is the first sign of madness. But she knows that's not true. Madness thrives in silence, when the only voice you listen to is the one inside your head.

And it's not like she could say these things to anyone else.

Kat churned through her regular weekend activities: visits to the garage to punch some of the tension out of her shoulders; walks across the common, her heart clamping down every time she saw an apricot cockapoo. But she was just killing time really. Waiting for the message that finally beeped through this morning. When she read Beth's text asking if she could walk Luna after work today, Kat had felt a heat spread through her, a warm glow down her arms and something hotter burning her neck and cheeks. It was happening.

She still needs to be patient, to give Beth time to feel relaxed around her, but she's chosen this path and she's walking down it.

Kat hadn't told Beth that it's her day off. Stopping at Beth's on her way home from Groom & Bloom was one thing, but if she revealed that she'd be making a special trip it might seem overzealous, or give some hint of her ulterior motive. Even worse, it might cause Beth to change her mind, and Kat couldn't bear that.

Kat pushes herself off the sink and away from the mirror. Her heart is already racing; she can't imagine how she's going to feel when she's stood outside Beth's house, ringing her doorbell, seeing her standing on the threshold. But she needs to hold it together because Beth mustn't get suspicious. With the way their friendship ended, Beth would be unlikely to welcome Kat with open arms if she knew her true identity.

Kat lifts her frayed parka off its hook by the front door and walks out of her flat. She nods at a neighbour she's never spoken to, a tired-looking woman clutching a sky blue Co-op bag for life in one hand and a small child in the other, then clumps down the stone steps, and out onto the road. It's milder today, but the sky is already black and there's drizzle in the air, so she heads for the tube station.

The house looks even bigger up close, Kat thinks as she tries to drum up the courage to walk up the steps and ring the bell. All the houses on this street have an air of ostentation, ornate archways over the front door and fancy shutters in the windows, but Beth's is double the width of all the others. The front door seems to loom over her while her feet stay welded to the mosaic-tiled pathway. Kat can hear noise inside, a child gabbling. The tale is too fast and high-pitched for Kat to decipher any of its meaning, but the sounds of normal life settle her nerves a notch and she takes three tentative steps upwards.

She wonders if Beth will invite her in, or just hand Luna over at the door. Will they chat for a while? As friends? Or will Beth treat her like staff, reel off a list of instructions and thrust a roll of poo bags in her hand? There's only one way to find out. She takes a deep breath and presses the doorbell.

A few moments later, the door swings open and Beth is stood there. She's so close, only inches away, and as her perfume wafts across Kat's pockmarked skin – a different scent to the one Kat remembers – she starts to feel dizzy. She wonders if she's going to faint.

'Oh hi, Kat. Thanks so much for this.' Beth smiles; it's warm, and her white teeth gleam in the overhead light. Then her eyes dip down, take in Kat's ancient coat, thick black cargo pants and dusty Timberland boots, and the smile fades. 'You know what, let me get Luna for you. You don't want to be hanging around here.' She swivels her head, but her body continues to block the doorway. 'Martha! Can you put Luna in her harness and bring her out here with her lead?'

Kat's itching to get inside now. She wants to reach out to the thin ceramic table lined up against the stairs and pick up each photo frame in turn, scrutinise the pictures of Beth's family. From this angle she can see only the far end of the table, and just make out the faces of two little girls in matching rainbow-striped dresses. Another picture is a family shot taken in one of those studios, a soft white background with the four of them smiling in loose linen clothing. She can't see the other side of the table. She wonders if there are pictures of Beth's mum and dad, and if they're beautiful like her; they were always a mystery, even back then.

One of the girls from the photo tumbles out of the kitchen, being dragged down the hallway by Luna, who's attached via the lead.

'Careful, Martha,' Beth says, a little tut escaping. 'Kat's going to think we have no control over our dog.'

That's her cue to speak, Kat realises with a start. 'Not at all,' she says. 'Luna's still a puppy really – she's bound to get excited when there's a walk on the cards.'

111

Beth smiles again, but her eyes slip behind Kat, towards the pavement. Kat allows herself one more look, then takes Luna's lead and turns back down the steps. 'I'll give her an hour on the common, then a wash at the salon, so we'll be back around seven o'clock.'

'Thanks, Kat, you're a real star.'

Kat turns left towards Wandsworth Common, the closer of the two commons to Groom & Bloom. Streetlamps cast their glow over the parkland closest to the road, but Kat isn't scared of the dark, so she heads deeper in, towards the trees. Luna clearly approves because her tail is up and wagging ferociously as she forages in the leaves. Kat watches her chase a squirrel until it disappears up a tree. But instead of losing interest, Luna sits patiently beside the trunk, nose up, waiting for it to reappear. Her unfailing optimism, against all the available evidence, feels like a message for Kat. *Keep going; you failed last time, but this time will be different.*

Kat feels the now familiar tug at her insides as she walks back up the hill towards Beth's house, a newly washed Luna trotting beside her on the lead. She pauses on the threshold, staring up at the light glowing through the glass panel above Beth's front door. Is she's doing the right thing? Following her instincts, taking these risks again? The focus saps her peripheral vision, so it's a shock when someone suddenly pushes past her, too close, clipping Kat's shoulder with theirs. Kat lets out a gasp. 'Sorry,' she says, on auto-pilot, wondering why she's apologising for being bumped into. But instead of returning the apology, or just walking away, the offender turns to face her. It's a young man, skinny but tall, with a pale face and dirty red hair poking out of a black beanie. He doesn't speak, but his expression – angry and resolute – is enough for Kat's heart to race. She wonders if he's going to pull a knife, demand Kat's phone and money. He'd be disappointed with Kat's second-hand iPhone 6 and the sole two-pound coin in her pocket if he did.

'Do you know her?' he finally says.

'Sorry?' Kat says again, but in confusion this time.

'The woman who lives in that house,' the guy spits out, nodding his head towards Beth's house. 'Are you friends with her?'

'No, I … What's it got to do with you, anyway?' Kat blusters, trying to meet his threatening tone with something close to assertive. But he ignores her question.

'Do you know what she did?' he says, stepping forward until his face is only inches from hers. 'She let a man die, caused his death, watched it happen.'

Kat shakes her head, trying to make sense of what he's saying. Is he talking about the drug addict Beth called the ambulance for the other night? Kat can smell the man now, the vinegary cologne of stale sweat. His lips are curled into a snarl, but his eyes don't quite match up. They're grey, like Kat's, but with a hint of blue that makes them look almost celestial in the glow from the overhead streetlamp. And they flicker with more than anger. He suddenly reminds Kat of her teenage self, and she feels a rush of sympathy for him.

'She wasn't responsible,' she whispers. Her face prickles in the cold air, and she suppresses the urge to scratch her skin. 'It's a tragedy, him dying,' she continues, 'the paramedics not being able to save his life. But it's not Beth's fault.'

'You don't know shit, you fat cow. Fat and stupid.'

Saliva forms in Kat's mouth and she tries to swallow it, but her throat constricts. She feels it gather like a sticky puddle at the back of her mouth. She's not fat; not anymore. Why did she feel any sympathy for him? 'I don't know who you are,' she growls. 'Or what the fuck you're talking about. But you need to leave Beth alone.' She takes a few steps forward. 'For your own sake. Do you understand?' She clenches her fists and broadens her shoulders. She knows she looks intimidating; she's trained hard enough over the years, turning all that jelly into muscle.

Her aggressive stance seems to work because he takes a step

backwards, and a few more. But then he pauses, resolve creeping back up with every metre of distance made. 'She did kill him,' he snarls. 'She deserves to be punished.'

'Heroin killed your friend. Pure and simple. You need to leave Beth alone.'

'You're wrong.'

'Stay away from her,' Kat hisses.

He juts out his chin. 'She's the real scum, not Jon,' he growls. Then he gives Kat one last look of disgust and turns back down the hill. Kat watches the black-clothed figure disappear into the dark night, then turns back towards Beth's front door. Despite what has just happened, she feels totally calm. Because she knows Beth better than he does. Better than anyone around here.

April 2003

Chapter 18

Katherine

Katherine zips her coat up to her neck. She knows it makes her look even more like a balloon, but she's freezing. If she tried moving a bit, she might warm up, but she can't risk it. Can't risk them seeing her.

Because how would she explain that?

Her mum doesn't know she's in town either, let alone in Victoria Park. Not that Katherine lied to her; it just sort of happened. She was hanging out on her estate, but then found herself walking down Becca's street. She nearly got caught too because two of Becca's friends turned up – one Katherine recognised, Clara, and another one she didn't – but luckily, she managed to hide behind a neighbour's car when Becca opened the door. The three of them left together soon after that, and Katherine followed. She even got on the same bus as them without being spotted.

The three sixth formers are in the skate park now. Sat on the edge of the concrete quarter pipe, legs dangling over the side, drinking cans of cider and talking too quietly for Katherine to hear. It's funny, watching them. Part of her aches to go over there, to sit down next to Becca, clink cans and lean in, create some distance from Clara and that other one with peroxide hair. But a bigger part of her enjoys watching, imagining what could happen, rather than risking sounding stupid, or worrying about how Becca might react.

Ever since that lunchtime when Becca stood up to Jade on her behalf, she's been doing a lot of imagining, daydreaming about them spending time together. She worked out that Becca uses public transport rather than the school bus, so she swapped her mode of transport too and they now bump into each other quite regularly. Becca always smiles at Katherine when they pass each other, and twice – when the seat beside her has been empty – she's nodded at it. That's when Katherine's heart has almost exploded, because she gets to sit next to Becca, their shoulders practically touching, for nearly half an hour. She's not sure what it means, the tingling on her skin coupled with the squirming in her belly. But she knows she likes it.

The older girls are sat with their shoulders touching now. There's plenty of space, so Katherine doesn't see why they need to be so close. She grabs hold of the low tree branch that's providing her camouflage, and grips it tightly, feeling the rough surface send tiny jolts of pain through her skin. Clara with her oh-so-cool afro drops an empty can over the edge of the pipe, and Katherine listens to it skitter along the smooth concrete. Then Clara lowers her head until it's resting on Becca's shoulder. Katherine takes a deep breath. Clara has good skin too. Her dad is Caribbean, and her mum is Irish, so of course she doesn't have to worry about being pale or using toxic eczema creams that don't fucking work. Kat bites the inside of her cheek and circles her tongue around the flap of dead skin.

Eventually Clara rights herself and a few minutes later they all push off the ground and unfurl their legs. Becca slips over the side, disappearing from view for a moment, then reappears with Clara's empty can in her hand. Katherine can still hear the other two laughing as she watches them walk towards the high street.

'Where have you been?' her mum asks, but her tone is curious, not accusatory. Singsong even. Her cheeks are flushed and there's a

118

smile dancing on her lips. She and Javier have got friends over for dinner, and Katherine can hear a mixture of squeals and bellows escaping from their dining room.

'Nowhere special,' she says. 'Just out.' She watches her mum run her finger down the page of the recipe book that lies open on the work surface, trying to make sense of the instructions.

'One and a half teaspoons of sugar per ramekin dish,' she reads. 'Can you remember that for me?' She opens the fridge door and picks out a small white dish in each hand. 'Where did you say you were?' She slides the desserts onto the kitchen work surface and returns to the fridge for more. Her hair hangs in pretty curls either side of her face, and she's wearing more make-up than usual. But her lipstick is smudged, the effect of having eaten two courses already, and the imperfection spurs Katherine on.

'I was with a friend.'

'That's good – I'm glad you're getting out. Who was it?'

Katherine pauses for a moment, then whispers tentatively, 'A new friend.'

'Oh?' As though sensing the thickening atmosphere, Linda stops moving, frozen in the middle of the kitchen, a ramekin in each hand. 'Do I know her?'

'She's a sixth former,' Katherine offers, her heart hammering against her chest. 'But we've become really close lately.' She watches her mum place the desserts next to the others – eight in total – and take a teaspoon out of the drawer. 'I really like her.' She speaks so quietly that her words are barely audible, but her mum's antennae are quivering on high alert now.

'How much sugar did it say?' she asks, staring at the pattern of pale yellow circles edged in white, buying time.

'One and a half teaspoons per ramekin,' Katherine murmurs.

Linda nods, like Katherine has just said something profound, then dips the teaspoon into the sugar bowl. She takes a deep breath. 'Is she more than just a friend, Katherine?' she asks without looking up.

Katherine's heart skips a beat, then races fast forward as she watches her mum shake her hand from side to side, grains of sand raining down onto solid custard. Because she knows what her mum is asking. And she's right, because Becca is more than a friend. She's a soulmate, the person who occupies Katherine's every thought, and the only living being who always makes Katherine feel better. Is that what love is? Does that mean they're in love? 'Would it matter if she was?' she asks.

'Of course not,' her mum says gently. 'I know it's a cliché, but I just want you to be happy.'

'She makes me happy,' Katherine promises, her voice still tiny.

Her mum's hand stills, and she looks up. Their eyes catch and Katherine can see tears glinting in her mum's eyes. Tears of relief probably, thinking there's finally someone to offload Katherine onto. But maybe a few of happiness. Katherine takes a breath and feels an unfamiliar urge to puff out her chest like a mating pigeon.

'That's great, baby. Really great,' her mum says, lopsided lipstick stretching out across her face.

Katherine can't remember the last time her mum called her that. Definitely before Sofia was born though. She suddenly loves the intimacy of this moment, her half-sisters in bed, forgotten, and her sharing this secret with her mum. She doesn't want it to stop. 'Can I help with the desserts?'

'Of course you can. I need to burn this sugar and I'm not sure I trust myself after the amount of wine I've drunk.'

Katherine takes the proffered blowtorch out of her mum's hand, curls her fingers around its grip and flicks off the safety catch. She angles it towards the closest ramekin dish and presses down. The sapphire flame is like a magnet, drawing her eyes closer. As she watches the golden grains bubble and meld into a burnt and blackened crust, she knows it will taste delicious, that its sweet crunch will mix with the soft creaminess beneath. Katherine wishes life was like crème brûlée. That you could be ugly and damaged on the outside and people would still want you.

'And does she have a name?' her mum asks finally. 'Your, um, girlfriend?' She starts transferring the finished desserts to a wooden tray with stainless steel handles, and the ceramic dishes chime as they clink against each other. She'll be gone in a moment, Katherine thinks. Back to her friends, her glass of wine, Javier's hand reclaiming possession as he strokes her arm.

And Katherine will be alone again, the odd one out. Too old to go to bed, too young to join the dinner party. All she's really got is … 'Becca,' she says. 'She's called Becca.'

December 2021

Chapter 19

Beth

Beth recognises the fumble of Simon's key in the door and steels herself for the inevitable mayhem. As usual, Luna is the first in the family to notice. She lifts her head at the sound and draws back her ears. After a moment of stillness, she launches out of her daybed and flies towards the front door, paws slipping and scattering on the wooden floor.

At least she's not leaving any muddy pawprints this evening; Kat did an excellent job of returning her both tired out and clean. When Beth first texted the groomer about taking Luna for a walk this evening, it was out of desperation rather than planning – Simon was working late, and she was still petrified by the memory of Mark's accusing words on Friday afternoon – and she still wasn't convinced it was a good idea. Then when Kat appeared to angle for an invite when she first arrived, that uncertainty had strengthened. But it had been a different story when Kat dropped Luna back. The dog was exhausted, and spotlessly clean, even by Beth's standards. She'd had a twenty-pound note ready, and Kat hadn't tried to linger.

The front door swings open and Luna jumps, but Simon is ready for her – the two of them perfected this trick many weeks ago. With his elbows bent, and forearms exposed, he catches her deftly. 'Hey, pup, how are you?' he asks, pushing the door closed with his foot, causing Beth to wonder whether he's left a mark on the white-painted wood. As she watches Luna lick his face in answer, and him respond with a muted laugh through zipped-up lips, she can't help visibly shuddering. Why does he let Luna do that to him? Does he not realise where her tongue has been?

A moment later, there's a clattering on the stairs and their younger daughter appears. 'Daddeee!' As Simon lowers Luna to the floor, Ava wraps her arms around his waist and pushes her head into the slight curve of his torso, her trusted companion tig-tig still scrunched in her fist. She's always been a daddy's girl, but Beth doesn't mind their closeness. Simon is the anchor in this family, not her, so it's something of a relief to see Ava gravitating towards him.

'Hey, gorgeous. How was your last Monday at school in 2021?'

Ava screws up her nose. 'Huh?'

Beth rolls her eyes at Simon before kissing him dutifully on the cheek (close to his ear to avoid the areas Luna might have licked). Then she turns to her daughter. 'How was your last Monday at school before Christmas, Ava?'

'CHRISTMAS!' Ava cries out, proving Beth's point in one high-volume screech. Magical elves and flying reindeers are much more exciting than some obscure concept of a new year.

Martha's head pops out from behind the playroom door. 'Hi, Daddy. Why are you talking about Christmas?' At 7 years old, Martha is losing her cuteness; chubby face replaced by elegant cheekbones, and milk teeth pushed out by giant slabs of enamel. Beth knows there's something beautiful forming underneath, but the transition still makes her sad. Because the older Martha gets, the more she looks like Beth. And the harder it becomes to pretend Beth's origins – her Romanian genes, the hardship of her

126

teenage years – aren't buried inside her. 'Are you talking about Santa Claus? Is he definitely coming, Mummy? Because Olivia said he's not real.'

'Huh?' Ava screws up her nose again.

'Of course he's real, Martha,' Simon says, gilding his voice with honey to hide the panic bubbling underneath. 'What would even be the point of Christmas if Santa Claus didn't exist?' Beth pushes her lips together. Simon picks Church of England every time a form asks for his religious identity, and she understands he was dragged to church quite frequently as a child, but he doesn't seem to hold any actual religious beliefs. For her part, she always ticks the non-religious box. But the ten or so years that she spent going to Mass every Sunday have left an indelible mark on her conscience, so Simon completely neglecting to mention the nativity isn't easy to stomach.

But of course she stays silent. Simon doesn't even know she was brought up Catholic, and revealing it is a risk she doesn't need to take.

'Olivia says there are two billion children in the world. And that there's no way one man could deliver presents to all of them in one night.'

'He has elves,' Ava points out hopefully.

'And Olivia is missing the point,' Simon says, sounding more confident now, warming to his theme. 'Father Christmas isn't a man – not like me or Grandpa, or Olivia's daddy. He's a magical creature, a symbol of what Christmas represents. Family, kindness, generosity, charity ...'

'PRESENTS!' Ava screeches, this time adding a spinning motion. Luna takes this as her cue to join in, and starts chasing her tail and barking at the frustration of not catching it. Martha drops to her knees, her suspicions cast aside for now, and dissolves into giggles as she tries to slow the manic cockapoo down.

'And presents,' Simon finishes, winking at Beth. She smiles in response and takes in the view. Two lovely daughters playing with their family pet. A handsome and loving husband, shrugging off his Hugo Boss overcoat and unknotting his Tom Ford tie. A beautiful home and privileged lifestyle. The perfect tableau.

So why is she struggling to breathe?

Because of a stinking teenager with a ridiculous idea in his head? Or the memory of her mum sobbing down the phone? She's worked so hard to protect what she's built, this perfect life; surely she's got the strength to get through this blip too? She takes a deep breath, smiles more warmly this time. 'Drink?' she asks.

'Well, it is the last Monday at school before Christmas, I suppose,' Simon answers. 'Let's open a bottle of red.'

Beth retreats to the kitchen and pulls an Argentine Malbec out of the wine rack, pretending not to notice that her hands are shaking again. As she slides it inside the electric bottle opener, she hears Simon drop onto the stool in front of the island unit.

'This is addressed to you,' he says.

'What is?' she asks, her back to him as she pours wine into two glass tumblers.

'A Christmas card, I guess. I found it on the doormat.'

Beth turns to face Simon, and hands him a glass. She takes a large sip from her own, savours the rich fruity wine as it trickles down her throat, then picks up the white envelope. Her name is written in capital letters. BETH. The flap isn't stuck down, but it looks used. She pulls the card out.

Except it's not a Christmas card.

And it's too late to hide it from Simon.

FEELING GUILTY YET, BITCH?

I'M WATCHING YOU …

Big letters, scrawled in black Biro.

She drops it onto the white quartz, can't stop a gasp flying out of her mouth.

128

'What the fuck?' Simon grabs it – not a greetings card at all, just a ripped-up section of Pret sandwich packaging in a used envelope – and lifts it towards his face, as though hoping it will read differently at close range. 'What's this about?' he demands when the message doesn't change. 'Who would send you this?'

Beth shrugs, tries to smile, but the air around her is too heavy, weighing down the corners of her mouth. 'I don't know,' she whispers. The words slide out slowly, but her thoughts are faster. The note has to be from Mark; did he follow her last Friday and find out where she lives? What should she tell Simon? He knows about Mark – DC Stone told him what happened outside the shop when the detective dropped Beth home – but he accepted her assurance that it was nothing to worry about, and he doesn't know about the squatter appearing on Friday afternoon. Will he want to call the police? She couldn't bear that. She needs this whole ugly event to be over, finished, not evolving into something bigger and more awful.

'Hang on, you don't think it's that homeless kid, do you?' Simon says, invading her thoughts, his face screwing up in disbelief. 'The one that shouted at you outside that squat?' He shakes his head. 'If he's still angry ten days on, there is something seriously wrong with him. We should call the police.'

'No, I …'

'He's dangerous, Beth.' Simon pauses, realisation creeping over his face. 'And he knows where you live. Christ, he must have followed you.' He pushes off the stool and starts pacing up and down the length of the island unit, sweat beading on his forehead. It's funny to see the fear that has lived inside Beth since that night, secret and shapeless, become something tangible as it spreads to her husband.

At least the girls are oblivious, Beth thinks. She imagines them cuddled up on the sofa in the playroom watching *The Snowman*; she can hear the familiar music as it slips under the closed kitchen door. The image calms her. Her children are still blissfully unaware that bad stuff ever happens; she's achieved that at least.

'Have you still got that detective's card? We should call him, make a complaint. Get the bastard arrested.'

'Simon, I don't think …'

'Why not? Because he's just a kid? Down on his luck? He's threatening you, Beth. Stalking you. What do you think happens next?'

What does happen next? If she calls the police, they won't do anything, not over one threatening note, even if they can prove it was him. She's listened to enough true crime podcasts to know the police need to see a pattern, with plenty of proof to back it up. They might have a word with Mark, but he'll still be free, and probably angrier, more determined to see her suffer. And more than that, she'll be connected to the vile teenager for even longer. No, she needs to keep her head down, ride the storm. She's navigated angry young men before, and she can do it again. But first, she needs to convince her husband.

'I don't want to give him more ammunition to hate me,' she says. 'He's just sad about that old man and has nothing better to do than take it out on me. He'll get bored eventually.'

'And until then?' Simon demands, not ready to accept her logic.

'I'll be careful.' Beth tries her smile again, begging her facial muscles to obey.

'I'm supposed to fly to Dublin tomorrow. How can I go now?'

Beth pauses. She hates the thought of Simon leaving her for three days, but she can't ask him to stay after downplaying the threat Mark poses. 'I'll tell Saskia what's going on,' she offers, while inwardly grimacing about what that will require, forgiving Saskia for her thoughtless MyNeighbour post for one. 'She sees everything on this street. And I won't go out on my own.'

'How can you be so cool about this?' Simon asks, his voice incredulous. He has no idea how tough her life used to be. How she's learned to cope with pervasive fear. She watches him pick up his phone, slide his thumb up the glass screen, stare blindly at the matrix of apps. His tick is so endearing; she thinks she might cry. She turns her back on him, blinks, hides her shaking hands as she reaches for the wine bottle, tops up her glass and takes a long swig. When she twists back, his phone is by his side and he's looking at her again.

'It's only three days,' she says. 'And I promise I'll keep myself safe.' Then she takes another gulp and hopes it's a promise she can keep.

Chapter 20

Mark

Mark's hands shake as he pushes his bank card into the cash machine. He's been relying on handouts rather than buying food lately, but his memory is sketchy about how much booze he's slid through the self-service check-out over the last couple of weeks.

And he needs a drink now. After delivering that note. And almost being caught by that brick shithouse with a dog.

Balance: £42.00. He breathes a sigh of relief and hits the ten pounds button. Enough for a third of a litre of Smirnoff Red Label, and that will do. He crosses the road and trudges into the Co-op, the only shop around here where he doesn't feel like a total imposter. Back on the pavement, with the slim glass bottle tucked into his coat pocket, Mark hesitates. He can't face going back to the squat just yet. He could go to Clapham Common. There'd be faces up there he knew, but the conversation would inevitably turn to Jon, and he can't stomach that either.

Without a plan, Mark turns right instead of left towards the squat and keeps walking, over St John's Hill, and under the mass of railway lines out of Clapham Junction station, rusted iron girders juddering above him as a train groans past. There's a patch of grass on his right, like a miniature park with bulbous trees and low fencing, and one empty bench at the back. It feels familiar somehow. Mark walks inside, drops down on the bench, and cracks open the bottle.

The more vodka he drinks, the less he cares about almost getting caught. The truth is, he wants Beth to know the note was from him, as long as she can't actually prove it, and he made sure to wear gloves and write with his left hand to avoid that outcome. He wants her to be scared of him. He wonders what she's doing now, double-checking her window locks perhaps, or even better, crying her eyes out, snotty tears descending down her not-so-pretty-anymore face.

The bottle is almost empty when Mark realises why this stretch of grass is familiar. He's been here before. It was daytime, too warm for autumn, and there were mums on picnic blankets entertaining kids with plastic bottles filled with fairy liquid. But it's definitely the same place. He was waiting for Jon while the old guy visited his dealer-cum-employer, choosing to stay one step removed from Jon's line of work, because that's not who he is.

Mark wonders if Jon's dealer misses his loyal servant now. If he even knows Jon's dead. Or that it was his smack that killed him. Not that it was the heroin exactly, Mark remembers through his vodka fug. It was the clumsy draw, caused by the bitch forcing Jon to drink too much of Mark's booze. But the smack played its part. If he hadn't been jacking up, he wouldn't be dead; that's for sure.

He knows the address off by heart. He's had the bit of paper Jon wrote it on for long enough, and he had to recite it to the guy with the bolt cutters only last week. Jon always insisted his dealer – Rudy – was a good guy, but that there was maybe a five per cent chance that things could turn nasty. Those were good odds, he'd explained, in the illegal drugs trade. But still, he liked someone knowing where he was.

Maybe he should go there now, Mark thinks, tell Rudy what

happened to Jon. Not to blame him of course – that wouldn't be clever – but to let him know. Just passing on information about a mutual friend. And if he manages to ignite a flicker of guilt, a momentary sense of remorse, that can't be a bad thing. It's about time the relentless 'what if' gnawed at someone else's gut.

He pushes off the bench and pauses, giving his legs time to catch up with his brain signals. Then he drops the empty bottle of vodka in the bin, and heads back onto the street.

Ingrine House is an ugly 1960s tower block striped with dirty concrete slabs and lines of grimy windows, some lit up yellow but most in eerie darkness. Mark pauses outside. It feels like the whole place is screaming at him to stay the fuck away, but of course that's just his imagination playing tricks, so he pushes on the main door to the block and keeps his head down as he trudges up the stairs. He feels a sudden urge to pee. Too much vodka, he decides, definitely not fear, because what has he got to be scared of? Rudy was Jon's mate; he'll be grateful for Mark stopping by. Mark sets his jaw, takes a breath and knocks on the flat's peeling front door. It opens a couple of inches. 'Yeah?' a voice floats out.

'Looking for Rudy,' Mark says in a low voice, even though the communal hallway is empty. 'I'm a mate of Clapham Jon's.' That's what he was known as, not exactly imaginative. Mark waits a moment, then the door swings open. The bloke looks like a bouncer. His chest is wide and curved, and he's wearing a thick gold chain around his neck.

'In here,' he says.

Mark stares inside the dimly lit flat. The carpet is grimy – mud, he hopes – and the smell is rancid. Sweat, weed, sick and booze; all mixed together like some hideous anti-perfume. Maybe this wasn't such a good idea after all. 'Can we just talk here?'

'Don't be a prick.' The man lumbers back into the flat, leaving the door open. Mark sighs – reminds himself that Jon came and went safely from this place for years – and follows him into the front room. A couple of kids are hunched over gaming controllers, *Call of Duty* crashing out of the TV, and an older guy is slumped in an armchair, eyes wide, like he's been zapped frozen by some Disney villain. 'Yeah?' Rudy says, ignoring the guy and easing himself down onto the chair's arm.

'Well,' Mark starts, feeling more sober now than he'd like. 'I've got some bad news.'

'I heard about Jon dying the other night,' Rudy says, 'if that's what you mean.' He says it so casually, without a hint of grief or guilt. The guy must know it was his gear that Jon was shooting up, and he still doesn't give a toss.

'Heroin overdose, they reckon,' Mark lies, suddenly desperate to cause a reaction. Yes, Jon was just some old homeless bloke with a smack habit, but he was also kind. Generous, despite having nothing; loyal to Rudy for a good five years. Mark shouldn't be the only one mourning him. But his plan backfires because it's shame he wants to see, not laughter.

'Fucking dickhead.' Rudy chuckles. 'You'd think he'd have worked out how to do it right by now.' Then he straightens out his face. 'Anyway, what do you actually want?'

What Mark actually wants is to scream at the guy, tell him he's a disrespectful piece of shit who deserves a fucking kicking. But Rudy looks like he could bench-press Mark without breaking a sweat, so he keeps his mouth shut.

'You after some brown too?' Rudy asks, mistaking Mark's silence for embarrassment. He walks over to an IKEA chest of drawers in the corner of the room, the wood veneer peeling at the edges, and curls his fingers around the top drawer.

'No,' Mark says quickly. Why do people keep assuming he's a smackhead?

'Oh.' Rudy screws up his face. 'You after Jon's job, then. Is that it?'

'No, I …'

Rudy pushes air through his nose like a horse. 'Well what the fuck do you want? Because all I'm seeing is a scrawny ginger pole wasting my time.'

One of the kids snorts, but the clatter of his controller doesn't slow down; apparently Mark isn't worth that amount of distraction. As Mark listens to the throb of gunfire coming from the TV, he feels the air around him grow heavy. He knows he should just go home to the squat, celebrate scaring the bitch with his note and fall asleep on the couch. After years of working for him, Jon never stopped being wary of Rudy, so that should tell him something.

But he's pissed off that no one is taking an ounce of blame for Jon's death. 'Thought you'd appreciate the warning, your smack killing people,' he mutters.

'What are you saying?' Rudy asks, his voice gruffer now. He tilts onto his feet and takes a few steps towards Mark. Their noses are almost touching.

'And maybe a sorry would be nice.'

Rudy shoves Mark hard in the chest. Mark lists backwards, and it's as though the movement wakes him up. What the hell is he doing? Why is he riling this guy? He reaches out to steady himself, but there's nothing to grab on to, and he stumbles backwards himself, falling onto the rancid carpet in front of the sofa. He can hear the kids laughing now, dropping their controllers, the real-life violence unfolding in front of them finally enough to warrant their interest.

Mark lifts his hands to his face, palms up, part protection, part surrender. He sucks in air as Rudy's foot connects with his ribcage. More kicks rain down, a heavy trainer against his ribs, his hip bone, the backs of his legs. He draws his knees into his chest, and pushes his face into the carpet, the stench of piss rising up his nostrils. The guy could pull a knife any moment, puncture his lungs or heart. He could bleed out on this floor. The images flood the backs of his eyelids as he prays for it to stop.

And finally, thank fuck, it does.

'Now get up,' Rudy growls. 'Get out of my flat. And don't

ever disrespect me like that again.' He kicks Mark again, a final warning.

Mark flips his head around, grimacing with pain. Then he rolls onto his shins, a knoll of damaged flesh, and gingerly pushes up to standing. He's shaking like an addict in withdrawal and his torso is throbbing with pain, but the adrenalin is still coursing through him. Even now, fear and aggression want to duel.

'Are you still here?' Rudy asks, his eyes smirking now he's reasserted his status.

'I'm going,' Mark manages. Then he edges his way towards the door, keeping as much distance from Rudy as possible in the small, overpopulated room. With his eyes focused on the dealer, he doesn't notice the small table jutting out beyond the arm of the sofa. His knee connects with its corner. Another jolt of pain travels through Mark's thigh bone as the table topples over. A plastic bag falls with it, revealing its contents. At least fifty brightly coloured foiled packets. Instantly Mark knows what they are; he's been living on the streets long enough to recognise packets of spice. Mark looks at the dealer and their eyes connect for a second.

Fuck it.

He grabs the bag and runs.

He slams the living room door closed. He hears it open again a moment later, but he's already out of the flat, pelting down the walkway, swinging off the banister and flying down the stairs.

'You'll pay for this, you thieving prick!' Rudy's deep scream catapults after him. 'You think I won't find you?'

Mark shakes the threat away, then smacks his palms against the main doorway. Out on the street, laughter starts to bubble out of him. God, he's fucking insane, but it's good to feel in control at last; it's been too long. It's busy on the main road, and he uses the cover of a double-decker bus to slip down one of the side streets. When he's sure he's not being followed, he stops, sucks in air. His body is still screaming with pain, but his heart rate begins to settle. He opens the plastic bag.

He's never tried spice, but he's heard about it. So many rough sleepers use it just to pass the time. Apparently it's like weed, but better at taking the edge off when life gets too shitty. He looks at the metallic packets, thinks about Rudy's parting words and wonders if they were worth risking another beating for.

Chapter 21

Beth

'Coffee?' Beth asks, hoping that the lure of caffeine will be enough to persuade Saskia to say yes, even if they didn't part on the best terms last Friday. Drinking coffee with friends is Saskia's second favourite pastime, and it's too early for cocktails.

'Well.' Saskia pauses, and Beth wonders if she'll need to do more, apologise for getting mad about the MyNeighbour post even. But then Saskia's shoulders drop a centimetre. 'Okay, just a quick one. But can we go to Sierra Rose? I've heard they've got some new Sumatran beans in.'

'Of course, sounds great,' Beth says with a silent sigh of relief, although not just because she's now got the chance to tell Saskia about Mark. When she first walked out of her house this morning, she'd expected to feel petrified about being out in the open. But after spending most of the previous night wide awake, listening to Simon's heavy breathing and wondering if she'd remembered to lock all the windows, being outside had the opposite effect. Being bathed in bright winter sunshine and surrounded by familiar people have put things into perspective;

it was just a stupid note, the pathetic actions of a man-child. Sticks and stones.

At least that's what she's trying to convince herself.

The two women fall in step as they walk down the hill, then take a right towards the café. Sierra Rose is part quintessential village store and part stylish urban coffee shop, and Beth adds three punnets of raspberries to her flat white order. There's only one empty table, and it's right at the back, Beth realises with a rising wave of concern. As they weave past buggies and discarded tote bags, Beth can sense people looking at her, some trying to work out why she's familiar, others – the ones she's met at school gatherings or street parties – wondering if there's a way they can grab her attention. She keeps her eyes resolutely focused on her feet, and is almost through the flock when a hand reaches out and curls around her own.

'Wow, Beth, I heard what you did. Well, I read about it. That's amazing. I mean, you're amazing.'

Beth swallows down a wave of nausea and draws her arm back, very slowly, making sure it doesn't look like she's recoiling from the woman's touch. It takes all her self-control, and Beth feels a heady sense of relief when the woman's fingers leave her skin.

'I would never have done that; I mean, I don't think I could. I would probably have called Giles or something – not walk away of course – but God, stopping the way you did. Amazing.'

'Thanks,' Beth murmurs, lifting her eyeline, willing herself to smile enough for the woman to not think she's rude while desperately trying to remember her name. 'That's very sweet of you to say,' she manages. 'Listen, I better …' She nods at the table where Saskia is now sitting, tapping on her phone, no doubt putting a photo of her coffee on Instagram, and tagging Beth in it, without asking for permission.

'Of course, of course. Enjoy your coffee.'

Beth smiles her goodbye – it's easier now, the memory of the woman's touch floating away – and then sinks into a wooden chair opposite Saskia. She stifles a sigh of relief and stirs a packet of brown sugar into her coffee.

'You don't take sugar,' Saskia notes, sipping her espresso.

'Bad night's sleep. I need the energy.'

'Makes sense.' Saskia crosses her arms and leans forward on her elbows. 'Why couldn't you sleep?'

Beth pauses. She needs to tell Saskia about Mark; she promised Simon that she would, and anyway, part of her likes the idea of her beady-eyed neighbour looking out for her welfare, putting her nosiness to good use for once. But she needs to get the balance right, provide enough information to put Saskia on the alert without her starting some rabble-rousing publicity campaign against him. 'There's this kid. Man, I suppose. He's called Mark.'

'Oh?' Saskia raises her eyebrows.

Beth rolls her eyes. 'He's said some things.'

'What things? Who is he?'

'No one important, just some dumb kid. But he kind of threatened me.'

'Shit, Beth. What did he say?'

Beth takes a sip of coffee. She can't let this escalate, nor does she want to give Simon an ally in his bid to contact the police. 'Something and nothing, I promise. I'm not worried really. But Simon's in Dublin until Friday evening, and he made me promise to tell you.'

'Wow, Beth, I can't believe you needed Simon to remind you who your number-one confidante is.' Saskia shifts her gaze, nods and smiles at the woman who accosted Beth – Lou, Beth suddenly remembers – and Beth can't work out if her friend is hurt or annoyed. Not that she has any right to be either. Saskia knew how unhappy Beth was about that MyNeighbour post, but she still took two days to remove it, and hasn't offered a word of apology since, even though Beth's made it very clear that one is required. Really, Beth wants to continue keeping her distance, to show Saskia that actions have consequences, but she can't do that now. She needs her friend's eyes.

But that doesn't mean Saskia can treat her as the guilty party. 'I guess I just don't want my problems to be content for your next social media post.' She shouldn't risk another falling-out, not now, but allowing the words to slip out is so satisfying. Like unclipping a corset. But the relief is short-lived as Saskia whips her head round, eyes ablaze.

'Jesus, Beth. How can you still be mad with me about that?' she demands. 'Did you even read it? I called you a bloody superhero.'

'You plastered my picture all over the internet!'

'Don't be dramatic,' Saskia says, lowering her volume, and digging her eyes into Beth's as an instruction to do the same. 'All I'm guilty of is telling our neighbours what an inspiring thing you did, and now you're throwing it back in my face.'

Beth looks at Saskia's wounded expression and imagines the child she must have been. Loved, idolised, always put first. Encouraged to think she's standing up for the little people when she's really just using their bad luck to boost her own self-esteem. She has no idea what a real wound feels like. 'And now you've got a top-post badge,' she counters, knowing she sounds petulant, 'and I've got a stalker.'

'That is not fair!' Saskia retaliates, her preference for low volume forgotten now. Then she narrows her eyes. 'Wait, a stalker? This guy Mark is stalking you?'

'I suppose you want to put his picture on MyNeighbour too now?' This is all so stupid; she should be backing down, apologising, blaming her outburst on stress or lack of sleep. Not making things worse. But she's developed a crack in her perfect persona, and she hasn't got the energy to fix it.

'Well, why not? Why are you so against it? You think the police will do a better job of protecting you? With all their problems?'

'I don't want people knowing my business.'

'Why the hell not? What have you got to hide?'

Beth freezes. What's happening to her? Why can't she smile warmly at Saskia and shrug off her question with a quip about a handsome tennis coach or Botox injections? Of course she's got plenty to hide, a whole past life, but that's nothing new. She mustn't let one impulsive decision to do the right thing harm what she's built. She picks up her phone, uses Simon's trick to give herself more time, then slips it into her coat pocket. 'I should go.'

'Now? No. You need my help, Beth. Pride's not going to keep you safe. Tell me about Mark, what to look out for.'

'I'll be fine. I told you, it's nothing.' Beth can't meet Saskia's gaze as she pushes the chair away and pulls her coat on.

'Beth, you can't do that! Tell me you've got a stalker, and then shut down. It's not fair; what am I supposed to think?'

Suddenly Beth can't stand Saskia's whining. She doesn't respond, just twists to go and zigzags quickly through the busy café, moving too fast for even the keenest yummy mummy to catch her eye. When she makes it out onto the street, she gulps at the air, but doesn't slow her pace. It's only a five-minute walk home, and when she reaches her house, her heart is still racing so much that she struggles to line her key up with the slim hole. Images start crowding her mind: Saskia's beady eyes drilling into her, then Mark running at her with a knife, smearing his note across her face, screaming 'BITCH!' at her, spittle flying out of his mouth. Into hers.

'Can I help you with that?'

'Fuck, fuck, fuck.' Beth drops the key and wonders if her heart is going to explode through her ribcage.

'God, sorry, Mrs Packard. It's me, DC Stone – I didn't mean to frighten you. That was really stupid of me, under the circumstances.'

Beth's heart skids to a halt. She watches the detective lean down, retrieve her house key, straighten up. 'What circumstances?' she asks.

'Shall we go inside?'

Beth wants to say no. When DC Stone walked out of her house last Tuesday, he said it was all over, and she scrubbed his presence away. But Saskia might be on her way home now, and Beth can't stand the thought of her friend – or ex-friend maybe – seeing the detective standing on her doorstep. 'Okay,' she agrees. She manages to slide the key in and pushes open the door.

Luna starts barking as soon as the detective comes into view. Beth holds a chew out to distract her, and watches the young dog take it from her hand, then retreat to her daybed, her tail wagging with excitement. It reminds Beth how effective generosity can be. She takes a deep breath and turns to face the detective. 'Tea? Coffee?' she asks, smiling warmly.

'I'll take a cup of tea, thanks.'

Beth pulls a mug out of the cupboard, drops in a teabag and covers it with spitting water from the hot tap. Then she pours some milk into a tiny jug and slides them both in front of him. The sugar bowl comes next, and finally she produces a teaspoon and a small dish for his used teabag.

'Thanks,' he murmurs. 'I never realised tea was this complicated.'

Beth smiles again, but it's tighter this time. 'You mentioned circumstances?' she prompts.

'Your husband called me this morning, to make an allegation about that man from the squat, Mark Sullivan. He told me about the note you received. I'm so sorry this is happening to you. You really don't deserve it.'

Of course she doesn't fucking deserve it. She tried to do a good deed and now she's got a threatening note and a fucking policeman leaving tea stains on her worktop. And a husband who lies, breaks his promise, thinks he knows best. 'Thank you,' she says, forcing herself to meet DC Stone's eye, to give the impression that she means it. 'But he really shouldn't have bothered you.'

'Don't be silly; that's what I'm here for. Have you still got the note?'

She pauses for a moment. 'Sorry, no. I shredded it this morning; I just want to forget about it.'

'Ah, that's a shame.'

'I don't want things to escalate.'

'It's harder without the evidence, but it's still a serious allegation. If I could take a statement from you, that would give us enough to caution him, and that might do the job of scaring him off.'

Beth allows herself a moment of hope. Could it work? Could a hard word from a man with a badge and a can of pepper spray stuffed in a desk drawer somewhere be enough to stop this? 'What if it annoys him?' she asks. 'And makes his behaviour worse?'

'Don't let him control this, Mrs Packard.'

Beth pauses for a moment, tries to shuffle her thoughts into some kind of order. 'I don't understand why he blames me. If he cared so much, why didn't *he* help his mate?'

'He was fast asleep in the back room when we found him, door shut, knocked out by vodka. In fact, that's probably it. Him feeling responsible, desperate to deflect the blame.'

'Sounds like you're justifying his behaviour now,' Beth murmurs.

'Definitely not. There's no excuse for what he's done to you.'

'I don't want ...'

'We just want to make sure you're safe.'

Beth looks at him. Could she trust him? Her teenage self would despise her for it. Like most people in her neighbourhood, she grew up suspicious of the men in dark blue uniforms, but it was later, when the police showed just how heartless they could be, that she learned to truly hate them. She's a new person now, and DC Stone seems like a decent enough man, but some memories run too deep.

Like the memory of that newspaper article, the one written without Beth's permission, just like Saskia's MyNeighbour post, and how the journalist who wrote it could only have got his information from the police leaking it. She reaches out for the work surface, blinks hard and turns to face the pig sitting in her kitchen. 'With all due respect,' she starts, carefully enunciating each word, 'I'm the victim, and this should be my call. Not yours, not my husband's. So please listen to me.' She pauses, swallows the acid in her mouth. 'I want to withdraw the allegation.'

'Mrs Packard …'

'And I don't want to make a statement.'

'I know you're scared, but …'

How dare he be so presumptive? 'Which means I'm wasting your time,' she interrupts. 'And I've got a busy day too.' Even while her insides buck and rear, Beth manages to make eye contact with DC Stone. He holds it for a moment, then shrugs in defeat and pushes off her bar stool.

Chapter 22

Kat

'Kat, I've got a splitting headache. Is there any chance you could stay a bit later tonight?' Sally's voice filters into the back room and Kat puts down her scissors, the final stage in making sure her current ward – Monti the maltipoo – is trimmed to perfection. 'I've got Rolo coming in,' Sally continues, the volume increasing as she walks in Kat's direction. 'And I'm not sure I've got the energy for that gigantic furball.'

Rolo is a Spanish water dog and one of their fluffiest clients. He's chocolate brown with four white paws, and however far you bury your fingers into his coat, you rarely reach skin. His owner likes to keep his fur long, which means he's a regular visitor at Groom & Bloom for a trim. He's usually a very welcome guest, but the playful two-year-old isn't so much fun if you're grappling with a headache. Kat looks at her watch. She's due to finish in ten minutes. 'What time is he booked in?'

Sally appears at the open doorway. 'Five. You'll be finished by six thirty latest.'

Kat looks at Sally's tired eyes, her hopeful expression. She scrapes her bottom lip with her teeth. 'I'm really sorry, Sally. I have plans this evening.' She watches Sally's face fall. Bites her lip a bit harder.

'Is there any way you could reschedule, delay your plans a bit?' Sally continues. 'I know it's a lot to ask but I'd really appreciate it.'

Kat considers texting Beth, asking if she can postpone Luna's walk by an hour or so. But what if Beth says no, and cancels their date completely? She's waited so long for this, a second chance. She shrugs her shoulders but can't bear Sally's desperate expression, so looks at the wall. 'Sorry, no,' she murmurs. 'How about some paracetamol? I've got some in my bag.'

Sally sighs and shakes her head. 'No thanks. I took some an hour ago and it hasn't touched the sides.' Kat watches Sally's head droop, then her body turn and retreat back to the reception desk. She feels bad, letting her boss down, but she's got to remember what's most important right now. Disappointing Sally is just collateral damage.

Kat uses the distraction of Rolo's arrival to slip out of the salon without saying goodbye. But her prompt departure means she's early for Beth's, so she takes her time, ambling slowly down and then up the road, scanning the pavements. As she passes the old Delphine's, she can see a shadow moving around beyond the glass shopfront. Tragedy is like that, she muses. It can stop *your* world from turning, but not *the* world. Life always goes on. And the death of one squatter just gives another rough sleeper the chance of a dry night's rest.

At 5.15 p.m. on the dot, Kat rings Beth's doorbell. It's still daunting, standing on Beth's top step, but she's relieved to discover that she doesn't feel quite as nervous as the day before. It's a while before anyone comes, but eventually the door swings open and Beth appears on the threshold. But she looks different today. Her hair is still perfect, shining with natural oils and curled neatly under her chin. And her skin is clear and smooth. But her eyes have a vacant stare, and her mouth is stained red.

And more than that, she's clasping a kitchen knife so tightly that her knuckles are white.

'Hi, Beth,' Kat stutters, her eyes flitting between Beth's face and the blade. Is it meant for her? Has Beth worked out who Kat really is? Or did that man come back; is it a weapon for self-defence?

'Oh, it's you. I forgot.' Beth blinks, looks down at the knife and draws it behind her back. 'Sorry, I was just, erm ...' Her voice peters out.

'I've come for Luna,' Kat offers slowly, assessing Beth more closely now that the initial shock has worn off. She doesn't look either angry or hurt; she looks wasted. 'Do you still want me to walk her this evening?'

'Luna?' Beth swivels her head and Kat follows her gaze. Luna is stood behind the glass kitchen door wagging her tail. 'Oh yes.' Beth stops. Starts. 'Sorry. Let me get her for you.' But as she turns, she stumbles. Instinctively, Kat reaches her hands up, but Beth is beyond arm's reach now. Kat watches her grab the side table to keep herself from falling. The table wobbles and three picture frames fall, slamming down like three shots firing. She can't be a bystander anymore. She takes a few steps forward, into Beth's hallway. The door to her right is shut and the muted sounds of a TV show trickle from underneath it. A sense of relief leaks in. The children are safe.

'Are you okay? Shall I take that?' she asks, nodding down at the knife.

'I'm sorry, I'm not feeling great.' Beth stares at the fallen picture frames; they look like three sharks now, with their fins jutting out. Kat reaches for the knife and their fingers touch for a moment before Beth pulls away. A jolt of electricity runs up Kat's arm, and she has to fight to stop a gasp escaping through her lips. She concentrates on righting the pictures instead. Two of them she recognises from the day before. The third is of an older couple, but they're both fair-skinned and blue-eyed. Not Beth's parents.

'Shall I put this in the kitchen?' Kat asks. 'Would you like to sit down?'

The corners of Beth's mouth lift, then drop, the effort of smiling seemingly too much. But she nods and gestures to the kitchen door. Kat doesn't have any difficulty finding her own smile. This is what she's been hoping for since she first saw Beth's picture on MyNeighbour. An invitation into Beth's home. And now Beth is the vulnerable one. She slides open the kitchen door, gives Luna a quick pat, then drops the knife safely into its block. By the time she turns round, Beth is slumped on one of the four bar stools lined up against the island unit.

'Um, can I get you anything? Glass of water?' Kat asks tentatively. It's strange to be stood in Beth's kitchen, playing the host, but it's also a golden opportunity to get closer to this woman who has occupied her thoughts for the last eleven days, and on some level, the last eighteen years.

'Thank you,' Beth whispers. 'I'm not normally …' She hangs her head, but more in exhaustion than shame. Kat uses the opportunity to feel for her phone, and is relieved to find it in the back pocket of her jeans.

'We all have difficult days,' she says, slipping the phone out, taking a clandestine photo, then putting it away again. She turns to the cupboards and tries to guess which one holds the glasses. The units are navy blue and gleam under a strip of LED lighting. There are no handles on the cupboard doors and Kat wonders if her touch will leave a smear. 'Is your husband here?' she asks, pushing lightly on the door above the wine rack. Her logic pays off. There are dozens of glasses inside, all sparkling, and regimentally lined up according to their purpose.

'He's in Dublin,' Beth murmurs. 'Business trip.'

Kat's mind races. Beth's children are here – Kat heard the TV playing in the room off the entrance hall – but otherwise she's alone while that angry kid is out there somewhere. But telling Beth about him could make things worse. She takes the glass over to the sink.

'There's a filter water tap.' Beth's voice, small and dulled, floats over Kat's shoulder. 'You just need to push the lever back.' Kat wonders how Beth can worry about water impurities when she can't stand up straight, but she follows the instructions, then slides the full glass across the island. The worktop is made of one of those composite materials, quartz or Corian, and shines white under the three brushed copper lights that hang down from the ceiling. It's perfectly clean except for the area where Beth is sitting, which is blemished by tiny red splatters arcing around her.

'Shall I get a cloth? Wipe that up?'

Beth looks down, then careers backwards, almost losing her balance on the stool. 'Oh God, I was eating raspberries. I didn't see …'

'It's fine,' Kat says again. 'I can clean it up.'

'No. I need to do it.' Beth swivels off the chair and lurches towards the sink. She opens the cupboard underneath, pulls out a fresh cloth and a bottle of cleaning spray. But her hands are shaking, and the bottle slips out of her grasp, falling to the floor. Beth stares at it, frozen.

Kat takes her opportunity. She puts her arm around Beth, breathes in her smell, feels the warmth of her slight frame against Kat's chest. The feeling is so powerful that her knees almost buckle, but she clenches her thighs and rides out the moment. 'Let me help you,' she whispers.

'I didn't sleep much last night.'

'You have a beautiful house. But I can clean to your standard, I promise.'

Beth turns to look at her and their eyes connect. Natural deep brown and imitation blue. Beth's face is so close now, ten centimetres at most. This is much better than Kat could ever have hoped for when she left work less than half an hour ago. She wants to take it further, but she can't; she mustn't risk freaking Beth out. So she leads her charge back to the stool, inhales one more time and lets go. She retrieves the cleaning products from the floor and sets to work on the island unit.

'Can I ask something, Kat? A favour?' Beth's voice is so small.

'Of course. Anything.'

'Can this be our secret? You seeing me like this?'

Kat stops cleaning and looks up. 'Who would I tell?'

'My husband. My children. The woman you work with. Your clients.'

'I wouldn't tell anyone. It's none of their business.' She feels an urge to reach out again, but instead she pushes her hands into her pockets. She runs her fingers over the smooth surface of her phone.

'I couldn't stand anyone knowing, not even strangers. Do you promise, Kat?'

'I promise,' Kat whispers. She understands Beth's need for privacy, the woman with a new name and a difficult past. She recognises it in herself too: the paranoia of living with something to hide. 'Could I ask you a favour too?' she asks. The image of that man is back, his angry words, and she slides her thumb across the glass screen, catching the ridge of her phone case with her nail.

'That's fair, I suppose.'

'Would you tell me what's happened today? You look scared. I want to help you.'

Beth stays silent, so Kat looks away, then resumes her task. She can sense Beth staring at her, those chocolate brown eyes leaving a warm glow on the back of Kat's neck as she scrubs the worktop, erasing its imperfections. Seconds go past, maybe even a minute, before Beth finally speaks. 'I did something a couple of weeks ago, got involved in someone else's mess. You probably know about it; everyone does.' Kat looks up at Beth, but she's staring into space. 'It felt like the right decision at the time,' she continues. 'But I regret it now. Too many repercussions.'

She must be talking about stopping for that squatter who overdosed. But what repercussions is she talking about? And is the man Kat met outside Beth's house one of them? She wonders if she should tell Beth that she saw him, whether that would help, or hinder the progress she's making. 'What kind of repercussions?' she asks.

'Police in my house. My so-called friend spreading all the sordid details on the internet. A man who wants to hurt me.'

Kat's heart lurches inside her chest. 'Who wants to hurt you?' she stutters.

'He's called Mark apparently.' Beth is so quiet, it's like she's breathing the words. 'He was there, that night, inside the old Delphine's that he and his mate had turned into a squat. And now he's found out where I live. He put a threatening note through my door.'

So that's why he was loitering outside Beth's house. Kat's stomach flips with unease at the thought of him – an unpredictable kid – hassling her childhood friend. 'Why would he do that?'

'I don't know. He's got this crazy idea.' It's like Beth is talking to herself now. 'He slept through the whole thing; the detective said so. But for some reason, he's decided that the man dying is my fault.' Beth falls silent and Kat listens to the hum of the fridge. 'I sent the police away today,' Beth finally continues. 'They can't help me. I just want it over, forgotten.'

Kat looks at her. The raspberry red lips and glazed eyes. Slumped shoulders and shaking hands. 'Do you know where he lives, this Mark person?'

'Of no fixed abode.' Beth elongates each word.

'But around here, you think?' Kat pushes. She needs to do something, stop him threatening Beth.

Beth sighs. 'The police moved him on from the squat, secured the whole place, so maybe he's sleeping on the common … I don't know.'

Kat thinks about her walk to Beth's. The shadow moving in the window of the old Delphine's; it's not secure anymore. *I do,* she thinks. *I know where he is now.*

April 2003

Chapter 23

Katherine

Fuck it. It's now or never. And it's a good decision. For once. Katherine takes a deep breath and slips her hand into the side pocket of her bag. Her trembling fingers find the folded piece of paper and she starts to slide it out.

But suddenly the hard plastic of a football bag pushes against her back. She lurches forward.

'Jeez, move down the aisle, you fat cow,' a surly voice drills into the back of her head. Anger explodes in Katherine's gut, but it's quickly eclipsed by horror as she realises that she's going to slip over. Fall flat on her face in front of Becca. Just in time, her fingers find the cheap velour of a seat headrest and she steadies herself. Then she twists her neck and glowers at the spotty teenager pushing from behind. Not only has he insulted her and almost floored her, he's also ruined her opportunity. There's no way she can stay invisible to Becca after the kerfuffle he's caused. She watches with resignation as the older girl turns her head towards the noise.

'Oh hi, Katherine.' Becca pulls off her headphones and looks up from her seat. 'Are you okay?' But she doesn't wait for an answer

before turning to the boy still wedged up against Katherine's back. She gives him a hard stare. 'Stop pushing her, or I'll get you done for assault.' She pauses. 'And using abusive language.'

'That's not even a crime,' the boy blusters, but with shrinking confidence.

'Oh yeah? Want to test it?'

Katherine's heart swells as she listens to this exchange, and when Becca winks at her, she thinks it might actually burst out of her chest. Yes, she's missed her chance to do the deed that she's been planning all weekend, but there'll be other moments. And witnessing Becca stick up for her in front of that dickhead more than makes up for any delay. 'Thanks, Becca,' she whispers. 'I better go and sit down.' She wafts her hand deeper into the bus.

'Sit with me,' Becca says, moving her satchel and patting the now empty seat. Katherine struggles not to yelp with glee; this is definitely a sign, she thinks. Proof that the voice in her head is right, that she's doing the right thing. A warmth spreads through her body as she throws the boy one last filthy look and sinks down next to Becca.

'God, boys can be such jerks, can't they?' Becca continues. She goes quiet for a while, as though a memory has disturbed her train of thought, and she turns her head towards the window. 'Do you have a brother, Katherine?' she asks without moving.

'No, only sisters,' Katherine answers quickly, desperate for Becca to look at her again. 'I mean, half-sisters,' she corrects.

Perhaps Becca picks up on Katherine's silent prayer because she turns back to face her. 'Well at least they're girls,' she says, smiling warmly. 'And younger. I bet they worship you.'

Katherine pictures her little sisters, the way their eyes dart to the door when she tries to make conversation. 'Yes, they do,' she lies. 'They're very sweet.'

Becca sighs. 'I love little kids. I would offer to baby-sit for them, but I suppose your mum and stepdad have you for that.'

Becca hasn't called them her parents, Katherine realises; she knows to make that distinction. 'You could come over anyway, help *me baby-sit?' The words are out before Katherine can stop them. She blinks as the stupidity of the suggestion ricochets around her brain.*

'What? Um, okay, maybe.' Becca looks confused, weirded out, and Katherine silently screams at herself. Why did she say that? Of course Becca wouldn't want to visit her house on those terms. But then, miraculously, Becca's face breaks into another smile. 'You know what, that sounds fun.' Then she points to her headphones. 'Listen, do you mind if I plug back in? I'm obsessed with Nina Simone at the moment.' She gives Katherine a sheepish look, then slips the noise-cancelling headphones back over her ears and tilts her head towards the window again.

Katherine slips her hand back into her bag and strokes the thin piece of paper inside. When the words tumbled out with her mum on Friday night, she even surprised herself. She's never used the label girlfriend for Becca. But the more she thought about it, the more it made sense. This is why her heart races, and her belly twists, every time she gets a glimpse of Becca across the playground. And maybe, hopefully, why Becca always has a smile for her. And now the idea of it being just the two of them makes her feel happier than she'd ever have thought possible.

Even her mum seems to like her more. On Saturday morning she suggested they go shopping together, and as they browsed the album charts in Woolworths (and Katherine tried not to ogle the pic'n'mix), her mum had asked lots of questions about Katherine's new girlfriend. The more she and her mum chatted, the better they got on. And the more excited Katherine became at the thought of being Becca's girlfriend. After that, writing a letter had felt like the natural next step. And now here they are, sitting together like it was written in the stars.

They'll be at school soon, Katherine realises. Becca will disappear along with her familiar leather satchel and Katherine won't see her for the rest of the day. She thinks about the words she wrote. How amazing Becca is, what a special friendship they've got, how it could grow into something even better. Surely reading it would

159

make Becca think more of her, not less? She steals another look at Becca's face in profile. The soft contours of her golden skin. Then she looks down at the sand-coloured satchel. There's a sleeve on one side with no clasp. Carefully she slides the letter out of her bag and slips it inside Becca's satchel.

December 2021

Chapter 24

Mark

Mark stares at the wall opposite. It's bliss, he thinks, this feeling. He's not cold anymore, for a start. And his body doesn't hurt even though the purple and yellow bruises all over his torso prove that he's taken a proper beating. He's floating more than flying; bobbing up and down in a cloud of cotton wool. He feels amazing.

Mark was never a fan of drugs growing up. And he knows – somewhere inside his head, or maybe as deep as his gut – that he shouldn't have dabbled today. But his whole body was in agony, the pain having grown rather than shrunk overnight, and the spice was calling him.

He looks at the spliff suspended between his fingers. It's only half smoked but the tip is smouldering, dreary grey without the spark of a flame. How long has he been staring at the wall? He's got no idea, but the sky is black again so it must be evening at least. With gargantuan effort, he picks his lighter next to him off the sofa and flicks it at the end of the joint. Then he closes his eyes and takes a long, hard toke, keeping the drug inside him for as long as he can hold his breath. Finally he exhales, but he can already feel its effect spreading through him, taking him deeper into paradise. Or oblivion.

He leans back against the matted velour sofa and turns to face the window. He watches a couple walk by, arms entwined, laughing at something, oblivious to him sitting in the shadows. The woman reminds him of Beth, something in her gait, and his mind meanders back to her again. He was half expecting the police to turn up today, and he'd been planning his mix of denials and no comments about the note he delivered. But no one came, which weirdly felt like a disappointment. Like even though he's making progress, she's still controlling things.

When he bumped into Beth on Friday, then found out where she lived, he'd thought he'd won. That if he hung around, reminded her what he thought of her, she'd start to feel trapped, too scared to leave her house. But he hadn't considered her little army. A husband holding her hand, two prancing daughters asking mindless questions, countless friends waving adoringly from across the street. Constant distractions that meant she didn't see him, or even sense his creeping footsteps behind her. That's why he decided to write the note, go for a more in-your-face approach. But it's him with the cracked ribs and a newly forming drug habit.

Not that it's going to become a habit. It's just medicinal, to get him through tonight.

He takes another draw. His head spins and he feels a faint urge to vomit. But then he takes a few breaths, and the nausea passes, so he sucks again. The joint is nearly finished, he notes, with a mix of disappointment and relief. He doesn't want the warm sunshine to wear off, the pain to return, the realities of his life to come back into focus. But he needs a straight head so that he can plan his next move. Something that Beth can't shake off. He thinks about her family's excursions at the weekend. Beth with the younger kid on Saturday morning, up on Wandsworth Common with hundreds of other ants in football strips. Then a family walk on Clapham Common on Sunday morning with takeout lattes and hot chocolates. The girls chasing their cutesy dog and giggling. Especially the little one with her chubby cheeks and that gap between her teeth. All of them so happy, so fucking *entitled*.

Mark drops the end of the joint over the edge of the sofa and slides his heel across it. His head is still rammed full of nothingness, but an idea seems to be forming, nonetheless.

Mark opens his eyes, tries to clear the fug inside his brain. Did he hear something? Someone? The back door doesn't have a working lock, largely down to him breaking it twice. He's been shoving a few boxes in front of the door to deter any uninvited guests (and no, he doesn't care if that's ironic), but he can't remember doing that tonight. A drug-fuelled paranoia starts to crawl over his skin. Has Rudy found out where he's staying? Has he come for his drugs, or payback for Mark stealing them, like he promised? Dealers all have knives nowadays, or machetes. Is he about to die? The pain in his ribs flares and he eyes the window, but it's a shopfront, not one that opens. Why the fuck didn't he secure the place? Protect himself?

He should go and check. It might be nothing: a fox or cat or even the spice messing with his sanity. He's always been a fighter; why isn't he backing himself now? He shakes his body, tries to instil some resilience, then stands up. He picks up a hollow metal tube from the floor – dress shop entrails – and slips through into the back room.

But before he has chance to react, a hand grabs him around the neck and shoves him against the wall of the storeroom. It's pitch-black without the glow from the streetlamps, and he blinks in the darkness, willing his night vision to kick in. The grip is powerful, cutting off his windpipe. It has to be Rudy, or one of his henchmen, but he can't see anything but dark clothing. His eyes swim with tears and sweat forms under his armpits. Belatedly, he realises his hands are just dangling by his sides. What the hell is he waiting for?

He goes to grab his assailant's hand, but it's like his arms are travelling through treacle. They don't even reach their destination before his neck is suddenly free again, but then he's being spun round by his shoulders. He can breathe now, but his cheek is pushed hard against the cold plaster. His beanie is whipped off his head and fingernails bury deep into his scalp, pulling at his hair, keeping his head from moving.

'You stay away from her, you fucking piece of shit.'

He screws his eyes together, trying to strip away the spice and confusion. The voice is deep, but it's a woman hissing into his ear, not Jon's dealer. He should push her away, twist out of her grasp, but he can't move. Is she too strong for him? Or has the spice turned him to jelly? 'You're pathetic, you know that?' the voice continues, swirling around his stoned head. 'No match for me. Leave this street now, or I'll come for you, hound you, just like you're doing to her. Do you understand me, Mark?'

The shock of her knowing his name jolts him; he can't help it. Who is this woman? Is she the one he saw at Beth's house? He'd called her fat then, but she was more than that; proper built. Could Beth have hired a bodyguard? With her frame so close and his face pinned against the wall, it's hard to make out her features, but he twists his eyeballs as far as they'll go. With his eyesight adjusted to the darkness, he can just make out that she's wearing a beanie pulled low over her ears, and a black jacket zipped up over her mouth. She's broad, solid, so just like that woman he bumped into. Does he need to factor her into his plans now? 'Fuck off,' he manages. 'You can't tell me what to do.'

'Yes I can, you stupid boy. You're still a child. In here, in your head.' She taps hard on his temple and tuts in disgust. 'And you need to leave Beth the fuck alone, okay? Or I'll make sure you regret it.' She gives him one final shove, then releases her grip on his hair and takes a step back. At her size, she should be slow and lumbering, but she's lightning fast and a few seconds later she's gone, slamming the door behind her.

He leans back against the tiny kitchen work surface, staring at the moon and waiting for his breathing to settle. That's why the police haven't come calling, he realises, because Beth has gone private, thrown money at the problem, like all posh people do. She's hired someone to protect her. He bets she's loving it, feeling like she's won.

A wave of fury rushes over Mark and he kicks out, connecting with the sole kitchen cupboard in the room. Once, twice, three times. He listens to the MDF crack and splinter, and then watches the door fall off its hinges. 'Not this time,' he whispers. 'This time you're going to fucking lose.'

Chapter 25

Beth

Beth uncrosses and recrosses her legs. She looks at her hands resting tautly on her knees. She daren't look anywhere else in case there are tell-tale signs on her face. She still can't believe the terrible mess she got herself into last night. When that detective left, she'd felt desperate to go for a run, to expel the cortisol racing around her body. But of course she was too scared to leave the house by then, all her earlier optimism extinguished. So she'd resorted to those familiar crutches instead. Cleaning out the kitchen cupboards and scrubbing every surface. Then when her heart rate still refused to settle, she'd crawled into her wardrobe and sliced open a new foil strip hiding in her old winter boot.

One pill wasn't enough though, so she made the stupid error of taking a second. Somehow she had the wherewithal to ask Lara to pick the girls up from school, used the well-worn excuse about waiting in for a tradesman. With Simon in Dublin, she thought she'd be able to float through the evening until bedtime, then sleep off her excesses, no real harm done. But she'd forgotten that she'd asked Kat to walk Luna that evening. Of course the salt-of-the-earth dog walker turned up bang on time, and somewhere along the way Beth told her about Mark.

She doesn't know why she did that. There was something in Kat's voice, steeliness mixed with kindness, a touch of familiar working-class dependability, that encouraged her to open up. But now she just feels more exposed.

Beth is one of about forty parents here, mainly mothers, sat in the school's main hall. She could name about half the audience, while they will all know who she is, or at least think they do. Capable mother, attractive wife. Brave pillar of the community, putting her safety on the line for a homeless drug addict. They don't know that she lies to everyone she loves. Or needs medication to stop herself cleaning relentlessly. She can sense the mums closest looking in her direction now. She knows they want to talk to her, to remind her that they met at a coffee morning once, and therefore have the right to press her for further details about her failed Florence Nightingale act. She keeps her head down and prays that no one has the nerve to tap her on the shoulder.

At least she doesn't have to face Saskia yet. In the past, the lower school has put on a big Christmas carol concert with all one hundred and fifty pupils sharing the space, but they've opted for a more intimate format this year, separate back-to-back concerts for each year group. The reception class went first so Angus will already have delivered his solo (and no, Saskia's four-year-old son didn't have an ounce of nerves, he announced on the way to school while she and Saskia painstakingly avoided eye contact; he's clearly inherited his mother's chutzpah) and now Beth is waiting for Ava's year one performance to begin. Unfortunately Saskia will be back in an hour for Martha and Olivia's festive turn.

Finally there's a rustling in the wings. Beth looks up and lets out a silent sigh of relief as the parents around her shift their gaze to the stage too. She even smiles a little as a line of five- and six-year-olds walk dutifully onto the stage and into their pre-agreed positions. All the children are wearing white clothes with bits of silver tinsel hanging around their necks and wrists, or wound into French plaits or pigtail buns. The effect is beautiful, a broad brushstroke of innocence, and Beth feels tears smart at her eyes. Ava is stood almost directly opposite – one of the benefits of knowing their positions in advance – and she gives her daughter the widest smile she can manage. It seems to be enough, and Ava gives her a quick clandestine wave in response.

The music teacher takes up her position at the piano and soon a multitude of off-pitch voices fill the room. The half-an-hour performance starts with 'Away in the Manger' (of course) and ends with a rousing rendition of 'Twelve Days of Christmas', which the parents are invited to join in with (Beth doesn't). There's a solo in the middle – Ava's best friend Chloe, who is luckily a better singer than football player – and a short speech by the head of lower school wishing everyone a happy 2022. Beth wonders whether that will be true for her. If she can somehow navigate a path through her estranged parents, an angry stalker and a growing dependence on prescription drugs. She takes a deep breath. She's dealt with adversity before, very effectively, and she will do it again.

There are coffees and mince pies laid on between shows and Beth gets caught in the general tide moving in that direction. But she wants neither and eyes the fire door instead, wondering if she can hide outside until Martha's concert starts. But before she gets chance to escape, she hears someone calling her name. Saskia has spotted her – she must have just arrived – and is holding up two cups like a peace offering. With a sigh, Beth shuffles over to her friend. She takes a deep breath, blinks and arranges her face into a warm smile. 'Sorry about yesterday,' she starts. 'I was tired. I shouldn't have taken it out on you.'

'Nothing to apologise for,' Saskia counters, shaking her head.

She eyes a plate of mince pies, then looks away. 'It must be awful, feeling like someone's watching you all the time.'

'It's not that bad.'

'I saw the detective leaving yours. You know, the police are tragically ineffective in stalking cases.' She sighs. 'But I'm still glad you called them. Are you going to get a restraining order? It's a legal faff, but I can help you with it. Then the police might actually be able to do something worthwhile.'

'I don't think …' God, why did Saskia have to spot DC Stone again? Why is she an expert on restraining orders? And why does she need to know every minuscule detail of Beth's life?

'Come on, Beth. Stalking is much more likely to escalate than de-escalate – you know that.'

Saskia's voice reverberates around Beth's head like a swarm of bees. And she's not sure that the pills are out of her system yet either. She's exhausted. Her head feels like mush. She mustn't let Saskia penetrate her shell again, but it's difficult.

'Beth? Are you okay?'

'Huh?' Her insides feel like they're buzzing too now, her heart on vibrate. But no wait, she is buzzing. It's her phone in her jacket pocket. She pulls it out on autopilot, looks at the screen. Eddie. Shit. She shoves it back in her pocket. But it only stops ringing for a moment before it starts again.

'You can get it,' Saskia says, nodding, probably desperate to know who Beth's not willing to speak to. 'The show isn't due to start for another ten minutes.'

'No, it's fine.' It rings again and Beth tries to ignore it, continue smiling, but Saskia is openly staring at her jacket pocket. She realises that she's got no choice. Blood rushes between her ears as she reaches inside, curls her fingers around the cool metal and accepts the call. She pushes it as hard as possible against her ear and sways slightly. 'Hello?'

'Elizabeth?' A tiny whisper but Beth can hear the Romanian accent. 'Thank you for picking up. I know you don't like us

171

leaving a message, clogging up your work phone, but I need to speak with you.'

'No problem,' Beth says, keeping her tone neutral as Saskia's expression moves from encouraging to intrigued. 'How can I help?'

'Help? Oh, *mea dragě*, we don't need anything. But I have some difficult news. I wanted to tell you in person but …' Beth's mum's voice trails off and the line goes quiet, just the thin gasps of someone trying not to cry. *But you never visit*, Beth silently finishes for her. Beth looks at Saskia's curious expression and grips the phone tighter. She wishes she could cut her mum off, say something to a dead line that will satisfy her awful friend and then call back when she's safely at home. But how could she possibly do that when her mum's obviously close to tears?

'Oh?' she tries, hoping it will be enough to prompt her mum to keep talking.

'A nurse came this afternoon. She's called Cathy; she's one of those community nurses.'

Beth's heart booms in her ears. Is one of her parents sick? 'That's nice,' she says blandly. 'Why?'

A pause. '*Mea dragabrě*,' her mum sighs finally. 'Your dad has lung cancer. Cathy's a Macmillan nurse. I didn't want to tell you like this, but Cathy thought I should.' A sob plunges down the phone, smacks Beth in the face. She sways again. Her dad's got cancer? She swallows hard. Smiles at Saskia. Wonders if she's going to faint.

'Are you there?' her mum asks. 'Did you hear me?'

Her chest isn't working. It's screwed so tightly that she can't release it. Her lungs, airway, voice box all clamped shut.

'Do you want to go outside?' Saskia mouths, pointing at the fire door. 'Talk out there?'

Beth looks at the door. If she'd been just a minute quicker, she'd be out there already. Talking to her mum without Saskia's questioning eyes digging into her. Her friend has given her permission to create some distance now, but at what cost? She nods at Saskia, manages some sort of smile, then backs away.

'I'm here, Mum,' she whispers into her phone, avoiding eye contact with the other parents as she weaves her way towards the door.

'Will you come and see us?'

Of course her mum would ask this. And of course she must go. Her dad deserves that at least, and her mum shouldn't have to face this journey alone. But has Beth really got the strength for it? With everything else that's going on?

'Please, darling. I know it's a long way, and your job is so busy. But say you'll come.'

Beth sighs. 'Of course I'll come,' she whispers. But she needs a moment to think it through, to make sure her lie is authentic. 'I'll get a flight back to Heathrow tomorrow,' she says. 'So it will be Friday in the UK by the time I get to yours.'

'Oh thank you, darling, thank you. Your dad will be so happy to see you; we both will.'

'Me too,' Beth whispers, and listens as the line goes dead.

'Heathrow, hey? Are you picking someone up?'

Beth twists round. Saskia is standing behind her. 'Were you listening to my call?' she demands.

'What?' Saskia asks, flustered by the venom in Beth's tone. 'I just caught the end—'

'I have a stalker following me,' Beth interrupts. 'And you think it's a good idea to creep up on me?'

Saskia's hand flies up to her face. 'Oh God, I'm so sorry! I didn't mean to scare you.'

'Well you did,' Beth keeps going. 'Look, I'm shaking,' she says, holding her hand up horizontally, anything to distract Saskia from what she overheard.

'God, I am so stupid. And poor you, darling. You seemed kind of relaxed about it yesterday. But of course you weren't, you were just being brave. Let me do something, anything. I could collect the girls from school? Pick up some groceries?'

173

Relief floods through Beth; she's managed to drag Saskia's attention away from her phone call. But she needs to keep going if she's going to stem Saskia's suspicion permanently and she doesn't know what to ask for. Then she thinks about Luna, and Kat's offer to walk her this evening after her aborted attempt last night. She accepted at the time, she remembers now, but she can't let that happen. She can't face that stoical dog walker ever again. 'Could you walk Luna later?' she spurts out.

'Luna?' Saskia repeats. 'Um, yes, I suppose I can do that, if it would help.'

'It would, thank you,' Beth whispers. Then she turns away from Saskia and stumbles back inside.

Chapter 26

Kat

Kat is putting in a rare appearance behind the reception desk when the bell above the door jangles. She looks up. But it's not a customer, not even a dog owner. 'What are you doing here?' she asks, her voice rising an octave with each word.

'Well, that's not much of a welcome,' her mum responds in a tone somewhere between offended and confused. 'I'm here because you invited me.'

'I did?' Kat walks out from behind the desk, and they share an awkward hug, Kat like a teenager in a sports car – heavy foot swapping between accelerator and brake – and her mum slow and formal, like she's trying to pinpoint the right muscle memory but having to rely on a stock response instead. As Kat pulls away, her mind starts rattling through the sporadic conversations they've had over the last few months. Her mum and Javier still live in Kat's childhood home, and she avoids visiting as much as possible, but she does still phone her mum from time to time, and usually after a few bottles of Brixton Pale Ale, so it's possible that she suggested a visit.

'You said that I should come and see where you work. That it would be nice for us to spend a bit of time together, just the two of us,' her mum explains, pulling off her tawny knee-length coat and draping it over one arm. She's wearing an elegant sage green woollen dress underneath, a stark contrast to her daughter's camo pants and sweatshirt. Kat considers her mum's words. That is the sort of thing she'd say once alcohol had loosened her tongue. Even at 34, she hasn't managed to completely cull her dreams about their building a better relationship. For one special weekend when she was 16, she'd felt like they were finding their way back to each other. It wasn't to be – it was just the final act before the curtain came crashing down – but that doesn't stop Kat reminiscing from time to time.

It's also entirely possible that Kat has since forgotten about inviting her mum to the salon. From the moment she saw Beth's face on that MyNeighbour post, she's wiped everything else from her mind.

'Before we meet up with the others,' her mum continues, filling the silence, still trying to jog Kat's memory.

'The others?' Kat asks, her heart starting to thud a little quicker.

'Javier and the girls; and Alex is coming too this year. It's our family Christmas outing, remember? We've come up to London because you're working right through the Christmas period and can't come home? Although why your boss is so keen to keep a dog grooming salon open over Christmas is beyond me.' While her mum shakes her head, Kat prays that Sally can't hear the conversation going on in reception, the fake excuse she gave to dodge another excruciating Christmas Day with Javier and his 92-year-old mother (who is both an outstanding advert for the Mediterranean diet and a cantankerous old cow). Luckily Sally is in the back room. One of her oldest clients, a majestic Afghan hound, is currently in for a groom, so the two of them have swapped places for the last hour of the day. 'I can't believe you forgot,' her mum goes on. 'I booked the tickets ages ago and emailed you the link.'

Kat blinks. It's like her mum is talking another language. 'What link?'

'*Pantoland at the Palladium*. And the reviews are brilliant so it should be really fun. Don't you remember anything?' she adds with an exasperated sigh.

Kat pauses for a moment as a faint alarm bell rings in some faraway corner of her mind. 'That's tonight?' she says, not looking for an answer – it's clearly tonight – but playing for time. Needing a moment to work out what to do. Last night Beth accepted her offer to walk Luna this evening, and after the progress she made in Beth's kitchen, she can't miss the chance to visit again. Especially with Simon still out of the country. But her mum has travelled all the way to South West London to collect her. How can she get out of their trip to the West End now? 'I'm sorry, Mum,' she starts. 'I've made plans tonight.'

'I know.' Linda's voice hardens as her patience wanes. 'A theatre trip with your family.'

'No, I mean plans here, in Wandsworth, plans I can't cancel.' Kat adds a level of gravitas to her tone, hoping that it conveys the importance of the event she's committed to, without her having to actually explain it. 'I can show you around the salon before you go,' she adds hopefully. 'Introduce you to my boss, Sally.'

Linda bats away the olive branch. 'Our Christmas family outing is a plan you can't cancel,' she counters icily. 'Do you not think that Sofia and Alex might be busier than you? They're working all hours at the hospital, but they still managed to book the time off. Gabriela is missing out on teaching two Pilates classes, and told her agent not to put her forward for any auditions today. It's not that difficult, you know. Prioritising your family once in a while.'

'They're not my family,' Kat mutters under her breath. She knows she's regressing, tumbling back into her petulant teenage self, but her sisters have always been a trigger. Sofia turned out to be a science genius and ended up at Imperial studying medicine. She's now working as a junior doctor at West Berkshire

Community Hospital, alongside her fiancé Alex. Gabriela isn't such a goody two-shoes, but she shows her value in other ways. Bit parts in *Casualty* and *EastEnders*. Millions of views for her stupid memes on TikTok. All topped off with a physique that's Pilates-moulded to perfection.

'Don't be ridiculous. Of course they're your family.' Her mum sighs and softens her voice. 'Look, forget everyone else. I'd love to have you there; please come, for me.' Kat looks at her mum's imploring face. She doesn't care about the others, but she hates rejecting her mum.

'I'm sorry, I can't,' she whispers. 'I would be letting someone down.'

'Who, Kat? Who is that important?' A light switches on in her mum's eyes; Kat can almost see it glowing. 'Is it some special?' she asks.

Kat scratches her chin and looks away. 'Maybe,' she admits.

'You like each other?' Kat's mum pauses. 'And it's mutual?'

Kat's shoulders tighten. She bites the inside of her cheek. 'I need to get on; you should go.'

'I'm sorry – that came out wrong.'

'It's fine. We all know what happened. How I fucked up.'

'It was a lifetime ago, Kat,' her mum tries. 'You need to let the guilt go.'

Kat turns back to face her mum. They share the same colouring, but otherwise they're opposites. Her mum is slight and pretty, while she inherited her dad's stocky frame and masculine features. But they do love each other, on some fundamental level, so it shouldn't be this awkward. 'I'm trying, Mum. And seeing my friend tonight is part of that.'

Her mum sighs, then pushes her arms into her coat, one by one. 'Well in that case, I forgive you.' She gives Kat a watery smile and nods. 'Happy Christmas, love.' She plants a quick kiss on Kat's cheek, then leans on the door and glides out of the salon.

Kat watches until her mum disappears down one of the

residential streets, heading for Clapham Junction and her festive family night out. Part of her aches to be walking next to her, then sitting in the Palladium and having her head filled with frivolous entertainment. But she can't miss this chance to be with Beth. She checks her watch, then picks up a pad and pen and walks over to the display shelves. Sally had asked her to do a quick stocktake before she finished for the day and it's good to have something mundane to concentrate on. As she's noting down the eight packets of Pet Munchies salmon bites, her phone buzzes in her pocket. She fishes it out and reads the message that has lit up on her screen.

Hi Kat, don't need you tonight after all.
Friend walking Luna for me. Thx Beth

Kat grips the phone. Rage jerks through her like a lightning strike. It's there, then gone, but it leaves her breathless. She's given up a night with her mum to help Beth out, she risked her own safety confronting Beth's stalker last night, and now she's being dismissed like she's staff? Kat pulls at the collar of her shirt. The stench of buffalo chews and rabbits' ears fills her nostrils.

She grabs her parka, then flings open the front door. It's freezing outside, and she lets the icy air cool her cheeks as she pauses for a moment to catch up with the thoughts swirling around her head. She thinks about Beth's text. *Friend walking Luna for me.* She bets it's Saskia, the woman who wrote that MyNeighbour post. She lives across the street too, something Kat discovered when she dropped the Groom & Bloom leaflet through Beth's letterbox, recognising her from the photos she found on the internet. And of course a woman like that would want to get involved, act the saviour, muscle her way further into Beth's life.

Kat flicks her hood over her head and zips it up to her chin, enjoying the sense of anonymity it creates. Then she walks up the hill, just shy of Beth's house, and slips down the next residential street where she still has a good view. She doesn't have to wait long to be proved right. At six o'clock Saskia leaves her house and knocks on Beth's door. Long blonde hair in a high ponytail and wellies adorned with pink and yellow flowers. An English rose, punctuated with thorns. Beth's younger daughter appears at the door holding Luna on a lead. Kat wishes it was Beth, just that one fix would help, but she won't even reward her with that.

Saskia heads up the hill towards Clapham Common, and Kat falls in step behind her. She watches her cross at the lights, then follows when the traffic allows, keeping those stupid floral wellies in her sights. Saskia lets Luna off the lead, so Kat has to be very careful, backtracking if the inquisitive cockapoo comes close, or dipping into the shadows if Saskia looks over her shoulder. As she watches, Kat wonders what kind of friendship they have, whether it's one of convenience, doing and returning favours, or something deeper. She remembers Beth's disparaging comments about Saskia last night, the so-called friend who posted Beth's story without her permission. And yet, she's chosen to lean on Saskia rather than Kat today. What does that say about how she feels about Kat? After everything Kat's done for her?

As she walks, Kat tries to clear her head, to convince herself that Saskia doesn't pose a threat. That she can get closer to Beth without Saskia getting in the way. But by the time they reach Beth's house again, and she watches Beth smile warmly at her neighbour, her skin is prickling with the thought of what she might be forced to do.

April 2003

Chapter 27

Katherine

Katherine can't move; she mustn't make a sound. Her skirt is bunched around her waist and the room is so cold that there are goose bumps on her naked thighs. But even behind the locked door – just a slab of thin MDF really, her feet exposed at the bottom – rustling her clothes feels like too much of a risk now. She slowly, carefully, leans back until the nylon of her school coat finds the cold plastic of the raised toilet seat lid.

Year twelves don't usually use this toilet block – they have their own in the sixth form centre – but of course they're allowed to go wherever they want. It's one of the perks of being top of the school. Katherine closes her eyes and wonders where Becca is standing. She imagines her leaning against the sink unit, but with her back to the mirror because she's too beautiful to need the reassurance of regular check-ins. Her friend Clara will be facing the opposite way, practising her pouts, or retouching her make-up. There's the muffle of conversation between them – Becca's voice instantly recognisable, Clara's gradually so – but it's muted, and Katherine can't make out what they're saying. It's probably nothing important, she hopes, just the humdrum of weekend gossip. But still, she feels on high alert. Waiting for something.

Elation hopefully. Catastrophe maybe.

'What the actual fuck?' *Clara's voice suddenly rises in the cold room and Katherine puts her hands to her face, her worst fears itching at her skin.* 'She wrote you a letter?' *Katherine's heart booms in her ears. Becca will defend her, she promises herself, cut Clara dead. The room is silent for a second, then another, and Katherine feels it spinning behind her eyelids.*

Then she hears Becca let out a sigh. 'It's my fault,' *she says, her words now pealing with clarity.* 'I can see that now. But I felt sorry for her.'

Katherine squeezes her eyes, then her cheeks and lips. Her whole face contorts. No, no, not this. Not sympathy. There's more to their relationship than that. They like the same TV shows, the same music. They share the same beliefs. Why doesn't Becca mention that?

'That's your problem – you're too nice. And then you get weirdos like her writing you freaky love letters. Makes me feel sick.'

Clara's calling me a weirdo, Katherine thinks, willing her message to get through to Becca. Surely you must defend me now?

'You wouldn't feel like that if it was a boy,' *Becca counters eventually. It's quiet, tentative, but Katherine can hear the conviction too. A warm breeze of relief flows over her skin. It's not all in her head; their relationship is real.*

'I would if it was a year eleven heffalump with a face full of acne.'

A herd of buffalo stomp over Katherine, the dust of its wake threatening to suffocate her. She hates Clara with every atom in her body. It's her fault that Becca's pushing Katherine away. She's warping Becca's mind, driving a wedge through the friendship they've built.

'Actually, there was something in the letter about you,' *Becca continues, her voice slowing down and dropping an octave, as though she's reluctant to share any more. Katherine leans forward, digs her elbows into the doughy flesh of her thighs.*

'Oh?'

'She said that I shouldn't be friends with someone who chucks cider cans around.'

'Hang on, what?' The room goes silent. Katherine imagines Clara's face screwed up, trying to wind her memory backwards. 'She must have been watching us on Friday night,' she finally says.

Katherine bites the inside of her cheek. She hears the squelch of flesh tearing, and tastes the metallic liquid as it slides down past her gums. Why did she mention Clara in her letter? Her mind flickers back to Friday night, watching them sat on the edge of the skate park. She knew Clara was poisonous then, so why didn't she just forget about her? Katherine's legs feel numb now. There'll be a red mark on the back of her thighs.

'Listen, Becca, I know I've been laughing, but this isn't actually funny,' Clara continues. 'What if she thinks I'm your girlfriend? And gets in a jealous rage?'

'You're being ridiculous; she's a harmless little mouse.'

Katherine thinks she might be sick and wonders how she'll manage it sitting on the toilet.

'Fat mouse, you mean.'

Katherine wants to vomit in Clara's face. Spew regurgitated carrots in her eyes.

'Don't say that. Look, she's just a lonely girl who's developed a crazy crush. It happens.'

'No, it's more than that,' Clara pushes. 'She's deluded. And that makes her officially mad. Which also means she's dangerous.'

'She's not dangerous,' Becca whispers.

God, of course she's not dangerous! Katherine tries telepathy, squeezing out her message and forcing it through the toilet door.

'I think you should tell Mr Thomas. You're his favourite student. He'll take it seriously.'

'I don't want to get her into trouble.'

'It's being too nice that got you into this mess in the first place; you need to put yourself first now. Anyway, where is the letter?'

'Still in my satchel,' Becca whispers.

'Come on. Let's take it to Mr Thomas before lessons start. Just to be on the safe side.'

The silence is back, but this time it feels oppressive. Katherine wants to break it with a blood-curdling scream.

'Do you really think I should?' Becca finally asks, her voice wavering.

'Definitely. And I want to read it too. If I feature, it's only fair.' Clara tries to disguise her giggle with a cough, but Katherine hears it. She wants to dig her fingernails into Clara's face and rip the flesh off her sticky-out cheekbones. The brazen bitch thinks that she can destroy her and Becca's friendship, and get the teachers on her side too. Well, she's wrong. Becca will put her straight. And if she doesn't, Katherine will do it for her.

She listens as the door to the toilets swings open, then shut. And finally, they're gone. She pulls up her knickers, smooths down her skirt. But her hands are shaking. With fear at what might happen next. But mainly with fury.

December 2021

Chapter 28

Saskia

Saskia walks into her hallway, steps out of her wellies and slides down onto her backside, with her spine pushed up against the radiator. That was a God-awful walk. Not because it was freezing cold, although it was, and that didn't help, and not even because she had to pick up two separate bags of poo. But because she got the fear. The scratching of panic between her shoulder blades that she was being followed. She reads all the horror stories about London parks after dark, the muggings, the senseless attacks. She reads about the women who have been murdered, often for no other reason than being in a killer's eyeline when they chose to strike. So she knows the risks. But she has always refused to let them curtail her life, because freedom, equality, are important to her. She believes that she is entitled to walk alone safely after dark, and so she must practise what she preaches.

But tonight she was scared. She couldn't stop thinking that someone was behind her, that she's got a stalker of her own.

While she can barely admit it to herself, she wonders if it's jealousy. When Beth first told her about Mark, Saskia's first thought

189

hadn't been for Beth's safety. It had been much less charitable – *well of course you'd be the one with a stalker, like some sort of celebrity, wouldn't you* – and she can't help wondering if she's created an imaginary stalker of her own as a way of competing with her supposed friend. But that doesn't really make sense because she doesn't have an imagination; she's not that kind of writer. She might embellish facts slightly to make them more exciting, but her brain isn't wired to make things up from scratch. Could she have dreamed up the feeling of eyes on the back of her neck? Or the shadow that seemed attached to her by some invisible, ominous leash?

'Are you comfortable down there?'

Saskia looks up and gives her husband a sardonic smile. 'Just thawing out.'

Tim nods thoughtfully. 'Would you move for a glass of wine?'

'Obviously.' Saskia shakes the strange thoughts out of her head and holds both hands out for Tim to pull her up.

'Jesus, your hands are freezing.'

Saskia sighs. 'It wasn't my all-time favourite walk. Cold, dark; a bit scary if I'm honest.'

'Well, at least you're back in one piece. And you're always saying that women should be able to walk alone at night without feeling scared.'

Saskia heads down the narrow hallway and into the kitchen. 'You're right, I suppose. Maybe Beth having a stalker has put me on edge. Reminded me that, very frustratingly, men's physical dominance means they've always got the upper hand.'

'I think you're being a bit dramatic. It's Clapham Common, not downtown Caracas.'

'Beth was too scared to walk there,' Saskia points out. Perhaps it's her own fault for always banging the feminist drum, but it would be nice if her husband could appear a little more concerned about her welfare.

'It's different for Beth though, isn't it? She actually does have a stalker – a genuine threat – so it makes sense that she wouldn't take the risk.'

'But it's all right for me, you mean, your wife?' Saskia suddenly feels boiling hot – God, this can't be a hot flush, she's only just turned 40 – and takes a long gulp of the crisp Chablis. At least he's poured her a glass of wine.

'Well, you offered to take Luna,' he reminds her. 'And you're, I don't know.' He pauses to find the right words. 'You're more robust than Beth.' He shrugs. 'She's just one of those people who's a bit more fragile.'

'Like a precious doll?'

'Exactly,' Tim says, relieved that Saskia is on the same page as him at last. She eyes her now half-full glass. She wants to throw it at him, bang her fists against his chest, remind him that she should be his precious doll, not Beth. But that would be over-dramatic. And a waste of delicious wine. She takes another sip.

'You could have walked Luna instead, you know; then you'd have been protecting both of us,' Saskia ventures.

Tim clears his throat. 'Sorry, what was that?'

'Well, she's your friend too, isn't she? You're happy to accept her hospitality when it's a dinner date, or an impromptu barbecue.'

Tim scratches his neck as the realisation creeps over his face. 'God, I suppose you're right,' he says slowly, looking sheepish. 'How very unthoughtful of me. I'll message Beth now, see if she needs someone to walk Luna tomorrow. In fact,' he adds, warming to the theme, 'I could do the morning walk for her too, save Beth going up there at all. Work won't mind if I'm a bit late in.'

Saskia drains her wine and tries to swallow down her annoyance too; her taunt seems to be backfiring. 'You're never late into work.'

'Yes but this is different, special circumstances. They'll be fine about it, I promise.'

Saskia watches her husband pick up his phone and scroll, looking for Beth's number, she supposes. She can tell that he's excited at the prospect of being Beth's saviour because there's something Marvel-esque about his expression. He won't be imagining anything more than that though, nothing romantic. Because he knows that he's not in her league. He's in Saskia's league instead. Division three maybe.

Chapter 29

Kat

Kat didn't plan to be here, on Beth's doorstep, knocking on her front door. Just like she didn't mean for the youngest daughter, Ava, to have seen her through the playroom window. But she couldn't pretend that her standing outside their house was a coincidence after being spotted, so here she is, wondering how the hell she's going to explain herself.

She should have remembered that watching people is only safe at night, when you can become part of the darkness, a sense of someone rather than a physical presence. But she'd had a restless night thinking about Beth, and how she turned to Saskia rather than Kat yesterday after everything Kat had done for her. By 5 a.m. she was in Jayden and Will's garage, trying to find the answer in a punchbag. But all she could see – on every wall, and in every direction – was Beth's face, both now and before.

Kat can hear feet pattering on the wooden floor of the hallway, and the effervescent buzz of children whispering. But the door remains closed. The delay provides a valid excuse for her to walk away, but something is keeping her rooted to the spot. The proximity is feeding her desperation to see Beth, but it's more than that; a tingle on her skin, a whiff of something not quite right. She looks at her watch. That's it. It's past eight o'clock on a Thursday morning and Ava is watching TV in her pyjamas with a cloth tiger in her mouth.

Why isn't she getting ready for school? And where is Beth?

Fear lurches in her tummy. Has Mark been here? Has he ignored her warning and come after Beth anyway? A thought suddenly blindsides her; could she have made things worse? She rams the door knocker hard against the wood. The whispers get louder, more frantic, allowing Kat to hear the girls' conversation.

'I'm going to answer it.'

'No, don't! Mummy says it's not allowed.'

'Why not? We're kids. We need help.'

Kat catches her breath. What help do they need? Why hasn't Beth appeared? Surely she heard the door this time?

'It could be a burglar.'

'It's not. It's the lady who walks Luna.'

'Are you sure?'

'Positive! I saw her through the window.'

Kat pushes her hands deep into her pockets. Adrenalin is flying through her, which she knows from experience means that she's not completely in control of her limbs. 'Open up,' she whispers to the closed door. 'Please.'

A second later, her plea is answered. The door swings on its hinges and Kat tries to smile at the two nervous-looking girls stood opposite. 'Hi there, I'm Kat,' she says in her most upbeat voice. 'Luna's dog walker.'

'We know,' the older one says. Martha.

'I told you,' Ava adds triumphantly.

'Is your mum at home?'

The jubilant look disappears as Ava shrugs, then lets her bottom lip droop. 'She's asleep,' she whispers. 'She won't wake up.'

Kat's mind races. Beth had clearly taken something on

194

Tuesday evening. Did she do the same again last night? Kat knows how pills can transform you from a caged tiger into a stoned sloth.

Or is it much worse than that? Has Mark found a way into her home?

'Did you try to wake her, Ava?' The words tumble out on top of each other. She tries to smile, to reassure the little girl, but it pulls her face out of shape.

'I did,' Martha says. 'I shook her arm. She opened her eyes for a bit, but then she rolled over and went back to sleep.'

Kat takes a deep breath and slowly exhales, enjoying the feel of her heart rate settling. Beth is alive. She imagines her lying in a king-sized bed, wrapped in a goose-down duvet, her dark hair splayed out across the pillow. Then a new thought enters her mind: opportunity. 'It sounds like Mummy is really tired,' she says. 'Maybe we should let her sleep a bit longer.'

Both girls nod, but Martha's face creases into a frown. 'But that means we'll be late for school,' she moans.

'And miss the register.'

Kat looks at their trusting expressions. It doesn't matter to them that Kat's almost a stranger; she's the adult in the room, so it's her job to solve this problem. 'I could walk you to school if you'd like.'

'But what about our breakfast?'

Kat laughs. She always approves of people who put their stomach first.

'We could have some of Granny's mince pies,' Martha suggests. 'They came in a big red box yesterday, with a ribbon and everything.'

'I'm not sure mince pies …' Kat starts, but doesn't get chance to give her (highly hypocritical) healthy eating advice before being interrupted.

'No. They're yucky,' Ava announces, crossing her arms.

'Liar, you love mince pies,' Martha counters.

Ava shakes her head primly. 'Only the ones that come in a cardboard box from that old man.'

Kat can't help smiling. Mr Kipling has always been her favourite too.

'But Granny uses Prue Leith's recipe! And she's from *Bake Off*,' Martha says in a voice that suggests her argument has clinched it.

'I don't care; they taste weird.'

'No they don't!'

As the girls' voices rise, Kat looks towards the kitchen in panic. She needs to stop the argument escalating. 'How about I make some pancakes?' she suggests.

'Pancakes?' Ava's eyes light up, and it reminds Kat of herself at that age. She was born with a sweet tooth and loved smearing Nutella on the wafer-thin pancakes that her mum would make as a Sunday treat. That was before her skin enflamed, and sugar became the enemy, and every forbidden bite tasted both better and worse.

'I'll do a deal with you,' she offers. 'If you get dressed in your smartest school uniform, and do it so quietly that you don't wake Mummy, I will prepare you the finest banquet of pancakes and Nutella.'

'Yay!' the girls cry in unison, their difference of opinion already forgotten. They spin and slide across the floor, then race up the stairs, but on their tiptoes, heeding Kat's warning not to wake Beth. She stands still, staring at the charcoal and cream runner that zigzags up the stairs, and fantasising for a moment about living here. And then, with a smile of anticipation, of making up for past mistakes, she walks into Beth's kitchen.

Saskia is stood outside her own house, checking her watch impatiently. When she looks up, her brow creases in confusion. This is good, Kat thinks. This drives a sturdy wedge through Beth and Saskia's friendship, even if Beth isn't aware of it. To further prove her point, she reaches out towards the girls, and miraculously

Ava takes the bait, curling her dainty fingers around Kat's rough hand. On Kat's instruction, which feels surprisingly natural to say she's hardly even spoken to a child since she was one, the three of them walk across the road.

'Hello,' Saskia says in a polite, condescending voice, as though she's interviewing a prospective cleaner. 'Where's Beth?'

'She's in bed,' Ava states solemnly.

Kat watches Saskia's expression darken. 'Beth's fine, just tired,' she says quickly. She needs to deflect both suspicion and any offer of help from Saskia. 'I'm walking Luna later and so she asked me to take the girls to school.' Kat can feel Martha's quizzical stare, but she doesn't meet her eyes and eventually the 7-year-old gets distracted by Saskia's daughter's new hairband.

'That must be why Beth didn't answer my husband's text,' Saskia says, looking triumphant for some reason. 'Well, why don't I take them? It seems silly both of us going.'

Of course Saskia would say this. Try to wheedle her way further into Beth's good books, make Kat look like the outsider. 'I promised Beth that I'd take them,' Kat counters. 'But I can walk your two as well if you think it's silly?' she adds in an entirely alien tone.

Saskia offers her something between a cool smile and an angry grimace in retaliation. 'Let's walk together.'

They don't speak again during the five-minute walk to school. There's enough chatter from the children for it not to appear too awkward but Kat doesn't care anyway; the less comfortable Saskia is, the better she feels. All four children race into school as soon as they arrive, and Saskia makes some excuse about a barre class and scuttles off. With a new level of hope rocking in her tummy, Kat looks at the unfamiliar door key in her hand and starts back down the hill.

Luna is asleep in her daybed when Kat walks inside, and the house is silent. She breathes in the now familiar smell – a mix of bleach and cedarwood diffuser – and wonders where to go first. She knows that Beth could wake up at any moment, and that she'll need to explain herself when that happens, but her urge to search, to discover, is too strong for that risk to hold her back.

She doesn't bother with the playroom, and the study turns out to be full of Simon's work stuff. A few books on the shelf, but mainly wires and cables snaking up from plug sockets and two big screens sat angled on the desk. The kitchen is clearly Beth's domain, but it doesn't reveal much either. Beth still craves cleanliness and order, but Kat had worked that out on Tuesday evening. There are half a dozen expensive hand creams under the sink and Kat rubs some Clarins lotion between her palms. She inhales its citrusy perfume – so different to the medical creams she's used to – and wonders if she's brave enough to go upstairs. Being found perched on a bar stool in Beth's kitchen is one thing; being caught lurking around bedrooms is quite another.

But there might be something interesting up there.

Kat saw windows in the roof, which means there's a loft bedroom, or more likely a full-on suite with wet room and walk-in cupboards. She's sure that's where Beth will be. Which means she can risk checking out the first floor. Carefully, silently, she climbs the stairs. Her heart is thudding when she reaches the top, but the stillness around her calms it. The bedroom door to her right is adorned with multi-coloured wooden letters spelling MARTHA. She gently pushes on the door and slips inside.

She opens the wardrobe door, stares at the perfect line of hangers and walks her fingers through the rainbow of clothes hanging off them, from navy to pale pink with a dazzling mix of colours in between. She reaches up on her tiptoes and slides her hand across the top shelf. What is she looking for? Beth's private journal, her innermost secrets neatly written down, like Kat used to do? As if it would be that easy. All she finds are a collection of Tiffany boxes filled with trinkets and jewellery. Saved for when Martha becomes an adult and has her own standards of beauty to retain. Eventually Kat closes the wardrobe door and turns back into the room.

The bed is unmade, so she pulls the duvet up to the pillow and strokes the creases out. There are two distressed wooden photo frames on the bedside table. She picks them both up and sinks onto the bed. One shows a couple, a younger Beth, much more similar to the girl Kat remembers, but with an added whiff of privilege, and a blond man wearing jeans and a racing green polo shirt. That must be Simon. The other photo is of the same older couple from the frame downstairs, clearly Simon's parents. Kat wonders why there are no pictures of Beth's family on display.

'Kat?'

She whips her head around.

'I'm sorry,' Beth says, giving Kat a warm smile. 'But what the fuck are you doing in my daughter's bedroom?'

'I'm sorry,' Kat parrots back, buying time.

'What's going on?' Panic rises in Beth's voice as the strangeness of the situation sinks into her just-woken brain. 'Where are my children?'

Kat needs to stem her fears before they escalate, before Beth throws her out. 'They're at school. They're fine, I promise.'

Beth's eyes flit around the room until they land on Martha's wall clock, then they widen. 'How can it be half past nine? Why didn't they wake me? And why are you here?'

'I was passing, I knocked, to see if you wanted me to walk Luna,' she stutters. 'It's my morning off.' She stands up and smooths down Martha's bed for a second time. 'Ava saw me. They told me you were sleeping, and I thought it would be nice, for me to take them, you to get more rest. After everything.' She tapers off and stares pleadingly at Beth.

'You took them to school? What about their PE kits? And an extra bag to bring their artwork home in?' She rubs the heel of her hand against her forehead. 'They didn't mind you taking them?'

Kat has no idea what the girls shoved into their backpacks when she instructed them to get their stuff, but she doesn't think now's a good time to admit that. 'They have everything they need,

199

and they liked it, I think. I made them pancakes for breakfast,' she adds. 'I cleared everything up.'

Beth leans back against the wall. She looks tired. Harassed and scared. Kat knows she should feel sad, but she can't help pleasure creeping in. Because Beth's vulnerability is a chance for her. 'Thank you, I guess,' Beth whispers eventually. 'I did have a bad night.'

'I'm sorry to hear that,' Kat lies.

'And thank you for getting the girls to school on time.'

Kat's heart booms silently. 'It's my pleasure.'

Chapter 30

Beth

Beth stares at the ever-changing view rushing past the window. The historic charm of Richmond-upon-Thames, followed by its grimier neighbours, Feltham and Staines. Then into the countryside, the genteel conurbations of Virginia Water and Sunningdale, and past the world-famous Ascot racecourse with its royal connections.

But she doesn't see any of it. Her head is too full.

She interlaces her fingers and squeezes them together. But they feel naked without the ridges of her engagement, wedding and eternity rings – the revealing jewellery that is currently stacked neatly on her bedside table – so she pushes them back into her jacket pocket. She's determined not to touch the seat.

Part of her is glad to be out of London. She's exhausted with the constant fear of wondering where Mark will show up next. Not knowing whether the shadows in doorways or behind parked cars are him watching, or her imagination taunting her. And with Simon still in Dublin, that fear permeates into her home too, making normal tasks impossible. On Wednesday night she dealt with it by drinking too much wine, then taking a tablet to help her sleep, which of course led to her oversleeping. She'd thought she never wanted to see Kat again after her breakdown on Tuesday, but thank God the dog walker showed up on Thursday morning. Beth has worked too hard at being the perfect mother for one mistake to have her branded as substandard, but that's exactly what Nightingales' pious receptionist Mrs Gilbert would have thought if Martha and Ava had been dropped off after the register.

But she is also dreading what comes next. A return to her childhood home, the house she lived in until she was 16. Her dad fighting cancer.

Finally, the train pulls into Reading station. It's the last stop so Beth waits until everyone else gets off before pushing out of her seat. As she does, a thought suddenly flashes up – what if Mark followed her here and is on this train? He could do anything to her; no one knows she's here. She was extra-vigilant at Clapham Junction, scanning the platform as she waited for the train to arrive, but still, she might have missed him. Her eyes whip left and right as she walks away from the platform and towards the concourse.

The station has had an upgrade since she last visited, lots of gleaming glass and shiny stainless steel, plus a curved roof with a nautical feel. As she walks towards the exit, she remembers how different it was when she was growing up here; the snack shop that wasn't much bigger than a cupboard but still managed to stock every chocolate bar you could think of, and the shabby flower stand with the owner who would try to flog bunches of wilting roses to every man in a suit.

Beth decides not to take a cab to her parents' house; the walk will give her time to prepare herself. As she veers left out of the station, she tries to conjure up the Beth her parents remember, then layer on a decade-long glamorous career in international finance. God, she feels sick. How on earth is she going to be able to hide who she really is? She finds their rare, short-lived telephone calls difficult enough, so how can she possibly keep up the pretence for hours in their company? Her only hope is that her dad's illness distracts them from her lies. She knows that's selfish, but survival often is.

Reading is a growing town, and Beth doesn't recognise half the buildings, the shiny glass accountancy firms that have sprung up close to the station, and the red-brick blocks of luxury commuter flats. But some things haven't changed. Forbury Gardens, where she hung out when things became too difficult at home; the crumbling ruins of the old abbey, where she would daydream about her escape. She crosses over the narrow river and gradually the landscape changes. She avoids making eye contact with a group of teenage boys and takes a left onto her parents' street. It's a long, deteriorating road and she walks for a good fifteen minutes, almost to the end, until she reaches number 205. She takes a breath and knocks on the white PVC front door.

An old woman with grey shoulder-length hair opens it. She lifts one hand to her chest and drops her head to the side. Tears sprout in her eyes. 'You came,' she whispers.

'Hello, Mum.' Beth's voice is croaky and she coughs to clear it.

'Such a long way, you must be exhausted after your journey. How long was the plane ride? Did you come from the airport?' The questions rain down.

'No, I arrived late last night.' The first lie of many. 'I stayed in a hotel close to Heathrow.'

'Still, you must be tired.' Her mum peers at her, looking for evidence of a long-haul flight. Beth doesn't need to worry – she's certain that she looks much worse than thirteen hours on a plane could achieve – but she still squirms under her mum's gaze.

'Are you going to invite me in?' she asks finally, smiling warmly, trying to break her mum's stare.

'Of course! Silly me. You must be hungry, thirsty.'

Beth waits for her to stand back from the doorway, and then steps inside. But the hallway is narrower than she remembers, and her mum is too close now. She'll want a hug, Beth realises, of course she will after ten years apart, but Beth can't allow that. She's already teetering on the edge, and her mum's touch will be like kryptonite. She needs to create more space, and knows the front room is just behind her. She reaches back for the door handle. It feels sticky under her grasp and a wave of nausea rises up, but she swallows it back down and manages to push the handle down.

Beth blinks. She'd forgotten about the large family photo above the fireplace. The only non-essential item she ever witnessed her parents buy. It's of the four of them, smartly dressed, heads together and smiling. Before Beth stopped being able to handle such togetherness. Before Eddie died. It's been almost two decades since her brother lived in this house, but his ghost is here in other ways too. The *Star Wars* VHS tapes that Beth can just about see in the open drawer under the TV, the faint sick and bloodstains in the carpet, the splinters in the wooden doors and the deep cracks on her mum's face.

She feels an intense urge to turn and run.

She was 15 when she first saw Eddie vomit on the floor. Her mum told her it was a stomach bug, but Beth knew that was a lie, her maternal instinct to protect them both at play. Because it's impossible to hide a secret like drug addiction when you share a bedroom. She remembers watching her mum scrub at the carpet with an old sponge, then squeeze the mix of sick and soapy water into a bucket. There was a small tear in her mum's rubber gloves, and Beth remembers imagining the remnants of Eddie's sick crawling inside and staining her mum's fingers.

It was around then when she started washing her hands in scalding water, cleaning her few precious things so ferociously that she ruined most of them.

Eddie was 19 when he died, but he'd been taking drugs for a few years by then. It started with hash, when he was supposed to be at school. Beth would find him lying on his bed when she got home from a run, smoking a joint and complaining about how shit his life was. She'd consider reminding him that he used to have ambition, that he'd talked about going to university or joining the navy. But she never did. She just hoovered her half of the carpet – all two square metres of it – and plugged her tinny Argos headphones in. The heroin started when he met some new mates at college. He lasted six months before dropping out, then died a couple of years after that.

And of course it was Eddie she pictured when she came across that homeless man slumped unconscious on the street. It was his memory that meant she couldn't walk past, even though she sorely wishes that she could have.

'Where's Dad?' she asks. She wants to see her father, get it over with.

'He's sleeping. Let's leave him for a while, give us a chance to catch up. Go on, sit down.' Her mum gestures towards the sofa. 'And I've got a surprise for you, hold on.'

The house is a tiny oblong box. One room that runs front to back, plus a kitchen behind the stairs. Beth watches her mum disappear, then perches gingerly on the sofa. She recognises it from when she lived here, and she can't let herself think about the number of dead skin cells that must be buried in the ancient polyester. A minute later her mum reappears carrying a tray emblazoned with an image of Bucharest. There are two mugs of tea on top of it, plus a huge Cozonac cake.

'I hope you're hungry,' her mum says with an anxious smile. 'Your dad's not interested in food much these days, so I don't get chance to bake anymore.' Beth wants to say thanks, but she can't shift the bile that's sitting in her throat. Cozonac is a Romanian festive tradition, a citrusy sweet bread with a cocoa and nut filling that gets swirled through the dough. She and Eddie rarely got actual presents when they were growing up – there wasn't money for that – but there was a Cozonac every Christmas. For a few years Beth tried to convince her mum that she deserved the first slice, but she never succeeded. Eddie was the eldest child and a boy – two attributes that were highly valued in their traditional family home. Beth accepted her fate after a while, and by the time she lost her competition, she'd moved in with her far less traditional aunt.

She wants to try some now, but her throat is constricted, and she can't imagine getting anything solid down it. She watches her mum drop a generous slice onto a plate and pass it over.

'You are still so beautiful,' her mum observes. 'But you look tired. You work too hard.'

Beth shrugs, breaks off a small piece of bread, and forces out another warm smile.

'I worry about you; you suffered terribly after Eddie died,' her mum continues, but avoiding eye contact now. 'All the cleaning.'

Beth swallows bile.

'We didn't understand it,' her mum admits. 'We didn't want you to leave us, but it felt like the right decision, to give you some space.'

'It helped, Mum; it was a good decision.'

Beth turns to look out of the window. A boy cycles past on a black and red bike and she tries to concentrate on the spokes of its wheels. But it doesn't work; the images still come. Eddie in the bedroom they shared. The tatty navy belt stretched around his bicep. The smell and mess, the humiliation of dying. She never set foot in that room again after witnessing that. 'It was a shock,' she says finally. 'I didn't handle it very well.'

'But you fought back. Getting your A levels at that new school. Then a place at university. You made us so proud.'

The bike has disappeared, but a man is walking past the window now. He looks like a builder, his large belly squeezed into a high-vis jacket. 'Can I see Dad now?' she asks. 'I can't stay long.'

'Really?' her mum asks, and Beth tries not to hear the disappointment in her tone. Then she shakes her head. 'Sorry, of course you can.'

Beth uses her thigh muscles, not her hands, to push up from the sofa.

'Cathy brought a proper hospital bed round; your dad is in your old room.'

Chapter 31

Mark

Mark eyes the packet of spice. Then he lurches forwards and pushes it off the arm of the sofa. Why the fuck is he wasting his life smoking that shit? He thought he was so clever, nicking all those packets off Jon's dealer. But that was four days ago, and he's hardly left the squat since. He's got no idea when he last ate or washed, and the only highlight was getting overpowered by a fucking woman. He needs to cut the spice out, and get on with his plan.

With way more effort than it should require, he pushes off the sofa and stands up straight. He can see the brightly coloured packets better from this angle. Maybe he should have a little smoke before he heads outside. To chill him out, stop him feeling so fucking angry. But the urge is strong enough to act as a danger siren as well. There's just enough of the old him left to know it's a stupid idea. That one smoke will lead to a second and third – like it has done since Tuesday night – and he'll spend another day holed up in this cold room barely conscious.

And she'll have another day to parade around like she's done nothing wrong.

He drops his face into his hands, fingers splayed out, and scratches at his hairline. His head is crazy itchy, but he's not sure if that's down to spice withdrawal, or his hair needing a wash. Both are equally humiliating. 'Come on, Mark,' he hisses to himself. 'You're better than this.' He scrunches his eyes closed and forces himself to think about his future. His design portfolio, floating on a cloud somewhere, begging him to give it some daylight. His dream to become a proper game designer one day. There was a text from his mum too, a few days ago. She's expecting him home for Christmas. He thinks about the decades-old Christmas lights flashing a greeting from the tatty hedge in his family garden. He takes a big breath, and without looking back at the drugs on the floor, slowly makes his way out of the squat.

The weak winter sunshine isn't bright, but the sun is low, and Mark hasn't seen daylight since Monday, so he takes a moment to adjust. As he watches people wander up and down the street, carrying shopping bags or chatting in pairs, the day smelling morning fresh, he feels like a vampire, struggling outside his natural habitat. The passers-by seem to think so too because they look away, or veer off the pavement to avoid him. He wants to scream that it's not contagious. That being a fucking loser takes practice. But they don't deserve his reassurance, so he puts his head down and walks down the hill in the direction of Clapham Common.

He knows this new plan is risky, but he's done with just following Beth like some pathetic stalker, feeling more and more impotent as she carries on with her life. Especially now she's got that bodyguard fighting her corner; he needs to up his game too. He doesn't have kids himself of course, but he knows how much his mum loves him and his sister. So if he can get to one of Beth's daughters, preferably the younger, cuter one, then that has to spark something. Fear, upset, guilt. She deserves them all.

He drops into the dip by the top of Northcote Road and starts walking up the other side of the hill. He quickly feels out of breath and it irritates him. He used to play football every Saturday morning, and mess around on the basketball courts after college most days. How can he have gone from that to an unfit mess in just six months? There's a discarded Coke can on the pavement, and he kicks it hard. It lifts into the air for a moment, then drops and skitters along the asphalt. It draws a dirty look from a bodybuilder type walking past on the other side and Mark glares back.

His eyes expand like popping corn. Holy shit, it's Rudy!

Mark drops his eyeline again and picks up his pace. With his heart hammering, he takes a swift right down a side road. When he's far enough away, he stops and leans against the wall, shaking his head manically. Was it Rudy? Or is this what spice withdrawal does?

He must be seeing things. He's not involved in the drug scene, so there's no way Rudy could have tracked him down, especially not to a posh neighbourhood like this. It's definitely the spice, messing with his head, making him paranoid, he decides. He's got a job to do; he can't be knocked off course again. He walks a bit further to settle his nerves, then doubles back. Whoever it was has disappeared by the time he reaches Brookhill Road again, so he swears with relief and carries on up the hill.

On his first approach, he walks straight past the school; he doesn't want to be captured on their CCTV. But after a couple of fly-bys, he realises that they don't have much CCTV anyway, just narrow-angled cameras at the different entranceways. Quaint London primary schools clearly don't worry too much about intruders. The iron railings across the front perimeter only reach Mark's ears, but he also counts three different entrances with only waist-high gates. This is going to be easier than he thought. The area immediately in front of the school is a playground with hopscotch squares and a chessboard painted on the ground. Around the side, Mark can see a short line of cars, a few spaces saved for the top-ranking teachers. With two four-by-four wagons jammed up close together, Mark decides it's the perfect place to hide.

He waits until the pavement is clear, then quickly vaults over the gate closest to the parking area, making sure he's facing away from the camera. He knows he's taking a massive risk – a teacher, caretaker, maintenance worker, or anyone, could spot him in a second, and there's a big chance they'd phone the police – but he reckons the prize is worth it.

With a clattering heart, Mark makes it across the ten or so metres of open space without being noticed, and quickly slides down between a Honda CRV and Volvo XC90. He bends his knees into his chest and leans against a tyre. His phone is out of juice – he hasn't thought to charge his battery while the spice has been the priority – but it doesn't matter. He's inside the school boundary, and it will be break time at some point. He remembers enough about school to know it will be mayhem for those twenty minutes, so as long as he's quick, he shouldn't get caught.

Especially as he knows exactly who he's looking for.

Chapter 32

Beth

Beth climbs the stairs one at a time, hoping the measured pace will slow her pulse rate. It makes sense that the Macmillan nurse would put a hospital bed in her and Eddie's old room; it's not like either of them has needed it over the last two decades. She just wishes she'd considered this in advance, given herself chance to prepare. She has so many reasons to hate the room – first the growing humiliation of sharing such a small space with her brother, then seeing his body lying there in all its filth, and of course the final humiliation, the revealing photo that made its way into the local paper. She'd promised herself that she'd never walk inside again.

But now she's got no choice.

The room is to the left of the staircase, but she needs a moment to compose herself, so she slips into the bathroom opposite and slides the lock across. She rests her head against the MDF panel for a few seconds, then turns to face the sink. She twists the tap and waits for the steam to appear, the tell-tale sign that the water is hot enough to clean her skin properly.

When it's ready, she pushes her hands under the burning tap and stares at her reflection in the mirror. She spends a lot of money on her face. She's never had surgery and hasn't yet resorted to thread lifts or fillers. But she uses the best make-up and luxury face creams. She visits expensive salons and invests in an array of different treatments. In the beginning the pampering felt alien, undeserved, and she kept imagining being exposed as a fake, of being dragged out of posh salons by her hair. But she persevered, and after a while she started to enjoy it. She's worked hard to build this life, and she won't let herself be pulled backwards.

She finally extracts her hands from the hot water and rubs them against the thighs of her jeans – the only material that she knows is clean. Then she unlocks the bathroom door, takes a deep breath and walks the few steps to her old bedroom. Her heart races as she pushes the door open, but the room looks different, thank God. The walls are painted white and are bare now, no sign of the Blu-Tack stains from Eddie's old posters. And its centrepiece is a high-standing hospital bed covered in crisp white sheets. She steps inside.

'Dad?' It's a question because the man curled in the bed doesn't look like the father she remembers. He's smaller, thinner, like an ageing tree root under a white shroud.

But he looks more familiar when he turns around to face her. 'My girl,' he whispers, his eyes shining with tears. 'I'm sorry that you're seeing me like this.'

Pain burns through Beth's chest. Why has she left it so long? She surges towards him, but then brakes. What happens if she touches him? Would she revert to the old Beth? She can't allow that, because she has a whole life in London, a successful one, and a family who rely on her.

And it's not like this estrangement is her fault.

She hovers, inches away from his bony frame.

'The fags finally caught up with me,' he whispers, his voice croaky and expression sheepish.

Beth smiles wanly at her dad's admission, but the urge to touch him has receded. She can smell him now, not clean like the sheets, but a musty old man odour. She feels numb suddenly, doesn't know what to say. 'Are you having treatment?' she tries.

Her dad shakes his head. A wave of sadness washes over his face and then disappears. 'I'd prefer to enjoy whatever time I have left.'

'You shouldn't just give up,' Beth says, but it sounds more like criticism than care.

'I've had a good life. My only wish was to see you again, and here you are, all the way from Singapore.' His eyes glisten. 'Can I ask you something?' he continues. 'And you promise to give me an honest answer?' His voice is thin and wispy, but Beth can't pretend she hasn't heard it in the small, quiet room. She nods, smiles warmly, steels herself.

'I know it's not really my place to ask, but I need to know whether it's our fault. My fault.'

'What do you mean?' she asks guardedly.

'Why you don't have children? Did we do such a bad job that it put you off?'

'No, of course it's not …'

'Because having children is the best thing in life. Even if it doesn't work out, if one dies and the other is too scarred by his death to come home, it's something to be proud of. Being a parent gives you purpose.'

Beth feels a desperate urge to tell her dad about Martha and Ava. To reassure him that she has that purpose, that all the lies she tells are to protect her babies. But she knows it would be too cruel to announce it now, when he's so frail, that he's been a grandparent for seven years already. And of course, there would also be the fallout of her mum finding out. A thousand regrets threaten to overwhelm her, but she must stay strong. A few more hours and she can go back to the cocoon of her luxury life. She scratches her palm, wonders whether she's trapped dead skin cells under her nails, and yearns to wash them again. 'Perhaps I'll change my mind,' she offers. Anything to soften the desperation on his face. 'There is still time,' she whispers.

'That would be wonderful,' he whispers back.

She sees him smile with relief and wishes that she could tell him about Simon too, the man who's protected her since university. Not in a physical sense – he's no broad-chested superhero – but by his privilege. His distance from the life she led before.

Beth's phone suddenly rings out in her pocket and she jumps. She usually keeps it on silent, but she switched the volume on when she left London, a way to assuage the guilt of her secret excursion. She draws it out of her pocket and looks at the name on the screen. Her eyes widen and she flips it over, just in case lung cancer has improved her dad's eyesight. 'I need to take this,' she says, standing up and pointing at the phone. For a moment her dad looks curious, like he might ask who it is – work, boyfriend, father to his now possible future grandchildren – but then his eyes droop slightly and he nods. With an invisible sigh of relief, Beth backs out of the room, and shuts herself in the bathroom again. She leans against the thin door and prods her screen. 'Hello? Are the girls okay?'

'Ah thank goodness. Mrs Packard. I was worried you weren't going to pick up.' Mrs Gilbert, the school receptionist, sighs into the phone. Mrs Gilbert is in her late fifties, stick-thin and wears her glasses on a silver chain around her neck. Beth imagines her calmly twirling the tiny links between her fingers.

'The girls, please, I need to know they're okay.'

'Of course you do, my apologies. Both Martha and Ava are safe and well. But there has been an incident, and Ava is a bit distressed. Mrs Crowmarsh thought it would be a good idea if you came to collect her.'

'Collect her now?' Beth's heart rate increases. She's two hours away from school. 'Why is Ava upset?'

'It's nothing really, a storm in a teacup, but there was a young man hanging around the playground at break time.'

'What?' A moan escapes from Beth's lips. Please don't let it be Mark. 'What do you mean hanging around?' she presses. 'Please God, tell me he didn't touch her.' A wave of nausea rolls over her and she grabs the radiator to steady herself. She wishes it would burn her, but it's cold.

'No! Well, we don't think so,' Mrs Gilbert admits. 'It was actually a member of the public who noticed him, through the gate, screamed at him apparently. That alerted the playground supervisor who sent him on his way. It was over in seconds, but unfortunately it seems as though he said a few things to Ava before he left. Miss Lewis should have called the police of course; she's extremely apologetic, just acted on instinct, she said.'

'What did he look like?' Beth interrupts, trying to keep her voice steady. 'What did he say?' There's a pause on the line and Beth eyes the tap, the promise of scalding water. Eventually Mrs Gilbert sighs and continues.

'Late teens, lanky and a bit, you know, unkempt, is how Miss Lewis described him. But I'm afraid we don't know what he said. Ava didn't want to tell us. She keeps asking for you, and her tig-tig.'

Beth scrunches her eyes together. The receptionist has described Mark. She pictures tig-tig, the cloth tiger that has been Ava's most reliable source of comfort since she was a toddler, faded from so many washes over the years. Currently lying on Ava's bed. 'I'm not in London,' she finally admits. 'And it's going to take me a couple of hours to get back.'

'Ah, I see.' Was that disapproval in the receptionist's tone, or understanding? 'Well, of course we can keep Ava here until then,' she continues. 'She can sit with me in reception. I'm sure you'll get back as quickly as you can, and she'll survive until then.'

Beth pulls the phone away from her ear and focuses on her breathing. She imagines Ava sat next to that uncaring woman for two hours, too traumatised to repeat whatever Mark said to her. Beth can't bear the thought of it. But she can't ask Lara to collect

Ava because she's Christmas shopping with her mum today. And she daren't ask Saskia with her hack nose.

Then she thinks about Kat, the stalwart dog walker who gave the girls breakfast yesterday and then took them to school. Beth can see her mum through the bathroom window now, hanging up tired sheets in their tiny, paved courtyard garden. Thinning grey hair, sagging jowls, no make-up and a shapeless cardigan. But something pure and good underneath, the same feeling that she gets from Kat. She returns the phone to her ear. 'A friend of mine will pick Ava up; her name is Kat, Ava knows her. And she'll take Martha too. I want them both at home until I've spoken to Mrs Crowmarsh about your inadequate security.' She finishes the call and then, with shaking hands, scrolls down her phone until she finds Kat's number.

Chapter 33

Saskia

What to do, what to do. Saskia paces up and down her hallway, hands on her hips, brow furrowed, no doubt adding deeper lines to a face that really doesn't need any more. God, what would have happened if she hadn't walked past the school at that exact moment? What would that repulsive man have done to poor little Ava? The playground supervisor was useless. There was a tatty beanpole of a resentful teenager in her jurisdiction, and she didn't even notice, just twirled her lanyard around her fingers and stared off into space. To be honest, Miss Lewis is barely in her twenties, too young to understand the high premium that children carry, so it's really the government's fault for paying such shitty wages.

She should have done more herself, Saskia realises. But once she'd screamed at the disgusting kid, and he'd stared back at her with those piercing, angry eyes, she'd felt exposed. Like the infrared dot of hate had been transferred to her own forehead. All she could think was that she wanted to get away from him, flee the scene and hide behind her locked front door. Does that make her a coward? Either way, it's left her stricken with indecision.

Because she has no idea what happened next. Is Ava okay? Has Mark been hauled off in a police car? Or did he run away before the school reacted? Judging by the responsiveness of the dreamy playground supervisor, Saskia can't help fearing it's the latter.

Normally she would call Beth in a heartbeat, fill her in on the details and offer to help in any way she could (while knowing that Beth would politely demur; of course she'd need to be the hero of her own story). But things are decidedly chilly between them at the moment. She thought walking Luna the other night would have warmed things up, but Beth still chose that steroid-popping dog walker to help out with the girls yesterday morning, and she hasn't replied to Tim's text, much to his disappointment (the only silver lining).

She wouldn't mind so much if any of it made sense, but what crime has Saskia actually committed? Championing Beth in their community? Worrying about her? Beth was so cross with her after taking that phone call at the school Christmas show, but for what? Mentioning that she'd overheard Beth talk about a trip to Heathrow? London's biggest airport is hardly an embarrassing destination; Beth was probably just arranging to pick Simon up from his flight home from Dublin.

In fact, didn't she say he was getting back today? A sense of shame fans out inside Saskia's chest and she drops down onto the naughty step. Is Beth at Heathrow now? She imagines her friend's phone ringing in the brightly lit airport concourse, the look of concern on her face when she sees it's the school calling, and then the guilt when she has to admit that she's not close by. That she's taken the school at its word and delegated her children's care to them. Do you even get phone signal in an airport these days? Perhaps Saskia should call her after all, check her line and offer to collect Ava until Beth can get back.

But what if Beth's not at Heathrow but at home, has even picked Ava up already? Would she think Saskia was calling to pry, or to demand some sort of praise for saving Ava in the first place?

Saskia rubs her fingers against her temples. God, it's not like her to be so indecisive.

A thought suddenly flashes up in her head and she whips her phone out of her back pocket. She can't believe she didn't think of it earlier; she knows exactly how to find out where Beth is.

Saskia has had access to Beth's location on Google Maps for months. Beth was reluctant to share it initially – almost offensively so, Saskia remembers thinking at the time – but her pink BP dot still appears every time Saskia opens location sharing on the app, so she must have forgotten to remove it. They'd been invited to see an up-and-coming band at some obscure venue in Camden – the drummer was the step-nephew of a mum at school – and Saskia had decided that she couldn't let a trip to north London go by without catching up with some old work colleagues. The detour meant that she was alone and lost in NW1 as the gig was due to start, hence asking (or more accurately, begging) Beth to share her location. The band turned out to be incredible and, helped on by a few pints of snakebite (Saskia's idea), they were dancing like groupies by the end of the night. Perhaps that's why the map sharing thing slipped Beth's mind.

Saskia opens the app now and taps on Beth's symbol. Then she watches the map shift west across London, in the direction of Heathrow. But no, it moves farther out of the city. When it stops, Beth seems to be in a residential area, a mesh of streets with a couple of cafés and a mosque. Saskia squints a little to read the street name (because the font is small, not because she needs reading glasses) but it's not familiar. She slides her fingers towards each other across the phone screen to zoom out, looking for a clue as to Beth's whereabouts. Royal Berkshire Hospital; Reading College; Reading train station.

Why is Beth in Reading?

Saskia drops her elbows onto the next step up and stares at the ceiling. Of course there could be dozens of perfectly innocent (boring) reasons: visiting an old university friend, or one of their many peers who moved out of London before the school years started. But if that's the reason, why the secrecy? And it doesn't explain why Beth snapped at Saskia for overhearing her phone conversation the other day.

Reading is farther away than Heathrow, a longer journey back to London, but even so, Saskia feels less inclined to offer to help her so-called friend now. Partly because her instincts are screaming that Beth won't be pleased about being tracked to Reading, and partly because why the fuck should she always be there for Beth, when Beth clearly doesn't extend the same courtesy to her? But mostly because her journalistic antennae have been stimulated and are now buzzing with curiosity.

Saskia pushes off the stairs and practically skips into her kitchen. Her laptop is on the island unit, and she slides onto the nearest stool and clicks on the mousepad (while she rarely admits it, she does prefer the bigger screen). She opens Google Maps, types in the street name from her phone, and then drags and drops the little yellow man (of course it's a man) to open up the street view. Interesting, she thinks. Unlikely to be a university friend, or a London escapee. The area is grey and scruffy, not helped by the heavy clouds overhead, as though Google chose weather that was on-brand with the landscape. The houses are hard to distinguish, just one long rendered building, probably painted white originally. The only demarcation is a line of PVC front doors, and they pop up with surprising frequency. Saskia thought London terraces were narrow, but these are on a different scale. A quick search on StreetCheck backs up the image of a deprived area, with high unemployment, drugs and antisocial behaviour.

Saskia swivels on the stool, stares into her postage-stamp garden and ponders what she's just discovered. Beth's secrecy makes sense now; the woman has built a reputation as the cream of the yummy mummy crop, and she wouldn't want anyone knowing that her life isn't picture-postcard-perfect. Woe betide the stain of a destitute friend, or even worse, family member. Beth's parents were killed in a car accident when she was a teenager (a tragedy that had seemed better suited to Hollywood movies until Saskia looked it up and discovered there were over three and a half thousand fatalities on British roads in 2003; some of them must have been parents, she'd figured) but Beth has never talked about her wider family.

Which seems odd now that Saskia thinks about it. She's always moaning about her own siblings – her baby brother who'll always be the favourite because he got a First from Oxford, and her sister who moved to Australia and now collects Iron Man tattoos like Saskia tots up hangovers – but Beth never mentions anyone. Not grandparents, or aunts or even fairy bloody godmothers.

Everyone comes from somewhere, don't they? Saskia watches a squirrel race up their only tree and wonders if Beth comes from the wrong side of Reading. And if she does, whether that makes her less of an adversary or more of one.

222

Chapter 34

Kat

Kat wouldn't normally answer the phone when she's with a client, but there's no way she's ignoring a call from Beth at any time of day. She flips off the shower hose, throws a towel over Aggie the cockapoo and picks up her phone.

'Kat, I need your help.' Beth's voice, tinny through the speaker, spirals inside her ear. 'I'm so sorry – I didn't know who else to ask. Can you help me? Please?'

Kat grips the phone tightly against her ear. 'Of course I can help,' she says, trying not to let her thudding heartbeat permeate her voice. 'What's happened?'

'It's that bastard,' Beth moans. 'Mark. He's been to the school, in the playground; he found Ava at break time. I've no idea what he said, did; she's too upset to tell anyone.'

Kat sucks in her breath as her mind starts clattering through possible scenarios, none of them good. 'Did he hurt her?' she whispers.

'No, at least not physically,' Beth stutters. 'But Ava's really upset.

He must have said something terrible to her, Kat, but Ava's not saying what, and the playground supervisor let him go.'

Kat's heart pounds. She thinks about Ava's sweet face, the innocence shining out of those young eyes. 'Poor Ava,' she whispers. 'How can I help?'

A deep sigh rustles down the phone line. 'I need to collect her, she wants to be at home, but I'm not in London. And it will take me two hours to get back from here.'

Despite the distress in Beth's voice, Kat can't help wondering where she is. Whether it's just Christmas shopping in Guildford or Bluewater, or somewhere else. 'Would you like me to pick her up?' she asks, pulling herself back to the phone call.

'Oh, Kat, thank you. I would ask one of my friends but, erm,' Beth pauses for a moment. 'But they're all so busy. I know you've only just started working for us, and as a dog walker not a nanny, but the girls loved you taking them to school yesterday.'

A rush of victory surges through Kat. Beth has chosen her over Saskia.

'And you know where to go,' Beth continues. 'Can you get away from the groomers?'

Kat thinks about her jampacked client list for the rest of the day. 'Sure, yes. But how will I get into your house?'

'I've told the school that you'll collect both the girls. What if he comes back at lunch break and tries something similar with Martha, or worse?' Beth's voice cracks. 'Honestly, why me? I just wanted to help that old man, and now everyone is gossiping about me and a vile man is terrorising my daughter. It's so unfair.'

Kat can't stop a warm glow filtering through her. She knows it's not appropriate, not amongst all these threats and upset, but Beth is confiding in her, trusting Kat with her two most precious things. She's not achieved what she set out to yet, but it's getting closer; she can feel it. 'Of course I can pick them up,' she whispers. 'I'll make sure they know that they're safe with me.'

'I knew I could count on you, Kat,' Beth whispers. 'There's a house key in Martha's sports bag, the inside pocket. I put one in there just in case I ever forget mine. You can use that to get in.' She pauses, but only for a second. 'And you'll go now?' she prompts. 'I told the school to expect you.'

Beth knew she would agree, Kat realises. Well, that's okay. Kat doesn't mind being the submissive one if that's what it takes to build a bond; it's the role she played before. 'Straight away. It will be fine, I promise.' She finishes the call, takes a deep breath and strides into the reception area.

'Everything okay?' Sally asks.

'Not really, no,' Kat says, faking a grimace. 'My neighbour just called. Apparently my front door is wide open, and it looks like someone has kicked it in.'

'Oh my God, Kat! That's terrible. Have they called the police?'

Kat didn't have time to plan for questions, so she improvises. 'I think so,' she stumbles. 'It wasn't a great line. Is there any chance I could go? See for myself?'

'Of course, you must!' Sally says, nodding her head vigorously. 'I'll finish Aggie's groom. Just let me know what's what, yes?'

'Thanks, Sally,' Kat says, grabbing her coat from the hook. 'I'll be a couple of hours max, I promise.' She gives her boss one last grateful smile, then pushes on the front door and steps into the cold.

Kat feels the school receptionist's stare wash over her and tries not to flinch. 'And you're a friend of Mrs Packard?' the skinny woman says, peering over her old-fashioned spectacles, the politeness of her words almost fully obscured by the suspicion in her tone.

'I walk their dog, Luna. And mind the girls sometimes,' she adds quickly.

'Ah, I see.' The receptionist visibly relaxes as she works out the connection between one of their most glamorous parents and the mound of solid flesh with red hair and a large tattoo standing in front of her. Staff clearly makes more sense than friend. 'Let me get

Martha and Ava for you,' she says, standing up. 'They're waiting in the nurse's room.' She pauses for a moment, as though assessing how much to say to this obvious interloper. 'Mrs Crowmarsh will call Mrs Packard this afternoon, once she's back home,' she finally offers, before disappearing through a side door. A few moments later, she returns with Martha and Ava in tow.

'Hi, Kat,' Martha says, adding a nervous wave.

'Where's Mummy?' Ava asks, her lip wobbling. 'I want Mummy.' She looks so vulnerable. Her once chubby cheeks seem hollow now, punctured prematurely by grim reality, and her eyes are red with rubbed-away tears.

A wave of revulsion slams down on Kat's chest. Ava is just an innocent child in all of this.

And it's her job to comfort that child, Kat realises, with growing panic. Sweat forms on her palms as the receptionist's glare burns into her skin. Because she's got no idea how; she's always been rubbish with people. But Ava needs someone to make her feel better, and she promised Beth that she'd take care of her youngest daughter. Kat scratches her chin and thinks about the scared puppies she has to put at ease at Groom & Bloom. Confidence, eye contact and lots of treats. Perhaps that works with small children too. She takes a deep breath, then bends down and takes Ava's hands into hers. 'Mummy is racing back to see you, I promise,' she says, looking directly into Ava's eyes. 'In fact, she's racing so fast that there'll only be just enough time for us to stop for hot chocolate with marshmallows.'

'Hot chocolate?' Ava asks, looking up at the receptionist then back to Kat. 'With marshmallows?'

'My Christmas treat.' Kat gives Ava her widest smile, and amazingly, Ava smiles back. Kat stretches up, takes the two book bags and Martha's sports bag from the receptionist without looking at her, then waits to be buzzed out of the school. As the three of them walk across the playground and then out of the gate, Kat wonders if she should ask Ava about Mark, find out what he said to her. But what would be the point? He's clearly crossed the line, and she doesn't want to cause Ava any more distress, so they continue their journey in amiable silence.

'Shall we watch a Christmas movie with our drinks?' Kat asks as she retrieves the key from Martha's school bag and slips it into the door. 'What's your favourite?'

'*Frozen*!'

'*A Boy Called Christmas*!'

'No, that's too scary. *Polar Express*?'

'Yes, *Polar Express*!'

Kat breathes a sigh of relief at not having to play referee again, then lets the girls lead her into the playroom. They both curl up on the sofa with their hot chocolates (on reflection, Kat imagines Beth wouldn't approve of hot drinks in here, but she's not stripping the treat away from the girls now). Ava strokes her cheek with a tatty cloth tiger while Martha picks up two remote controls, and toggles between them until *Polar Express* appears on the huge screen attached to the opposite wall. Kat has a Netflix account too, but only an ancient laptop to watch it on. It's not quite the same experience.

Gradually the girls get drawn into the movie, transfixed by the magical train and its northward journey. Kat looks at her watch. It's been an hour since Beth called her, so it will be another hour before she gets back. Now that Ava seems calm, the itch that she felt yesterday is growing again.

'Girls, I'm just popping out to the toilet, okay?'

Ava turns her head towards Kat for a moment, smiles, then looks back at the screen. Children appear to bounce back from trauma easily, but Kat knows that's not the case. Every bad experience nestles itself somewhere, ready to pounce when life gets more challenging. She gives Ava's arm a gentle squeeze, then slips out of the room, and pulls the door closed behind her. Carefully, she walks up the first set of stairs, then takes the second flight a bit faster.

She guessed right; Beth has a suite, not a bedroom. A sprawling master with super-king-size bed, layered with velvet throws and silk cushions. An en suite, tiled from floor to ceiling in cream limestone, with an enormous shower and wide double basin. And a walk-in dressing room with fitted wardrobes running the length of each side. A mix of emotions tingles on Kat's skin as she takes it all in. Fear, excitement and hope, all fighting for dominance. She runs her hands over the different materials, the cool tiles and soft bed linen, then eventually steps into the dressing area and slides open the left-hand wardrobe.

It's Beth's. Kat isn't surprised to find every item of clothing hanging neatly: jackets, dresses, skirts, blouses and an assortment of jeans, ordered according to their cut, colour and wash. The bottom of Beth's wardrobe is dedicated to footwear. On the left, there's a wall of designer shoeboxes, like a scene from *Sex in the City*. On the right, there are about ten pairs of boots lined up in height order from knee length to ankle. They are all regimentally straight, except for one single boot that sits slightly askew. Kat frowns. She's never cared that her own flat is a blur of mismatched angles, but seeing Beth's boot out of sync feels wrong. She leans in to straighten it and notices the sparkle of foil glistening from inside.

Kat pulls out a strip of pills and reads the name. Diazepam is a powerful sedative – she knows because she was given it herself during her first week at the unit. She burrows her fingers further into the boot and discovers seven more strips. Without the packaging, she can't tell how long ago the pills were prescribed, but the collection suggests it's not a recent thing. And here, hidden away. She thinks back to when she knew Beth as a teenager, and the traumatic way their friendship ended. Has Beth been hiding her anxiety all this time?

Shame lurches inside her. And her head spins with too many memories.

She drops the strips back in the boot and returns the boot

to the wardrobe. But she can't help delving further. The other boots first, and then the shoeboxes. She wants to tip them all over at once, but she fights the urge; Beth could be home at any moment. So she pushes up the cardboard lids one at a time. Stilettos, wedges, trainers. And finally, a small drawstring bag. With trembling fingers, she slides it open and starts pulling out its contents. She finds a spoon first, old and stained, then a silver Zippo. She flips open the lighter, and pushes down on the wheel, but the spark flickers and dies, the lighter fuel long since evaporated. She closes it up and turns it over in her hand. A chill runs down her spine as she reads the inscription etched into the metal. *Please fucking stop.*

She puts the spoon and lighter back in the bag, runs her fingers over some rough material inside, then finds a photo and pulls it out. It's of a young man with long dark hair and gaunt features. He's a stranger to Kat, but his eyes betray him. The similarity is too striking. There's also a newspaper cutting in the bag, neatly folded. With shaking hands, she starts to open it.

'Kat? Where are you?' Ava's voice floats up the stairs. 'I'm feeling a bit scared.'

Kat freezes. She scrambles the stuff back into its bag. 'Just coming!' she shouts down, dropping the bag into the shoebox and shoving it back into the wardrobe.

'Are you upstairs?'

Kat can hear footsteps below her. She flies out of Beth's bedroom and grabs hold of the banister, launching herself down the top flight of stairs. Shit, did she straighten the boxes enough? But it's too late to check. 'I just used the bathroom,' she calls out. 'Coming straight down!'

May 2003

Chapter 35

Katherine

Katherine watches a droplet of rain slither down the windowpane. She's not sure why she picked that one to stare at, there are hundreds of identical ones across the bank of windows, but she's invested now.

'Good morning, girls. This is Tabby. She'll be joining us today.'

The droplet reaches the window frame, but the climax is disappointing. It just spreads across the cold metal for a moment then disappears, morphed into a tiny stream, then washed along with the rest of the rain. With an almost inaudible sigh, Katherine shifts her gaze to the woman speaking. Dr Fay Sharp. Her protector and gaoler.

'Tabby is in the final year of her clinical psychology doctorate,' *she explains,* 'and will be with us at the unit for the next six weeks. I'm sure you'll all do a great job of making her feel welcome.' *A ripple of greetings works its way around the group, but Katherine doesn't bother adding to it. She's already met Tabby, at lunch the day before. The not-quite-a-doctor had asked to sit next to her in the dining room and Katherine didn't have much choice but to nod. Tabby had curled her long blonde hair around her ear and shrugged at her good fortune to have found a spot in the less-than-half-full*

233

room. But Katherine can't blame the psychology student for planning the encounter. Who wouldn't be curious about the girl in bandages brought here by the police?

'It's lovely to meet you,' Tabby says to the group. Then, excruciatingly, she shifts her gaze. 'Although Katherine and I met yesterday, didn't we?'

Everyone in the room turns to look in Katherine's direction. Instinctively she puts her hands up to her face, hiding her shame, or maybe just the red-raw skin around her mouth and chin. Her eczema is like a rat. When everything good in her life dies, her skin disease continues to thrive. 'Yeah,' she mumbles, silently begging for that to be enough to halt the exchange. It's her gaoler who comes to her rescue.

'Great,' Dr Sharp announces, drawing her hands together, and producing a muted clap that Katherine doesn't think was intended. 'Of course there's no pressure to say anything this morning, but does anyone have something they'd like to share? And please, everyone, remember that this is a positive space,' she adds.

With her head low enough to avoid all eye contact, Katherine scans the circle of her peers. She hasn't attempted conversation outside the group – she knows that she's incapable of making friends; what happened with Becca is proof of that – but they all know her story because she blurted it out in only her second meeting. She's not quite sure why she did that. Maybe it was the sedatives loosening her tongue, but it felt more like self-flagellation; wanting to see the horror, the disgust, on the faces of this rag-tag group of teenagers with a variety show of mental health issues.

'Um, could I say something?' Everyone turns towards the ghost-like girl sitting closest to the door. Her pixie-cut hair is dyed so blonde it almost looks blue, and her ears shine with tails of silverware.

'Of course, Molly. And take your time.'

'Thanks.' Molly blinks at the clinical psychologist. 'In my one-on-one session, I talked about why I self-harm. Not the big why,' she says, raising her hands and flickering her fingers, 'not the existential reason why I hate myself. But the smaller why. The pleasure it brings.'

'And you'd like to talk about that here?'

'I wondered whether other people felt the same. And why it happens. I mean, if I cut my finger on a piece of paper or whatever, it hurts like hell. So why do I like it when I do it to myself?'

'That's a really good question.' Dr Sharp nods, then scans the room. 'Does anyone else feel like Molly?'

'I know why she enjoys it,' another girl mutters. Tasha, Katherine remembers. She's only 14 and this is her third stay in a residential unit, so she gets a bit of kudos for that. 'My therapist on the outside explained it once.'

'Thanks, Natasha. Do you feel comfortable sharing your therapist's explanation with the group?'

Tasha shrugs, looks down at the laminate floorboards. 'It's to do with your brain,' she says. 'There are two parts – I can't remember what they're called – that process your pain. And that's both emotional and physical pain. When you're feeling really shit, if you cut yourself, you reach peak sore. But physical pain always subsides somehow, and it takes the emotional pain with it.' She slides her socked foot along the floor and the shushing sound is louder than Katherine would have expected. 'It doesn't last long, but you know, whatever.'

'That's exactly right, Natasha,' Dr Sharp coos. 'And thank you for also pointing out that the relief is short-lived. Our job here is to come up with ways to reduce the emotional pain in a less destructive, and longer-term, way. Does anyone have any ideas on how we might do that?'

Silence follows for a while, every girl hoping someone else will fill it. But eventually one of them surrenders. Katherine can't remember her name. 'Talking?' The girl says it as a question, as though Dr Sharp might disagree with her. Which she never ever does.

'Absolutely, Emma. Talking through problems is fundamental to recovery.'

'Writing things down?'

'Journalling is another excellent way of processing negative feelings, Amira.' Dr Sharp smiles at the dark-haired girl, then widens her gaze to take in the whole group. When she zeros in, Katherine knows what's coming. Three, two, one … 'Katherine, do you have any ideas on how to lessen any emotional pain you might be feeling?'

Of course she does. Travel back in time and not go to that assembly, or not storm out of her house on her birthday. Not meet Becca at all. But would she really want that? To miss out on what they had even though it ended so badly? Because the images are still vivid in her mind. Becca's beautiful face and perfect skin, her kind eyes and wide smile, her protective hand on Katherine's arm. But there are the other images too now. The way her body fell and crumpled. All that blood.

'I've got one,' a small voice chimes, saving her from Dr Sharp's encouraging stare. Katherine looks up. It's the girl sitting right next to her, her fingers tightly interlaced in her lap. She gives the girl a grateful smile for taking the clinician's focus and enjoys the tentative one she gets in return. 'Keeping busy, having tasks to focus on,' the girl continues.

'That can be really helpful, Ellie,' Dr Sharp says, although her voice is uncharacteristically reticent. 'Katherine, what do you think?' she tries again.

She bites her cheek. 'Absolving for my sins,' she murmurs.

'Sorry, I didn't hear …'

'Doing something good,' she says louder, looking at the new girl who came to her rescue. 'Helping someone in need.'

December 2021

Chapter 36

Beth

Beth skids to a halt on the corner of Brookhill Road. Her knees start to buckle. She reaches out, finds the rough surface of yellow London brick, someone's garden wall. But it feels grimy. She imagines the dirt seeping into her fingertips. Her heart starts galloping and she pulls her hand back, rubs it against her jeans. What's she going to do?

She raced back from Reading – a screeching taxi to the station, then a fast train to Clapham and a sprint from there – and she's only a stone's throw from home now. But she can't make the final steps, not with Mark curled up on the pavement opposite her house, his lanky legs folded under his chin. He looks like a victim, she realises. A sad, homeless man who's missed out on life's chances. Not at all like the truth of it: a nasty piece of shit who's happy to traumatise a little girl.

And what else is Mark capable of? If he's reckless enough to approach Ava at school, what would he be willing to do to Beth?

She's heard the stories. Stalkers who follow their victims night and day, whom no one takes seriously because they seem so passive. Then one day it changes. Except it's all too late by then. Because they're sitting in a police cell claiming mental illness and a woman somewhere has had her life ruined forever. Acid in her face, a knife in her chest, or even just a memory that she can never erase. Is that what's going to happen to her?

Maybe she should get it over and done with, walk right up to him and tell him to do his worst. Perhaps it's what she deserves after all the lies she's told, the people she's let down. Like her ill father – she didn't even say a proper goodbye. Just made some excuse about a difficult client as she waited for the cab. What kind of daughter does that? The kind who puts her nuclear family first of course. Simon, Martha and Ava. The three people she loves most in the world. She's got nothing to apologise for.

She can be faster than him, she decides. Slide her house key between her fingers just in case, then sprint the hundred metres, slam it in the keyhole and be inside her house in seconds. Yes, she can do this. Hold the panic at bay for long enough. She fumbles in her bag, finds the cold metal and takes a deep breath. Then she runs. As she gets closer, she can hear him calling her name, his voice too deep for a skinny teenager, but she doesn't look in his direction. Her heart is pumping madly, but she slides the key in, pushes hard on her front door.

And slams it shut. She closes her eyes and takes a deep breath.

'Mummy!' Ava races up and flings her arms around Beth's waist. 'There was a man,' she whispers into Beth's midriff. 'He said mean things about you.'

The man who is lurking outside their house right now.

She inches them both away from the front door. Her throat constricts. 'Let me just wash my hands,' she pleads. She wants to be reassuring – like a mum should – but she's too tense. She needs a moment to collect herself.

'I was scared, Mummy.'

'I know, honey.' Of course it could have been so much worse; in those moments that Mark was with Ava, he could have done anything. Part of Beth wants to know what Mark said to Ava, the accusations he made about her. But she can't bear hearing her daughter repeat his words out loud, letting his poisonous beliefs into their home. 'You're safe now,' she says instead, but her voice still cracks.

'Are you okay, Beth?'

Her eyes flick open. Kat is standing at the bottom of the stairs. She looks out of breath, as though today's events have knocked the wind out of her.

'I'm fine, thank you.' She coughs to clear the tears from her throat. 'I just need to freshen up. Can you hang on another five minutes?' Beth scratches her palms. She does it discreetly, but Kat must notice the tiny movement because she drops her eyeline. A cloud of concern darkens her face.

'Of course, take your time,' she says. 'We can hang out a while longer, can't we, girls?'

Beth gives her a grateful smile and walks towards the stairs. As she reaches for the banister, her hand brushes against Kat's arm. Usually she despises touching people, but there's something reassuring about the solidity of Kat's frame today, and the deep greens of her cactus tattoo. Beth pauses for a moment, draws as much strength as she can and then pulls away.

She almost cries with relief when she reaches her bedroom. The bed is perfectly made, and the line of cushions at the top is uniformly plumped. Every surface is sparkling and as Beth breathes in, the faint scent of cedarwood adds to her growing sense of calm. She picks her rings off her bedside table, then walks into her bathroom and turns on the tap, the hot water providing a more powerful tonic. She edges the temperature up higher as her skin craves more, and scrubs her hands with Aesop exfoliating wash. As its tiny pieces of pumice scratch away her skin, the memory of her decrepit father and decaying childhood home fades a little too. Finally she feels strong enough to reach for a towel and place her rings where they belong.

That's when she notices that her wardrobe door in the adjacent dressing room is open a fraction. Fear tingles on the back of her neck as her eyes dart around the room.

Has he been here? In her most private of spaces? Can she sense his presence now?

Don't be stupid! the rational part of her brain screams. She saw him outside, only a few minutes ago. He can't be in her bedroom. But could he have been here earlier? She takes a few jagged steps towards her wardrobe. But the irrational side is fighting for dominance again. Was it definitely him that she saw outside? Could he have come in via the garden? What if he is behind those doors? Ready to attack her as soon as she opens them? But she needs to know what's he done. She takes a deep breath.

The knocker on the front door rattles below her. She gasps; her head spins. Of course he's outside! Has he got the audacity to try to muscle his way in through her front door? She twists on her heels and races out of her room, and down both flights of stairs. 'Don't answer it!' she screams, but it's too late. Kat is opening the door. Beth sucks in a scream.

'Sorry! Can't believe I forgot my key.'

Beth almost cries with relief. She's never felt so happy to see her husband. 'Simon,' she whispers.

Simon scans the hallway, three scared faces. 'What's happened?'

'Oh, Daddy,' Ava cries out, curling herself around his leg. Then the playroom door swings open. Luna arrives first, flying into Simon's arms, oblivious to the dense atmosphere. Then Martha comes next and soon it's a tangle of limbs and fur. Beth tries to draw strength from the scene, at least enough to work out how much of what's happened to tell Simon. She wonders if she's got enough energy to conceal the bits that must stay secret.

'A scary man came to the school,' Martha pipes up.

Simon's head swerves towards her. 'What?'

'He spoke to Ava. He made her cry.'

'I didn't cry.'

242

'Simon, can we talk about this later?' Beth squeezes the words through her constricted throat. She watches him pull his phone out of his pocket, then seconds later, slip it back in.

'No. I want to talk about it now. Is it this Mark character?'

Beth bites her lip and stares at the floor. There's a tiny indent in the mahogany wood, next to the table leg. She imagines dust collecting there.

'Have you contacted the police? Because if you haven't, Beth, we're doing it now.'

'Simon, not in front of the children,' she whispers.

'But he's targeting our children now, isn't he?!' Beth blinks in shock; Simon never raises his voice with her.

'Or in front of Kat,' she pleads.

Simon turns to face Kat. 'You're the dog walker,' he spits out, but his face instantly drops. 'Sorry, that was rude.'

'Kat picked us up from school,' Ava interjects. 'I wanted to go home.'

'Why didn't Mummy pick you up?' He turns towards Beth. 'Where were you?' He sounds so accusing.

'She bought us hot chocolates.' Ava's voice trembles.

'Shall I go?' Kat's voice. Calm and strong. 'Now that you're both back?'

'How much do we owe you?' Simon pulls a slim wallet out of his back pocket. Following etiquette, despite the circumstances. Only his trembling fingers defy him. Beth watches him squeeze it open, like a Venus flytrap, revealing a wad of different-coloured notes. Her phone vibrates in her pocket. She sways, lets it ring out.

'Is fifty enough?' Simon mutters, still agitated. Beth wishes Kat wasn't leaving, she suddenly realises; she doesn't want to be alone with her husband. 'We don't ever use nannies,' he mutters. 'So I've no idea.'

'Will you look after us again, Kat?' Martha asks plaintively.

'Ooh yay!' Ava squeals.

The voices swirl around Beth's head. Her phone vibrates again.

She wonders if Simon is going to leave her. Or if Mark is still in her wardrobe. Or if her dad has died. She wonders if it was actually Eddie lying outside that shop, his ghost come to haunt her in an old man's body. The dent in the floor is growing. Opening up like a seismic ravine.

She watches in horror as it grows and grows.

And finally swallows her whole.

May 2003

Chapter 37

Katherine

Katherine pulls the long sleeves of her oversized sweatshirt over her knuckles and concentrates on the sound of Ellie's fingernails, the almost inaudible scratch-scratch as they brush up and down her palms. Some girls at the unit smirk if they witness Ellie's anxious tic, but Katherine finds it strangely comforting, as though the simple melody of it anchors her, and makes her believe that everything will be okay. That Becca will survive, and the police will choose not to prosecute.

And that Ellie will be her friend forever.

Since the group therapy session when Ellie came to her rescue, the beautiful 17-year-old seemed to migrate wordlessly towards Katherine – pulling her chair close and glancing in Katherine's direction every time she spoke, as though seeking her approval. Katherine couldn't believe it, someone as beautiful as Ellie caring what she thought, but she kept her true feelings private – after what happened with Becca, she's never admitting those again – and followed Ellie's lead.

After the third group therapy session, when Katherine's bandages had finally been removed, Ellie invited Katherine back to her room. Katherine had waited for Ellie to use the toilet adjacent to the therapy room (or that's what she said, even though Katherine only heard the rush of the tap running), and then followed her up the stairs and along the first-floor corridor, all the way to the end. Ellie had sat on her perfectly made bed, and she'd curled up on the chair, and not quite facing each other, they'd talked.

Ellie had opened up about her brother Eddie, how he died on her bedroom floor, and how ashamed she felt when the police photos appeared in the local newspaper. She talked about how her anxiety disorder had spiralled after that, and that Dr Sharp had diagnosed mysophobia, a debilitating fear of germs. In return, Katherine had expanded on the tale she told in group therapy. And especially the devastating consequences when Becca rejected her.

They're walking in the direction of Ellie's room now, and Katherine wonders if it's okay to assume she's welcome there again, or if she still needs to wait for an invitation.

'Do you want to come back to my room for a bit?'

Katherine's shoulders relax and a smile creeps across her face. 'Yes, thank you,' she says, trying to sound casual while flickers of anticipation dance inside her belly. Katherine ticks off the noticeboard, fire extinguisher and crack in the plaster where some previous patient punched the wall before they reach Ellie's room.

While they're complete opposites in many ways, they both seem to like the familiarity of routine, and Katherine slides onto the hard-backed wooden chair in the corner of Ellie's room without discussion, and then watches her new friend climb onto her (still crease-free) bed and cross her legs neatly underneath herself. The room is warm, and Katherine can't help scratching her chin.

'Does it hurt?' Ellie asks, staring at the scales of red skin on Katherine's face, while reaching for a tube of prescription hand cream on her bedside table. Katherine should feel embarrassed by such a direct enquiry, or annoyed, but there's not much Ellie could say that would offend her.

'It itches sometimes, but no, it doesn't hurt. Not physically anyway.'

Ellie nods her understanding. 'I suppose there were kids at school who made comments. It was the same for me.'

'You? But you're beautiful!' Katherine can't help spurting out, but the compliment goes either unnoticed or unaccepted.

'My parents are from Romania. Everyone called me gypsy.'

'That's crazy. I bet they were jealous.'

'Or they called me poverty case, because my clothes were too small for me, or too tatty.'

'I can't imagine that; you always look immaculate in here.'

'You're very loyal, aren't you?'

Katherine shrugs. 'No, I … I just like you, I guess,' she admits shyly.

'I like you too,' Ellie counters. 'But it's not just me. You're loyal to Becca too.'

'Becca? I did something terrible to her,' Katherine whispers, the weight of guilt dropping on her chest like a fallen tree trunk.

'You still talk about her like she's perfect, even after she turned the letter you wrote her into ammunition.'

Katherine sighs. She doesn't regret talking to Ellie about Becca – she was kind and compassionate like always – but it does mean that Ellie can spring the subject on her at any time. 'I owe her,' she finally whispers. 'After what I did to her.'

With the confession, the images come – just like they always do. The blood starting as a spot, then spreading. All the noise and chaos. Students staring in horror, a PE teacher trying to help, shoving a bunched-up football shirt against Becca's head. She never found out how well it worked, because the police turned up before the paramedics moved Mr Cannock out of the way.

'You were ill,' Ellie says. 'Scared and let down. You couldn't help it.'

'I remember being so mad with her,' Katherine whispers. 'For choosing Clara over me. I thought I was the victim, but I got that wrong.'

'You were a victim, just of a different crime.'

'It felt so real, my and Becca's friendship,' Katherine murmurs. 'I thought we were destined for each other. How crazy is that?' She feels exposed suddenly, sat tall on the hard-backed chair, so she slides off it and onto the floor. Belatedly she worries that Ellie might think her flabby body will contaminate the carpet, but, to her relief, Ellie doesn't react to her change of position. Katherine shuffles backwards until her spine connects with the wall beside the doorway, and then she pushes hard against it. 'I suppose you think I'm insane too?'

'We're all insane, aren't we?' Ellie counters. 'That's why we're here.'

'Not you; not really. You're just grieving for your brother. It makes sense that you need a bit of support. Whereas me, there's no excuse. Everything I've done, Becca's injuries and my own, it's all my fault.' Katherine tries to laugh, but it sounds more like a bark followed by silence.

'You took a risk. Yes, it went wrong, but you were still brave to try.'

'Why are you being so nice to me? Do you even like me?' Katherine holds her breath. She'd promised herself that she wouldn't push it, but here she is, doing it again.

'Of course I like you,' Ellie says, smiling. 'We're friends, aren't we?'

'Actual friends?' Katherine whispers, still struggling to believe it.

Ellie's expression shifts to serious. She leans forward and rests her elbows on her out-turned knees. 'Listen, I know that you think you're worthless, that your shape is too big, and your skin too damaged, and so how could anyone possibly like you.'

'Yes,' Katherine whispers. 'Exactly.'

Ellie shakes her head. 'But being a good friend isn't about how beautiful you are.'

Katherine stares, wide-eyed, transfixed.

'It's about loyalty, being there for each other, forgiveness for past mistakes.'

'I'll always be there for you,' Katherine whispers.

'I know you will. And that's what makes you the best friend I've ever had.'

December 2021

Chapter 38

Kat

Kat draws her knees up to her chest and pushes her back against the wall. She used to do this as a child, push as hard as could in the vain hope that she would disappear into the plasterboard. Become part of something there but unseen. It was a ridiculous hope, with the bulk of her then as well as now, but she feels the compulsion all over again.

Because the vision of Beth fainting, dropping with a thud onto her polished wooden floor, is on replay in her mind. Reminding her of when Becca collapsed, and everything that came after.

Like meeting Beth at the unit eighteen years ago, or Ellie as she called herself then. Kat had been broken when she first arrived there, slash wounds on her wrists and deeper ones inside her. But then Ellie sought her out, and gave her just enough hope to see a sliver of light. Ellie was damaged, like her, but also beautiful like Becca, with smooth skin and eyes big enough to listen as well as see. And for some unfathomable reason, Ellie wanted to be her friend. Kat couldn't understand why – not until the day Ellie fully explained it – but she bathed in the glow of Ellie's attention. From that first group therapy session, they slowly became inseparable. Kat didn't comment on Ellie washing her hands a hundred times a day, and Ellie didn't seem to mind Kat knocking on her door with a similar regularity. In fact, she seemed to like it.

Their friendship came to an abrupt end when Kat left the unit. It all happened in such a whirlwind. She found out the police had dropped all charges on the same day Dr Sharp confirmed that she was well enough to leave. On finding out the news, her dad announced that he'd booked her an airline ticket to Australia, and her mum offered to pack her stuff so that Kat could avoid going back home. Her whole life changed in twenty-four hours, but still, her last encounter with Ellie – with all that emotion coursing through her – was what she remembers most. And how utterly devastating it was.

At least now she's got a chance to make things right.

It felt like fate when Ellie's face appeared on the computer screen at work. She didn't look exactly the same of course – she was older, richer, more polished – but the post underneath her photo gave a bigger clue. After what she went through with her brother, stopping for a homeless heroin addict was exactly the sort of thing she'd do. Ellie didn't like to talk about Eddie much at the unit, but she'd given Kat the facts of his death, and how it led to her mysophobia and anxiety spiralling out of control – that and the newspaper article which followed. Ellie didn't bring any photos with her to the unit, so Kat never knew what her brother looked like. But the picture that she found in Beth's shoebox earlier today must be him; the resemblance is too stark for it not to be.

And as there were no other photos of him – or Beth's parents – around the house, it seems like Beth is hiding her whole past from her new family. Kat can't imagine how tough that must be, although the strips of diazepam in Beth's boot give her some idea. But she's not surprised. She remembers how ashamed Ellie was about growing up poor, her mum working two cleaning jobs. Kat

254

pushes the heels of her hands into her eye sockets. But it's not Beth's hidden past that's threatening to break her now.

It's him. That stupid boy who thinks he's a man. Who believes he can hassle a woman, traumatise an innocent child, and not suffer any repercussions. Kat tried to warn him off, and he seemed scared at the time; she thought she'd done enough. But her meddling seems to have made him more determined to punish Beth. So that's something else she needs to make amends for. When Beth finally came round after fainting in her hallway – and petrifying her children, Ava for the second time in a day – she'd accepted Simon's demand to call the police. Kat knows how difficult that must have been, for Beth to trust the police after what they did to her – that she's kept the newspaper article about Eddie's death for all these years is testament to how much it still hurts. She must have felt completely trapped into a corner.

Simon first tried to speak with the detective who interviewed Beth that night, DC Stone, but it had gone through to voicemail. Kat had heard the message he left – cold, angry, with a whiff of privileged condescension. She can't imagine that approach is going to get him very far. He eventually got through to someone when he phoned 101, but from the half of the conversation Kat heard, it didn't sound like he got the urgent response he was expecting from them either. He just got even more irate and then stormed off into his study when he ended the call, mumbling about finding a lawyer to sort a restraining order. Beth had looked embarrassed – although whether that was due to his behaviour, or her fainting in the first place, Kat wasn't sure.

Part of her felt desperate to stay, to keep an eye on Beth, but she had to remember that she wasn't part of their family, and to outstay her welcome would risk the progress she's made. So she'd said goodbye, taken the money with a sting of shame, and reminded Beth to double-lock the front door once she'd gone. She couldn't face going back to the salon, so she'd headed home and phoned Sally from there, mumbled that the break-in wasn't bad enough to bother the police with, but that she needed to wait in for a locksmith. Of course Sally had been characteristically understanding, and guilt had flared in Kat's chest once more. But she'd swallowed it down; Beth is her priority now.

Which means she can't sit scrunched up on her bed, disappearing into her teenage shell. Taking a deep breath, she opens her eyes, unfurls her legs and pushes off the bed. She wants a beer, something to take the edge off, so she navigates through her messy living room and into the kitchenette. She pulls a bottle of Brixton Pale Ale out of the fridge and flicks the cap off with a fish slice. The action reminds her of her dad, and she lifts the bottle, says a silent cheers to the man who finished the work of putting her back together. She wishes he were here to guide her now. There's also a big bar of Cadbury Fruit and Nut in the fridge, and after a moment's hesitation, she grabs that too.

She takes her stash over to the sofa and lowers down into its familiar lumps and bumps. Clearing up this mess feels like her responsibility now. It has done since she saw Beth's photo really, payback for the way things ended between them, but the feeling has grown as they've reconnected. When Beth brushed against Kat's arm on the stair earlier, and looked straight into her eyes, Kat had panicked for a second, worried that Beth had recognised her, even though there's nothing of Katherine left. But once the fear subsided, Kat had realised what Beth's eyes were asking. The same as they asked eighteen years ago: help me.

But Simon has called the police now.

Except, realistically, what difference will they make? Kat has kept herself away from the law, and the people paid to impose it, since their investigation into Becca's injuries all those years ago. But she's heard the stories. How stalkers are able to hound their victims unchecked for years before the police take it seriously.

256

And even then, the onus is still on the victim to collect enough evidence to prove their stalker's guilt.

Mark has already shown that he doesn't scare easily, and Kat can see that Beth hasn't got the strength to live with his toxic behaviour. Which means she needs to do something.

Chapter 39

Mark

Mark kicks the wall. Harder. Listens to the satisfying thud of more plasterboard cracking. What the hell kind of worthless prick is he, trying to freak out a kid? Turn a little girl against her own mother? From the minute he saw her little face crumple, he knew he'd gone too far. But of course it was too late by then. He'd already called her mum a cold-blooded killer, an arrogant bitch who was happy to watch a defenceless old man die. How fucking ironic that it was Beth's neighbour who caught him, stopped him from doing anything worse. What, is he supposed to feel grateful to her now?

He thought the school would phone the police, almost wanted them to by then, but that girl with a lanyard just pointed at the gate with her jaw quivering. He'd left sharpish, of course he had, but he hadn't gone far. He wanted to wait outside Beth's house again. Not to scare the little kid, or even Beth, but just to check she was okay. Kids bounce back, that's what people say, but he needed to see it with his own eyes.

The little girl had turned up a while later with her sister and a takeout cup in her hand. Her eyes were dry, but red and puffy, and it was that bodyguard with them, not Beth. For a moment, he'd felt justified – the woman couldn't even be bothered to pick up her youngest daughter after what she'd been through – but then he'd realised that the kid was getting punished twice.

And then Beth appeared, her face like a ghost's, her perfect hair all messy from running. She'd nearly collapsed against that brick wall, and he'd questioned his judgement for a second time.

Now, with a sudden urge to throw himself to a pride of lions, he chooses the only thing in his arsenal, and drops backwards onto the sofa, his arms flailing over the back, and his legs splaying out at different angles. With his arms high, he can smell his own stink and it makes him feel sick. What the hell has happened to him? Was it only six months ago that he came to London with a rucksack full of (fake) designer gear and a head full of hope? Now he's just a homeless dickhead with a spice habit and a baseless grudge. Of course it's not her fault Jon died; it's his. His booze, his encouragement, his selfish need for a drinking buddy.

He looks at the packets of spice now, still scattered across the floor where he left them this morning. Maybe it *was* Rudy he saw earlier in the street when he kicked that Coke can on his way up to the school. Maybe the hard-as-fuck drug dealer has worked out where he's staying, and is going to bring his machete and slice him up, or stab him with a little kitchen knife, but right in the heart because Rudy will know how to do that.

Fuck it. Fuck the shame, and the inevitable piss-taking. He needs to get out of this city and sort his life out. Stop terrorising innocent people. Stop smoking spice. Stop living like a rat, scared of being attacked by gangsters. But he can't turn up in Cambridge looking like he does now. And he needs to charge his phone. He'll stay here for one more night, he calculates, then go to the drop-in centre tomorrow. Even if he has to queue for hours to use the shower, he'll do it. Maybe get a haircut if that woman with the sun tattoo and pair of clippers is there. And take advantage of their complimentary plug socket. Then when he looks half decent, he'll get over to Stratford somehow and then use his last twenty quid for a bus ticket to Cambridge.

It's a plan. A good one.

As long as he doesn't think about his parents' disappointed faces, or his inevitable spice withdrawal, or the fact that his shame will travel with him.

He pulls the sofa cushion from behind his back and flings it across the room, right at the mirror resting on the mantelpiece opposite. The cushion is soft, but it's heavy, and the mirror sways in protest. The cushion drops first, but bounces away, so when the metal frame hits wood, the glass inside shatters. The noise splinters his hearing as tiny shards of glass land on his skin. 'Fucking metaphor,' he mutters to the empty room, but he gets no response, so he tries again. 'Fucking metaphor!' he screams.

But after bouncing off the walls, that cry dies unanswered too.

Everything is fine again. Chill. What he said to that little girl doesn't matter. What he stole from Rudy doesn't matter. No one cares that he stinks, including him, and his mum and dad are too far away to worry about. He sucks on the joint and feels the pure joy of it.

Tomorrow is another day. It'll be his day.

With all his dreaming, he doesn't hear the intruder come in this time. Not until he can see them too, at least a part of them, in a sliver of mirror that didn't make it out of the frame. A solid calf, black trouser leg, blacker trainers. Fucking Rudy has found him after all. Mark's too tired to fight this time. He smiles, sinks against the hard back of the cushion-less sofa and waits for the machete to land. Or the stubby knife to stab him. Or maybe a baseball bat that will knock him sideways.

He smells stink, Rudy's, as the burn grabs him around his throat. A ring of fire, scorching his skin and cutting off his windpipe. He tries to gag but the grip is too tight. His survival instinct kicks in, at last, and he pushes his arms up and reaches back. He feels a rustle of heavy material, a jacket, but he's got no power to create fists, or to find flesh and pull Rudy's arms away, to stop his own throat from being cut in half by a piece of rope, or whatever slice of hell is strangling him. His chest convulses, begging for air. But the pressure on his throat gets tighter as Rudy leans further over him. Mark catches his image in the sliver of mirror. It's blurred, monochrome in the darkness, but still, Rudy looks different tonight.

Then the darkness becomes black.

And his chest stops searching.

Chapter 40

Beth

There's a thin line of light between the blind and the Velux window. It's bright enough to wake Beth up and she stares at it now, picking at its meaning. There's the promise of a beautiful day – the line is too bright for the sun to be hampered by clouds – and it also tells her that it's late, at least nine o'clock. She's not surprised that she's slept in though; Simon encouraged her to take a sleeping pill last night. She'll be slow for the rest of the morning too no doubt, but it's worth it.

Beth rolls from her side onto her back and lifts her hand to brush Simon's side of the bed. She's also not surprised that he's gone. He will have got up for one of the girls, or the dog, whichever dependent was the first to demand some attention, leaving Beth to sleep because he will have wanted to feel like he's helping. He'll be sat in the kitchen now, she imagines, with a coffee and his laptop, the girls munching on Cheerios by his side. He always checks his email first – in case one of the partners at his investment bank has summoned him – but this morning she guesses that he'll move swiftly on to the mission that consumed his evening yesterday: getting Mark arrested, or at least under a restraining order, and away from their family.

Beth pushes back the duvet and stretches her lean frame against the mattress. She likes that it's sunny. Yesterday was such a terrible day – seeing her father so ill, letting Ava down, finding her private things tampered with, disappointing Simon – that she didn't think she could survive it. In that split second when she fainted, she wished it was something more permanent. But by the time she came round, with both Simon and Kat peering over her, wide-eyed with worry, she'd started to feel better. Like she'd been put to the ultimate test, and had made it through, and now a prize was due. The prize of something good happening for once, she prays.

She usually showers before bed, but she'd been too exhausted last night, so the urge is strong now. As she walks through her dressing room on the way to their en suite, she notices that her wardrobe door is shut now; Simon must have noticed and closed it. She shudders at the memory of finding it askew when she got home yesterday, then sets her jaw and looks away. She has never seen Simon as angry as he was yesterday afternoon, and he continued to blaze when no one from the police called him back. She knows he won't rest until Mark's under investigation – involving Ava was a red line for him – and of course Beth will support him (she'll have to now). But she won't mention the possibility that Mark might have broken in. She will not have the police's grubby hands looking through her things.

With the pleasure of underfloor-heated stone tiles beneath her feet, Beth leans over and turns the shower on, its powerful jets instantly creating a cloud of steam. She's slept well, the sun is shining, the children are safe, and Simon is back to take care of her. Today will be a good day, she promises herself. Then she twists the heating dial another couple of degrees, slips out of her pyjamas and steps inside.

* * *

Beth feels even more positive when she walks into the kitchen. At some point during her twenty-minute shower, she remembered that she'd booked the festive family trail at Painshill Park for today. It's a stunning eighteenth-century garden, and its Santa's grotto is reputed to be the most authentic outside Lapland, so she's certain the girls will love it. It will also be a chance for them to reset as a family and spend some time away from the epicentre of their problems. She knows there's more to come with both her dad and the police, but if she can have one day surrounded by Christmas magic, and focused entirely on her family, she hopes that she'll be strong enough to face it.

'Morning.'

'Hi, Mummy,' Ava sings. 'You really like lie-ins at the moment, don't you?'

Simon looks at her quizzically, but she's too caught up in her daughter's innocent gaze to provide any explanation. Ava seems more at ease than Beth could ever have hoped for after what she went through yesterday. Beth knows that could change, and going back to school next term might be difficult for her, but for now it's good to see her smiling. 'Hey, guess who we're going to see today?' she asks, while reaching down to both pat Luna and check her paws aren't dirty.

'Granny and Grandpa!'

'No,' Beth starts, straightening up.

'Well, actually yes,' Simon pipes up, looking sheepish now. 'I called Mum this morning, asked if we could stay with them for a couple of days. Sorry not to run it past you first. I just thought, with everything going on, it would be nice to get some country air.' He pauses. 'And have a break from London for a while.'

His meaning is clear – a break from Mark and his threats – and Beth understands why he would want that. But the Surrey countryside will provide that too, and the girls shouldn't have to miss out on seeing Father Christmas. 'We can't go today,' she says, shaking her head. 'At least not until later.'

'Why not?' Simon asks. 'Football has finished for the season.' He pauses, glances at the girls, then lowers his volume. 'And it's not safe for you to be here.'

'Don't worry, we won't be here,' Beth explains. 'I've booked the Christmas trail at Painshill Park, with Santa's grotto as the grand finale, so we'll be out of town anyway.'

'Wait, what?' Martha pipes up.

Ava gasps open-mouthed and pushes her palms against her chubby cheeks, like she's auditioning for *The Sound of Music*. 'Are we seeing Father Christmas today?'

'Will we get a present too?' Martha asks.

'I told you he exists,' Ava mumbles victoriously.

Simon smiles, but it's tight and doesn't reach his eyes. He's clearly not happy with Beth sabotaging his plans and she wonders why; he's usually so easy-going. 'The booking is eleven until one, so we could go to your parents' this afternoon?'

'Please, Daddy?' Ava slips her hand inside Simon's and gazes up at him.

He sighs. 'Well okay, but let's at least take our overnight bags with us. Then we can go straight to Granny and Grandpa's from there.' Simon's parents live in Hertfordshire, the opposite side of London from Painshill Park, which means they'll almost drive past their road on their journey northwards. Beth feels sad that he's so desperate to avoid his own home, because it reminds her of how she felt growing up. A new surge of anger wells up as she realises how much damage Mark has caused.

'A weekend away to recharge,' she whispers. 'Then we'll sort this Mark problem together, okay?'

He smiles at her, but she can't help feeling like there's a new barrier between them.

Chapter 41

Joseph

Joe Stone parks up next to the line of ambulances and kills the engine. He hates hospitals. He's hated them since he was 15 when his appendix burst, and the school decided to call 999 rather than wait for one of his parents to pick him up. They were both there in time to sign the forms for the operation, but having to writhe in agony in front of his 25-year-old (and super-hot) history teacher was enough to put him off all things medical for life.

So it's a shame that, with his job, he ends up in the hospital fairly regularly. 'Ready then?' he asks, clicking his seatbelt free and reaching for the door handle.

'Yep. Let's do it,' Jason says in response, his colleague in CID and best mate in the force. Everyone reckons they look alike – the two J's as they're known – but Joe is quietly confident that he's the better-looking of the two.

They push on their respective doors and climb out of the unmarked Vauxhall Astra. They're heading for the St James' wing of St George's Hospital, which means going through the main entrance. Joe nods pleasantly at the three patients in wheelchairs sucking on cigarettes outside, while silently passing judgement. Then the two of them walk past the sweeping reception desk and towards the lifts. He notices a few passing glances from other visitors – however averagely they dress, people always seem to be able to spot a copper – but the staff don't bother to look up. A detective heading up to ICU is too run of the mill for that.

As the lift light shines that they've reached the first floor, Joe waits for the door to slide open and takes a deep breath. He's been with Wandsworth CID for nearly five years and has been involved in hundreds of attacks on teenagers over that time, from drunken fights between mates gone wrong, to stabbings initiated by warring gangs. It's all too easy to treat new victims as just one more, forget that they are all the centre of someone's world, and most with mothers who still remember tucking them in at night. This kid they're seeing now might be half a foot taller than him, and full of patter on the night they met, but he's still got his whole life ahead of him, and last night someone tried to take that from him.

The pair of them walk up to the reception desk and wait to be noticed. It was Joe's day off yesterday, so he only found out about Mark's attack when he came on shift at eight o'clock this morning. He was reading the details in the handover book when his sergeant, DS Flackwell, had wandered over and offered to give him the lowdown personally – while also neatly dropping the case in Joe's lap.

A member of the public had seen Mark Sullivan sparko through the shop unit window in the early hours on their way home from a Christmas party. Apparently inspired by the post about Beth Packard dabbling in heroism a couple of weeks earlier, they'd assumed a drug overdose and phoned the emergency services. By the time the paramedics arrived, the good Samaritan had wandered off and Mark was crawling around on the pavement. He was clearly under the influence, but there was also a deep red ligature mark around his neck. With a suspected spinal fracture, he was collared and blocked, and taken to A&E at St George's, where he was treated overnight. His condition has been described as stable, but he's currently unconscious in ICU.

It hadn't taken the on-duty CID long to work out Joe's connection with Mark – the initial arrest for drug offences, and the allegation made by Mr Packard against him – or for them to flag to DS Flackwell that Joe might just be the man for the job. Luckily, it seems they were also out of the blocks quickly with the initial investigation. The on-call forensics officer has already been to the hospital, and shared photographs of Mark's wounds. And a SOCO team are heading to the crime scene this morning.

'Can I help you?'

'DC Stone, Wandsworth CID,' Joe says, showing his badge to the nurse who's appeared behind the reception desk. 'And this is DC Worthing.'

'Is this about Mark Sullivan? Because you know he's not actually conscious?' The nurse sounds a bit exasperated, but nurses work twelve-hour shifts on this unit, so Joe's not going to take it personally. Her name badge shows that she's called Gloria Faithful, which feels like the perfect name for a nurse. 'And your forensics guy left an hour ago,' she adds.

'Yeah, we know,' Joe says, trying to sound grateful for her insight. 'We just wanted to have a quick word with whoever's in charge of Mark's treatment. To get a likely prognosis, and check if or when we'll be able to interview him.'

Gloria sighs. 'Of course you do, sorry.' Her face relaxes. 'That's Dr Rahim. She's not here at the moment, but I can page her for you.'

'Thanks. We'll wait over there,' Joe says, nodding towards a row of plastic chairs attached to the wall. Only one of them is occupied, and Jason guides them to the opposite end, conscious that visitors in a place like this don't usually like police sitting too close. But this particular visitor keeps looking over at them.

'Excuse me,' she finally says. 'Are you police officers?'

'We're with CID,' Jason says in the polite voice he saves for members of the public.

'Are you here about my boy?'

Joe pushes forward in his chair. 'Who's your boy?' he asks gently.

'Mark,' she whispers. 'Mark Sullivan. Someone strangled him. Why would they do that?' Her face crumples and tears snake down her cheeks. She looks like the kind of mum who would remember tucking Mark in at night, Joe thinks.

'You're right, Mrs Sullivan, it is hard to understand why anyone would behave like that.' He sighs, to prove that he's still not immune to the horror of violent crime. 'But DC Worthing and I are investigating what happened, and we will find out who did this to Mark.'

'The nurse said he'd been sleeping rough, in an old shop. That he'd been doing drugs. But it doesn't make any sense. Mark hates drugs. He was working, trying to get a job with one of those game designers. Why would someone want to kill him?'

Her eyes plead for answers, but Joe doesn't want to share their working theory. He hasn't visited the crime scene yet, or interviewed a single person of interest, so he's trying to keep an open mind. But the uniforms first on the scene said it looked like a fight over drugs that escalated. The place was a mess apparently, a smashed mirror, boot holes in the wall, furniture flung around. And there were dozens of packets of spice scattered over the floor. Spice may be the value brand of the narcotics world, but that kind of quantity is still way more than someone like Mark could afford to buy. It doesn't take a genius to work out he nicked the stuff and then got punished for it.

But it's not Joe's only working theory. He thinks about the voicemail still sitting on his work phone. The angry voice of Simon Packard demanding that he arrest Mark. *Or do something, for Christ's sake!* Joe wonders what his failing to pick up the message until this morning might have led to.

'It's early days, Mrs Sullivan. But I promise we'll be investigating this fully.'

'He was coming home, you know. Back to Cambridge, for Christmas. We were all looking forward to seeing him, hearing his news. And then I get a call from the police at six o'clock this morning saying Mark's in hospital.'

'I'm sure he'll appreciate having you here when he wakes up.'

'DC Stone?'

Joe turns his head, then stands up.

'I'm Dr Rahim, the SHO here. I've been treating Mrs Sullivan's son.' She nods at Mark's mother and smiles. 'I understand you want to know more about Mark's condition?' she continues, looking back at Joe.

'Yes please,' Joe says quietly.

The doctor gestures back towards the reception desk and Joe follows. Jason, always the best at building a rapport with distressed mothers, stays put. When they reach the desk, Dr Rahim pauses. 'So Mark was transferred to ICU from A&E at about five o'clock this morning,' she says, sounding more at ease now she's got facts to relay. 'He is in an induced coma on a ventilator; he was intubated by the A&E team because he was very combative on arrival.'

'You mean he was lashing out at staff?'

'Well yes, but don't be too quick to judge, DC Stone. Mark has clearly been strangled – there are ligature marks on his anterior neck and the pattern is relatively flat, which rules out hanging. Strangulation causes cerebral hypoxia, which is essentially lack of oxygen to the brain, and this can lead to distress, disorientation and, as you call it, lashing out. If Mark was suffering a bleed on the brain, this could also explain his erratic behaviour. And of course in Mark's case, his actions could also have been the result of him smoking synthetic cannabinoids. It was impossible for the A&E team to determine which of these were the actual cause without tests.'

'And now?' Joe asks.

'Mark has been thoroughly assessed. He's got fairly significant bruising on his torso, and two broken ribs. But these injuries are a week or so old, so not related to last night's attack. Otherwise, he's been lucky. He's had a CT scan of his brain and C-spine and that's come back normal, which means no spinal fracture and no bleed on the brain.'

'So does that mean you can wake him up now? We're really keen to talk to him.'

'I'm not going to extubate Mark just so that you can have a chat, DC Stone.' Then she softens her tone. 'The signs are looking positive, but we need to take things slowly. I'm going off shift soon, but my colleague – Dr Melnyk – will be doing the ward round this morning and he'll decide about the next stage in Mark's treatment. But yes, he may ask the nurses to hold the sedation so that some preliminary checks can be carried out on Mark's cognitive function. And if that goes well, the next stage is to wake him up fully.'

'Okay, thank you.' But Joe isn't willing to let her go yet. He has one more question, but he needs to tread carefully. 'Could I ask your opinion on something?'

'You can ask,' she responds, her voice suddenly heavy with suspicion.

'You said that Mark was lucky. From the impact of the strangulation, do you think someone was actually trying to kill him, or was it more about wielding power over him?'

Dr Rahim doesn't answer straight away, but Joe is relieved to see she seems to be considering his question and not giving him the familiar line about it not being her job. 'When you cut off someone's oxygen supply,' she eventually explains, 'the body reacts very quickly, and can lose consciousness in seconds. But to kill someone, you need to apply pressure for minutes. That's why we often see strangulation in domestic abuse cases – it can make victims feel like they're dying, give abusers that power, but without causing major physical injuries. So in answer to your question, I would say it depends. If the perpetrator is familiar with violence, then no, they weren't trying to kill Mark. But a less aware attacker could have seen Mark stop breathing, lose consciousness, and believe him to be dying.'

'That's helpful, I think,' Joe says with a smile. 'It makes me wonder whether I could ask one more,' he adds sheepishly. Dr Rahim rolls her tired eyes, but crucially doesn't walk away, so Joe keeps talking. He knows the forensic officer will have swabbed Mark's neck for fibre residue, and taken lots of photos, but he's a believer in the more expert advice, the better. 'From the markings, can you tell what kind of ligature was used to strangle Mark?'

Dr Rahim tips her head to one side in thought. 'It's hard to say,' she says thoughtfully. 'Something thinner than a belt, but thicker than a washing line. Maybe a tie, but I wouldn't be confident enough to say that in court. Your forensics officer was here earlier; I'm sure he'll have a better idea.'

'Thanks, I appreciate your help. And you'll let us know as soon as he wakes up?'

'Not me,' she says with a smile. 'My shift finished three hours ago. But yes, I'll make sure someone calls you.'

'Thanks,' Joe says again, then ambles back to Jason who is now sat next to Mrs Sullivan. 'Time to go, mate.'

'Yeah, coming.' But before he gets up, Jason takes Mrs Sullivan hand in his. 'Mark will be fine, and we'll catch the man who did this, okay?'

'Okay,' she whispers back. 'And thank you.'

The pair of them walk back to the lift, and out into the fresh air. 'Where next then?' Jason asks. 'The crime scene?'

'Yeah, that's what I was thinking. But I just want to stop somewhere first. It's on the same road.'

Chapter 42

Saskia

Saskia lets the rich coffee trickle down her throat. She closes her eyes for a moment and imagines the caffeine entering her bloodstream, like a personal trainer shouting motivational quotes to the rest of her sluggish body. Last night started as a civilised kids' tea at Emily's, but gradually morphed into dancing around her kitchen until the early hours, the children collected by tight-lipped husbands at some hard-to-pinpoint moment during the proceedings. The ramping up had been Saskia's idea of course. Partly as content for her Instagram story, but mostly as a way to punish Beth for rejecting her yet again.

She couldn't believe her eyes yesterday, looking out of her living room window and seeing that hulk of a woman merrily let herself into Beth's house with Martha and Ava in tow. Just because Saskia didn't offer her services, doesn't excuse Beth for ghosting her. Saskia had checked her phone straight away in case there was a missed call, evidence that Kat wasn't Beth's first choice for comforting Ava after her harrowing experience, but there'd been nothing, not even a text. Once again, Beth had chosen to entrust her children to her new dog walker rather than her best friend, even after Saskia had been the one to save Ava from whatever misdeed that man was planning. (Surely the school would have told Beth that?) Well fuck her, Saskia had thought. Being born in poverty generally corresponds with being raised without morals. She'd quickly banished that thought and then mentally sworn at her parents for indoctrinating her with their judgemental views.

Beth and the girls had also been invited to Emily's tea party (naturally), but no one had been surprised when they didn't show up. While there had been no official word from the school, news of the intruder had spread like wildfire, and the mums had been gossiping about the incident in Emily's kitchen. Vitriol for the school (how the hell could their security be so lax in this day and age?) and sympathy for the children affected (apparently Ava Packard got the brunt of it, poor darling, and after Beth had been such an angel with people like him). Saskia had also found out that the school had let Mark get away, which meant he was still out there, able to continue stalking Beth and her family. In fact, perhaps it was that discovery, her scuttling off rather than making sure he was apprehended, that persuaded Saskia to open another bottle and tell Alexa to turn the volume up.

'Another coffee, Saskia?'

Saskia smiles at the handsome Brazilian barista and nods. 'Thanks, Paulo. But can I get this one in a takeaway cup? I only came out for croissants.' He laughs and his eyes scrunch up in a cute way, and Saskia vaguely wonders what he might look like topless, and then two minutes later he presents her with an espresso coffee in a paper cup. She pushes off the wooden chair and lowers her sunglasses to avoid the vicious glare as she steps outside.

She takes it slowly up the hill on her route back home. With her eyes protected, she lifts her face to the sky and enjoys the half-hearted attempt at warmth filtering out of the sky. She knows from experience that her hangover will disappear by mid-afternoon, just in time for her to think a glass of something around 6 p.m. is a good idea. Unfortunately it's only mid-morning, so she's got a few more hours of suffering to contend with. As the hill gets steeper, she pauses to take a much-needed breath, then lifts her glasses and narrows her eyes.

The men stood outside Beth's house look like police officers. Are they expecting to interview Ava about yesterday's incident? She's only 5 for goodness' sake. Or has something else happened? An unwelcome wave of guilt washes over her; damn, why didn't she stick around and make sure Mark was arrested yesterday? When did she become such a wimp?

Saskia watches the two men knock at Beth's door and then start peering through her living room window when it goes unanswered. Are the Packards ignoring the detectives? Or are they genuinely not at home? Saskia pulls her phone out of her pocket and opens Google Maps again. She clicks into location sharing, and a quick tap on Beth's pink dot shows that she's at Painshill Park in Surrey. As Saskia looks back at the sky, the memory of a weeks-old conversation starts filtering through. A trip to Santa's grotto. Something nauseatingly lovely for the whole family. Beth's absolutely fine, she realises, then she sighs, and continues up the hill.

'They're not in,' she calls out helpfully to the two identikit detectives still languishing outside Beth's house.

'Thanks,' the slightly better-looking one answers. 'Any idea when they'll be back?'

Now that he's initiated conversation, Saskia feels qualified to cross the road and lean on Beth's gate. 'Not sure; they've taken the kids to see Santa in Surrey. Who are you anyway?'

'Sorry,' the man says. He's wearing a navy bomber jacket over a grey hoodie. 'I'm DC Worthing. And this is my colleague, DC Stone.'

'I recognise you,' Saskia says, squinting behind her glasses. Now that she's closer, she realises that it's the same detective she

275

spotted leaving Beth's house on Tuesday morning. 'Are you here about Beth's stalker?'

DC Stone smiles tightly. 'We just wanted a quick word with Mr and Mrs Packard. We'll come back later.'

'Well, I hope you've caught the little prick. It makes me sick, scumbags like him preying on women and children.' She pushes away the nagging voice that's calling her two-faced.

'So you know about Beth's concerns then?' DC Stone asks casually.

Something snaps. It's her patience. 'Excuse me, did you say Beth's concerns? That's bloody typical.' God, her head is pounding now. 'Shift the blame to the victim, especially if they happen to be a woman. He's the scumbag here, not Beth.'

'You probably want to be careful what you say,' the other one pipes up.

'Oh so it's my fault now, is it? Do you want to arrest me, or shall I get in line behind my best friend?'

DC Worthing lets out a loud, exasperated sigh. 'Listen, the man Beth claims to be her stalker is currently unconscious in St George's Hospital with his mum crying by his bedside, so maybe cut down on the insults, yeah?'

Saskia blinks. It's not like her to be speechless, but the wind has definitely been knocked out of her sails. 'What's wrong with him?' she finally asks.

'We can't say,' DC Stone interjects. 'We're heading back to the station now; I'll give Mr Packard a ring.' Both detectives move towards the gate, and Saskia steps back to let them through.

'Is it drugs, like his so-called friend?' she asks.

DC Stone pauses and turns to face her. 'I understand that you're worried about Beth,' he says kindly. 'But it wouldn't be appropriate for us to share those details.'

'I only ask,' Saskia persists, 'because two overdoses so close together might mean there's stronger-grade heroin on the street. Or that it's been cut with dangerous impurities.' She tries to sound knowledgeable. 'I read an article about it. I support a local drug charity, you see, write content for their website, and I'd like to let them know if there's anything to worry about.'

'That is true,' DC Stone admits, nodding. He seems to have more time for her now that he realises that she's not just a champagne socialist. 'But it would have been flagged directly after Jon Smith's death, the man Beth called the ambulance for, if the street heroin was deemed a problem.'

Saskia creases her forehead. 'I don't understand?'

'Jon died of a stroke, an air aneurism caused by a bubble getting into the syringe, rather than the drug itself,' DC Stone explains. 'Which actually isn't that uncommon.'

'Really? I've never heard of it,' she counters, not quite understanding why she's positioning herself as a drugs expert.

'Perhaps you should try reading an article about that too, then?' the detective says with a distinctive smirk in his voice, before following his colleague back to their car.

'Maybe I will,' she spars back, although too quietly for him to pick up the petulance in her voice.

Chapter 43

Kat

In hospital. Mark is in hospital. Alive. Blood pounds in Kat's ears as she tries to process what she's just overheard from the familiar spot around the corner from Beth's house. Her heart stutters then lurches, and she leans against a parking meter to catch her breath. What does that mean? For her, and for Beth. And what happens now?

She wishes she knew how serious Mark's condition was. The detective said that he was unconscious, and something about his mum crying by his bedside. Is he dying? Or will he wake up?

Will he remember?

She blinks furiously. Maybe she should go to St George's Hospital, try to find out for herself. But she got up early this morning to see Beth, not Mark. They connected so powerfully yesterday that she feels she's earned the right to knock on her door now, to check how she is. She can't let their new closeness drift away just because Simon is back home. But Saskia said that Beth was somewhere called Painshill Park, visiting Santa's grotto with her family. That means she'll be gone for a few hours at least, so maybe Kat should go to the hospital; she'd be back before Beth anyway.

Except there's Saskia to deal with too now. Kat felt sick listening to her with those detectives, describing herself as Beth's best friend, casually telling them where Beth is today, as though they confide in each other about everything, which Kat knows for a fact isn't true. When Beth asked Kat to pick up Ava and Martha yesterday, she seemed to be singling Kat out as special. Not only entrusting her with her two most precious things, but also revealing that she was out of London. Details that she didn't seem willing to share with anyone else, not even Simon. But did Kat get that wrong? Were Beth's friends just too busy with their glamorous lives to trudge up to school in the middle of the day for someone else's children?

She pushes her clenched fist against her breastbone, trying to calm her ragged breathing, but it doesn't work. Maybe she is the mug after all. The one who risked her job, and her friendship with Sally, to pander to Beth's needs.

Her growing confusion creates a surge of frustration through Kat's limbs, and she suddenly feels the urge to lash out, to find a punchbag and pummel it to death. Just when she was rebuilding her friendship with Beth, starting to make up for the mistakes of her teenage years, someone comes along and threatens to undermine everything she's achieved. And of course it would be Saskia with her flounce of blonde ponytail and sneering, over-confident expression.

Once the detectives had driven off, Saskia had got her phone out again, tap-tap-tapping on it like the addict she is, before she finally walked inside her own house across the road. The woman is so prolific on social media that she could have been typing anything, but Kat bets she was messaging Beth, telling her about Mark and the detectives knocking at her door, scrabbling for Beth's gratitude for providing the warning. Kat wonders how Beth will react to the news. Will she be relieved that Mark's no longer a threat, or horrified about being dragged further into a scandal? Will she race back home to face the detectives or stay away for longer?

This all matters; Kat knows it does. But her mind's not working properly, and she doesn't know what to do. She pushes away from the gate and starts walking, onto Brookhill Road and down the hill; she'll get the bus to Tooting, check on Mark. But she stalls, shakes her head. No, that's a stupid idea, far too risky. She turns back up the hill. She should go home. Ask Jayden if she can have an hour in his and Will's garage. Expel some energy, for everyone's sake. But surely she needs to find out how Mark is? She turns back down the hill, shaking her head and muttering to herself.

'Are you all right, Kat?'

She looks up. Shit. Saskia is supposed to be in her house; Kat watched her walk inside. Why is she on the street again? 'Yeah, I'm fine,' she answers, but her voice warbles. She puts her hand to her throat and tries again. 'Why are you asking?' But now she sounds defensive.

'Okay, sorry.' Saskia raises her palms. 'You just look a little upset, I suppose. Are you due at Beth's? Simon usually runs with Luna on a Saturday morning, so I doubt they'll need you today. But maybe you got your wires crossed?'

Fear and frustration collide and explode. 'God, you don't stop, do you?'

'Sorry?'

'Acting like you know everything about Beth's life. Always digging, digging, digging.' Kat curls her fingers and scratches at the air, her face pulling into a grimace.

'Now hang on …'

'She doesn't like you, you know.' The words tumble out. 'She told me how nosy you are, always wanting to know her business.' Kat teeters forwards, imagines shoving Saskia in the chest.

Saskia narrows her eyes and holds her ground. 'Fuck you, Kat.'

'She told me how pissed off she was with you,' Kat continues,

280

oblivious to Saskia's growing anger. 'For putting that post up on MyNeighbour.' Somewhere within her spiralling thoughts, Kat knows that it was Saskia's post that led her to Beth in the first place, and that she should be grateful. But the cyclone is too strong for rational thought.

'How dare you speak to me like that. In fact, who even are you?' Saskia asks, her pitch rising.

'I'm Beth's friend,' she counters.

'No you're not. You're Luna's dog walker. And somehow, you've weaselled your way into Beth's life, her home, her children's lives.' She takes a step closer, but Kat doesn't back away. She wants to slap Saskia's stupid face. 'Why would you do that?' Saskia continues, tilting her head. 'It's not for the money, is it? You want her, her beauty, her celebrity.'

'No,' Kat mumbles. 'It's not like that.'

'You're obsessed with her, aren't you? And too blind, too stupid, to see that Beth would never feel like that about you.'

'You know nothing about our friendship,' Kat warns. Her skin is fizzing now. She wants to headbutt Saskia, knock her out, remove the problem in one swift movement.

'I'm going to tell Beth that you were skulking outside her house, you know.'

'Tell her what you want!' Kat blurts out. Her head feels like a spinning top, spiralling dangerously towards a cliff edge. 'She won't mind; Beth and I go back eighteen years!'

'What?'

'Nothing.' Kat sucks in some air. What has she said? Saskia mustn't know about that, about Katherine and Ellie. It will disrupt everything.

'You grew up with her? Is that what you're saying? You knew her before her parents died?' Saskia pushes.

The words land on Kat's skin, but she can't absorb them. 'What?' She shouldn't have said anything, but now Saskia isn't making sense.

'Did you live in Reading too?' Saskia presses. 'Is that why the two of you are so pally?'

'Reading?' Kat stutters. 'Are Beth's parents dead?'

'Hah!' Saskia shouts in triumph. 'You can't know her, then. Because they died when she was a teenager, in a car accident. Which means you're lying, or delusional! How could I have ever thought you and Beth were friends?'

But Kat's not listening anymore. Her throat constricts. Beth's parents must have died after Kat left for Australia. While she was recovering under the warmth of her dad's acceptance, his unconditional love, Beth was experiencing tragedy for a second time. Two more lives cut short. Kat blinks furiously, but she can't cry in front of Saskia. She needs to see Beth, the urge is almost unbearable now, and she needs Saskia out of the picture. 'Beth hates you,' she spits out. 'Calls you nosy, a has-been, a jealous leech.'

Saskia swallows, then scoffs. 'More lies, I see. Beth is my best friend; she would never say those things.'

'And a hypocrite,' Kat continues. 'Pretending to care about the little people when you just want some glory in your sad, selfish life.'

Saskia pushes her lips together and furrows her brow. 'Well, let's just see who Beth believes, shall we?'

Kat gives Saskia a hard stare. Is she really this thick-skinned? This stupid, like Mark? Is Kat going to have to teach her a lesson too? Suddenly a noise makes her jump, a shrill electronic sound. Her phone is ringing in her pocket. It might be Beth; maybe she needs Kat's help again. She twists away from Saskia and prods at the screen. 'Hello?'

'Kat? Where are you?'

Kat scrunches her eyes closed, rams the heel of her hand against her forehead. 'Sally?'

'You're an hour late!' Sally protests. 'Look, I can't keep covering for you!'

Kat gasps, blinks wildly. Sally never raises her voice.

'Saved by the bell?' Saskia asks, scowling, but then her eyes widen.

'So are you coming in?' Sally pushes.

Kat can't think straight, can't speak.

'Hey, Kat, are you okay?' Saskia's hand is on her arm.

'I need you here; I'm drowning. Please, Kat,' Sally begs. Sally. Her warm, thoughtful boss. The only person who believes in her, accepts her, treats her with respect. Kat's head surges with shame and she stumbles backwards, reaching for something solid to stop herself from falling. Of course she must go. She turns, lurches for a moment, her arms flailing, then finds her balance and charges down the hill.

Chapter 44

Beth

It's always a couple of degrees colder outside London, and Beth feels the extra chill now. But she's grateful for it, because the freezing temperature also means that the frost has settled in for the day, and she can't remember seeing a landscape quite so beautiful as the grounds of Painshill Park glistening in the sunshine.

'It looks magical,' Simon observes, reaching for Beth's hand. They're walking the Christmas trail and the girls are a few metres ahead, crunching the iced puddles, Martha carefully, Ava more haphazardly. 'I'm glad you persuaded me to come,' he adds.

'It's nice to be out of London,' Beth agrees. 'It feels like the first time I've properly breathed in weeks.'

'Since that night,' Simon reminds her. 'The night when you crossed paths with that idiot.'

'Yes, but it's not only about Mark.' An image of her shrunken dad hijacks Beth's thoughts suddenly, but she shakes it away. She'll need time to process her dad's illness, what it means, but not now, not on this special day with her family. 'I don't like strangers commenting on my business,' she chooses. 'And after Saskia put that post on MyNeighbour, it felt like everyone was gossiping about me, judging my actions.'

'I agree she should have asked you first,' Simon starts carefully, 'but people are just proud of you, and I don't think you should blame Saskia for how tough things have been when that vile Mark character has been pushing threatening notes through our letterbox and terrorising our children.' Simon pushes his lips together so hard that they almost disappear.

'He's really got to you, hasn't he?'

Simon forces air through his nose. 'Wouldn't it be stranger if he hadn't? I mean, sometimes I wonder why he hasn't got to you more.'

Beth doesn't answer him. There's a chocolate treat wrapped in red and green foil shining on a tree branch, and Beth tries to draw some strength from Martha and Ava's squeals as they spot it. Simon doesn't know about those tiny white crutches that live in her old winter boot. 'I just thought that ignoring him would be the best way to strip the oxygen out of his anger.'

'And now? After what he did to Ava?'

'It's different now,' she says quietly.

Simon smiles with relief – kindred spirits again – and Beth lets herself be pulled closer as his arm snakes around her shoulder. They walk like that for a while until they spot Santa's grotto, and then all four of them quicken their pace, while Beth also searches her bag for the antiseptic wipes.

Both girls choose Simon to chaperone them. It could be because they've missed him over the last few days, but Beth suspects it's more to do with their feeling nervous, and wanting his reassuring presence. Children are good at picking up signals, and Martha and Ava seem to know that she's the more anxious parent; they're clearly harder to con than the mums at Nightingales. So Beth is left in charge of Ava's tig-tig and the communal rucksack, complete with water bottles and snacks. There's a small marquee next to the grotto serving stewed tea in plastic cups, so she picks one up and sinks down into a child-sized chair.

As she sips the hot drink and stares at the blemished view through the plastic marquee window, the rucksack trembles on the table in front of her. It's the buzz of a phone. Hers is in her pocket, so it must be Simon's. She considers leaving it – it's probably a work call and she's not in the mood to play secretary – but eventually curiosity overrides her reticence. By the time she fishes it out, the screen has labelled it a missed call, but also displays that it is the third time the mobile number has tried him this morning. Beth's forehead creases. Simon checks his phone every five minutes. Beth taps in his code to open the phone – 2306, their wedding anniversary – then clicks into his recents. Sure enough, the same number is listed three times in red. There are two new voicemails. She clicks on the first one – left at eight thirty this morning, when Simon will surely have had his phone to hand – and lifts the handset to her ear.

Good morning, Mr Packard. This is DC Stone, returning your call regarding Mark Sullivan. There has actually been a development in the case, so I'd be very grateful if you could give me a call back as soon as possible on this number. Many thanks.

The voicemail finishes, and Beth looks at the screen. Simon was desperate to talk to the detective yesterday. Why didn't he pick up? Or at least listen to the voicemail and call DC Stone straight back? But there is also an undercurrent in the detective's voice that Beth doesn't like. She wonders what the development is, and why DC Stone didn't elaborate. She clicks on the second voicemail, left half an hour ago, and puts the phone back against her ear.

Mr Packard, it's DC Stone again. I'm not sure if you've picked up my voicemail from earlier, but I am very keen to talk with you regarding Mark Sullivan. My colleague and I are heading in your direction now, so we'll stop by, see if you're in.

The weight of something unpleasant drops onto Beth's shoulders. It's invisible, but she can feel it wrapping around her. As she stares at the phone, a third voicemail magically appears on the list. It must be from the call she's just missed.

Mr Packard, no luck trying you at home. Listen, you may hear from your neighbour that Mark Sullivan is in hospital. There's nothing to worry about, but I would be grateful if you could return my call at your earliest convenience.

The phone feels slippery in Beth's fingers. She fumbles for it, but it drops, hitting the table with a bang. Four teenagers dressed as elves turn to look at her. Mark is in hospital? What's wrong with him? And why hasn't Simon acknowledged any of DC Stone's calls? Suddenly she doesn't want him to know that she's listened to the voicemails. Simon has never kept secrets from her, or demanded any sort of privacy, but she still feels like she's stepped over a line, broken his trust. She picks up his phone between her finger and thumb and drops it back into the rucksack.

Beth pushes her hands through her hair. It feels greasy and she realises the skin on her fingers is now mired by it. She needs to wash them but there's no sink in the marquee. She pulls a wet wipe from the packet in her bag and wipes furiously at her fingers. But now they feel worse. Sticky. She needs running water, piping hot. She takes a long breath. Suddenly she wonders if DC Stone could have called her too; her phone is in her pocket, but her coat is thick and it's on silent. She pulls it out, but there are no missed calls. Just a WhatsApp message from Saskia. She remembers DC Stone's warning and clicks it open.

Your stalker in hospital. Unconscious.

Not drugs. Did you know?

PS Hope PP Santa grotto fun xx

God, why does that woman have to know everything first? And how does she even know where Beth is? She blows out some air and focuses on the content of Saskia's message. Mark isn't just in hospital; he's unconscious. The man who has followed her, threatened her, stripped away her daughter's precious belief that the world is good. For a moment Beth allows herself to wish he would die. Be gone from her life. But then she shakes her head and tries to process what it means. Why is DC Stone so keen to talk to Simon? Even if Mark's injury is violence-related, surely the detective is more likely to suspect another rough sleeper, or gangs, rather than a respectable banker with no history of violence?

She can see the girls now, standing at the grotto's exit, each with an identical present in their hand, staring at a tree trunk wound tight with fairy lights and wiring. A camera flashes. They'll be by her side again soon; she needs to get her head straight, reapply her happy face. She visibly jumps as another message buzzes through on her phone. It's Saskia again. Her eyes widen, her breathing stops. What the fuck? Colour drains from her face.

'Mummy? Are you okay?'

Chapter 45

Saskia

Saskia closes her front door and leans against the wooden frame. She never cries, at least hardly ever, so she's not sure why she feels the urge now. She was scared, she realises, arguing with Kat in the street. For all Saskia's lofty beliefs about championing mental health awareness, when she comes across someone who is clearly unwell, she becomes a frightened animal and goes on the attack. When did she become such a bitch?

Saskia wonders where Kat is now. Whoever she was talking to on the phone clearly upset her – she was staggering so blindly that Saskia thought she might fall over – but then she righted herself and ran off towards Wandsworth Common. It was a relief at first, the sense of a threat diminishing – especially with Kat being so physically intimidating too – but now that the adrenalin has worn off, Saskia can't help feeling worried about the strange woman, and what she might do. She seemed so out of control.

Saskia pulls the unfamiliar phone out of her pocket and stares at the blank screen. It's an old iPhone, a 5 or 6 maybe, and looks tiny compared to her own. It must have slipped out of Kat's hands when she reached for the wall, but Saskia was too wired to notice at the time. It was only once Kat disappeared that she'd seen it lying on the pavement. She taps on the glass now and the screen comes to life with the photo of a weird-looking dog, a skinny Alsatian with rabbit ears. Saskia taps it again, and sighs when the usual grid of numbers comes up. *Enter passcode.* She tuts and puts it back in her pocket.

Not that she wants to spy on Kat. But if she could get into the phone, she'd be able to check Kat's call history, work out who had upset her, and possibly even where she disappeared to. She needs to return the handset somehow. And if it also provides some intel on who Kat really is, that can't be a bad thing. Like whether there's any truth to Kat's claims that she and Beth knew each other when they were growing up. The two of them being friends is so hard to imagine that Saskia jumped on the first hole in Kat's story and accused her of lying. But Kat not reacting to Reading doesn't mean anything – the only evidence Saskia has that Beth spent time in the town was the fact she visited a shitty house there the day before, and that's weak even by Saskia's standards. It's harder to explain Kat not knowing about Beth's parents' car accident, but Beth was 17 when that happened, so it's possible that they'd lost touch by then.

Saskia wonders if she should let Beth know what Kat's saying about her. All this time, Beth has been scared of her stalker, Mark, and with good reason. But his threat has always been from outside her home, while Kat burrowed her way inside. She even walked Martha and Ava to school on Thursday. Kat said that Beth was sleeping, and Saskia hadn't questioned it at the time – of course she hadn't; she was too busy being offended that Beth hadn't asked her to take the girls – but what seasoned mother sleeps through school drop-off? Was there something dodgy going on even then? She needs to talk to Beth.

But then, she's only just sent that message about Mark being in hospital. Is she really going to ruin Beth's blissful family excursion for a second time?

With a jolt of frustration, Saskia pushes away from the doorframe. She eyes the coffee machine that sits centre stage on her island unit. An injection of caffeine is just what she needs to help her decide. At least the house is empty, she thinks as she drops in a capsule and waits impatiently for the thin line of coffee to fill her cup. The children were desperate to go swimming, but luckily Tim knows that chore sits squarely in his camp, along with putting the bins out and sorting the MOT on the car. He'd even offered to make an afternoon of it – swimming at Latchmere Leisure Centre followed by tea at Franco Manca. Saskia had been waving goodbye to the three of them when she noticed Kat pacing up and down the road outside Beth's house.

She opens WhatsApp on her own phone; the two grey ticks show that Beth hasn't read her message about Mark yet. She's clearly having too magical a day with her family to check her phone. Despite everything, Saskia can't help bristling at that, but at least it gives her more time to decide what to do. She cradles her cup of coffee and thinks. Perhaps she should do some digging first. See if she can find out a bit more about the mysterious Kat. If she finds a link between her and Beth, it means Kat's telling the truth, so is neither delusional nor dangerous (if you ignore the circumference of her biceps). And it explains why Beth would lean on her more than one might expect of a dog walker. If she doesn't find any link, she'll still have more background information to share with Beth.

She flips open her laptop and hovers her fingers over the keyboard. The only thing she knows about Kat is that she works at Groom & Bloom, so she starts there. The website is rudimentary at best – not even a blog – but it does list the names of their groomers: Sally Greenwood and Kat Wilson. There's a short biography too, and Saskia learns that Kat got a taste for dog grooming while living on a farm in Australia, then earned her qualification from Lywood Grooming Academy near Newbury after she returned to the UK. Saskia pauses for a moment, takes another glug of coffee, then picks up her phone. After a short online search, she taps in a number.

'Hello, Lywood Grooming Academy,' a gruff, slightly bored, voice answers.

'Oh, hi there,' Saskia responds, trying to sound upbeat. 'I hope you don't mind me calling on a Saturday.'

'It's not ideal, to be honest. What do you want?'

Saskia sighs. Maybe she should get straight to the point. 'My name is Sally Greenwood,' she says, transferring to her professional tone. 'I run a dog groomer's in London, and I'm after some information on one of my groomers.'

'And you're calling me because?' The word hangs in the air, somewhere between a question and an accusation.

'Because she qualified with you and got a rosy reference along with her distinction,' Saskia counters, silently praying that her assertive tone works in her favour, and that grooming comes with the traditional categories of awards.

'I take it she's done something you're not happy with?' the woman with no name surmises, making Saskia wonder how reputable her course can be.

'In a way. But I'm more concerned than unhappy,' Saskia ad-libs. 'There have been a few incidents. Her mental health seems to be deteriorating. Of course I'm not suggesting that's your problem, I just wondered whether you knew of any relevant history, to help me work out what to do. There was nothing in her reference to explain it,' she adds, hoping a soupçon of menace doesn't backfire.

The voice expels a heavy sigh. 'Name?'

'Kat Wilson.'

'Hold on, I'll get the file.'

While Saskia waits, she types a few combinations into the search engine. *Katherine Wilson + Beth Packard. Beth Packard +*

Reading. Beth Packard + tragic car accident. But she knows it's pointless. Packard is Simon's surname, so only Beth's married name. She has no way of tracing her friend further back than that. She wonders if that's weird, knowing so little about someone she's supposed to be best friends with. Beth's Facebook link comes up on the search too, but Saskia doesn't bother clicking into it; she already knows there are only saccharine pictures of Martha and Ava on there. The same with Instagram, and Beth doesn't even have a Twitter account.

'Still there?'

Saskia snaps her focus back to the grumpy woman on the phone who is – she has to admit – doing Saskia's bidding. 'Did you find her file?' she asks.

'Yeah, there was some mental health stuff,' the woman starts.

Saskia's pulse quickens and she leans forward. 'Oh?'

'Not while she was here, but before, as a teenager. She put it in the notes on her application form because it disrupted her education – she missed her GCSEs and got some random Australian qualifications instead.'

'Disrupted how?'

'She spent a couple of months in a mental health unit in Newbury.'

'What for? What was wrong with her?'

'How am I supposed to know? I'm not a bloody doctor. Anyway, it's confidential that sort of stuff, isn't it? And grounds for discrimination if I turned her application down, not that I would. I remember her now. A bit awkward with humans, I'll give you that, but a natural with the dogs; they all loved her. I'm sorry to hear she's struggling again now.' There's genuine sadness in her voice and Saskia feels a stab of guilt for stretching the truth. She shifts on the stool, eyes the bottle of wine on the island, looks at her watch.

'Don't worry, I rate her too,' she appeases. 'I'll make sure she gets the help she needs. Anyway, thank you. I'd better go.' Saskia ends the call and taps her fingernails against the quartz surface, one at a time. So Kat does have a history of mental illness. And being in residential care for two months, forgoing her education, all points to it being a serious condition. Surely that's enough of a red flag for Saskia to tell Beth, to warn her what Kat's been saying. Although maybe she should keep quiet about researching Kat; ironically, that could make it look like Saskia's the obsessive one. She clicks into WhatsApp and scribes a message.

Beth, your dog walker is WEIRD. Stood outside your house. Said she knew you 18 yrs ago. That you were FRIENDS. Assuming not?? Maybe delusional? Idk. Hope you're okay xxx

She stares at the two ticks, willing them to go blue, and then they do, and she lets out an involuntary gasp, which is ridiculous because what else was she expecting to happen? But as she waits, gripping her phone, nothing more happens. There's no *Beth typing* flag. Why isn't Beth responding? 'Shit,' she mumbles under her breath, suddenly deflated. Surely her message warrants an immediate reaction?

Saskia eyes the bottle of red wine standing suggestively next to the coffee machine, then reaches for it and unscrews the top. In lieu of a glass to hand, she splashes some into her now empty coffee cup and takes a generous gulp. With nothing better to do, she picks up Kat's phone and runs her thumb over the screen. Kat, the broad, brawny tomboy. The woman who prefers animal company to human, who wears comfortable clothes and zero make-up. 'Fuck, of course,' Saskia exhales slowly. She taps 1-2-3-4 into the phone, and watches the screen come to life. Kat clearly isn't the type to dedicate thinking time to a phone passcode.

With a wide smile and a small whoop of triumph, she scans the home screen. She taps into the messages, but there's nothing much in there. Beth, Sally, someone called Jayden. The Notes app is empty, but there are a few voice memos. Saskia clicks into the first and a chill runs down her spine. It's slurred and distant, but it's Beth voice she can hear, not Kat's. And she's talking about

Saskia. *My so-called friend spreading all the sordid details on the internet.* God, she sounds so drunk. She never gets into that state with Saskia. A worm of jealousy wriggles across her shoulder blades, but she shakes it away. The important fact is that Kat was recording Beth. Why would she do that? So she can listen to Beth's voice whenever she wants?

Saskia shudders and clicks into Kat's photos.

And there it is. In both black-and-white and full colour. Evidence of Kat's obsession.

As she scrolls, Saskia starts to feel sick, the red wine turning to vinegar on her tongue. Photo after photo of Beth, from different angles, close and long range. And other photos too. Martha and Ava. Beth's stalker, Mark. And even Saskia herself. Her hands are trembling now, but she keeps scrolling, wide-eyed, heart racing. And then she sees it. A photo from last night. Mark. She throws the phone on the work surface in horror, and watches it slide onto the floor.

Chapter 46

Joseph

Joe slides his phone into the back pocket of his jeans and releases a sigh of frustration, although Mr Packard not picking up his calls is hardly damning evidence of guilt. Of course the guy's going to be pissed off with Mark after the idiot frightened his daughter half to death – Christ knows how Mark managed to get into her school at all; Joe has already briefed the school liaison officer about the incident – but that doesn't mean the ex-public-school boy is going to slip out in the middle of the night and try to strangle a homeless teenager in a dirty squat. In reality, it's much more likely to be a fight over the spice he clearly nicked – either the original owner wanting payback, or another addict taking issue with Mark's little windfall. The older injuries that the doctor mentioned back that up, and as Joe looks around the squat, he's even more inclined to think it.

'Bit of a mess,' Jason surmises, which is a massive understatement. There's damage to the walls, flakes of plaster on the floor, and a huge, smashed mirror with shards of glass refracting in the sunshine. The only furniture in the room is an old IKEA sofa, dumped in the middle, but most of its cushions have been flung around the floor too. And the final addition to the smorgasbord of debris is a few dozen brightly coloured metallic packets, like football cards with added hallucinogenic. The last time Joe was here, it was night-time and he was in and out in a few minutes, and more focused on trying to caution a lanky drunk kid than taking in his surroundings. But his impression was that it was a fairly civilised place to bed down. It doesn't look like that now.

'Found anything useful?' Joe asks Isobel, one of the two scenes of crime officers methodically working their way around the squat. The other one – Annie – is a county netball player, and the only woman Joe would consider marrying without a first date, so he tries to avoid conversation if he can.

'No sign of forced entry at either the front or rear,' Isobel starts, her voice quick and efficient. 'But the back door wasn't locked and there's access from the road via the alleyway so no massive mystery there.'

'Any other good news?' Joe asks sarcastically.

Isobel gives him a look. 'The five dents in the plasterboard over there look fresh,' she says, pointing to the wall that runs from the front door. 'And consistent with a kicking action.'

'Suggesting a fight,' Joe murmurs, but Isobel just shrugs; supposition isn't her job.

'The measurements suggest that all the dents were made by the same footwear,' she continues. 'Most likely a boot or heavy trainer.'

'Interesting.' Joe looks a bit closer at the wall.

'Maybe Mark kicked the wall himself,' Jason suggests. 'We already know he's got a temper. Although his mum reckons he's a good kid underneath his fucking imbecile exterior.'

'Don't they all,' Joe muses.

'No sign of blood splatter on the walls,' Isobel continues. 'Annie is going through the shards of glass, but nothing there yet either.'

'Any chance of DNA at all, do you think?'

'I've found a couple of head hairs on one sofa cushion, but

they're likely to be Mark's based on the photos that came back from the hospital. The packets of spice will obviously be removed, and we'll send a sample batch for fingerprint analysis, so that might give us something.'

'Any luck with the ligature?'

'Possibly. There was an old tourniquet belt on the floor, which looked fairly consistent with the pattern of abrasions on Mark's neck. That will go to the lab, and if we're lucky, we might get DNA from the sweat or skin scrapings on there.'

'Tourniquet belt? As in what nurses use to take blood?' Jason asks.

'Phlebotomists,' Isobel corrects. 'And yes. Except this one hasn't been used by a medical professional in a while.'

'Bit skanky?'

'More likely to belong to a drug user,' Isobel opts for.

'Maybe it belonged to Jon and was just lying around here,' Joe suggests. 'Picked up in the heat of the moment.'

Isobel looks affronted. 'I worked this scene the first time around, and we did a comprehensive sweep of the place. There's no way we'd have missed something so relevant.'

'How long were you here?' Joe can't help asking. He knows a suspected drug overdose of an NFA – a person of no fixed abode – wouldn't be considered a priority.

'We wouldn't have missed it,' Isobel repeats defensively, narrowing her eyes, reminding Joe that he shouldn't make an enemy of her.

'Of course, sorry. Any idea when the forensic report will come through?' he asks, changing the subject.

'Middle to end of next week maybe. How's he doing by the way? The assault looked pretty nasty from the photographs.'

'Lucky, apparently. Other than that, I'm waiting to hear from the hospital. Hopefully he'll wake up soon.'

'Yes,' Isobel says with a sigh. 'Did you say his mum is there? I bet she's desperate.'

'I meant for me. Much easier to find the assailant if you get it from the horse's mouth.'

'That's if he knows anything,' Isobel counters. 'Looking at the scene, he may not have seen his assailant. There's no electricity, so it will have been dark, except for the light coming in from the street. And the ligature mark shows that he was strangled from behind.'

'You're a bundle of joy, aren't you?'

'Just pointing out the facts, DC Stone.'

Isobel's expression is serious, and Joe's trying to work out if there's a smile hiding behind her eyes when Jason's phone rings. He watches his colleague listen, nod, grunt a few times and finish the call. 'Work-related?' he asks.

'Yeah, it was Sagal. I asked her to check if there was any CCTV that could help us, but apparently Brookhill Road is a CCTV black spot.'

'There's a camera at the dog groomer's a few doors up,' Isobel offers. 'I saw it on my way here.'

'Very observant,' Joe notes. 'You know, you'd make a great forensic scientist.'

'Yeah, I heard that.' Isobel rolls her eyes, and Joe decides to consider it a friendly gesture.

'Shall we stroll up there?' Jason asks, but it's a question that doesn't need an answer. With a camera positioned so close to the scene, they have a very good chance of spotting the assailant either arriving or leaving the property. Joe says goodbye to Isobel, nods self-consciously at Annie, and follows Jason out of the shop.

There's a bell above the groomer's door and it jangles as they walk inside. It reminds Joe of buying sweets from the village store – which is weird, because he grew up in Lewisham – and the warm feeling grows when the woman behind the desk smiles at them both. On second glance, her face looks a little tired and her shoulders sit higher than they should, but she has a hazy glow about her that Joe feels drawn to.

'Morning, gentlemen, how can I help? I'm guessing that you're more interested in what happened at the old Delphine's than my price list? I'm Sally by the way.'

'Good guess,' Jason says, beaming at her, his skills with middle-aged women at play again. 'There was an incident at the property in the early hours of the morning.'

'I thought I saw that the same squatter had moved back in,' Sally says sagely. 'My heart goes out to him, poor lad, but two incidents in one month.' She shakes her head vaguely and lifts her eyebrows. 'What happened?'

'A young man was assaulted,' Jason offers. 'And we noticed that you have a CCTV camera outside your shopfront. Is there any chance we could take a look at the footage from last night?'

'Assaulted? Is he going to be okay? And of course you can; it's a pleasure to help. The camera only records when there's motion detected outside our front door, but I guess that's what you're looking for, why you asked.'

'Thanks, Sally.'

Sally smiles again, but then she crinkles her nose. 'The only thing is, I don't have a clue how to retrieve the footage. Let me get my partner in crime.' She pauses and two pink spots sprout on her cheeks. 'Sorry, I didn't mean … Anyway, Kat's much better at the technical stuff than me. Hold on.' She disappears behind an orange-and-charcoal-striped curtain at the back of the shop. She's gone much longer than Joe would have expected for such a small shop, but eventually returns with her colleague in tow. With dyed red hair, broad physique and fierce expression, the partner in crime is definitely more wildcat than friendly tabby. Jason gives Joe a look that says *your turn*, and he picks up the mantle.

'Thanks for helping out with the CCTV.'

Kat nods. She looks nervous, which Joe is used to, but also slightly hostile. Joe wonders what her background is, and whether a run-in with the police has featured in it at some point. 'It's only got a ninety-degree view angle,' she says, her voice carrying a defensive undertone too. 'Did Sally tell you that? It won't pick up anything outside the squat.'

'Don't worry,' he says, using his good-natured voice. 'We're looking for anything in the general vicinity that might help us. Could we start from about 10 p.m.?'

'Ten?' Kat repeats, unnecessarily, as though buying time. Joe doesn't respond, and eventually she clambers behind the desk. As she types something into the keyboard, Joe can see that her fingers are trembling. Then she swivels the screen so that Joe can see it across the desk and loads a security company website. Finally, some footage emerges on the screen. Joe leans in.

About half an hour, and thirty-seven fragments of footage later, he leans back.

'Nothing of interest,' he sighs. 'Just the usual Friday night foot traffic.'

'Sorry,' Kat says, although she doesn't sound like she means it.

'I guess there was only ever a fifty-fifty chance that the assailant would come from this direction,' Jason surmises. He doesn't look particularly bothered either. Like Joe, he knows that detective work is at least ninety per cent wasted time.

'Sorry we couldn't help,' Sally says ruefully. 'Is there anything else we can do?'

Joe feels his phone rumble in his pocket and pulls it out. It's the hospital. 'No, it's fine, I should probably take this.' He points at his phone, but doesn't wait for their response before backing out of the shop, the jangle of the bell more irritating now. 'Hello?'

'DC Stone? This is Samantha at St George's ICU. I thought you'd like to know that Mark Sullivan has just woken up.'

Chapter 47

Beth

Beth's skin crawls. She wants to be sick. She reaches for the antiseptic wipes. 'I'm fine, darling,' she whispers to Martha, trying to lower the mask that has served her so well over the years. But it stalls as the image of Saskia's WhatsApp message flickers behind her eyes. Who the hell is Kat, and why did she say she knew Beth eighteen years ago?

'How was Santa?' she asks, desperate to buy time, to work out how to function around her family. Beth watches her eldest daughter's lips move, but she doesn't hear the words. Her head is too dense. Her life swerved eighteen years ago when Eddie died. Her fear of dirt and germs escalated so much that life became unbearable. She was sent to that place, the mental health unit. Dr Sharp gave her tools to cope – medication first, then CBT – and she worked out some strategies of her own. But the memory of being there is still shameful. Living amongst such hopelessness.

She spent five months in the unit, eighteen years ago. Did Kat know her in that place? Beth squeezes her eyes shut and tries to position Kat's face next to her shrouded memories from that time. But there's nothing.

Perhaps Kat knew her before she left home. Or more accurately, knew of her. Yes, that makes more sense.

In the article that the local newspaper ran when Eddie died, they wrote lots about his poor, struggling family, including a photo of the tiny bedroom she and Eddie shared. Suddenly everyone in the local area knew how she lived. Some felt sorry for her, others looked away, but most people wanted to know more. To get closer to the drama. That's why Saskia's MyNeighbour post was so excruciating: the threat of history repeating itself. Kat could be any one of those voyeurs from years ago. A girl from school, or just someone who read page three of the *Berkshire Gazette* that week.

Except would someone like that really recognise Beth after all these years?

And why would she want to be part of Beth's life now?

Kat has been in her home, Beth realises with another wave of nausea, alone with her children. She found her in Martha's bedroom on Thursday morning when she was still groggy from sedatives. Beth thinks about finding her wardrobe door askew when she got home yesterday.

Is it Kat who's been riffling through her things rather than Mark? And if it is, how hard did she look? Did she find Beth's pills? Or the bag with Eddie's most precious possessions? Beth gave him the Zippo lighter to convince him to give up the smack. The engraving – *Please fucking stop* – cost an extra ten pounds but she thought it was money well spent at the time. A dose of guilt with every hit. But guilt requires caring, she realises now, and Eddie was long past that.

'Mummy? Did you hear me?'

Beth blinks. She can't fall apart. She can't let Kat ruin what she has. 'Sorry, darling,' she murmurs. 'What did you say?'

'He gave us presents, look,' Martha says, proffering her gift. 'Can I open it?'

'And me!' Ava pipes up.

'Why not, it's almost Christmas.' Beth watches her daughters rip at the wrapping paper and uses the distraction to take a breath. She needs to go home. Alone. Mark isn't a threat to her anymore; he's unconscious in a hospital bed. Of course she needs to get her head around that too, talk to Simon, find out why he's avoiding DC Stone's calls. But she can't deal with that yet, not without knowing who Kat is, and what she wants. She takes another deep breath, then gestures for Simon to walk a few steps away. 'I need to go back to Wandsworth.'

'What? Why?'

'Saskia has fallen out with Tim,' she improvises. 'She needs a shoulder to cry on.'

'We're supposed to be going to my parents.'

'I know. I'm sorry. But Saskia is in a terrible state. I can't abandon her. You go though, your mum will never forgive me if I sabotage a visit from her grandchildren. And I promise I'll come by train this evening, or tomorrow morning at the latest.'

'You can't stay in the house on your own, Beth,' Simon says, shaking his head. 'Not with Mark wandering the streets.'

Beth pauses, breathes, absorbs the electric current of her daughters' chattering voices. 'He's not wandering the streets,' she finally says in a low voice. 'He's in hospital.'

'What?'

'Saskia messaged me. I don't know how she knows,' Beth lies.

'It's probably drugs-related,' Simon blusters. 'Maybe she heard through that charity she's involved with.'

'Probably. Maybe.'

'A relief in a way, I suppose. For us. Not that I'd want …'

'I know.'

Simon pulls his phone out of the bag, taps at the screen, sees the missed calls and blinks. 'Do you think I should brief a solicitor?'

Beth suddenly feels the urge to laugh. At her husband's petrified face, at her blindly inviting Kat into her home, at her belief

304

that a single act of kindness would bring her peace rather than just more pain. But instead, she grazes Simon's cheek with her lips, promises him that it will all be okay and opens the Uber app on her phone.

Chapter 48

Mark

Mark feels like shit. Like he's got a stonking hangover, a killer sore throat and a bucketload of shame. He didn't want his mum to see him before he had a shower, and yet here she is, sat next to him in a hospital bed, not only contending with his pervasive stink but also having to watch a machine breathe for him, and various tubes and medicines keep him alive. He's been conscious for about half an hour now, the breathing tube pulled out by a nurse called Samantha, but his throat still feels like it's lined with sixty-grit sandpaper.

'The doctor said you were lucky, no long-term injuries,' his mum says, trying her best to sound upbeat. 'He said you'd be able to come home soon.'

Mark doesn't respond. He's been in the hospital for less than a day, and aware of being there for less than an hour, but he can't imagine leaving. It's like he's locked in the present. The past and the future both feel out of bounds.

'But also that the police are on their way,' she continues gently. 'I met them this morning. Two detectives. I forget their names, but they seemed nice enough.'

'I don't want to talk to the police.' He thinks about the drugs in the squat, the primary school he crept into.

'I know you don't like to make a fuss about stuff, Mark, but someone strangled you. They could have killed you. That kind of dangerous criminal shouldn't be roaming the streets.'

An image of Rudy comes into his head. His mundane expression when he kicked Mark in the ribs. That was a punishment for nothing, so it's not surprising that he'd up his game when Mark nicked his gear. 'This is London, Mum,' he grumbles. 'Stuff like this happens all the time.'

'Between gangs, maybe. But not to people like you. Why were you even in that old shop? The nurse said you'd been sleeping there?'

Mark closes his eyes. He deserves this inquisition, and so much more, but he doesn't know how to answer his mum's questions. How to tell her that he got chucked out of two homes for being violent, and then lost his job. That his friend died, but instead of honouring his memory, he turned his grief and guilt for the part he played into hatred, terrorising an innocent woman, and then her child. That he stole from a drug dealer, smoked what he nicked and probably deserved to be taught a lesson.

'I don't need to know though, not if you don't want to tell me. I'm just glad you're alive, and that I can take you back to Cambridge.'

Mark's face cracks. Her generosity is too overwhelming. He lifts his hands up to hide his tears, but he knows his body gives him away.

'Oh, love. It's going to be okay.'

He feels his mum's arms around his shoulders. He leans into her warm body and sucks in her familiar smell.

'Is this a bad time?'

Mark drops his hands, looks at the two detectives loitering in the doorway and wipes frantically at his cheeks.

'Mark hasn't been awake long,' his mum warns, moving her

body slightly to shield Mark from their view, to give him a moment. 'He's still quite groggy. The nurse said you were coming, but I can't remember your names.'

'DC Stone and DC Worthing,' Mark hears one of them say. A mix of the voice and the names registers in his misty brain. They're the same detectives who nicked him on the night Jon died. Christ, this gets worse. He swallows hard and shudders as the equivalent of a Samurai sword slices his throat. He watches the two of them walk into the room and stand at the end of his bed.

'Hello, Mark. How are you feeling?'

'Not bad,' he says stiffly.

'I hear you were lucky.'

Why does everyone keep saying that? He shrugs and makes some non-committal sound. But he can't hold their gaze, not now they've seen him crying, so he turns to face the window.

'Listen, I know we've had a bit of history,' the broader one says – DC Stone, Mark remembers. 'And we will need to have a conversation at some stage about the drugs we found. But you suffered a serious assault last night, and we really want to find out who did this to you.' His voice is kinder than Mark remembers it. He sighs, risks looking in their vague direction.

'I don't remember much.'

'Just tell us what you can. You were in the disused shop?' the detective prompts.

'Yeah.' He looks at his mum, sighs. She knows this already, but it's still hard saying it out loud. 'I'd been smoking a bit of spice. And I'd forgotten to block up the back door. I heard something, and then, lightning fast, there's someone behind me.' The words bring the memory into focus and his heart rate increases. Even in this bright, sterile room, fear taps at his skin. He thought he was dying last night. It wasn't the pain, although that was intense, it was not being able to breathe. Life being sucked out of him.

'Take your time, Mark.'

He leans over, takes a sip of water. 'I didn't even get a chance to turn round. I felt something around my neck, a piece of elastic maybe, and then he was pulling it so tight, I couldn't breathe.' Mark blinks, swallows, puts his hand to his neck.

'The shop looked like there'd been a bit of a struggle,' DC Worthing says.

Mark shrugs again. He can't look at his mum. 'Nah, nothing like that.'

'You said he,' DC Stone points out. 'Did you see your assailant?'

Mark thinks back. He assumed it was Rudy attacking him at the time, and again when he woke up. But he didn't actually see him. 'No, not really. There was a broken mirror on the floor – an accident from earlier – and I saw bits of him in that. Black trainer, black cargo pants.' He's back in the squat again. Confused, terrified, his arms flailing. He wipes his sweaty palms against the hard cotton sheet. 'And then maybe ...'

'Maybe what?'

'Just before I lost consciousness, the grip got tighter.' He can see the dark figure now, looming over him, face contorting with the effort of pulling. 'They sort of leaned over me, and I got a flash of their face.'

Those cold eyes.

'Fuck,' he exclaims.

'Mark!'

'What is it?'

'I know who it was! It wasn't Rudy!'

'Who's Rudy?'

'It was that woman!'

Chapter 49

Kat

God, that was terrifying. She knew that she'd been careful last night, and had made a huge effort to avoid Groom & Bloom's CCTV camera. But she hadn't thought to check the footage, so when she retrieved it for those detectives, it was the first time she'd seen it. Thirty agonising minutes. But her vigilance had paid off; there was no video evidence of her being anywhere near the squat last night.

She's also relieved that the detectives didn't show up any earlier. When Kat first arrived at the salon, her mind was so scattered that she could barely function. She gave Sally some lame excuse for being late – that she overslept, even though she was wide awake by 6 a.m., still wired from the previous night – and disappeared into the grooming room. As always, it was the dogs who calmed her down, at least enough to pretend. Cookie the tail-wagging cavapoo, Bella the maltipoo with prima donna tendencies, and then Ziggy, the cockerpoo who always persuades her to part with one extra treat.

But she knows her sanctity is only a temporary reprieve. She can't hide forever; there is still so much to do.

Yesterday she thought she was making progress, getting closer to Beth, almost enough to reach the truth. She'd worked out a plan, and it was supposed to go smoothly. But now Mark is in hospital and Saskia won't release her interfering tentacles. And she's just found out that Beth's parents were killed in a car accident not long after the two of them fell out. So much tragedy in one family; how can that be allowed? Kat thinks about the Beth she knew – Ellie – and how badly her brother's death affected her. What kind of mental state must she have been in when her mum and dad died so soon after? Kat's heart almost bursts with a yearning to have been there, by Beth's side. Attentive. Vigilant to her needs.

And to top it off, Kat dropped her phone in the street. She doesn't care about the handset itself – she bought it when she first got back from Australia – but there's stuff on there. Potentially incriminating content. She needs it back, but she can't disappear on Sally again to look for it. She'll have to wait.

She stares at the clock on the wall then looks down at the dog under her hand. Sirius, with his lion's mane, wags his stubby tail under her gaze. The knots of tension each side of Kat's neck release a single notch and she sighs. One more hour. One last dog. Then she can do what she needs to do. Go back to Beth's. Find her phone. Make things right.

How stupid she was, thinking she could find her phone five hours after she dropped it, and with no daylight to search by. If it fell somewhere obvious, someone will have nicked it. And if it's obscured from view, there's no way she'll be able to spot it in the shadowy darkness. Kat kicks the low wall of some rich man's border in frustration. She'll come back tomorrow morning to resume her search, but for now, all she can do is pray that it's nestled somewhere elusive. That no one has found it, broken her worthless passcode and come to the wrong conclusions. Someone like that meddling cow Saskia.

311

She looks back at the Packards' house. Their car, the spotless Mercedes four-by-four, is still missing from the side of the road, but the hallway lights are on. Kat wonders what that means. The lights could be on a timer, the house still empty, the family escaping London for the whole weekend even. But she remembers that the hallway lamps are antique with traditional switches, and she's never noticed any of the wires and buttons you need to add smart technology.

Suddenly the living room gets swathed in light too. On instinct, Kat swivels away from the window and backs up a few steps. She wants to see Beth, but not like this, hovering outside like a stalker. Like Mark. She imagines him lying in a hospital bed and wonders how he is, if he's regained consciousness. But then Becca's motionless body from all those years ago suddenly comes into view, and it's all too much, too confusing, so she grabs hold of a gate post and forces herself to breathe, from the diaphragm not the lungs, like Dr Sharp told her once.

She's not a bad person, she reminds herself. Her intentions are always honourable. Yes, she made a mistake with Becca, but Ellie picked her up from that. Things went wrong with Ellie in the end too, but that is salvageable now. With what happened to Mark, and him alive not dead, and Saskia sticking her nose in, and Kat's phone still missing, the stakes are higher. But she's still got a chance to make things right; she's sure of it. She watches Beth walk over to the living room window and pause for a moment before drawing the curtains, except they're voile drapes, so gossamer-thin, and rather than hide Beth, they turn her into an alluring shadow.

The playroom to the right of the front door is in darkness, and there are no lights upstairs either; Kat feels certain that Beth is alone in the house. She takes a deep breath and starts towards it, but a movement across the road grabs her attention. It's Saskia's front door opening. Kat freezes, then retreats a few steps; she can't have another showdown in the street with that woman. She

312

watches Saskia look up and down the road, then walk across it with a bottle of some type of sparkling wine in her hand. She's going to Beth's house. Rage surges through Kat. Why the hell can't Saskia leave Beth alone for one minute? This is her chance, her moment. Not Saskia's.

Beth doesn't even like the stupid blonde. Not really. Saskia is just a friend of convenience, living across the street, their daughters' best friends. Beth doesn't trust Saskia with her secrets, and why would she when the drama junkie just splashes them all over her social media? She hopes that Beth turns Saskia away now. *Take your bottle back home, darling. You're not welcome here.*

Kat watches Saskia rap on the knocker and wait. *Please don't answer it,* she prays. *Or if you do, please send Saskia away, back home to drink on her own.* The door swings open. Beth looks tired, but still beautiful of course. She crosses the threshold. Walks down her steps. Beth doesn't want Saskia inside, Kat realises with growing elation. She watches them talk on Beth's pathway, Saskia proffer the bottle, Beth shake her head slightly. Kat tries to stay calm while she waits for Saskia to drop her head and retreat.

But suddenly the tableau shifts. Beth's arms spread open, and Saskia folds into them. They're locked together, like two best friends. Then with their arms still around each other, shoulders, hips, thighs, they walk up the steps and into the house.

Kat's vision freezes. The image of their embrace is like a camera still, to be imprinted on her mind forever. Because it's wrong. The whole scene is wrong. And she needs to stop it.

Chapter 50

Beth

Beth collects the champagne glasses with shaking hands; they chime as they clink against each other, and she wishes she could enjoy the thrill of anticipating a fun evening. But she needs a clear head tonight. To work out what to do about Kat. To find out how much Saskia knows, then get rid of her. To stay safe. She peels off the foil cover and untwists the wire muselet. Then she grips the exposed cork and turns it slowly. She finds the ritual calming, and she takes her time to fill each glass with the effervescent liquid.

'Thanks, darling.' Saskia accepts the proffered drink. Beth watches her take a sip, then place the glass down on the coffee table and lean back against the sofa. Saskia's long woollen coat is slung to the side of her, a creased mound of mess, and Beth itches to straighten it. It's rare for Beth to host girlfriends in the living room, but the open-plan kitchen felt too exposed when Saskia swept into her hallway; she wants to contain the woman's insatiable curiosity within four solid walls.

'God, what a terrible time you're going through at the moment,'

Saskia muses, sighing. 'So much different crap to contend with. And alone in the house; I can't believe Simon's putting his mother's festive summons before your safety. Mark may not be a threat anymore, but Kat? She is seriously unstable.' Saskia's voice trails off as she takes another large sip. 'Why on earth would she claim to know you, do you think?'

Beth used to consider Saskia the perfect friend, so preoccupied by her personal drama and faddish principles, that she never noticed Beth being tight-lipped about her own life. But she didn't account for Saskia's journalistic nose, how the sniff of something not-quite-right sets her off like a terrier. Or that one day she'd become the story. 'Can I see it, Kat's phone?' she asks, trying to sound casual. When Saskia mentioned on the doorstep that she'd found it in the street, Beth knew she must have it. She ached to just demand it, but was aware there'd be a dance involved in getting possession.

Saskia smiles but doesn't reach for anything. Beth feels a sudden urge to fly over the coffee table and scratch the patronising look off her face. Rip at Saskia's clothes until she exposes the handset. She shifts on the sofa and runs her nails up and down the heel of her hand, absorbing the thin line of pain.

'You can, of course,' Saskia starts slowly, 'but are you sure you want to? The images are quite chilling; I don't want to upset you.'

Give me the fucking phone. 'It can't be anything worse than I'm imagining,' Beth explains. 'I just need to see it for myself.'

Saskia hesitates for a moment, then reaches across to her coat and pulls a small phone out of the large pocket. 'There are audio recordings of you,' she explains. 'But it's the photos you'll want to see.' Saskia puts the phone on the coffee table and gives Beth the code. With the screen unlocked, Beth takes a deep breath, taps into the photos and scrolls through the images.

'I would say it's lucky you're so photogenic, but I don't suppose that's appropriate under the circumstances.' Saskia has never liked silence, but Beth isn't in the mood for pandering to her wishes right now. She's too busy trying to make sense of what she's looking at. Dozens of photos of her on Kat's phone. Taken in secret, Kat spying on her. Beth looks towards the window; the voile curtain that she once loved now seems so inadequate. Kat's phone dropped just metres from here. Would she come back for it? Is she out there now?

Panic rises in Beth's gut, and she concentrates on breathing. Kat is clearly obsessed with her, so much more of a stalker than Mark ever was. But why? And who is she? Kat told Saskia she knew Beth eighteen years ago, which was when Eddie died. Is her fixation related to his death? Or what came after? Beth can't go to the police, not after everything that's happened with Mark. So what can she do? Tears prick at her eyes, but she can't let them fall; she needs to hide her fear from Saskia.

Why did she let Kat into her life? She never trusts anyone, not wholly, so why did she let her guard down with a scruffy dog walker? Perhaps that's why. In Beth's world, where wealth and beauty are the only currency worth trading in, Kat just wasn't an adversary. But could it have been more than that? She thinks about her mum hanging the washing out in her tiny garden yesterday, how she reminded Beth of Kat. The community Beth grew up in always leaned on each other because managing alone wasn't an option. She found it repellent at the time, the neediness of it, but perhaps a dormant part of her was drawn to the familiarity of Kat's selfless urge to help.

She should have known better.

'Have you seen the last picture yet?'

Saskia's voice is loaded with meaning and Beth steels herself before scrolling to the end. A gasp escapes from her lips, and she rams her lips together to ride the swell of nausea rising up.

'Kat must have strangled him,' Saskia says, her voice finally sombre. 'Then taken a photo when he passed out. There's a bright red line across Mark's neck, and a snake of material next to him. One of those cheap ties maybe. You know what this means, don't you?' she says gently. 'Kat is more dangerous than Mark. We need to tell the police, urgently, especially now you're here alone. Kat clearly did this for you, to protect you, but minds like hers, they can swerve faster than Lewis Hamilton. You could be her next victim.'

Beth swipes her thumb across the screen to scroll away from the photo. She can't bear to look at it. She knows Mark survived the attack, but not whether he'll fully recover, or even regain consciousness. Is Beth supposed to feel guilty, responsible, for that too? And what will she say to DC Stone? That it wasn't her husband who attempted to kill Mark, but her mentally ill dog walker? But swiping away from the photo only exposes another one of her, taken, like them all, without her knowledge. She tosses the handset onto the coffee table in disgust, then changes her mind and shoves it down the deep crevasse of the sofa.

Every muscle in Beth's body feels taut now. She looks at Saskia on the opposite sofa, her long limbs softly draped over the cushions. Is that smugness on her face, or sympathy? Excitement or concern? 'How did you know I was at Painshill Park today?' she asks suddenly.

Saskia's face twitches. 'I didn't.'

'Yes, you did, you mentioned it in your message, said you hoped it was fun.'

'Did I?' Saskia looks away, clearly buying time, perhaps hoping that Beth will notice her discomfort and change the subject. Beth waits, and eventually Saskia surrenders. 'Um, maybe I saw your location on Google Maps,' she mumbles. 'When I was, um, checking some directions for Tim.'

'Google Maps?' Beth has a sense of tumbling, but her body doesn't move.

'Yes, you shared your location with me, remember? That night out in Camden?'

Beth's mind careers backwards. A gig in north London. Saskia arriving late. Getting swept up by the live music. 'You track me?' she asks, trying to keep the horror out of her voice.

'No,' Saskia squeaks. 'Well, hardly ever. Only when I need to know where you are and I don't already, which is rare, like today, with those detectives on your doorstep.'

Beth tries to breathe normally but it comes out in shudders. 'And yesterday?' she whispers.

Saskia pauses, her expression morphing from guilt to sympathy. 'There's nothing wrong with having a past, you know,' she starts. 'I take it you were visiting someone from your past in Reading? Was it family? You know, being born with a silver spoon isn't all it's cracked up to be, there's nowhere to go but down. Coming from nothing, achieving all this.' Saskia lifts one arm and wafts it around the room. 'You should feel proud, not embarrassed.'

Saskia is the worst of them all. A fucking hypocrite, slagging off Mark and Kat for stalking Beth when she's doing the exact same thing. And now she has this knowledge, the power to destroy Beth. Will she tell Simon? The girls? And who does she mean by family? She can't know that Beth's parents are alive.

Can she? Has she somehow used her journalist nose to sniff out the truth?

This is all too much. Kat could be out there, prowling around, and now Saskia has the tools to expose her too. But Beth can't cause a scene, not when her whole life is teetering on the edge of some fatal abyss. 'Are you hungry?' she asks suddenly. Time to herself in the kitchen, a moment to breathe. 'Shall I get us something to eat?'

Saskia takes another gulp. 'Lovely,' she says, with a relieved smile, so quick to assume she's been forgiven. Saskia always looks at ease, Beth realises, as though the cotton wool of privilege not only softens, but also obscures what normal people fear. She pushes off the sofa and walks out of the living room, pulling the door tightly closed behind her.

Beth opens the fridge door, but even with the food in neat rows, the garish Christmas packaging overwhelms her, and she pushes it closed. A loud rustle from outside startles her and she twists round to face the wide glass doors, but there's just blackness. A pigeon or fox?

Or Kat, waiting for her chance to break in?

Perhaps she should want it, Beth thinks. A showdown, winner takes all. But of course that's crazy; that's not who she is. She's measured, careful. She acted on impulse with that stinking drug addict, and that's when everything started to go wrong. She needs to be smarter now.

Beth spots the expensively wrapped box that arrived in the post a few days ago, a batch of Simon's mum's mince pies. It's a Christmas tradition that has always irritated Beth, why Mary has to use such excessive decoration when she's just following a widely used recipe from *Bake Off*, but it does seem like the most appropriate treat for this evening.

She pulls on the red ribbon and lifts off the lid. As she switches on the oven to warm them through, Luna tip-taps along the floor and stands beside her. 'Do you think I can survive this?' Beth whispers as she slips four mince pies onto a tray. 'Navigate my way past an obsessed dog walker and a neighbour who knows too much?' Luna drops her head to one side and wags her tail. A bell pings. There's a melody now. Beth slides the tray into the oven. Then she sets the timer for five minutes and waits.

April 2003

Chapter 51

Katherine

Katherine's eyes swim. It was all such a big mistake.

How could she have been so stupid? Thinking that Becca might be interested in her?

She throws some cold water on her face, then reaches for a paper towel. It's hard and it scratches her skin. Good.

She needs the letter back. Before it's too late, before Becca shows it to Mr Thomas and someone else reads her words, an old, staid teacher peering into her soul. The idea is too sickening; she can't let it happen.

But that means asking Becca for the letter back. Begging her to pretend she never found it in her satchel in the first place. To roll back time.

She might do it, Katherine thinks. She heard kindness in Becca's voice earlier, when she was talking to Clara, Katherine eavesdropping from inside the toilet cubicle. She hasn't got Becca completely wrong. But Clara won't let her. Katherine knows the bitch is just jealous. She doesn't like Becca having other friends, good friends like Katherine.

But are they even good friends? She's not sure anymore. It's all so confusing.

She needs to see Becca. Get the letter.

The quickest way to the sixth form centre is across the playground. Katherine heads down the long corridor, walls lined with noticeboards and artwork, towards the main doors. But as she gets closer, a barrage of students surges in the opposite direction. Maybe break time is over. She doesn't care about missing her lesson, but is she too late to stop Becca? With rising urgency, she jostles against the tide until she reaches the exit. She looks out of the window and discovers the reason for the sudden influx. It's pouring with rain. A proper spring deluge that she knows will be over if she waits for five minutes.

But she hasn't got five minutes.

She pushes open the door and runs into the rain. It's not warm, but it's not freezing either, and she enjoys the feel of it slithering down her face. She feels giddy suddenly, doing something so crazy, while everyone else is shaking themselves dry and bitching about studying in wet socks. She laughs manically as she crosses the playground and yanks open the door to the sixth form centre. The rain disappears, and away from the crazy, she falls silent again.

She shouldn't be here really. Year elevens aren't welcome. But she just needs to find Becca, get the letter, then she'll be gone and no one else will even notice her being there.

Except that twenty-odd eyes are staring at her now.

'What are you doing here?' a boy asks, not disguising his horror at a non-sixth former stepping onto his hallowed ground. But her tongue is too thick to speak now, and her brain isn't firing. She stares at him, dumbstruck. 'Are you looking for someone?' he prods.

Yes! She's looking for Becca, and she needs to find her before it's too late. She scours the room, the sofas and coffee tables, old desks and crappy TV on a stand. Then she sees them. Becca curled up in an armchair, with Clara sat right next to her. They're joined at the hip, and the knee and shoulder. Like lovers, she thinks.

And Becca is holding up a piece of paper. It's her letter, Katherine realises, held in both hands and slightly towards Clara so that they can read it together. They're smiling and laughing. They think Katherine is just one big joke.

How could Becca do this to her?

She needs the letter.

They're not far away, not in strides, not when you're running. Katherine reaches out, but her hands are fizzing. She misses the letter. Her fingernails connect with Becca's cheek.

Becca screams, lifts her hands to her face.

Clara pushes to standing. 'What the fuck?!' Her shout is like an angry ripple and suddenly there's commotion everywhere. Katherine looks left and right, sees angry faces, all staring at her.

'I just wanted the letter,' she whispers, to no one at all. Why do things always go wrong? Why can't she make herself be understood? Then she stumbles backwards, twists on her toes and lurches towards the door.

'Katherine, wait!' Someone is calling her name, maybe Becca, but she can't slow down; she needs to get out. She pushes on the door and tumbles outside. It's still raining, which means the playground is empty, and she can hide in a torrent of water. She pauses for a moment, face upturned to the sky, then notices the school gates, wide open. Of course she can't stay here now, not for the rest of the day, or ever again.

She hates the school anyway. Hates her home too. Her body, her face.

'Katherine, please hold up!'

It's definitely Becca, but she's not stopping for her. Fuck her. And her girlfriend. Katherine picks up her pace.

'Where are you going? It's chucking it down!'

Katherine runs. Sprints. Her lungs are screaming but there's something glorious about running without a destination. Pain jolts in her ankle as she stumbles off the pavement, but then it's gone and her legs are still lifting and pushing.

'Come back, Katherine! Where are you going?'

Becca's voice is loud, so she must be close. Katherine hates to admit it, but she likes being chased. In the rain. It feels more special somehow.

The noise is like nothing she's ever heard before. A screech. A thump. A car alarm going off. And still the pulse of rain falling. Not five minutes after all.

Katherine stops. She looks at the tarmac. Then she dares to shift her gaze, just slightly, until Becca's body comes into view. She's lying on her back, rain and blood submerging her beauty. There's a woman too now, wailing and shaking, her head in her hands, standing next to a car in the middle of the road.

There are teachers running over, Mr Cannock with his first-aid bag. Students crawling out of holes. And there's Clara. Collapsing beside Becca, curling her arms around her lifeless friend.

December 2021

December 2021

Chapter 52

Kat

Kat stares at Beth's front door and wills it to open. For Saskia to leave and Kat to take her place. Because she's ready now. Ready to open up, tell Beth who she is, roll the dice and hope that this time it works. She can't let the memory of Becca's accident hold her back forever. Yes, it was her fault – the police might have concluded differently, but she knows the truth – yet that doesn't mean risks are never worth taking. And after revealing too much to Saskia in the street, and losing her phone, all those incriminating photos, and with Mark in hospital, time is running out.

But she needs Saskia gone. Like she wishes Clara wasn't there all those years ago. Accidental villains, blindly making things worse. Should she just knock? Barge in? Pull Saskia out of the house by her stupid blonde hair? She wishes she knew what Beth was thinking. Saskia will no doubt have relayed every word of their conversation, so of course Beth will be suspicious of Kat now. Would she be grateful to have Saskia out of the way so that she could grill Kat for an explanation, or is her focus elsewhere? Is it with Mark, worrying about him lying in a hospital bed? She

329

remembers the hug Beth and Saskia shared on the doorstep, how Beth crumpled into the stupid blonde's arms. Or is her focus with Saskia now?

There are too many swirling thoughts and unanswered questions in Kat's head; she can't second-guess every outcome. She needs to be brave.

She crosses the road and opens Beth's gate. Then she walks purposefully up to the front door. She lifts her hand, grabs the knocker, and with her heart pounding ferociously, bashes it against the wood. Once, twice, three times.

But nothing happens. No one comes.

She tries again but gets the same result.

Fuck. She knows Beth and Saskia are inside. Why are neither of them answering? As her panic grows, Kat tries to stop the images coming, but it's too hard. First Becca, lying in the road, rain turning her blood pink. Then Ellie, lying next to her in bed, staring into Kat's eyes, revealing her deepest secrets. And Mark, lifeless, his threat extinguished.

There are other images too. Not memories, but the work of her imagination. There is Eddie, Ellie's brother, dying in a pile of sick. And the old homeless man, losing his life with the same addiction. And Beth a witness to them both, doing her best to survive.

Kat flips round and leans against the front door. She senses the flash of a shadow to her right; it's a figure moving behind the living room window. She looks back at the street – it's empty – and then drops to her knees. She carefully works her way over to the window and peers over the sill. Someone is sitting on the sofa, but leaning forward, pouring from a bottle with a shaking hand. Her hair is longer than Beth's, and she's taller, broader. It's definitely Saskia. Hunched on the sofa, she seems scared. Of Kat? Have they guessed it's her at the door? A surge of frustration rushes through her. She just needs to see Beth, to explain, to atone for her mistakes. Why won't someone let me in?

There's more movement, and the living room door opens. Kat

watches Beth walk inside, carrying a plate of something, mince pies, like the ones Martha wanted to eat for breakfast on Thursday. She proffers it towards Saskia. The Christmas tree lights are twinkling; it all looks so civilised. Best friends, a festive drink and a mince pie to soak up the alcohol. It couldn't be more perfect.

Except.

Kat watches the silhouette of Saskia take a bite, then stares in horror at her reaction.

June 2003

Chapter 53

Katherine

'Katherine, wake up.' A voice slowly infiltrates, and a hand pushes gently on Katherine's shoulder. 'I couldn't sleep.'

A shadow of someone causes Katherine's heart to race. But the voice is too familiar for it to be more than a temporary flicker of adrenalin. She turns onto her side and assesses the slight figure, dressed in pyjamas, crouching at the side of her bed. 'Ellie?'

'I keep thinking about you leaving tomorrow,' Ellie says, her voice still tiny. 'Or today now. I'm scared about being left here without you.'

Katherine's heart swells so much that she catches her breath. No one has ever needed her before. She's excited about her trip to Australia, meeting her dad for the first time, and starting a new life ten thousand miles away from Becca, but she hates the thought of leaving Ellie. She stares into her friend's eyes; the white bits glistening in the strip of light that's seeping over Katherine's door, and the brown irises reminding her of exotic gems. 'We can stay in touch,' she whispers back. 'Maybe you could visit me in Australia?'

Ellie shakes her head vehemently, then shivers. 'It's freezing out here. Can I get in with you?'

Katherine can't quite believe what's happening, and wonders for a moment if it's not. If this is all a dream, a generous gift on her last night at the unit. She pinches her thigh to check and enjoys the sting of pain it creates. She slowly lifts the duvet, and shuffles back towards the wall, rolling onto her back. Suddenly they're lying next to each other, attached at the joints, two halves of a whole, staring at the ceiling.

'Do you think you're fixed?' Ellie asks. 'From your illness?'

Katherine thinks about the question. She's relieved that the police aren't pressing any charges for the road accident. Against her or the driver, so she won't have to carry the guilt of ruining someone else's life on top of Becca's. And she's more optimistic about the future than she's been since the accident. But how can the darkness inside her ever fully disappear after what happened to Becca? She runs her fingers over the deep scar on her wrist. 'I don't feel suicidal anymore,' she says, 'but the rest, I don't know; it's hard to feel good about myself.' She wants Ellie to respond, to tell her she's got every right to, but her friend stays mute. Katherine listens to the soft swish of Ellie's hands wringing underneath the duvet.

'I'm not fixed,' Ellie finally says.

'You will be soon.' Katherine hopes she sounds genuine. She's out of her depth really, trying to counsel; she can barely function herself. But Ellie is her best friend. And it's easier to scrabble for something to say in the dark.

'I wash my hands a hundred times a day. When I'm not washing them, I'm imagining disgusting things worming their way into my skin. Then I wash them again.'

'Why do you do that?' Katherine whispers, her heart thudding, hoping she's not breaking some unknown therapy rule.

'When I was little, my mum was too busy cleaning other people's homes to have time for ours. There was always this layer of grime. I tried, but I just made it worse, and it freaked me out. So instead, I stayed away as much as I could. When I was older, I figured out how to keep the important areas clean, my

side of the bedroom, the bathroom. If I kept to myself, I could just about cope. But then Eddie started vomiting. Everywhere. I'd watch Mum clean it off the carpet, but she'd never do a good enough job. And of course they could never afford to replace it. The bacteria would float around our house, and I'd dream about it landing on me.'

'Do you think …' Katherine starts, pausing for a moment to build up some courage. 'Are you sure it was your brother's sick that upset you?' she spurts out.

'What?' Ellie pulls away, a centimetre maybe. Katherine squirrels closer, desperate to regain the connection.

'I just mean that you could have been doing that thing that Dr Sharp talks about: projecting. You thought you hated the dirt, but really you just hated Eddie being ill.'

'No, that's stupid,' Ellie spits out. 'You're stupid.' She flips onto her side with her back towards Katherine.

Shit. She didn't mean to offend her. 'I'm sorry,' Katherine says, trying not to sound whiny. 'I always say the wrong thing.'

'I don't like you talking, telling me what to think. That's not how you'll fix me.'

'Can we rewind? Pretend I didn't say anything?'

'I just need to look at you.' Ellie's whispered moan wafts up in the darkness. She's not making sense, but Katherine is too scared to ask her to explain now.

'Just tell me what to do,' she says instead.

'Be here, every day,' Ellie murmurs. 'Let me see you.'

'But why?'

'Because you make sense of everything.' Slowly Ellie turns back to face Katherine. Her dark eyes look different, more dangerous, at close range. 'I look at you, and I know I did the right thing.'

'What thing?'

'It's not your fault that you're fat, is it? Your dad's this big Australian farmer, so it's in your genes.'

'I guess,' Katherine mumbles. She has the sense that she's moving

337

towards a precipice, but slowly, still with a chance of surviving, if she can change course in time.

'And having such red-raw, ugly skin, you didn't ask for that either.'

The tears are coming now. Katherine can feel them stinging, but Ellie seems oblivious to the pain she's causing. Her eyes are staring through Katherine, not at her.

'Like Eddie,' Ellie continues. 'It wasn't his fault that he vomited, or that he never washed, or that he stole money from mum's purse. Not really. Not once the drugs took hold.'

'Not his fault,' Katherine agrees. 'But I don't understand why you're saying this?'

'How can you not understand?' Ellie's voice rises with incredulity. 'Life isn't even, Katherine. Some of us are born to do well, to succeed, while others are destined to fail. You will always fail, Katherine. It's not your fault, it's pre-written. There's too much wrong with you. And Eddie was the same. That's why I did it, the kindest thing. Because who wants to spend their life failing?'

'Did what?' Katherine whispers. But Ellie shows no sign of hearing her.

'And that's why I need to see you every day,' she continues. 'You are my constant reminder that I did a good thing. That dirty people will always be stained with their imperfection. There was no hope for Eddie, like there's no hope for you.'

'Did what?' Katherine repeats, her voice louder this time.

'Freed Eddie of course, from his tainted existence. He was in our bedroom, slouching against the wall, ready to inject more of that dirty stuff into his body. He'd already been sick; there was a pile of watery vomit on the carpet. In that one moment, I knew what to do. How to help him. I'd read a leaflet about it, you see, how an air bubble in the syringe can cause a massive stroke. It was so simple.'

Katherine's mouth goes dry. She blinks under Ellie's blind stare. 'You did that?' she whispers. 'You injected him with air? You killed him?'

Ellie's body shivers, an almost imperceptible movement. 'Not killed him, Katherine. I freed him. Just like you tried to free your-self, but you failed, because of course you would. Eddie was lucky to have me.'

'You're not like Becca at all.' Katherine pushes away, her back against the wall, burrowing into the plaster. 'You're a murderer; I need to tell Dr Sharp.'

Ellie smiles, as though she's won, which doesn't make sense. 'Yes, do it. Then I'll tell her it's all lies, and she'll believe me, not you, because you're desperate and deluded, and she'll make you stay. And I really want you to stay, Katherine.'

Katherine stares at her friend, a ruthless killer but also beautiful and clever. She's right; everyone will take her side. Then Katherine thinks about her dad, and the future he's promised her, and knows that the only way to escape is for Ellie's secret to become hers too.

December 2021

December 2021

Chapter 54

Kat

Kat pushes away from the window and launches herself out of Beth's gate. She looks left and right, then runs over to a yellow skip at the side of the road – piled high with rubble from yet another extension – and grabs the biggest piece of concrete she can carry. Holding it in two hands, she races back to Beth's house, and without thinking twice, hurls it through Beth's living room window.

There's the high-pitched screech of shattering glass and then a deep thud as the concrete slab hits Beth's living room floor. Kat surges forward. She needs to get to Saskia. With the thick sleeves of her parka pulled over her fists, she frantically pushes the loose fragments of glass out the window frame, then heaves herself through the hole. She can hear the snagging of material, and feel the sting of cuts where her skin is exposed, but neither slow her down.

Saskia is slouched on the sofa, her hands at her throat, swollen lips open as she searches for breath, the creaking drone of her wheezing filling the room. Kat knows she's in anaphylactic shock, and that she could be dead in minutes. Beth isn't moving at all. She looks like a young deer caught in a car's headlights. Beautiful, startled, innocent. But Kat knows the truth.

'She needs an EpiPen!' Kat screams. 'Does she carry one?' Kat's eyes spin around the room. 'Where's her bag?!'

'I don't know what's happening to her,' Beth finally says, her voice trembling. Even now, she's playing the role perfectly; only her hands give her away, the sound of nails scratching skin.

'You poisoned her – that's what's happening,' Kat spits out. She spots Saskia's coat on the sofa beside her and starts rummaging through the pockets. Nothing in the deep outside ones, but she sees the slim ridge of something inside the breast pocket.

'No, I didn't,' Beth counters. 'I didn't know she had an allergy.'

'Bullshit!' Kat exhales loudly. She reaches inside and yes, it's an EpiPen. 'Even I know she's allergic to nuts; it's all over her social media. She volunteers for an allergy charity, for fuck's sake!' Living on a farm five hours from the nearest medical centre means that Kat has had first-aid training, including how to administer epinephrine. She flips off the blue cap, takes a second to line it up with Saskia's thigh, then jabs the orange tip in at a right angle.

'No, sorry, I didn't mean that,' Beth stutters. She takes a step backwards, unsteady on her feet. 'I mean, I didn't know there were nuts in those mince pies. That's it. Simon's mum sent them to us, you see. I didn't think for a moment that—'

'That's a lie too!' Kat screams, turning back to face Beth. 'If Martha knows which recipe your mother-in-law uses, there's no way you don't.'

'Beth?' Saskia's hoarse, tired voice crackles through the air and both Beth and Kat turn towards it. Her face is still puffy, but there's some colour in her cheeks now. 'You fed me nuts on purpose?'

'Of course not, darling. I would never do that. Thank God you're okay.'

'Yes she did. You were too close to working out the truth.'

344

'Ignore her – she's crazy,' Beth says, her voice settling. 'You know that; you're the one who warned me about her.'

'She saved my life,' Saskia whispers.

'It all happened so fast,' Beth pleads. 'She threw concrete through my window; I would've looked for your EpiPen if I wasn't distracted by that!'

'You found my phone, didn't you?' Kat continues, trying to recapture Saskia's attention. 'And told Beth about it. That's why she changed her mind on the doorstep, hugged you, invited you inside.'

'Yes, but so what?'

'Beth never hugs anyone, does she? She hates touching people – you know that. That's how desperate she was to get my phone off you.'

Saskia pauses a moment, realisation mixing with confusion. 'But it incriminates you, not her.'

'Did you look at the photos?' Kat asks.

'Yes, you strangled Mark,' Saskia croaks, but there's no fear in her voice. Perhaps her body is too weary for that.

'I mean properly look at them,' Kat presses. 'I was there, but it was Beth who attacked him. After Mark approached Ava at school, and Simon called the police, I knew she'd try something, anything, to get rid of him. So I followed her.'

'That's madness!' Beth laughs, but it sounds more like a cackle. She must realise it too because her hands fly up to her mouth.

'Did you see the previous photo, Saskia, the one of Beth?'

'I saw all of them.'

'But did you look carefully?' Kat keeps on. 'See where she was, or check the timestamp?'

'No, I …' Saskia's eyeline shifts to the opposite sofa, and Kat follows it. There's a dark shadow between the off-white cushions. It's her phone. She lurches towards it, but Beth is faster, spinning on her toes, and swiping the phone before Kat reaches the sofa.

'That's mine,' Kat says. 'Give it back.'

345

'Why, because it's got evidence that you strangled Mark?' Beth asks, her eyes blazing now. 'And that you've been stalking me, taking photos, making voice recordings, for weeks?'

Kat turns back to Saskia. 'She's twisting things; I promise she's the dangerous one.'

'But you followed me too, didn't you?' Saskia says, her voice the quietest. 'I felt it at the time, on the common. And I was right, because there are photos of me.'

'I was scared for you,' Kat explains. 'Once you'd put that post up on MyNeighbour, risked exposing Beth's secrets, I thought you could be in danger. I tried to warn you off, told you Beth didn't like you, so that you'd distance yourself from her. But you didn't listen. Like Mark didn't take any notice when I told him to back off either.'

'This is all fantasy, darling,' Beth pleads. 'Don't listen to her.'

Saskia's face curls into a grimace, but with pain not confusion this time, the aftereffects of her anaphylaxis. She closes her eyes, takes a few breaths, then steadies herself. 'If you were watching Beth at Mark's squat, like you say, why didn't you stop her attacking him? Even if you're telling the truth, that's cruel in itself.'

Kat's face crumples, an involuntary reaction to Saskia's stinging words, because of course she's right. Yes, Kat phoned for the ambulance, but she should have done more than that; she should have stopped Beth before one was needed. But instead, she froze. Petrified. Still cowed by Ellie's threat after all this time. 'Eighteen years ago, Beth made me believe I had no voice, no power,' Kat explains, her voice pleading. 'She told me that everything I do will always fail. That's why I took the photos, made the voice recordings; I needed real evidence to back up what I knew before I could contact the police. But she was right; I was failing. When I was too scared to stop her attacking Mark, I realised it had to stop; I needed to be braver. That's why I came here tonight.'

'But I still don't understand,' Saskia exhales. The colour has drained from her face again, and there's a film of sweat across her cheeks. 'What have you known all this time?'

Kat turns towards Beth and sees a growing realisation cross her beautiful face, her fiery eyes turning to ash. Finally she's worked out who Kat is. 'I met Beth in a mental health clinic when we were teenagers,' she says. 'Although she was called Ellie then. She had anxiety disorder and mysophobia, a fear of germs.'

'She's lying, she's crazy,' Beth mumbles, scratching her palms.

'I thought we were friends, until the night Beth admitted to murdering her brother.'

'What?' Saskia spits out.

'He was a heroin addict. But he died of a stroke, an air bubble in the syringe. Everyone thought it was an accident, but when we were in the unit, Beth told me she did it.'

'No, I would never,' Beth whispers, too quietly to drown out the sound of her fingernails scratching. 'It was an accident.'

'You had a brother?'

'And then you told me that her parents died in a car accident,' Kat goes on, her voice starting to break. 'And I'm scared she caused that too.'

Beth's head snaps up. She catches eyes with Saskia, whose face is filling up with disgust. 'They're not dead, okay?' she implores. 'They live in Reading. That's where I was yesterday, visiting my parents. Maybe I haven't been completely honest with you, with Simon, but I just wanted to leave that part of my life behind.' She reaches her arm towards Saskia but holds it mid-air. 'I didn't kill Eddie though; I loved him.'

'And the homeless man?' Saskia asked.

'He reminded me of Eddie,' Beth murmurs. 'I wanted to do what I couldn't for my brother, save his life.'

'He died of a stroke too,' Saskia continues. 'An air bubble in the syringe. That detective told me today.'

Kat runs her hands through the red spikes of her hair and blinks back hot tears. Of course deep down she knew that Beth had killed that man, but hearing it out loud is still like a heavy weight dropping on her chest. Is his death on her hands too? For not having the courage to defy Ellie all those years ago?

'You hated having squatters on our road, didn't you?' Saskia continues. 'You said they were dirty.'

'No, I just meant they needed help,' Beth protests. 'How can you choose her side? You're my friend; she's not like us.'

Saskia's eyes flit between them both. A siren sounds in distance, but Kat suddenly feels calm. Soon it will be over, one way or the other. She's played her hand and all she can do now is hope she's done enough for others – Saskia, the police – to see through Beth's beauty, her wealth, her smile. To believe Kat instead, a skint dog groomer with a fifty-inch chest and a history of mental illness.

But then a shriller noise erupts. It's Beth's phone, buzzing on the side table. Beth looks, then reaches for it. Saskia groans, an animal sound. Kat turns to look.

And watches her vomit all over the carpet.

Chapter 55

Beth

The smell, oh my God, it's vile. Beth watches the putrid liquid seep into the fibres of her carpet.

'Elizabeth, are you there?'

Beth drags herself back to the phone call, tries to use the cold glass screen of the handset to cool her burning face.

'He's gone, *mea dragă*. Just taken his last breath.'

Her dad is dead? 'Please, no,' Beth whispers. It's too soon – she hasn't had chance to say goodbye. She closes her eyes, but her eyelids are infested with Saskia's vomit, worming and burrowing its way into her eyes. She flicks them back open. Kat is kneeling beside Saskia now, her bulk obscuring the stain on the carpet, but even her presence is sickening. Fat, ugly Katherine. How dare she intrude on Beth's life?

'It's his time, don't be sad,' her mum says. 'He's with Eddie now.'

Beth stares at her hand. Red raw from scratching, but also littered with marks from years of abuse. She tracks each faint scar with her eyes. Will Eddie tell her dad the truth? That his last vision was watching his sister hand him the syringe, and how he didn't think for a second that she'd tampered with it, until the hit wasn't what he expected? That instead of euphoria, he felt his body shut down. Will her dad know that she did it for him and her mum? Eddie was destroying all their lives, not just hers. Will he remember that?

'Are you there, my darling?'

'Eddie wasn't so great,' she whispers.

'You're upset. It's a lot to take in.'

'He was a smackhead, Mum. And a thief.'

'He was ill. He would have recovered if he'd been given the chance, just like you did after your stay at the unit.'

A ball of fury fizzes inside Beth's head. 'Don't compare us!' she cries. 'Eddie and I weren't the same.'

'Oh you were for a long time, inseparable even, like twins. But then you changed. You started staying out until late, and being withdrawn at home. Eddie missed you. He wanted to help, to draw you out of your shell, but we seemed to be the problem, not the solution.'

'Eddie was the problem,' Beth reminds her. The fat lump is pulling Saskia to her feet now. There's a trail of bile snaking down the nosy bitch's chin. Beth feels her chest sinking inwards, tightening up. 'He was the drug addict, Mum. The poison. Throwing up on our carpet.'

'He only did that once, Elizabeth. And that wasn't the drugs – it was when he had a stomach bug.'

Beth's mind crashes and bounces. 'No, that's not true. It was all the time.'

'Dr Sharp talked about this, do you remember? How your illness would distort your memory. Eddie was an addict, yes. And at times that made him behave badly. But mostly, he was his old self. Kind and funny, full of ideas. Like you, I suppose.'

Beth can't listen anymore. To the lies. She drops her arm, feels the handset slip out of her grip. The tinny sound of her mum calling her name repeats a few times, but she pushes them away, and finally the sound dies. How dare her mum make such ridiculous claims? Beth is not like Eddie. He was the fuck-up, the failure, the weak link. She was the saviour, the one strong enough to get away, to build a perfect life. An image of her winter boot comes into her head, the shimmer of a dozen pill strips, but she pushes it away.

'I think you strangled him.' Saskia's voice is so quiet, void of drama, not like her at all really. 'And you tried to kill me.'

Beth looks at her neighbour. Dishevelled, clammy, sick-stained. Then she looks at the woman who's the size of a rhino but has somehow managed to slither her way into Beth's life. Something snaps inside her, like an elastic band, so powerful that her arms flail outwards. Of course she strangled Mark. He was threatening her family, and their lives are worth a thousand times more than his. She lied to Simon about the sleeping pill – that was easy – then when he was asleep she took Eddie's old tourniquet belt from the pouch in her shoebox. It felt apt to use it after she'd kept it for so long, carrying her brother's shame to help her live with her own. She can't believe Mark is still alive, but hopefully he'll never regain consciousness; it's what he deserves, his own fault for behaving so despicably. Like Kat, like Saskia.

'You're all so stupid!' she screams at the top of her voice. 'So blind to the truth!' She's shouting too loudly; she needs to think about her next-door neighbours, but it's flooding out of her now. She looks at her ex-friend, the dribble of saliva that's worked its way onto her collar. The sweat at her temples. Her unkempt hair.

'The police are coming,' Saskia warns. 'I'm going to tell them.'

How dare she act so calm? So smug? Beth is the one in control here, not Saskia. She needs to understand that. Beth looks at the floor, sees the lump of concrete, imagines launching it at Saskia's stuck-up face.

Then a moment later, it's in her hands, and she's smashing it down with a blood-curdling scream.

Chapter 56

Joseph

'What do you reckon then?' Joe asks as they walk back to the car.

'Can't discount it, I suppose. But Beth Packard? It's hard to imagine, and Mark's account isn't exactly crystal clear. First, he thinks his attacker is some big drug dealer called Rudy, then suddenly he sees Beth's face – the woman he hates; let's not forget – just before he blacks out. I don't know.'

'Yeah,' Joe muses. 'There's a lot that points to it being a work of fiction, but I can't help thinking he sounded genuine.'

'Let's talk to Beth tomorrow,' Jason suggests. 'See how she reacts to our new witness statement.' He starts the engine and the police radio sizzles into life. They don't need to listen to the constant thrum of instructions as uniformed officers are sent to various disturbances around the borough, so Joe leans forward to turn it off. But with his fingers on the dial, he pauses. 'Did you hear that address?'

'The smashed window?'

'I'm sure that's the Packards' house. Busy day for them, isn't it?'

Jason lifts his eyebrows, then wordlessly switches the button that turns on the emergency response. With blue lights flashing in the grille, and the siren wailing above them, they fly out of the ambulance bay and head up Blackshaw Road towards Wandsworth. They take a right up Burntwood Lane, skirt around Wandsworth Common and pull up outside the Packards' house in just over five minutes; the first to arrive.

And one look at the smashed window, what's happening inside, is enough.

Joe throws open the car door and sprints towards the house. He knows the rules, the green light he's got to enter the property without back-up because there's an imminent threat to life, but he's not sure it makes much difference. Seeing someone get whacked with a concrete block is incentive enough. He watches the woman fall to the floor. 'Get an ambulance!' he shouts as he hurtles forward.

'On it!' Jason's voice, loud but controlled, filters out from behind him.

Joe reaches the window, covers his hands with his jacket, his face with his hands, and hurdles into the room. He takes in the scene in a split second, then turns to the woman lying unconscious on the floor, blood seeping out of her head. He drops down beside her, checks her airway and pulse. She's alive at least. He grabs a coat from the sofa and pushes it against the wound. He recognises her, he realises. She works in that dog groomer's a few doors up from the squat; he was looking through her CCTV footage only a few hours ago. Kat, he remembers her name. But what is she doing here? Is this about Mark? Is she his friend, avenging his attack? But if that's true, why didn't she tell Joe that she knew him when he and Jason visited the groomer's earlier?

'She broke into my house,' a small voice whispers in his periphery. 'Smashed my window.' Joe shifts his gaze towards its owner. Beth Packard is trembling, but is she scared of the intruder in her home, or just coursing with the adrenalin of hitting Kat with a concrete block? Is she a victim defending her home, her friend, or a dangerous assailant, like Mark claims?

'Paramedics will be here in seven minutes,' Jason says, climbing more gingerly through the gap. 'Hey, are you okay?'

Joe watches Jason turn towards the other woman in the room. It's the neighbour they met earlier, but she's lost her mettle now. She looks dreadful, slumped on the sofa, her face pasty white and puffy. Her eyes aren't focusing, and she's sweating even though the exposed room is freezing cold.

Jason crouches next to her. 'I'm DC Worthing,' he says gently. 'We met earlier. I think you're in shock, so I'm just going to lie you down, okay, and put your legs up on the sofa? It will help, I promise.'

'I just need to …' Saskia rasps, pushing Jason's arm away. She sounds like Mark, her voice in shreds.

'I get it, it's a lot to take in,' Jason reassures her, trying again. 'Someone smashing their way in. But just concentrate on your breathing.'

'No,' she says, with more force. 'I need to explain.'

'She's got it wrong,' Beth murmurs. 'Please; she doesn't understand.'

'No, it's the exact opposite of that,' Saskia says, wiping her mouth and pushing herself to sitting. 'For years I've misunderstood.' She gives Beth a wounded stare. 'I was blinded by her, her big, innocent eyes, just because she's so beautiful and rich. Because she plays the perfect mother, the perfect wife, so well. But that should have been a clue, shouldn't it? Because no one's perfect, so it had to be a lie.'

'I can be perfect,' Beth whimpers. 'If you just give me a chance to show you, to clean up this mess.' Beth wafts her arms around the room, but her left one knocks the side table. It wobbles with the impact and a picture frame falls onto the floor, the glass shattering as it connects with the table leg. 'No!' Beth cries out, reaching for it, not noticing, or caring, that her hands are being sliced by the shards. She stares at the photo. It's a family shot, all four of them dressed in different shades of white clothing. But now it's bare, exposing how the photo has faded over time. She looks back up at Joe. 'I just wanted to protect my family. Keep life perfect for them. Don't you see?' She looks down at the floor, her features pinched. 'They shouldn't be exposed to people like her. Life's failures. It could rub off, couldn't it? I couldn't risk my children being stained by her.'

'She's worth ten of you, a hundred,' Saskia says, vehemence breaking through her hoarse tone. 'She saved my life tonight, twice. She only broke in because Beth fed me nuts, tried to poison me, so that she could give me my adrenalin shot. And that concrete block was meant for me; Kat jumped in the way, took the hit so that I didn't have to.'

'She did that?' Joe looks down at the woman, an unlikely hero, but aren't they all? As he stares, he sees movement, followed by a low moan. When Kat opens her eyes, Joe sees that they're different colours. One eye is bright blue, like the sea.

The other is a light grey, and it reminds him of an early dawn.

January 2022

Chapter 57

Kat

Kat takes another look at the address on her phone, just to be sure she's got the right house. Then she smooths down her dress – another risk she's trying, like agreeing to go on a date with Jayden, and so far, so good, on both counts – and stares at the house with hopeful, newly grey eyes. It's modern, red brick and detached. A wide pathway splits the front garden into two squares, then spreads around the perimeter of the house. It's smooth and flat, and wide enough for a wheelchair, Kat thinks as tears start to burn at the back of her eyes.

Kat sets off up the path, putting one foot in front of the other until she reaches the white front door. Then she presses the bell. As she waits for it to be answered, she thinks back to the first time she stood on Beth's doorstep. She'd felt proud of herself for getting that far, for finding a way into Beth's life. But she was scared too. Not of Beth, even though she knew what the woman was capable of. Fate had given her a chance to make things right, to stop protecting a murderer with her silence, but she was scared that Ellie's prophetic warning would turn out to be true.

That she would fail. She almost did too – a week on ICU and an operation to release the pressure on her brain are testament to that – but in the end, she got there. Perhaps she should have had more faith in herself.

The door swings open. 'Katherine?'

Her face instantly folds inwards and her eyes clamp shut. She puts her hands up to hide her distress. She shouldn't be behaving like this; it's rude. She's a guest; she should be smiling, proffering the small gift she's brought, politely accepting her host beckoning her inside. And yet, the sobs keep coming.

'It's okay, you know.'

'I'm sorry. So sorry.'

'You did nothing wrong.'

Kat dares to splay her fingers and look at Becca through the gap they've left. She rubs her eyes with the sleeve of her new coat, then her nose.

'Are you going to stay out there all day?' Becca asks.

'It's just a shock. Seeing you like this.'

'On two feet, do you mean? Without my wheelchair?'

'I just thought …'

'You're right. I used the wheelchair for years after the accident. The doctors didn't think I'd walk again, but it turns out miracles do happen, if you complement them with daily physio sessions, that is.' Becca softens her voice. 'Please come inside.'

With the last of the sobs still obstinately refusing to leave Kat's chest, she nods and returns Becca's smile. When she steps into the thickly carpeted hallway, she notices that Becca is barefoot. Becca gives her a sheepish grin. 'For years we had to have a hard surface in here, easy access for the wheelchair,' she explains. 'So now we have thick pile carpet, and I don't think I'll ever tire of digging my toes into it.'

Becca leads Kat into the living room and gestures for her to sit on the sofa. Then she lowers herself down into the armchair opposite. There are four cards on the mantelpiece, each following the theme of a happy first wedding anniversary, and a photo of Becca in a white dress, stood next to a man with wide eyes and a generous smile.

'You're married?' Kat asks timidly. Even now, she can't help feeling awestruck by Becca's beauty, inside and out.

'Yes, a year ago. It rained all day, but that's our fault for choosing a winter wedding. I wouldn't get married until I could walk down the aisle unaided, but of course as soon as I could, I wanted to do it straight away. So late January it was.'

'Your life was on hold for such a long time.' Kat feels tears smarting again.

Becca leans forward. 'Would you like a cup of tea?' Kat watches her go about the ritual of pouring two cups from a pot on the coffee table. Milk? Sugar? The distinctly British way of giving Kat a moment, but also an example of Becca's compassion, perhaps the result of her being so badly bullied for her Jewish heritage that she was forced to change schools. 'They weren't wasted years,' she finally answers. 'I learned a lot about myself; and I promised myself that I would walk again, that I just needed to be patient. And here I am.'

'You always had such strength,' Kat whispers. 'Principles.'

Becca takes a sip of tea. 'It wasn't very principled to show Clara your letter.'

Kat's hand trembles and she places her mug back down. 'I shouldn't have written it,' she whispers. 'Put you in that position.'

'You were vulnerable and showed nothing but love. And I laughed at you.'

'That's not true,' Kat mumbles. 'You came after me, that's why you were hit by the car. That's why it's my fault.'

'You felt guilty about my car accident. And I felt guilty for putting you in that position. That's why I worked so hard to walk again. So that we could both be free of it.' She pauses. 'Because I knew one day you'd come. I just didn't think it would take this long.'

Kat looks at Becca. She can't believe that she once thought she looked like Ellie. Where Ellie is closed, Becca is open. And where Beth wears a mask, Becca radiates authenticity. 'I'm sorry you had to wait,' Kat whispers. 'I had some other guilt to get rid of first.'

'And did you?'

Kat smiles, the tears all dried up now. 'Yes,' she answers. 'I did.'

Epilogue

January 2022

The service is over now. Beth's dad has been sent to his final resting place, and he should leave too, Simon thinks. The girls are with his parents in Hertfordshire. Their house in Wandsworth is on the market, and his mum is dropping heavy hints that he and the girls should move closer to them. But for now, they have school tomorrow, and it will be a long drive home in the rain.

But he can't leave the crematorium yet. Not without introducing himself to Beth's mother – a stranger to him for all these years – and showing her the precious photos that he keeps in his wallet.

Beth left as soon as the service finished, led away, back to her new home on remand in Bronzefield prison, flanked on both sides by prison officers. She didn't cry at all during the service. She sat blank-faced, looking straight ahead. If you weren't watching carefully, you might think she didn't move at all. But Simon noticed the way her hands slid and scratched as her father's coffin disappeared behind the curtain.

The investigation is ongoing. DC Stone has phoned Simon a

couple of times, but he barely listens to the detective. Beth has been charged with the serious assault of Mark Sullivan and Kat Wilson. They're hoping the footage of her crouching down by Jon Smith's side will be enough to prove she was responsible for his death too, the passer-by who put filming the event above helping suddenly labelled a hero for first compelling Beth to phone for an ambulance, and then providing the vital evidence to prove her guilt. The police video analysts have already determined that she picked the needle off the ground, and their working theory is that she used it to inject air into Jon's vein after he had injected himself with heroin, when he was pliant. Thames Valley police have decided there's not enough evidence to charge Beth with her brother's murder, but she's paying in other ways for that.

Simon didn't believe it at first. When DC Stone phoned him at his parents' house that night, he'd called the detective's accusation ridiculous, defamatory, dangerously inaccurate. He'd known Beth for sixteen years, he'd said, and she'd never even lost her temper. It took Saskia to convince him otherwise. Sitting with her and Tim in their warm kitchen, she'd taken him through Beth's list of crimes. Deep down, he'd known that Beth was aware there were nuts in his mum's mince pies. But it was when Saskia explained Beth's motivation, her craving for some elusive form of perfection, that he'd surrendered to the truth. For sixteen years he'd admired her quest for the perfect life, and had felt honoured that she considered him worthy of being part of it. It took her fall from grace for him to realise how damaging, how arrogant, it is to have such a narrow view of what perfect means.

He looks over at Beth's mother. She's stood by herself, reading the messages on a line of bouquets. Simon hesitates for a moment, then walks over to join her.

'They're beautiful,' he murmurs. He doesn't look up, but he senses Beth's mother turn towards him.

'I don't normally like flowers like this,' she says quietly. 'Cut at the stem. It feels wrong, finding something beautiful, then cutting off its energy supply.'

'I've never thought of it like that.'

'But I find it comforting today. I want them to die, you see, so that Stefan's surrounded by beauty on his journey. Do you think that's selfish?'

'No,' Simon says quickly. 'Stefan was your husband. They may be beautiful, but these are just flowers. His happiness, your wishes, those are more important.'

'Love before beauty,' she whispers.

'Always.'

Simon smiles at his mother-in-law, and pulls two photos out of his wallet.

Acknowledgements

A lot of writers warn debut authors about second book syndrome, but for me, my third book – *My Perfect Friend* – was my most challenging to write. Tens of thousands of words were virtually screwed up and thrown into a cyber bin before the story finally began to flow. Hence, I have a lot of people to thank for keeping me going.

But first, I would like to thank the experts who gave me their time. Thank you, Dr Mike Forsythe and Dr Sophie Lane, for your advice on Mark's injury and treatment. Not only did you answer my many questions, but you provided the perfect solution for waking Mark up at just the right time. Thank you, Susan Clarke, for explaining the dog grooming process, and a big thank you to Inspector Simon Stone for sharing your knowledge and insight as a police officer in the Metropolitan Police. I hope your namesake Joe Stone meets your expectations – we can both look forward to the movie version! Thanks also to Hannah Smith for your eleventh hour social media insight.

I also wanted to give a blanket acknowledgement to the 'between the commons' area of my borough. Brookhill Road is fictional, but local readers may recognise some of the real land-marks I include in the book. Thank you for 'lending' me your lovely area for inspiration – I'm sure there's no one as dangerous as Beth living amongst you!

Thank you also to everyone at HQ and especially my brilliant editor Cicely Aspinall. Your thoughtful suggestions were all 'perfect' and made for a much-improved book. Thank you also for being so positive about everything book-related and more.

The whole writing community is incredibly supportive, but I'd like to particularly thank Sophie Flynn, Liv Matthews, Meera Shah, Catherine Cooper, Jane Jesmond, Simon Van der Velde, Jac Sutherland and Lucy Martin for making me feel part of something. Thank you also to my friends closer to home, my Chuffing Bats tribe who always make me laugh, and especially Becky and Rachel. Thank you, Bex, for forgiving my absences, and Julia, Louise and Jane for the pep talks on dog walks.

I'd also like to thank my readers, especially those who have taken the time to review my books. From the early reviews given by Pigeonhole readers, NetGalley members and the book-blogging community, to every reader who has taken the time since. Reading your positive comments reminds me how incredibly proud I am to do this job.

And finally, my family. Thank you, Dad – your role as my chief beta reader remains secure – and Mum, for always listening. Thank you, Scarlett and Finn, for raising yourselves for a few months. And thank you, Chris, your Sunday roasts got me through.

A Letter from Sarah Clarke

Dear Reader,

Thank you for reading *My Perfect Friend*.

I have always been interested in first impressions, and how we make judgements about people based on the way we look. As a thriller writer, I wanted to take this inclination into the world of crime, which is why my murderer is beautiful and fragile, and my hero awkward and intimidating. Mark is a rough sleeper, but also a talented game designer with big dreams.

While the book's title might suggest otherwise, all of my characters are far from perfect. While Beth could never be forgiven for her actions, do you feel any sympathy for her desperation to provide the perfect life for her family? Did your opinion of Kat or Mark change as you got to know them better? And was Saskia a likeable altruist or just a spoilt brat? I'd love to hear what you think!

You can reach me by email at sarah@sarahclarkeauthor.com or via social media. I am on Twitter as @SCWwriter, and on Facebook /sarahclarkewriter and Instagram as @sarahclarkewriter. You can also sign up to my newsletter to hear all about my new books, competitions and offers.

I loved the brilliant feedback I received for *A Mother Never Lies* and *Every Little Secret*, and I would be hugely grateful if you could spare a few moments to review *My Perfect Friend* too. It really makes such a difference.

You can also follow my publisher @HQstories for lots of book news and great giveaways.

Happy reading,

Sarah

A Mother Never Lies

'Brilliantly tense, with an unexpectedly dark
heart – a totally compelling read.'
Sophie Hannah, *Sunday Times* bestselling author

SOME TRUTHS CAN'T BE TOLD.

I had the perfect life – a nice house, a loving husband, a beautiful little boy.

But in one devastating night, they were all ripped from me.

It's been fourteen years, and I'm finally ready to face the past.

I'm taking my son back.

He just can't know who I am … or why we were torn apart.

**A nail-biting thriller packed with twists and turns, perfect for
fans of Lisa Jewell and Shalini Boland.**

Every Little Secret

'A fast-paced, twisty story … A thrilling read.' Catherine
Cooper, bestselling author of *The Chalet*

From the outside, it seems Grace has it all. Only she knows
about the cracks in her picture-perfect life … and the huge
secret behind them. After all, who can she trust?

Her brother Josh is thousands of miles away, and he and Grace
have never been close – he was always their parents' favourite.

Her best friend Coco walked away from her years ago, their
friendship irreparably fractured by the choices they've made.

And her husband Marcus seems like a different man lately.
Grace can't shake the feeling that he's hiding something.

But when her seven-year-old daughter makes a troubling accusation, Grace must choose between protecting her child and
protecting her secret … before she loses everything.

Read on for the gripping opening chapters.

Prologue

It's widely understood that unconditional love is reserved for a child.

Not for your brother or sister. Not your husband or wife. It's not even expected for your mother or father.

Unconditional love is one-way. And it can be a lonely journey.

If you're not sure that your child deserves it.

If they say hurtful things. Make selfish choices. Turn on the people who love them the most.

Can you push back against the forces of motherhood? Put your hand up and plead: *it's different for me – my child is not to be trusted anymore.*

I choose to give my unconditional love to someone else.

I don't know the answer to that question. Soon I will be tested, but not yet. Tonight I can look down at my sleeping child, so perfect and innocent in slumber, and still enjoy the miracle of motherhood. I can graze their forehead with my lips, tuck in the duvet, whisper that I love them. And mean it.

Then I can close their bedroom door behind me, walk downstairs and return to my husband.

Chapter 1

GRACE

2019

Grace gives Marcus an imploring stare, but he's immune to her plea. *Just do it*, his eyes say. No sympathy there. She stares around the room, but there's no option for escape either. She feels vulnerable, still in her pyjamas, sleepy dust lurking in the four corners of her eyes, her body trapped by their increasingly unnecessary winter duvet. She takes a deep breath and surrenders to the inevitable.

'Do you like it, Mummy?'

Grace swallows the tepid liquid and tries to ignore its pallid tone and the suspicious brown dots floating on the surface. 'It's delicious, honey. The best cup of tea I've ever tasted.'

Kaia smiles, relief etched into her face. She's always been like this, carrying the weight of an in-built urge to succeed. 'I made a card too.'

Grace takes the folded piece of cardboard from her daughter's proffered hand and sneaks a look at her husband, who's loitering behind the bed like a spare part. Perhaps that is his role today. This is the eighth Mother's Day that they've celebrated as a family, but even now, with Kaia's glittery *I love you, Mummy* sparkling from inside the card, it causes a lump to form in her throat. Theirs wasn't the smoothest route to parenthood, and Kaia still feels like a gift.

'Kaia has offered to make breakfast too,' Marcus offers, the tease in his voice apparent to everyone over the age of about 10.

'Gosh, what a treat,' Grace spars back. 'Perhaps you could make breakfast for Daddy as well. I'm sure he'd love that.' He's avoided the milky cup of tea; she doesn't see why he should miss out on burned toast or stodgy pancakes too.

'I'm not making Daddy's breakfast.'

Grace sits up straighter in bed. Kaia is usually such a Daddy's girl. 'Why not?' she asks.

'It's Mother's Day,' Kaia replies quickly, as though surprised Grace hasn't worked that out. 'It's not his turn.'

Grace relaxes back against the headboard and smiles. 'Yes, of course. Perhaps Daddy could help you make breakfast then?'

'I'm nearly 8. I can do it by myself,' Kaia announces.

'It appears that I'm redundant then,' Marcus says, holding up his hands with mock offence. 'In that case, I'll go for a shower instead.' Grace watches her husband walk into their en-suite bathroom, the muscles in his back expanding and sliding over bone as he stretches out his shoulders. His professional career ended seven years ago, but he still trains with the determination of an athlete. Then she turns back to Kaia, who's eyeing the bed with a longing expression. Grace smiles her approval, lifts up the duvet and lets Kaia wriggle inside until their heads are parallel. Kaia cups her small hand tightly over Grace's ear. 'But, Mummy,' she whispers, her warm breath crackling down the shadowy tunnel to Grace's brain. 'Will you make *my* breakfast? Because you're the best at that.'

*

Marcus offers to buy croissants from the local deli in the end. They sit at the breakfast table together, ripping apart the soft dough and smothering it with Grace's mother's famous damson jam, and Grace allows herself a moment of reflection. Life hasn't always been easy, and at times she's found it hard to stay optimistic, but here she is, eating delicious food in a home she loves, with her two favourite people in the world.

'Hey, Kaia, help me clear the table.' Marcus picks up the three plates dappled with crumbs, and gestures for Kaia to collect the rest of the crockery. As Grace watches Kaia walk between the table and the kitchen, she wonders what her daughter is thinking about. Usually she'd be giggling at Marcus's atrocious dad jokes by now, or calling shotgun on the washing up and barging him out of the way. But she seems miles away today. Perhaps this is just a sign of her growing up, claiming her independence one clandestine thought at a time.

Marcus looks at his watch. 'Time for rugby, Kaia. Race upstairs and get your kit on.' It was always Marcus's dream to have a child to share his biggest passion with, and he never allowed Kaia's gender to be a barrier. He signed her up with the local rugby club as soon as she was old enough, two years ago, and it's since become a Sunday morning ritual from September to April, the highlight of both their weeks.

'I don't want to go.'

Marcus looks up in surprise. 'Huh?'

'I want to stay at home with Mummy instead.'

'But you're the best player in the squad,' he reminds her, fatherly pride oozing out. 'Faster than all the boys. Awesome ball skills. You love it there. Why don't you want to go?'

Kaia shrugs and leans into Grace.

Marcus adds a bigger smile and tries a different tack. 'How about I promise to get you a hot chocolate at the end?' He winks. 'Marshmallows on top if you score a try.'

Grace watches her daughter weigh up his offer. Kaia has always loved rugby and comes home recounting stories of her achievements on the pitch. And she's a big fan of hot chocolate too. Perhaps Grace should give her one more push. 'And Grandad will love to hear all about it later,' she cajoles.

Kaia turns to looks at her. 'But what if someone kicks me in the eye?' Her expression is open and her tone innocent, but the question still causes Grace's croissant to rear up inside her stomach. She crouches down. 'It's non-contact rugby, Kaia. It's not the same game as Daddy used to play.'

Kaia stares at her, as though she's searching Grace's face for further reassurance. Silence sits between them for a while, but finally Kaia's eyeline drops and she sighs. 'Okay, Mummy.' Then she plods up the stairs and returns two minutes later in her Wimbledon Rugby Club strip.

'Thank you,' Marcus says, his low voice showing he hasn't fully recovered from Kaia's question, the arc of white skin next to his right eye a constant reminder of his own accident. He guides their daughter out of the front door and the house falls blissfully silent. The air feels looser with them gone, and Grace sucks it in.

She runs a bath, adds a generous dollop of bubble bath and climbs in. As always, her hand drops to the scar on her belly. She runs her finger along the slight ridge and wonders what it would have been like to have more children, multiple Mother's Day cards and unappetising cups of tea. But it wasn't to be. She sinks under the bubbles and listens to the gentle whoosh of water in her ears.

Dear Reader,

We hope you enjoyed reading this book. If you did, we'd be so appreciative if you left a review. It really helps us and the author to bring more books like this to you.

Here at HQ Digital we are dedicated to publishing fiction that will keep you turning the pages into the early hours. Don't want to miss a thing? To find out more about our books, promotions, discover exclusive content and enter competitions you can keep in touch in the following ways:

JOIN OUR COMMUNITY:

Sign up to our new email newsletter:
http://smarturl.it/SignUpHQ

Read our new blog www.hqstories.co.uk

🐦 https://twitter.com/HQStories

f www.facebook.com/HQStories

BUDDING WRITER?

We're also looking for authors to join the HQ Digital family!
Find out more here:

https://www.hqstories.co.uk/want-to-write-for-us/

Thanks for reading, from the HQ Digital team